THE ORCHID FILE

R. J. STRONG

For my son, Rhett.
*My reason to keep fighting. Without him, this book would have
been done two years ago.*

Hell is empty and all the devils are here.

— WILLIAM SHAKESPEARE

What can I say? Treason is in my blood.

— MAISIE SHEPPARD

1

Piazza Navona
Rome, Italy
February 27
1432 Hours Local Time

Killing them was easier this time. At first, they reminded him of his new life so much he almost stopped. He'd dined with friends at cafes and rode on buses. Enchanted by the sprawling European cities, just like them.

This time he felt no remorse as he approached the square and feathered the throttle of the tiny three-wheeled truck. Two large cardboard boxes marked 'fragile' occupied the open bed. Loving one or two similar things does not make people alike.

The lives he took were a coincidence; their stories no more than worthless accidents while they lived a life of convenience. They paid nothing for their happiness.

He fought fiercely for those sweet days on the sunny Madrid sidewalks. His life was deliberate, forged from the scrap heap he inherited. He viciously labored to purge his fear and remake himself in a decade-long effort to leave the wreckage of that night behind. The old Nasir was weak. No more.

When he fled Iraq in '06 all he could carry with him were memories, even if they were nightmares. Nightmares of American soldiers storming his house leaving death in their bootprints.

Nasir eased off the accelerator and coasted to a stop inside the plaza.

The American soldiers had all worn masks and night vision goggles. He never saw their faces, except one. The man that shot his mother had his goggles up. His mask had been pulled down and he had blood on his face.

Nasir closed his eyes. Yes, he remembered the blood on the soldier's face. Such a small amount compared to the crimson pools left in his childhood home that night.

A year ago, a news clip about corruption in the American government flashed across his television screen. He instantly knew the suited FBI Agent walking to a table surrounded by a bank of stern faced politicians. There to testify about something no one cared about.

Nasir was fourteen the first time he saw that man. The soldier with blood on his face. Only then he'd held a rifle instead of a thick binder, and wore battle dress instead of a tailored suit.

In the time it took his coffee cup to hit the floor, Nasir's purpose crystallized. His murdered family would finally have justice. Months of planning and execution led to this day. Today the FBI Agent from the news would see his face.

Nasir took a deep breath and studied the scene. It was a bright, cold day but the cool weather had not dampened foot traffic in the famous Piazza Navona. The plaza buzzed, tourists and Romans alike basking in the afternoon sunshine.

Two hundred feet ahead, Nasir spied a red umbrella

bobbing through the crowd. Just like it always did on the second and fourth Tuesday of the month.

A tour group had disembarked from a gray bus and followed the obnoxious umbrella-carrying tour guide. The red umbrella stopped beside the showy centerpiece fountain with its well-heeled American customers in tow.

Nasir pressed the gas pedal and made his way through the plaza toward the largest group of souvenir vendor stalls, one of five carts bringing replenishments of cheap, gaudy souvenirs and baubles. He skirted the group until he came to a line of vendors next to the fountain.

No one looked at him. He had scouted this location so thoroughly, he knew how to blend in. The boxes on the back of his golf cart looked like a hundred others.

The cart rolled to a stop. He pulled the parking brake and slipped out. When he glanced at the tour group he hesitated.

Most of the group had their phones trained on the sculpture snapping photos. But a couple stood off to the side smiling at each other. They were old but their expressions were no different than love-struck teenagers. A life he would never have.

A sudden wave of sadness washed over him. Never again would his girlfriend fall against him giggling when she was tipsy. No more walks through the park hand in hand. Somewhere in Madrid, she was wondering why the man she knew as Sergio said he never wanted to see her again.

Her heartache was his biggest regret. But that life was never his, no matter how hard he tried to make it so. He was not born for happiness.

Nasir flipped up his collar and pushed his hands inside his pockets as the tour group began to circle the Fontana dei Quattro Fiumi. He walked to the mouth of a narrow alley that cut through the tall buildings bordering the piazza before he turned around.

Leaning casually against the stone, he watched the tour group move within three meters of his abandoned cart.

His finger hovered over the car key remote in his pocket, his thoughts on the old couple. Then he mashed his thumb down on the alarm button.

Nasir slipped into the alley as the blast rocked the sun-drenched piazza. The center obelisk in the fountain cracked, and the marble sculptures chipped, pitted by metal shrapnel. Behind him, the concussion shattered windows as it roiled down the plaza. Screams replaced conversation.

Halfway down the alley, he stopped and looked at the security camera fixed to the side of a building. He held his collar away from his face and gazed at the camera until he heard sirens fire up in the distance. Then he was gone leaving a plume of smoke and dust swirling behind him.

2

———

Boca la Caja
Panama City, Panama
March 13
1500 Hours Local Time

Steamy sun beat down on sacks of fruit, green coffee beans, and crates of vegetables lining Carron Pier. Boats bobbed up and down in the muddy water while men hopped on and off with sacks and crates. The emptied vessels were quickly reloaded with outgoing cargo once the offload crew was done.

Most of the men working the pier wore long sleeve shirts. Some darker-skinned locals braved the ruthless tropical sun without protection, but regardless of dress everyone was drenched in sweat.

A short stocky foreman yelled in Spanish that the boat was clear. The man nearest the cleat bent over and unwound the mooring lines so the captain could cast off.

At 5'11", the man unwinding the rope was taller than the men around him. Once he'd been paler than his indigenous co-workers, but months in the sun had turned his skin brown.

Like everyone working the pier, he shouldered hundred-pound sacks and crates onto waiting craft. His dark brown hair and beard were thick and unkempt and he wore shabby clothes. His long sleeves were pushed up to his elbows exposing black ink that scrolled from the crook of his right arm to his wrist.

Hell is empty and all the devils are here.

Luke Marshall straightened and tossed the rope across the water to the waiting crewman. Then he wiped the sweat from his face and slung a few more sacks while the next boat maneuvered into the empty berth.

It took a while. The skipper was inexperienced and the boat yawed with each overcorrection. Luke watched him annoyed when the distant whump whump of a helicopter distracted him.

Helos carried tourists over the canal or some shipping bigwig to his next appointment. They stayed clear of this part of town. Poverty isn't exactly a draw for tourists or shipping magnates.

Luke, however, was here for precisely that reason. The hubbub of the Canal and the glitter of the city were miles away. Carron Pier saw mostly local imports and exports that circulated outside of Panama City's richer areas. The local Panamanian goods he slung day after day stayed right here in Boca la Caja. It was grueling work but it kept him busy.

A salty breeze off the ocean ruffled his hair. These people might be poor and rough, but he had great respect for them. They were better humans than the ones he'd left behind in America riding in limos on the way to ten thousand dollar-a-plate fundraisers. Here they worked hard and didn't hurt anybody.

That's all it took to impress him anymore. Live your life,

don't destroy anyone and you had Luke Marshall's full and undying approval.

Luke dumped another sack of coffee on the pallet, irritated that he stood in the sun doing nothing while this idiot played around in the water.

The beat of the helicopter drew his attention again. It was louder now. He twisted and squinted at the sky. He saw it coming in low over the rusted metal roofs.

His chest tightened. That bird was headed his way.

The helo swooped low over the pier office drawing everyone's attention.

The bumbling captain threw out a line, but it thumped on decaying wood and splashed into the water. Luke was halfway down the pier already vetting his exit routes.

The Carron office was a low cinderblock building at the base of the pier. The office doors stayed open so the sea breeze could substitute for air conditioning. Behind it, the busy street was visible through a large gate in the high wall. A crumbling warehouse bordered one side of the office, and a concrete pad with weeds growing through the cracks lined the other side.

The helo swung to a stop over the abandoned concrete pad and hovered. By the time the skids touched concrete Luke was at the office. He glanced back at his co-workers to see if any of them followed him.

They all stood slack-jawed at the improbable sight of a chopper touching down at Carron Pier. Whatever was coming out of that bird was meant for him.

Luke retreated to the shade of the roof overhang ready to slip away if he didn't like what he saw. The empty warehouse next door would offer cover out to the bustling street.

The blue and white helo had two doors on each side. The back door swung open as soon as the engine whine lowered and the rotors slowed. An older man with an expanding middle stepped out and stooped to walk under the blades. He wore khakis, an olive polo shirt, and was slipping a black O's ball cap over his silver hair.

The old man cleared the rotors, then craned his neck at the dockworkers gawking at him. Luke saw his shoulders drop in defeat.

Luke fought the desire to melt into the shadows and disappear. Had anyone other than Frank Longer shown up here, he would have. Instead, he crossed his arms.

The movement made Frank's head snap toward him and their eyes met. Frank made for a gap in the fence and headed for Luke. He stepped into the shade and took off his sunglasses hooking an earpiece over the back of his collar. "Hello, Luke."

"Colonel." Luke reluctantly reached out.

Frank shook his hand hard. "Good to see you, Son. How are you?"

He greeted Luke like they'd just run into each other at the grocery store.

"You didn't come all this way to check on me." Luke urged the old man toward the point. There would be no questions about how the family was doing.

The Colonel pointed to the empty office. "Can we talk?"

With a cautious glance around, Luke nodded.

"It's just us, Son." The Colonel flashed Luke a cigarette-stained smile as they walked in.

"It is good to see you, Frank, but this clearly isn't a social visit."

"No. No. You have to leave a forwarding address for it to be a social visit." Frank grinned again. "You're a hard man to find."

"That's because everyone in Washington wants me dead."

Frank laughed. "Fair enough, Luke. I need your help.

Believe me, I wouldn't have come if I'd had any other recourse."

Luke squinted at him but didn't say anything.

Frank's face sobered as he saw Luke's expression harden. "There's some disturbing intelligence on...."

"No," said Luke, his voice flat.

"Hear me out."

"No. You're going to ask me to work for you and I won't do it. You know that. Why are you even asking?" Luke turned his back on his friend and mentor and walked to the door hoping to catch a breeze. The room was stifling.

"Look, I know it's been difficult for you since...lately, but..."

"Started way before that, Frank."

"I know." Frank studied the floor, his brow furrowed. "Luke, you're already involved, you just don't know it."

Luke looked back.

Frank sighed and continued. "You know about the bombings? Targeting Americans?"

Luke shook his head. There was no TV in his tiny place, and he made it a point to look the other way in the presence of a newspaper. The only news he got was chatter from the dockworkers, and that was local.

Most of these men didn't know how they would pay the medical bills for the new baby *and* put groceries on the table. Attacks on Americans didn't rate very high on their give-a-shit-ometer.

"There have been three bombings in the last six months. At first, it seemed random. After the second and third, it became obvious that American tourists were targeted. First in London, then Paris, and three weeks ago in Rome."

Luke said nothing. Frank hurried on. "The London attack was the least surgical. The bomb was on a bus, but they still managed to kill their American targets. At the cafe attack in Paris, it was a backpack dropped right next to them. In Rome, he drove the device right up to them and parked it. The intel community is squabbling with each other, Luke. Nobody has taken responsibility, although ISIL is definitely this guy's cheerleader."

"There's a lot of lone wolf assholes running around out there. How do you know they're related? Bomb type?"

"Well, they did have similar composition and detonators." Frank hedged.

"But," Luke prompted.

"Whoever this guy is, he's all over the map. We don't even know if he's tied to any known terrorist group, although some of them have tried to claim the bombings. Even after three attacks, we're no closer to finding out who is responsible."

It irritated Luke that Frank avoided his question. He turned to face Frank and saw how uncomfortable Frank looked. "And now you're here."

The old man nodded.

"Put the fodder where the calf can get it, Frank." Luke used his mentor's old saying for 'get to the point'.

It worked. Frank straightened. "I said we had no leads, but that's not entirely true. We have one. Luke, your name has popped up in chatter since the very first attack. It's the damnest thing. Each subsequent attack your name popped up. In all the monitored chat rooms. Al-Qaida, Hamas, Syrian rebels, and ISIL.

"Except for Al-Qaida and Hamas, most of these groups solidified after you got out. They were still shitting in diapers in '04 when you were kicking doors in Mosul. They shouldn't know you exist. Yet someone is throwing your name around, Son."

Luke felt sick.

"CIA has been all over me to find you. They're looking to

me because you served under me. For months I've told them no, but I've put it off as long as I can, Son. This time makes three."

"Who else in Washington knows about this?"

"To my knowledge, only the SecDef has been briefed, so I assume the President has been too. The SecDef is my boss, so I don't have much choice in the matter."

Frank grinned. "You don't have a lot of fans in Washington, son, but Secretary Neelen's on your side. The spooks have their own team working on the bombings. So far I've been able to keep them pacified, but they're not exactly known for their patience."

"You think the attacks are related because my name pops on the dark web? I testified in front of Congress so much last year everybody and their grandma knows who I am." Luke dreaded the answer as soon as he saw Frank's grin die.

Frank pulled a cloth handkerchief from his pocket. He took off his ball cap and ran it over his damp forehead. "Son, every single American killed was from Colorado," he said folding the handkerchief and shoving it back into his pocket. "Eleven in total."

The tightness in Luke's stomach hardened into a boulder. He felt the sweat on his face turn clammy. Looking away from Frank, he hooked his thumbs into his pockets and watched the foreman browbeat the men back into a hustle.

"It's a coincidence." He tried lying, mostly to himself.

The Colonel took a step and joined Luke in studying the innocuous scene on the pier. "Sun getting to you? Eleven people dead from your home state, Son."

Frank pulled a fat envelope from his back pocket and handed it to Luke. "This guy's blowing up all of Europe to get your attention. Just help me find out who he is. That's all I'm asking."

Luke's face was stone as he reached out and took the envelope.

Frank clapped him on the back and fished his aviators from the back of his collar. "I'm sorry to ask this of you, Son. I truly am. But it is good to see you again." Frank slipped on his glasses and strode out into the sunlight.

"Yeah, you too," Luke lied. Before he even heard the rotors whine, Luke had walked through the gate out onto the crowded streets of Boca la Caja.

Thirty minutes later, Luke dropped the kickstand of his battered dirt bike into the sand. He followed a narrow sand path through mangrove bushes until a small deserted beach opened up among the palm trees.

A tiny hut sat fifty feet back from the water. Luke walked to it and pushed open the unlocked door. Inside, he peeled off his sweaty clothes and slipped on swim trunks.

Home was simple - a room with an outhouse and shower and tap fed by a rainwater cistern. The structure had no power. It was a ramshackle lean-to with a lumpy mattress really, but Luke had been drawn to its isolation.

The shack's meager feel evaporated outside the door. Steps away lay his own private beach and the warm clear water of the Caribbean Ocean. The persistent ocean breeze cooled him all night. Rundown paradise is still paradise.

Luke threw the envelope down on the bed and pulled a beer out of the large cooler by the camping stove. He popped the top off and drained half of it before crossing to the windows and flinging them open.

The cool evening breeze dried the sweat on his body. When the bottle was empty, he tossed it into a box and started walking toward the sea. He had a little extra daylight since he skipped out early.

In seconds he was waist-deep in the gentle water. He dunked his head then swam away from shore. Luke swam until his muscles burned, then he swam harder.

He could go. Just go wherever and never talk to Frank again. He mentally flipped through a list of countries he could disappear in.

Not that his attempts at running away had ever been successful. He resigned his commission and managed to land in a bigger shit storm in Savannah than the one he ran away from.

The truth was his war would never be over. These days his enemy lived in a mirror.

Everything he owed his country had been paid, and then some. But when he tried to hide, to fade out of existence, trouble still found him. It found him in the desert, dive bars in little Georgia towns, and a god-forsaken barrio in Panama. It didn't matter where he went.

The burn in his shoulders intensified and Luke kicked harder savoring the feeling.

Frank had unlimited resources and the entire Defense Intelligence Agency at his disposal. He didn't need Luke. Frank had done just fine without him. The world was still spinning. Frank knew why Luke was tucked away on this remote stretch of beach; one of the few who knew everything.

Without warning her face swam into Luke's thoughts. He might as well have been surrounded by her hair instead of salt water. He could smell her and feel her. The memories crushed down on him like the equatorial sun at noon.

Luke stopped swimming so suddenly that his wake overtook him and lapped over his back. Flipping over, he grabbed two fistfuls of hair. No one heard the agonizing scream he let out, floating in the deep water. He let the water rock him and allowed the pain to wash over him. It was a way to keep her close.

She was their scapegoat, so he'd spent the year after her death ripping through Capitol Hill. He successfully indicted three Congressmen and two Senators.

Endless hours of committee hearings resulted in one successful charge and one resignation. The evidence was deemed insufficient to continue with charges on the rest, including Senator Onessa.

His prime target slipped away with a muddied but intact career, and Luke was left with a lot of powerful enemies.

And still Frank showed up on Luke's doorstep. It wasn't like the old war dog to mince words, but that's exactly what Luke saw. He would rather have his fingernails pulled out than go back to his former life, but if the unflappable Frank Longer was rattled, things were bad indeed.

The good news for Frank was that Luke had nothing left. The only thing he wanted was gone. He would help Frank ID the bomber, then get the hell out and back to comfortable anonymity. The Philippines were nice this time of year.

Luke swam back to the hut thinking about the flight confirmation included in the packet Frank gave him. A confirmation for Washington, D.C. bearing his name. His ticket back to hell.

3

———

Indian Ocean
275 Miles off the coast of Somalia
March 14
1125 Hours Local Time

Drunk men never lie about women. And the men who recommended Maisie Sheppard gushed about what they saw her do to four Somali pirates on the processing deck of a Russian trawler. And her price was right.

The Mbaraki Bar in Mombasa, Kenya was the place to go to find the baddest of the bad, and Francisco Telles bought into the stories. In the sober light of day, however, she seemed less sexy badass and more prickly porcupine. Francisco swallowed hard. He'd worked hard to advance himself to first mate.

Now his first crack at a security hire stood there mouthing off to the captain as Somali pirate craft bore down on them.

Maisie draped her arm over the stock of her slung rifle. "Couple things, Cap. One, your idea of 'a great deal' of money differs vastly from mine. And B, other contractors charge double my rates. So you're welcome."

"Other contractors are more reliable."

"Whatever, Holmes. I was thirty minutes late to shove off."

Captain Burns' steely eyes narrowed at being called 'Holmes'. "Cast off," he corrected her.

"Whatever. Look, if you want security that comes with 401Ks and matching polos, you shouldn't be poaching tuna out of restricted Somali water."

Deep lines around Gill Burns' mouth disappeared as he frowned.

Maisie gave him a dark grin. "Those pesky insurance companies ruin everything, don't they? But then I don't report to insurance outfits, so I'm what you get. Relax, Holmes. No ship under my protection has ever been taken."

"Is that so?" Captain Burns crossed his arms.

Maisie leaned against the panoramic bridge windows looking out on the ocean and let her binoculars hang around her neck. She flicked an old soggy toothpick at the garbage can and missed.

"Out of how many attacks, young lady?"

"Ten." Maisie pulled out a thin metal canister and popped a fresh toothpick into her mouth. "And don't call me young lady. I can assure you I'm neither of those things." She winked at Francisco. "Right, Franny?"

Clearly, the Captain doubted her ability as much as the sweating first mate. Her black tactical clothing and sweat-stained boonie hat overwhelmed her fit 5'5" frame. The delicate gold chain and locket hanging around her neck clashed with her ensemble. A tactical magazine carrier, her SCAR 17 CQC, and iron-sighted Colt 1911 strapped to her right thigh made her look like a high school girl cosplaying Call of Duty.

That was the point. She didn't want the pirates taking her seriously, and she didn't give a rat's bottom lip if this chain-smoking Brit did.

Another blip sounded from the console. Captain Burns walked to the forward bridge windows and raised his binoculars to scan the horizon. Maisie joined him looking through her own pair of binos. Nothing but looming grey storm clouds.

"Radar says two now," Francisco said in a shaky voice. He wiped his palms on his pants.

"How fast?" The Captain's voice held no emotion.

Maisie realized this wasn't his first go with Somali pirates either.

"Approximately forty knots."

"Francisco, sound the alarm if you please. At current speeds, they should be here in under twenty minutes."

Francisco fumbled with a microphone, his thumb hovering over the button. "What should I say it is?" His whisper was hoarse.

"Just say it, Franny. They'll figure it out anyway," said Maisie still gazing out over the water. The swift-moving outboards were just now coming into view. "And make that three boats," she said.

Francisco's shaky voice came over the ship's loudspeakers announcing the incoming craft. When he finished, he turned to the Captain for orders.

Burns hung his binoculars on a peg by the window. "Go help prep the deck before this thing goes tits up. I'll be down in a moment," he said to Francisco.

"Good luck, Maze," Francisco muttered as he scurried off the bridge.

Burns turned and faced Maisie. "So you're to be tested on your first voyage with us, Miss Sheppard. Are you ready?"

"Don't worry, Cap. You're as safe with me as you are in your mother's arms. And I'm gonna be your mommy today." She lowered her binos and smirked at him.

His smile was strained. "Bunch of arseholes, that lot."

"Eh." She shrugged. "So was my ex."

The captain threw his head back and laughed.

"Just make sure the deck is locked down and the crew is sequestered." Maisie flipped the toothpick to the other side of her mouth.

"Ten minutes and it will be." His face grew serious again. "Good luck, Miss Sheppard." He disappeared down the stairs.

Maisie stepped out the bridge door after him and watched the twelve-man crew of the Starfarer secure fishing lines and retract the rigging from the twin cranes that hauled up the massive tuna nets. A practiced waltz to make the thirty-foot climb from the water as hard as possible.

Piracy along the horn of Africa had been all but eradicated in the last decade. In the absence of the threat, illicit fleets flouted international maritime law to cash in on the blossoming demand for tuna. Knowing they couldn't report it to authorities without exposing their illegal operations, Somali brigands now targeted the illegal fishing vessels. To avoid pricey ransoms and crippling fines, the fleets turned to private security to defend against pirates. Once again piracy flourished.

It was in this salt-crusted quagmire that Maisie had buried herself scraping together a life. Escaping the past takes money, and her particular skill set was in high demand around Kilindini Harbor. So she lived cheap, took dangerous work, and hoped one day it would be enough to get out.

Maisie stepped back onto the bridge and hung up her binoculars. The fast-moving skiffs were easily visible now.

She slipped off the locket and kissed it before securing it in the smallest velcro pocket in her tactical pants.

Moving to the main control console, she flipped up a clear plastic cover and pressed a red switch marked in a language she didn't speak. Below her, in the belly of the ship, pumps ground to life. The water cannons were the ship's only defensive weapon. The grinding steadied to a roar as the pumps reached full power. Torrents of water shot out the sides of the ship, strong enough to take off skin or capsize a small boat.

Locking the bridge behind her, Maisie stepped out onto the narrow catwalk that ran along the side of the ship's bridge. Sliding the SCAR to her back, she climbed a narrow ladder to the top of the superstructure. A long thin pad was lashed down between eye hooks.

The ocean spread out around her, gray and restless. It wouldn't stay that way for long. Once the storm hit, things would get rough.

She reached back and brought her rifle back around then bear crawled to the pad. Laying on her belly, she kicked her left leg out and settled into a prone position. She chambered a round and flipped the safety off. It took only a second to find the pirates through the Elcan Specter DR.

The boats were about four hundred meters out. Well within range in ideal circumstances, but the sea grew rougher by the second pitching the ship with it. She sighted the lead craft and ran through the sequence in her head, while she waited for them to get close enough to cull the herd.

The largest boat led, flanked by two more. They ran wide open. No doubt those khat-chomping assholes hoped to find the ship unprotected. Some captains didn't pay the high security prices gambling that they wouldn't be spotted.

That knowledge sometimes worked for the pirates. Today it would get them killed.

Three hundred meters. She waited. Missing was not an option.

Two hundred fifty meters. Maisie nestled the polymer stock into the hollow of her shoulder and cradled the fore-end in her support hand. The crosshairs aligned high on the forehead of the lead boat driver. She waited for the down roll.

One breath in.

The ship pitched down bringing the red dot between her target's nipples. Her teeth ground down on the toothpick. As she slowly exhaled, she pulled the trigger and the rifle burped fire.

The man stiffened and red mist coated the dingy bucket seat behind him. The other two men crouched but grabbed for the wheel and brought the boat back on course.

The skiff on the starboard side had two men. Maisie picked one and exhaled again. This time the passenger clinging to a handrail with an AK-47 pitched backward and fell into the water. The driver crouched, but all three boats kept coming.

Persistent fuckers. Then again, if they failed to produce any ransom money, their respective warlords would kill them anyway. Maisie counted seven total. Three in the lead boat and two in each of the secondaries. All with AKs. Two down. Five to go.

She lined up her sights on the lead boat again and waited for the roll. This time paint exploded off the steering column of the port side. The two men flinched but stayed upright. A trigger pull later the passenger hit the deck, dead.

Three down.

Maisie flattened as bullets skimmed the superstructure's

metal skin below her. The skinnies figured out where the rounds were coming from. One hundred meters out. Time to move.

She inched back to the ladder on her belly. Putting a foot on each rail, she slid down to the catwalk.

The clouds thickened and grew dark. Drops of rain hit her face as she sprinted to the starboard side of the Starfarer. Peeking over the rail, she saw two boats. The lead had split off. Most likely gone to port.

They flanked her. Running the numbers in her head, she decided to deal with the three men in the two skiffs first.

Now the boats bobbed twenty feet out trying to dodge the surf churned up by the water cannons. After several failed attempts to come alongside, a rail-thin, dark-skinned man in a torn Hawaiian shirt managed to slip his boat behind the water cannon.

Metal reverberated as his craft bumped the Starfarer's waterline. A few seconds later she felt it again. The second skiff made it between the cannons. A grappling hook clanged on the railing twenty feet ahead.

Yanking on the SCAR, Maisie jammed it into her shoulder and duck walked toward the hook staying below the railing skirt. She pivoted to square up on the railing. The rain came down hard now.

Taking a deep breath, she popped up and slung her support elbow over the railing looking for her quarry. One of the pirates had shimmied halfway up the slick rope faster than she'd ever seen it done. He stopped when he saw her.

His yellow eyes were huge in his head, his tattered shirt much too big on his emaciated body. The craze in his eyes turned to fear. At least he was smart enough to be scared. One round and he dropped into the roiling water.

Seeing his partner fall seemed to infuse the remaining man with energy. Ignoring the stinging rain, he leaped out from behind the wheel and lunged at the rope. Maisie pulled the trigger again and he dropped to his knees on the bow, then pitched forward into the sea.

Maisie twisted and saw the second skiff astern near the propeller. She ducked as a hail of bullets slammed into the steel railing skirt.

Ahead, she spotted an orange foam life preserver and grabbed it. Waiving it above her head, she ducked again as another wave of bullets bit through foam and the steel hydraulic boom arm above her.

Maisie picked up the life preserver again and thumbed the SCAR's toggle switch to full auto. Then she heaved the foam circle out like a frisbee. It sailed thirty feet in the air along the gangway and the lead followed it, pinging off the hull.

She rose to her feet and brought her elbow over the railing. The lone pirate on the second boat still aimed in the direction of the life preserver. Her muzzle dipped, and she pulled the trigger raking the deck of the small boat. The man had barely turned toward her in surprise before she mowed him down.

Maisie whipped around, reloading as she sprinted across the trawling deck to port side. The rain fell in sheets now, obscuring her vision. The Starfarer pitched hard in the rough water. One more.

She threw herself over the port side railing with a reckless disregard for cover. The lead boat bobbed in the choppy sea. It was empty. A long rope hung from the grapple hook down to the white tips.

They were boarded.

A white-hot thrill of fear pulsed through her and she threw herself behind a five-foot pile of rope dripping with seaweed. She scanned high for him along the deck and bridge catwalk.

Their usual play was to take the bridge and bring the ship closer to the Somali shore. Closer in, more of his underfed buddies would board with welding gear and punch through the engine room door to take the crew.

This guy hadn't had time to make it to the superstructure from the back of the boat. She waited, hoping to see him dart across the open expanse of the trawling deck.

A loud clang made her look toward the bulwark door leading to the lower decks. It creaked open and shut with the rocking boat. He'd gone below. The damp toothpick flattened as her jaw tensed.

The belly of the ship was full of hiding places - the perfect place to ambush her. Exactly the scenario a single operative needed to avoid. She'd messed up badly by letting him board unchallenged. Rage sank into resignation, and she shouldered her rifle again.

Maisie scanned the deck one last time before sprinting to the bulwark and sliding through the door.

The stairwell was dark, lit by only a single bulb. The dark sky added little light to the gloom. At the bottom of the stairs, she whipped around and swung her muzzle over the railing.

A dozen doors led off the long narrow hall. If he decided to pop out of one, she stood in a kill box with nowhere to move. She tried each door handle as she passed. They were all locked per protocol.

Ahead she saw the large secondary processing room. The crew didn't use this room since they froze their catch whole. It functioned as a storeroom and unofficial pot smoking area for the crew. She swept the room quickly and moved to the final stairwell on the far side that led down to the lowest level of the ship.

Only two compartments made up the bottom level. The engine room astern, where the crew hunkered down behind two inches of piston-locked steel, and the brine tank that occupied the entire aft section of the Starfarer. The refrigerated twenty thousand gallon holding tank held icy, salty brine so cold it could freeze a hundred pound tuna solid in less than twenty minutes.

Maisie tucked her elbows in tight to navigate the narrow staircase. She shivered in her damp clothes. Next to the brine tanks the temperature sunk.

The stairs ended beside the engine room door. It appeared intact. The crew was safe for now.

The short hallway ended at an insulated door that allowed access to a small platform above the brine tanks. The platform held two men max and was the only way to observe the payload without being exposed to the lethal brine.

A clank made her press herself behind a large pipe running from the ceiling. Slowly her eyes adjusted to the dark. An eerie red glow came from the emergency exit light above the stairwell. She left the flashlight mounted on the rifle off so she didn't mark her position.

All she could hear was the storm raging above. She spat out her toothpick and risked a look. The tank access door sat open.

With her rifle up, Maisie stepped out and moved down the hall. Gray light spilled into the dark hallway through the access door. The light came from two shafts originating at the trawler deck sorting tables. A stout net divided the holding tank down the middle and the sorting shafts dropped the graded fish into the correct side.

A quick movement blocked the light. Maisie threw herself to the wall just in time. She felt the concussion as rounds whizzed by her. He fired blindly around the door with one hand and missed her by inches.

Her finger twitched on the trigger, but she fought the

instinct. He stood behind two inches of insulated steel. Patiently she waited without making a noise, her SCAR trained on the door. Sure enough, a moment later his head broke the dismal light.

Maisie fired. Her rounds went through the opening and a few bounced off the far tank wall. She had no idea if she hit him, but she scored a victory.

Instead of slinging his rifle, he'd shot cowboy style. At her return fire, he dropped his AK-47. Now it lay useless on the floor.

Thanks to crew safety concerns, the access door couldn't be secured from the outside. She couldn't lock him in.

Maisie pitched the rifle around to her back and drew her Colt. She'd get jammed up with a long gun in that tiny space. The ridges of the worn wooden grip felt familiar in her hand.

She barely brought the gun to plane before the pirate came flying out the door in a full assault. He flew at her with a curved six-inch knife in his hand. Her father always said guns were business, knives were personal. This khat and adrenaline-fueled skinny was fifteen feet away from getting very personal.

Even with her gun already up, Maisie could only pull the trigger once before he slammed into her. Her scalp dug into the serrated steel grating, and she felt his blade glance off her magazine carrier and slice the skin across her left pec. Her breath caught in her throat as pain seared from her chest and shoulder. The SCAR's sights snagged on the rough flooring wrenching her back.

Her bullet punctured his right shoulder. The .45 round should have stopped him. Instead, it infuriated him. His wide eyes shone bright while the rest of his skin receded into the darkness.

As they struggled, he tried to hold down her gun hand

and get his knife back into her flesh at the same time. She saw him raise the knife again.

He was strong, but not strong enough to hold her with one hand. A quick twist of her gun hand brought the muzzle around and she pulled the trigger. The round whizzed by his cheek and he threw himself to the side.

Maisie bent her knee and slammed her boot sole into his chest. She yanked the hand holding her gun down and heard him yell in pain. The knife flashed again, and Maisie felt a sear across the back of her right hand. Her Colt bounced down the hallway behind her.

He brought the knife down again, but she caught both arms as he struggled to bury the blade in her chest. They fought, neither able to overpower the other. Maisie yanked both of his hands to the left while thrusting her body to the right. A powerful kick put him on the floor.

While he righted himself, Maisie yanked the SCAR back around but her sights snagged on a rat's nest of piping jutting out from the wall. She abandoned it rather than turn her back to the enemy.

Her adversary let out a ragged laugh. Blood shone on his forearms from cuts inflicted by the floor.

"Give us de boat and we let choo live," he said showing yellow teeth. This pirate knew English.

"You mean the royal 'we'? I killed all your brethren."

"If you kill one, four take the place," he said standing to his feet.

"Yeah, well unless you've got 'em in your pocket they won't help you right now." Maisie angled herself away.

He knew her rifle was useless. She'd never get it around in time; the space was too small. And her 1911 lay halfway down the hall.

"What do you want?" She knelt slowly as she talked, pretending to check an imaginary injury on her leg. In a smooth motion, she straightened, the dagger from her boot hooked in her index finger. Her fingers gripped the cutouts and five inches of cold steel pressed against her wrist so he couldn't see it.

He grinned. "I want to be rich."

"So you're after like thirty dollars."

"No, we want more than that."

"You," she corrected him.

It worked. He advanced on her, eager to make her understand. She backed up through the access door and saw the floor fall away beneath the platform grating. The air temperature plummeted.

"It's just you and me," she said.

His eyes flicked to her wrist and he realized she had a knife. An animal growl came from his bared teeth as he leaped toward her. Maisie was ready.

Sidestepping his charge, she slammed the dagger deep into his back, narrowly missing his spine. Before his screams finished echoing in the cavernous space, she slammed his knife hand against the railing and swept his legs from under him.

His knees hit the jagged grating tearing them open as his knife plopped into the frigid water below. Maisie grabbed his filthy pant leg and hoisted his bony frame over the railing. His flailing legs knocked her dagger from her hand. It landed on the grating and spun to a stop three feet away.

"Maya," he begged, clutching the railing, "please."

A hard shove sent him over the railing headfirst toward the floating chunks of ice and tuna.

She was already turning to retrieve her dagger when she felt a hard yank around her throat. Her back slammed against the metal railing.

The Somali's reach was long. Long enough to grab her rifle as he fell. His one hundred and fifty pounds pulled the nylon sling across her throat, pinning her to the railing, choking her.

Her vision blurred and she heard the sound of another knife being unsheathed. A second later it plunged into her upper thigh, the lowest point on her body he could reach from where he hung.

Stars seared across her already blurring vision and she clutched at the sling as it crushed her throat. A vicious yank pulled it tighter. He was trying to climb back up.

On the verge of blacking out, Maisie stretched out her foot and tapped around. The sound of scraping metal rewarded her effort. She bent her leg dragging the knife under her boot tread. She patted the grating softly, afraid of knocking the dagger off the platform edge.

Her fingers closed around frosty steel. She flipped it so the blade pointed up. Feeling along the bulging skin of her neck and slid the blade into the hollow of her collarbone. Thrusting it out and downward, she prayed it would bite. If it bounced back, she would slice her own throat.

The taunt nylon didn't resist the razor-sharp edge. The few remaining threads snapped under the man's weight. A guttural cry echoed in the chamber as he fell into the icy water still clutching her rifle. The moment he hit the water his screams cut off.

Gulping in air, Maisie rolled onto her hands and knees coughing violently. Through the grating she watched the pirate pump his arms, swimming in vain for the wall of the tank.

His breathing grew shallow as the water froze his body even as it remained liquid around him. She watched until his arms slowed and his eyes grew wide. Soon his body would be as solid as the tuna drifting beside him.

Maisie sat down gingerly and leaned against the railing

listening to the storm howl above. She could feel the blood on her injured leg grow cold on her skin.

The threat was gone. She was alone again. From where she sat, she could see the steel door sheltering the crew; a pitted, rusted reminder that no one was coming to help her. No hand would reach down to pull her off the cold grating or stitch her up. Or warm her bed.

Maisie Sheppard was on her own.

4

———

Kilidinia Harbor
Mombasa, Kenya
March 17
1300 Hours Local Time

Three mornings later, Maisie slung her backpack over her shoulder and walked through crowded Kilindia Harbor.

Outside the chain link gates marking the pedestrian entrance, the streets of Mombasa teamed with people. Vendors of every kind, working out of minivans and tents, filled every inch of curb peddling food and wares to dock workers. Maisie crossed the street and headed away from the port district.

Half an hour later she was deep in the city. She made sure to stay on the shaded side as much as possible. Eight weeks in the blistering sun was enough. Soon she turned left onto a narrow side road with dingy stucco apartment buildings on both sides. Some had small porches and some didn't, but they'd all seen better days.

Ahead a metal-roofed lean-to shack stuck out from a three-story building. The upper half was painted white, the lower half purple. A sign on the door said 'Mwagni Cafe'. Above the door, a hand-painted sign read 'Karibu Guest Rooms'.

The smell of something frying drifted through the open windows and the interior was gloriously dim. Maisie stepped inside. She bypassed the tables and took a seat at the bar.

The place was ragged, worn, and fastidiously clean. Three fast ceiling fans kept the heat tolerable.

The bartender came up to her with a wide grin. "Hello, Miss Maisie. Did you have a good voyage?" He spoke with a thick Swahili accent.

"Hi, Samuel. Yes." She smiled back while delivering the lie required of everyone in her line of work. "Smooth seas."

"Same as always, eh?" Samuel popped the top off the sweating brown glass and set the bottle on the peeling veneer in front of her.

"Same as always," she said drinking half the bottle in one swig.

Samuel could tell from her haggard face, and the bandages on her body, which voyages had truly been smooth, and which ones weren't. She'd grown fond of him over the last two years. He was a good listener and knew which questions not to ask.

"Hungry?" Sam asked her.

Maisie smiled and nodded. She hadn't eaten for twenty-four hours. "I'm a little hungry."

He flashed her another bright grin and hurried away. Soon he came back with a steaming bowl of stew and rice. On top was a generous pile of warm chapatis, a fried flat-bread. "And here is a spoon for you foreigners." He grinned again as he handed it to her.

Maisie devoured the stew slowing only when it was too

hot to swallow. She scooped up the last of the stew with a scrap of bread then pushed the bowl away, satisfied.

Maisie shrugged off her slouchy long-sleeve button-up. Her tank top was more comfortable in this heat.

Everyone at Sam's knew she was a regular. Still, a white woman in a Mombasa cafe was unusual, and almost every head turned toward her bare arms. She ignored them. What caught her attention was the lone head that didn't turn.

He'd come in halfway through her meal and sat alone near the door. The man had been careful not to look at her as she watched him in the cracked bar mirror. He wore a t-shirt and a tattered ball cap with his head dipped forward so the brim covered his face.

Like that would keep her from recognizing him.

Maisie sighed. All she wanted to do was drink three more beers, walk the two blocks to her tiny flat, take a shower, and drink herself into oblivion. When the dread and pain from the last gig faded, she'd go out and find somebody else willing to hire a woman.

Right now she needed her wits about her. That man was a mistake she couldn't afford to make again. With a disappointed look at her bottle, she pushed it back.

Samuel saw the movement and promptly moved to replace it. He stopped, confused when he realized it was half full. Their normal dance was Maisie saying she didn't want another, and Samuel putting another in front of her anyway. She shook her head a fraction and slapped some money down on the bar with a tired smile.

Maisie turned on her stool and looked at the man. The way he twisted his bottle was as familiar as his olive skin. He held one shoulder back instead of staying square to the table. Always, even alone, one side bladed away. Only when he trusted someone intimately did those broad shoulders loosen.

She grabbed her pack but didn't sling it in case she needed to drop it quickly. God only knew what he was doing here. Under her breath, she cursed herself for letting him get between her and the only exit. She was in such a hurry to get food and sleep she missed it.

For a moment she calculated her odds of losing him if she skirted his table and ran. They weren't good. Her leg was still sore. And if he knew she was in Mombasa, he knew where she lived. As far as he'd traveled to have a conversation, there was zero chance he'd leave without one.

As she approached his table, one of the metal chairs slid from underneath blocking her path.

"Hello, Maze." He finally looked up.

Maisie saw the brown eyes. After all this time, his voice still made her heart thump, but he could never know that.

She hunched her shoulders and contorted her neck in an exaggerated roll. "I thought I felt a knife in my back," she said giving him a cold look.

"I'm sorry to barge in on you like this." He offered a reserved smile with only a hint of the mischief he still couldn't quite hide. It made his eyes crinkle at the corners, a little more these days, but the same way.

"You got a minute?" He motioned to the chair he'd just kicked out.

Maisie shot the door a wistful look but dropped her bag and sat down.

Adrian Romero was the last person she expected to see in her town, but she mastered her surprise and slipped into the icy mode that served her so well.

"You look tired, Maze."

"I'm sorry. I didn't know you were coming or I would have put on some makeup."

His look of concern faltered. "I...."

"How did you find me?" She cut him off. He knew damn

well how much she hated small talk. It seemed especially heinous that he'd tracked her down, deprived her of anonymity, then sat there talking about bags under her eyes.

Adrian avoided her squinty glare, confirming her suspicion.

"I see. You already knew where I was. Do you have a list of my former addresses and lovers too?"

"Eh, you kept changing credit cards. There are some gaps." A smile flitted around his mouth.

Maisie's nostrils flared, but she was so disarmed by his easy charm she got tongue-tied. So not that much had changed.

"It was a joke, Maisie." Adrian took a sip of his beer. "I see your sense of humor hasn't aged well."

She glowered at him. "I don't remember having one."

"I used to make you laugh."

The glare died on her face. It was just like Adrian to waltz in here and pretend as if nothing happened. To him, she was just an ex-girlfriend.

"I'm sorry it was a bad joke. We haven't been following you. I knew you went to Israel after your father died. After that...." He shrugged. "The Department of Energy doesn't have the resources to keep tabs on former operative's kids."

"Still working for the ol' nuke dukes, huh? The Agency didn't come calling?"

"They did. The CIA is a little ivory tower-ish for me. You know I don't have the diplomatic skills for that nonsense. Didn't really want it anyway." He took a long pull from his bottle and gave her a sheepish smile. "The DOE is home."

"Too bad. You would've fit right in with those dum dums."

"Maze, I need your help."

Maisie guffawed and pounded her fist on the table so loudly that every head in the cafe turned. "That's the funniest fucking thing I've heard in a long time," she said, pretending to wipe a tear from her eye. "See, I do have a sense of humor."

Adrian sat quietly until the table stopped shaking. "You done?"

"I was done a long time ago, baby." Maisie dropped the fake laugh.

"This is a matter of national security."

"Which is no doubt why you're entrusting it to me." Her voice oozed sarcasm. "Why don't you tell me why you're here, so I can say no." She kicked her feet up onto the table.

He focused on her for a few long seconds. "It's about your father, Maze."

"What about him?" She knew the strain showed on her face, so she shifted in her seat allowing herself to look uncomfortable. Of course she was uncomfortable talking about her father.

"I need to find the uranium, Maze."

"A little late for that don't you think?" She relaxed in her chair but fought the lump swelling in her throat. The pain she thought she'd buried long ago bubbled up, raw and seething. After all these years, how fucking dare he?

Keep control, she told herself.

Adrian leaned forward and put his elbows on the table. Outside the open door, a loud group of men walked by laughing and talking. He waited for them to pass. "Maisie, someone knows about the missing U."

"And how would they know about it? The truth was buried in a DOE vault after they buried Dad. I'm the only person outside the agency that knows the truth about Orchid. Right?"

"Keep your voice down." Adrian looked around.

"Right?" She prompted, louder this time.

"Three months ago, a vigilante hacker group released

emails from a known Al Qaida operative in either Syria or Pakistan. We don't know exactly where, but the email included the words 'uranium' and 'Project Orchid'. The context is hard to figure out from the translation, so we had to reopen the case. Here's the thing. The IP address belonged to Al Qaida operatives, but the keywords were in the inbox of the email account.

"Someone is advertising."

"Exactly," answered Adrian.

"Who?"

Adrian looked uncomfortable.

Maisie's boots thunked on the floorboards as she sat bolt upright. Her voice was half growl, half whisper. "Who?"

"I have new information that he's alive, Maze."

"John Bressler," she whispered. Her father's old partner.

Adrian nodded.

Charles Sheppard had been accused of stealing highly enriched uranium and murdering John Bressler after they worked on the top-secret project. Accused by the man that now sat in front of her asking for help.

Maisie shook her head. "There was a body. They identified his remains."

"His body was ID'd by dental records. The rest of the body was burnt beyond recognition. It's possible the whole thing was faked. Charles and John were Cold War legends. I doubt there was a trick they didn't know."

"Dig up his bones. Test the DNA."

"The body was cremated."

"Fucking convenient," Maisie spat out.

"Yes."

"So," Maisie spoke slowly, "You're saying he faked his own death. That means Dad didn't kill him. You testified that Dad killed him."

"I testified that it was a suspicious accident. Come on,

Maze. What was I supposed to think? I found newspaper clippings of the car accident in Charles's apartment."

"Did he kill Dad?" Maisie felt cold despite the heat. She felt squeezed and the room slid out of focus. The scenario running in her head was not new. Fifteen years later, she was more convinced her father would never have taken his own life.

A hand touched hers and she started. She yanked her hand away from Adrian's.

His face softened. "Maze, all I know for sure is that everything pointed to suicide. The trajectory and the gun in his hand don't suggest anything else."

Maisie shook her head and shrugged like she didn't care. She swallowed the lump forming in her throat.

"Who killed who is not our biggest problem right now. We've got five tons of highly enriched uranium that is now known to some of the world's most dangerous men.

"Does Bressler have it?"

"I don't know who else it could be. I have a source saying he's alive, and then the hacked emails show up. It seems more likely now that they were working together. Maybe Bressler backed out on the deal or double-crossed Charles and tried to sell the U on his own. I don't know.

The only thing I know for sure is I have to find that second file. It wasn't in your father's apartment. But if Bressler's alive he has it, mark my words. And if he has it, then he knows where the U is.

"What makes you think I can find him?"

"You knew your father's work habits. You knew his contacts, his drop spots."

"I was seventeen when it happened. I was barely drinking age when you found out about it. It's not like Dad briefed me on his assignments."

"No, but you were with him constantly after your

mother died. Prague was no place for a little American girl in the early 90s, but there you were. Hell, half the time you were his cover story. You absorbed his knowledge and his methods. You ate dinner with his assets and went to school with their children. He groomed you, Maisie, even if neither of you realized it was happening at the time."

Maisie pressed her lips together and drew in a long breath. No. She realized it. And Adrian damn well knew it too. It's why he was here.

"Help me find the U before this goes sideways on us, Maze."

"Not my problem. I haven't been American for a very, very long time."

"That's not fair."

"What happened to me after Dad died wasn't fair." Maisie stabbed the table with her index finger. "I didn't hear you bleating about that. You just let it happen."

"Look, I don't blame you for not wanting to see me," said Adrian. "You have a right to be angry."

She looked away in case her face betrayed her.

After her father died in disgrace, she had no one to blame. No one to hate. Now the one person responsible for the ruins of her life had risen from the dead. Adrian just plopped a chance for revenge into her lap, along with the resources to pay for it.

The scattered drifting of the last years melted into the operational focus she was good at. She'd prayed for this chance. Her last chance.

Still, things would go more smoothly if Adrian got the wrong idea.

She forced herself to relax. "I'll do it for one," she said.

"One what? One million? You want money?" Adrian sounded surprised. Hurt clouded his face.

An evil spark of pleasure flickered. So he could feel hurt.

Maisie sat back. "I'm a freelancer. The goodness of my heart doesn't pay the bills."

"Oh, you do have a heart?" Adrian's voice was hard. "How patriotic of you, Maze."

She threw her hands up and shrugged. "What can I say? Treason is in my blood."

Adrian's chair scraped on the chewed-up linoleum as he stood. He reached into his pants pocket, pulled out three Kenyan shillings and tossed them next to his beer bottle. "Okay. One it is. Be at Likoni Ferry at nine AM tomorrow. See you then, Benedict."

When he was gone, Maisie pulled on the long gold chain around her neck. She reached for Adrian's beer and drained it as she ran her fingernail along the groove of the worn clasp. The locket popped open.

Inside was a creased picture of a pretty woman with long hair and green eyes smiling next to a young man sporting a bushy beard. Maisie's own two-year-old face grinned below her parents; the only proof she had that life had once been happy.

She snapped it shut and grabbed her bag. Without a look back she walked out.

5

Defense Intelligence Agency HQ
Joint Base Anacostia-Bolling, Washington D.C.
March 17
1300 Hours Local Time

A bulb was on the fritz. Luke heard a low buzz above his head every time the light flickered. It grated on his dwindling patience, although not as much as the group of people trying not to look at him. Four chairs separated him from the nearest person, and she looked like she would have preferred a few more.

Binders, coffee cups, and laptops cluttered the conference table. Modern, curved back office chairs surrounded it. People displaying various levels of stress occupied the seats.

Most of them were younger than Luke by about fifteen years. The young'uns all sported fashionable clothes. At least, Luke assumed it was fashionable. Wasn't that the lingo for wearing something that ugly? Every intelligence briefing he'd ever attended was filled with camouflage, not couture, but that was a lifetime ago.

Not that he could cast any stones about appearance.

He'd rolled in sporting clean but stained 5-11 tactical pants, and a faded plaid button-down cuffed at the sleeves. Even with the tear on the shoulder, it qualified as the nicest shirt he owned. His boots were the same ones he'd worn at the pier five days a week for the last eight months. The soles were separating and the leather was more gray than black. He kept his beard but trimmed it to look more presentable.

Luke scanned the group for the twentieth time. He knew two people in the room. That meant he trusted two people in the room.

Frank Longer, whom he'd served under, and the former head of Navy Intelligence, Rear Admiral James 'Moby' Brandis who now helmed the Defense Intelligence Agency. The only man above Frank at the DIA.

Luke never served under Brandis, but the man was a legend. It spoke volumes that men of Frank and Moby's caliber were unable to stay retired because the rest of these thumb suckers couldn't handle their shit.

What did he have to say to them?

Did Frank really think he had something to offer? He'd told Luke he was looking for a fresh perspective. Luke had perspective, but it certainly wasn't fresh.

The group around the table talked among themselves ignoring him.

"Are they trying to come across as hard-liners?" A young man with an unlined face and a sleek comb-over gestured with a tablet stylus in his hand. "We've got all the major players taking credit for something they clearly didn't do. We need to know why."

"What if they're manipulating fundamentalist groups," said a young brunette that looked fresh out of grad school. She wore a structured blue jacket with short fuzzy strings hanging from it that looked like blue worms. "Or paying them for a job? Terrorism outsourcing, maybe?"

"There are cheaper ways to get the job done," answered Comb Over.

Fuzzy shrugged. "Just brainstorming."

"Confusion could be their play. Keep everyone looking the wrong way. It could indicate a larger plan," chimed in a young black man whose shirt was a size too small. The buttons strained and he kept straightening in his chair trying to relieve the pressure on the fabric.

Luke thought Buttons sounded marginally less clueless than the others. More like he was thinking, and less like he had verbal diarrhea.

Frank stood and pointed a remote at a large TV on the wall. When nothing happened, Frank cussed and slapped the remote.

Out of nowhere, a mousy little gamer type with dirt brown hair and a gap in his front teeth appeared and took the remote. He mashed several buttons and the screen sprang to life. He whispered something to Frank who nodded, then he backed up still holding the remote.

Leaning over his armrest, Luke watched the young man recede to the corner and sit crossed legged on the floor. It looked like he was doing his best to become one with the carpet.

Luke immediately liked him. The nerd's social dread was his own bristling posture minus the age and experience. The young man pulled a wireless keyboard onto his lap and watched Frank approach the screen.

"Alright everyone, let's get started. Thank you for being here. This group is comprised of some of the best this agency has to offer. I appreciate those of you who volunteered for this assignment."

Frank motioned to the nerd sitting in the corner. "We need all the help we can get to shut down this threat before more Americans are killed."

Frank pointed to the screen as the flaming torch and red atomic ellipses of the DIA seal faded and a photograph popped up on the screen.

The image of a mangled, smoking red double-decker bus snapped Luke to attention. The first attack in London.

"Over the last six months, there have been three different bombings all targeting Americans. The first was October of last year." Frank pointed to the charred bus. "One American dead, four injured."

Frank pointed to Tommy who clicked.

The next photo was a street scene somewhere in Paris. Bistro curtains still hung in the shattered windows, the fabric pitted with holes from glass and shrapnel.

On the sidewalk under the window, tables and chairs lay tipped over. The scene was ashen gray and white except for a narrow ribbon of vivid red blood snaking through cobblestone.

"In December of last year, it was Le Bon Plat Bistro." Frank uttered the French in his South Carolina drawl. "It's a favorite of American tourists. The bomb detonated at supper time while the restaurant was full. This was the deadliest. Seven Americans."

Frank pointed again and the screen flicked to a pitted sculpture in the center of a fountain. This photo must have been taken soon after the bombing. Bodies still littered the ground.

Luke counted three figures around the fountain. Two huddled protectively together in a pool of blood. He felt his heart rate spike as he looked at the mangled Americans lying in the sunny Italian plaza. This briefing was for his benefit. Everyone else at the table knew this information.

"And finally, three weeks ago in Rome three more Americans were killed. We are no closer to identifying the responsible parties, but I'm hoping that's about to change. We're not the only ones working on this, but," Frank gestured to Luke, "*we* have help."

Luke ignored the furtive glances sent his way and watched his old commander continue speaking.

"Both al-Qaeda and ISIL have taken the blame for the first two bombings, and al-Nusra is copping to the third. But none of them did so until recently. Al-Qaeda and ISIL both piped up one week after the third bomb went off. Al-Nusra issued a statement two days later.

"Most of us, including me, think they did so because nobody else spoke up. As detailed as these attacks were, there would have been some kind of chatter. Even going back over the mountain of data we collected, there is nothing that supports the involvement of any of these groups.

"Not to mention al-Nusra has never carried out an attack outside of Syria and Turkey. Ever," said Brandis.

Frank nodded in agreement.

"Are we sure they're not working together? A syndicate of some kind," said Comb Over.

"Cooperation is unlikely. The groups that cooperate are few and far between. The only people they hate more than us are each other," growled Brandis with his arms crossed. "They kill each other when they're not targeting us."

Comb Over sounded defensive. "Unlikely maybe, but it is a new generation as you regularly point out, sir. Methods evolve. It's not impossible that they've brokered a peace to increase their reach."

Brandis scowled. "You might want to write that in pencil. Methods may change, but people never do. I've been around long enough to see hate passed from generation to generation like eye color."

"It would be unprecedented and a departure from the hardliner norm, but we'll keep it on the list," Frank said, ending the conversation. He pointed again and the picture gave way to a bullet point list.

"Here's what we do know. All three attacks clearly targeted American tourists abroad. One American in London, seven in Paris. Two Australians also died in Paris, but we believe they were in the wrong place at the wrong time. In Rome, the bomb was placed five feet from a tour group. It was surgical.

"Immediately after the London bombing, a known ISIL operative, and several lower-level al-Nusra members showed up on a monitored chat room - the same chat room - asking about you." Frank pointed at Luke.

"The same thing happened after the second and third attacks. Different forums, different operatives, but they were all discussing you by your real name, Luke."

Frank turned to address the table. "For those of you who don't know, Luke Marshall began his career as an Army intelligence officer and later transferred to the 75th Ranger Regiment. Before long he was selected for the 1st Special Forces Operational Detachment serving under my direct command during the war. Lieutenant Marshall has graciously agreed to assist us."

Luke sighed. He wished Frank wouldn't call him Lieutenant.

Frank turned back to the screen. "Unfortunately, the forum chatter is not Lieutenant Marshall's only link to this case. Every single American killed was from Colorado. Luke's home state."

Shocked murmurs rippled around the table. Everyone except the nerd feverishly rifled through notes or tapped on keyboards. Luke smiled. They didn't know that little fun fact. Frank played that card close, no doubt trying to protect him.

"So that's why he's here," said Comb Over loudly as the table erupted in strained whispers.

Frank held up his hands to silence the questions they were shooting at him. When that didn't work, he approached the table and began to soothe feelings hurt by the lapse of information.

An argument broke out over what else Frank might be withholding from them and how they were supposed to do their jobs without all the information.

Luke watched the scene around the table for a few moments before settling on the nerd in the corner. He was still on the floor tapping away when he caught Luke's gaze. The young man grinned awkwardly. Luke nodded in reply.

Ignoring the bickering group, the young man rose from his corner and approached Luke. He stuck out a pale, thin hand. "I'm Tommy Byrne. NSA." He looked at the floor more than Luke.

"Luke Marshall," said Luke, shaking his hand firmly.

"There's something else you need to see," said Tommy with a twitchy head jerk at the screen. "Frank was getting to it before he got," Tommy glanced at the table, "interrupted."

Luke turned. A video was cued up, and he could see the frozen figures ready to move at the touch of play.

"We've all seen it. We got the video from the Roman Police two days ago. It took weeks to get, and I had to talk their OIT guy through the process of uploading it." He laughed. "Italians, am I right?"

Luke smiled.

"Anyway, it's CCTV footage from an alley off Piazza Navona right after the bombing. "Most of their cameras suck, but luckily this is a newer camera. The footage isn't terrible. This guy's behavior is weird, which probably makes him the bomber. Or a delivery guy, or some schmuck. I don't know."

Tommy hit a key on the keyboard cradled in his arm. "No facial recognition hits on our end. I have our lab working with Italian authorities to see if we can get any hits on their facial recog platforms." Tommy grinned. "I'll probably have to tell them how to do that too."

Luke looked at the screen. The camera looked down a narrow brick-paved alley with tall buildings on each side. At the end of the alley, a slice of the crowded plaza could be seen.

As the next few hours ticked by in fast forward, only a dozen people walked under the camera. It was a quiet alley, not a main entry or exit point.

At 1432 hours the black and white picture rocked briefly, and the movement of the people in the plaza turned to panic. Moments later, a cloud of smoke obscured the square. Only the alley was visible onscreen.

Tommy slowed the video.

Figures in the video crouched and cowered in the alley trying to flee or take cover. Except for one man.

A young man in skinny jeans and a parka walked upright past a huddled family taking refuge in the alley. He strode away from the piazza until he came within yards of the camera capturing the footage they now watched.

The man stopped and looked up. For nearly five seconds he looked straight up at the camera. Then he dipped his head and resumed walking as two Italian constables ran past him toward the plaza.

Even on the black and white footage, the man looked dark-complected. He could have been of Middle Eastern descent, but he looked very European hip. He was young, maybe Tommy's age. His face, however, made the hair on Luke's neck prickle.

It wasn't possible.

6

———————

"Rewind that," Luke muttered to Tommy. He stepped forward.

Tommy tapped on the keyboard and they watched it again. As soon as the young man looked up at the camera Luke barked, "Pause it now."

Behind them, everyone stopped talking and looked. Frank abandoned the table and walked to Luke's side.

Luke took a step toward the screen and crossed his arms as he studied the man's face.

Was he imagining it? He squinted at the screen. No. It was right where he was afraid it would be.

The man's left eyebrow was less full and shaped differently than the right. A gap in the hair ran through the middle of the left brow. The skin hadn't scarred, the eyebrow just didn't grow back the same after it was blown off.

The man's stylishly ruffled hair distracted from a pronounced widow's peak. It wasn't visible in the footage, but Luke knew there were scars inside his hairline. His hair had been shaved close the first time he saw the boy. Cut close so the village doctor, with a gun to his head, could sew up the boy's scalp.

Luke raked his fingers through his hair and locked them behind his head.

Frank watched his reaction. "What is it, Luke? Do you recognize him?"

Luke dropped his hands and spun to look at Frank, his voice a strained hush. "Are my old ops declassified?"

"I highly doubt it. Tier One operations are seldom declassified. Why are you asking?"

"The king of hearts."

Frank raised an eyebrow.

"Mahmoud al-Din Arazi. Remember him?"

Recognition spread over Frank's face. "Yeah. He was an HVT killed during a raid on his compound in...oh six or oh seven."

"February, oh six," said Luke. "I killed him. My team took point on that op, remember? Not just him. His wife and most of his entourage returned fire." Luke turned back to the screen and straightened his shoulders. After a deep breath, he pointed at the screen. "I think that's his son, Nasir."

Frank pursed his lips and studied the paused screen for a moment. Everyone at the table hushed, and Luke sensed Brandis leaning forward.

"You're plowin pretty close to the cotton, Son. You sure about that?"

Luke made sure his voice was high enough for everyone to hear as he spoke. He wasn't going to say it twice.

"At the time, his son was twelve and recovering from an accidental detonation that killed Arazi's principal bomb maker and injured the boy. Learning family trade, I guess. It happened two weeks before the raid and was the reason we were able to pinpoint the compound.

"Al-Din Arazi sent for a doctor from the neighboring town of Bazwaia, who turned informant shortly after. Mahmoud and his wife, Amirah, both had weapons. When we breached the bedroom, I broke right. Coots went left. When they started firing I spotted Amirah. Coots hit the elder Arazi. They never made it off the bed." Luke paused as that night played back in his head. "We didn't know Nasir was sleeping in the room with them until we went in."

Luke looked back at the face on the screen. "He's the right age. Nasir would be about twenty-six or twenty-seven now. He wouldn't need much information to figure out who led the raid on the compound."

"Even if the mission was declassified, personnel are never named," said Admiral Brandis. "How would he know it was you?"

Luke closed his eyes briefly before he spoke. "It was a gunfight from pretty much the second we breached the outer wall. Halfway up the stairwell my NVG's took a round headed for my face. Probably saved my life. It destroyed my NVGs, but I ended up with only a wing. But I had to finish clearing the house without them.

"After we engaged al-Din Arazi the building was cleared, or so we thought. We turned on flashlights and I pulled down my facemask to check my face. It was then we realized Nasir was in the room."

"Shit," said Frank. "He saw your face."

Luke plowed on. "We cuffed him and put him with the women and children. However briefly he may have seen my face, I doubt he'd ever forget it."

"Not to mention, he's seen your face on every news outlet in the world over the last year," Buttons said. "The bombings started after you made national headlines, now that you mention it."

Luke grimaced, wishing Buttons wasn't right. "Yeah."

Frank looked at Luke, incredulous. "Is it possible?"

"Looks that way," said Luke, tense. "I've got a lot of enemies, Colonel, but none of them are blowing up buses to get at me."

His heartbeat raced as the memories of that night rushed back. The only people left alive in that compound were the ones with enough sense, or enough fear, not to pick up a gun.

Luke and Frank looked at each other, the full weight of Luke's revelation bearing down on them.

"I find it hard to believe that he's pulling off attacks the most sophisticated networks in the world can't, all to get back at you for killing Daddy," said Comb Over.

"It's not unusual for a terrorist to fixate on a specific person. Jimmy Carter for example," offered Buttons.

"Yeah, the President of the United States. Not a homeless lumberjack." Comb Over looked at Luke. "No offense."

"What happened to him after the raid?" Fuzzy was leaning forward addressing Luke directly now.

Luke shrugged. "Not sure. To my knowledge, there was no follow-up on anyone who wasn't an intelligence asset. And he," Luke pointed at the screen, "wasn't. We barely worried about secondaries back then, and we definitely didn't have the manpower to follow family members."

Frank and Brandis both nodded in agreement.

"He seems to like viewing his own handiwork. Did we check any CCTV possibilities at any of the other bomb scenes?" Fuzzy directed the question at the nerd.

"Yes," said Tommy, "all CCTV in the blast areas were checked. Nothing."

"He wanted us to see him this time. Why?" Fuzzy challenged the Admiral.

Brandis pointed at Luke. "I'm guessing it has something to do with him."

"What about DNA?" Comb Over looked around the table.

Fuzzy shook her head. "None of the bomber's DNA was on any of the devices. Not that it would have survived that heat anyway. Even if they collected a DNA specimen from the mother or father that night, we can't confirm an ident without the suspect's sample. Any biological evidence is a dead end."

"We don't need to confirm the ident." Brandis addressed the table.

"We always confirm...," Comb Over started but Brandis cut him off.

"The ident is good. We need to find him," Brandis said directly to Comb Over who scowled.

"At least we have a name," said Fuzzy, trying to sound positive.

"He probably hasn't gone by his real name since his father died," said Luke.

Fuzzy nodded in agreement. "We're still working with Interpol. Maybe he popped up somewhere else in Europe and we can find something. Driver's license databases or employment records. Maybe an alias will show itself," she said shrugging. "Sometimes the easy stuff works."

"Lone wolves don't have the resources to do what he did. They drive trucks into crowds because it's cheap," said Comb Over.

"I agree. I'll get my team on finances." Buttons was all business now. "The recon required to research and target the victims would take money. He picked expensive cities too. His network is probably small, but if he's got a bomb maker, he has to pay him and his suppliers. Any freelancers we like for that?"

"Maybe...." Fuzzy shuffled through a pile of paper, then

consulted a spreadsheet on her computer and rattled off several names that Luke didn't know.

"No, they're solid Al-Qaeda," said Comb Over. "Try the Syrian set. A lot of Iraqi refugees settled there after the war. Plus they're the most active right now, at least online."

She scrolled through the computer then made a note on paper. "Bomb makers in Syria," she muttered as she wrote.

"If you were going to find him through traditional means, you would have done it already. I know you did your jobs. The problem is he knows it too." Luke looked at Frank. "His father was highly intelligent, we have to assume the same about him."

"If you're a terrorist you need bombs, and you can't get them from the local hardware store. That's how it works," huffed Comb Over.

"Where are you getting your intelligence from? CNN?" Luke couldn't keep the anger out of his voice.

"He's not acting like a terrorist," Tommy finally spoke, sounding meek next to Comb Over's aggression. "That's why it's so hard to find him."

"What is he acting like?" Comb Over turned on Tommy, who shrunk a couple of inches.

"A vigilante," answered Luke before Tommy could formulate an answer. "This isn't politics."

Comb Over forgot about the nerd and rounded on Luke. "That doesn't change the fact that he still has to get supplies and money to operate. So where and from whom?"

Everyone in the room looked at Luke including Frank. Luke looked back at them. He racked his brain for something to tell them. He needed to point them down the right path so he could pick up his tattered rucksack and leave.

That was a problem. They hoped he was full of answers, but he wasn't. Luke had one lead and he wasn't going to share it with this crowd. He wouldn't even tell Frank in order to protect his old asset. He sighed and looked back at the screen. "I don't know," he said.

"Well, it's a good thing the Colonel brought you in on this." Comb Over threw himself back in his chair and slapped his stylus on the tabletop.

"Backtrack and start with his father's old network," Luke said to Frank. He was determined to give them something, even if it was small. "We left it largely intact and went after the head of the snake instead. We didn't have enough warm bodies to do anything else."

Buttons spoke up. "Are the old guys gonna hand over money to some noob and open themselves back up to intelligence authorities?"

"He's al-Din Arazi's son. That name alone would open doors for him," said Brandis. "Some of them might even owe his father favors."

"The old school are all dead or retired," said Comb Over dismissively to the old war dog.

To Luke, it sounded like disrespect. He opened his mouth to rip Comb Over a new asshole when he saw Brandis looking at Frank with a knowing look. The words vaporized on his lips when Luke saw Brandis nod.

"Luke, can I speak to you for a moment?" Frank strode to his office and held the door open.

Luke walked through and stopped, stiff, in the middle of the office. Frank eased the door shut and the noise around the table faded. The Colonel crossed to his desk and eased onto the edge rubbing his bad knee.

Luke knew what he was about to say.

There had been a day when Frank's word was his command, but that day was long gone. If Frank Longer thought Luke was going to work with the wet diapers sitting in the next room, he was about to be set straight.

"You're really going to make me tell you no?" Luke crossed his arms.

The Colonel shook his head. "Luke, I need you on this. You'll have full operational control."

"No."

"Who am I supposed to send?"

"Send the twenty year old with the comb over who still lives with mommy."

"You knew al-Din Arazi inside and out. Hell, you developed the asset that led us to him. If this guy is dusting off his dad's Rolodex, you're the man for the job. Son, those guys read about him in a history book. You tracked him down."

A history book. When had he gotten so old?

"Frank, you asked me to ID him. I did."

"I need you on this," repeated Frank.

"I won't do it, and you know why?"

"We all lost someone in the sandbox, Son."

"Don't give me that bullshit." Luke pointed a finger at Frank. "Not everybody lost what I did."

"I know," said Frank sadly.

"Every intelligence agency had files on Arazi. Get on the horn to old dogs, see what they can dig up. That's your starting point. They can take it from there." Luke jerked his head toward the conference room.

"We are the old dogs, Luke."

Luke scowled. "They can handle it."

Frank shook his head looking tired.

"They'll learn, Frank. Just like I did. You learn to put out fires real quick when your pants are burning."

"We don't have time on this one. What if he kills again before we find him?"

"I'm not going back in, Frank. I'm done." Luke turned his back, but the Colonel wasn't done.

"The Luke Marshall I knew would never turn his back on his duty."

Luke whipped back around, his teeth clenched. "I've done my duty. And I don't like the choices that life forces you to make. I didn't like it then, and I hate it now."

"The FBI wasn't the shelter you thought it was going to be." Frank's tone was respectful but direct. "And don't tell me you were happy slinging bags of rice in the jungle. The only thing you hate more than this life is inaction. Every time you run away you end up worse off than before."

At the mention of the FBI, Luke took a menacing step toward his old friend. He froze, surprised and ashamed of his impulse. Luke's anger told him one thing - the old man was right. Few things make people angrier than the truth.

"And Son, you've got no reason to run," continued Frank. "The world needs more people like you. People who stand up for what is good, even if it makes them enemies. People who give a hoot about what's right, not what's easy."

Luke's anger ebbed as he realized that even Frank didn't know the truth. Heartbreak and blind fury drove him, not some overdeveloped sense of justice.

Eighteen months ago, he'd left Georgia and ripped into Washington with a vengeance born of pain and rage.

Cheered by the average, condemned by academics, and feared by the powerful, it was an outrageous crusade to get revenge, and the whole nation thought it was justice.

"I'm not running. I just...," Luke trailed off and his shoulders slumped as he realized he wasn't convincing anybody in the room.

Now, once more he looked down the barrel of a choice too hard for anyone else to make. Consequences too heavy for anyone else to bear. And once again he was unable to walk away. Still paying for his sins.

Luke looked up. Frank was eyeing him.

"Alright," said Luke, sounding defeated.

The Colonel strode over and clasped a hand on Luke's stooped shoulder. "Son, it's a damned shame you got so good at hard and holy things. I wish you knew how sorry I am, for everything. It's not fair, and I can't make it so."

Luke said nothing.

"You'll have whatever you need. Just say the word."

"I need Tommy." Luke's voice had a hard edge. He'd wallowed in self-pity long enough. Time to work.

Frank clapped once and rubbed his palms together. "You got him. Anything else?"

"Just keep the rest of them away from me."

Frank laughed.

7

Sharq Souk Marketplace
Kuwait City, Kuwait
March 21
1945 Hours Local Time

As evening fell, long strings of lights along the rooflines flickered on bathing the waterfront promenade in a warm glow. Offerings of every nationality and quality drew a large crowd to the open-air market. Kuwait City natives' love of dining out was evident in the crowds that packed the restaurants.

Crowded was good. It would be easier to lose his tail in a crowd.

Luke stopped and feigned interest in a men's clothing store window, acutely aware that his blue Columbia shirt and brown 5.11 tactical pants were the opposite of the high fashion he pretended to consider. At least he'd sprung for new ones.

To see better in the gathering shadows Luke took off his sunglasses and slipped them into his chest pocket. He focused on a tailored dishdasha behind plate glass trying to get a view of the man following him.

He watched as traditional Kuwaiti and Western clothing all blended together in the flow of people behind him. The crowd was large and diverse, but Luke still looked foreign among them. So did the blond, obviously American, man following him.

Luke and Tommy arrived in Kuwait City two days before, and no one except Frank knew about it. At least that's what Luke demanded upon agreeing to the operation. Too many fingers in the pie made him nervous. If Frank wanted his help, Luke would do it his way.

Frank had done what he could to keep Luke's piece quiet, but the cat was out. This guy screamed spook. He wore a stylish fitted linen jacket over an open-collared button up and his light coloring stood out in the crowd.

Luke sized him up when he noticed his presence five minutes before. Who knows how long he'd had the tail, or if the man knew Tommy was back at the hotel monitoring.

"Where are you going, Arrow?" Tommy's voice piped up in his ear. "That was your turn."

Unconsciously, Luke touched his ear to dig at the tiny earbud. He wasn't used to hearing voices in his head. Catching himself, he redirected his hand to rake through his hair. The transmitter Tommy gave him was so small it completely disappeared into his ear canal. That was the point of course, but it felt as comfortable as having a large grain of rice jammed into his head.

"Standby, Wizard. I've got a shadow."

"Shit." Furious typing came through the earpiece. "Who?"

"Not sure," Luke said.

"Okay, Arrow," came Tommy's reply. "Let me see if I can find out who he is."

Luke heard more typing. He closed his eyes in brief annoyance before he said Tommy's code name again. The nerd had tried to make his call sign Kalashtar, which Luke immediately vetoed.

"Wizard, make sure the door's bolted first. Put out anything you've got for early warning."

"Roger."

Annoying code names aside, Luke felt better about the situation with Tommy back at the hotel doing what the nerd called 'magic'. The kid had a gift, no doubt about that.

Luke heard shuffling and puffing as Tommy left the hotel room desk he'd rigged as a makeshift tactical operations center. Then keys clacking.

"You good? Are you safe?"

"If anyone comes through that door, they'll set off the entire building's fire alarm. Best I can do right now. Let's concentrate on your tail," said Tommy.

Luke took the next right and walked away from the waterfront. "He looks American. No idea if he's friendly or not, but he'll blow Adder's cover." Adder was the man Luke came to see.

"What are you gonna do?" Tommy sounded relieved at the news that the tail was American.

That same fact infuriated Luke. His own side spying on him.

"If I can't lose him I'll break his nose," Luke said.

"You're probably better at the second one, Arrow. I'm on the neighboring frequencies to see if I pick up any other encrypted comms. We won't be able to listen, but it would indicate some secret squirrel activity. An educated guess and a few calls, I can probably find out who it is and if they're here for you."

"If they admit it. And he's definitely here for me." Luke

made a left and stopped again pretending to window shop at a booth selling Persian rugs.

The pretty young woman with big brown eyes and heavy black eyeliner smiled at him as she approached. He angled himself so he could see the wide promenade without turning his head.

Luke smiled at her tapping his watch. "Excuse me, Miss. Do you know what time it is? My watch is still on New York time." His rusty Arabic made him sound American, but it worked in his favor.

Her smile broadened, impressed that the American spoke her language. "Yes, it is ten minutes to seven."

"Ah, yes, thank you." Luke placed his hand on his chest dramatically like he was relieved he wasn't late.

In his peripheral vision, he saw the blond man walk by without glancing at him and continue down the promenade. Luke swung his head to peek over his shoulder to make sure the man was out of sight.

The man was gone, no doubt watching from some staggered point further down the promenade.

"Thank you for your help, Miss," Luke flashed her a dazzling smile which she returned. Her smile faded when he turned and walked away without another look.

Instead of continuing down the waterfront, Luke moved quickly among the stalls of the open-air bazaar. "Wizard, you hearing anything?"

"Nothing besides the usual military and police traffic."

"Get on the horn to Eagle and update him," said Luke.

Frank refused to be called by any other sign than Eagle. "Roger."

Ducking around stalls and hopping over a few tables, Luke sliced off a corner in the direction his tail went, hoping to cut him off.

Soon the open-air portion of the market gave way to a

large cobblestone plaza with storefronts and restaurants. Tables with umbrellas and flickering candles crowded the plaza, all filled with people. Another pedestrian-only street bisected the plaza, and the shops and restaurants continued in both directions. Luke went left.

Two blocks ahead he saw the promenade end in a four-lane highway with cars whizzing by. Across the busy street soccer games were underway in a large park lit by stadium lighting. Beyond it, the Kuwait City skyline spiked into the soft blue and pink twilight.

Luke saw two narrow streets cutting across before he reached the highway. He took the first right. Inwardly he cringed as he realized he was passing the Al-Abib Coffee House, his destination, but he walked by without so much as glancing at it. After a turn back toward the highway, he saw the blond man reappear behind him, this time very interested in lamb kebabs at a food cart.

Ahead a narrow alley cut behind the stores facing the highway. It was lined with trash bins. When he reached it, he saw that it went all the way through to the street paralleling his. He stopped long enough to gaze around like he was lost, then ducked into it.

Luke ran to the other end and checked around the corner. Clear.

He sprinted toward the highway, then down the sidewalk past glittering luxury storefronts. At the corner of the street he just left, he posted up and peeked through the storefront glass.

His tail peered into the alley he had just run through. Luke saw the man start as he realized he lost his mark, then hurry into the alley.

Luke moved slow and quietly. When he reached the alley for a second time, he waited. The man checked around every trash bin as he passed, wary of an ambush.

With stealth and speed born from thousands of hours of training, Luke stalked the man to within ten feet. His pursuer whipped around when he finally heard Luke's footsteps.

Lightning quick Luke closed the gap and snatched the man's left arm. Spinning him around, Luke slammed him against the building, with the arm twisted behind him. He threw his full weight against the man pinning him to the wall.

"Who are you? Why are you following me?"

"Whoa. Whoa. Whoa." The man held up his other hand.

Instead of looking afraid, he gave Luke a toothy smile over his shoulder. "We're on the same team, Buddy."

Luke wanted to wipe the grin off his face. "Call me buddy again, fuckstick. Who are you? Why are you following me?" Luke cranked his forearm against the man's neck jamming him further into the wall.

"The name's Simpson and I'm not the bad guy." The man kept his free hand up while he tried to keep his nose out of the stucco.

"Swearzies." Simpson flexed the pinky finger of his hand as he looked at Luke over his shoulder.

"Start talking." Luke ran his hand around the man's belt line feeling for a weapon. When he didn't feel one, he yanked the man around and slammed his back against the wall.

"So you're the infamous Luke Marshall." Simpson's voice was controlled and, to Luke's annoyance, amused.

Luke shoved him making the man's shoulder blades bounce off the wall. "Answer me."

The man dropped his right hand and held it out, offering to shake. "Jay Simpson. Nice to meet you."

Luke took a step back, releasing the man. No way that was his real name. "Who do you work for?"

"Come on, Marshall. You already know that." When Luke didn't shake his hand, Simpson dropped it and smoothed his jacket.

"Why is the CIA following me?"

"Did you think you were the only one hunting the guy blowing up Americans?"

"Hold on, I'm checking him." Tommy's voice sounded so loud in Luke's ear that he flinched. Simpson grinned.

"That doesn't answer my question," growled Luke.

Simpson shrugged. "We're having trouble finding this asshole too. When I heard Longer brought you in, I was intrigued, to say the least."

"You're working for Frank?"

"Nah, man. I got my own gig. You know how it is."

"You 'heard', huh? Were you just gonna follow me around? Is that the company's operational guidance these days?"

"Okay, you got me there. I was taking a shortcut. That's my bad." Jay grinned again.

"He's legit," Tommy said in Luke's ear. "Langley's owning him."

"But," Jay rolled his shoulders to straighten his shirt, "your name starts popping up everywhere. Then Longer pulls you in from whatever cave you were hiding in and, boom, we have a name. The real question is, why would I *not* follow you?"

Luke finally loosened his fighting stance. "You should have come to me. Poaching my asset is not okay."

Simpson was an inch shorter than Luke with none of Luke's hard-packed muscle. He had the fit physique of a runner and bounced from foot to foot with pent-up energy.

"Sorry. I know I'd feel that same way. It's just that you're not really known for...," Jay trailed off.

"For what?"

"Reasonable...ness? Friendliness?" Jay grimaced at having brought it up. "Look, I didn't know how you'd react." He rubbed his shoulder. "I don't know that I was wrong about that."

"You were poaching my asset."

"Yeah, I just apologized for that."

"I should break your jaw and leave you in a trash can, you goddamn spook," growled Luke. "I'll do whatever it takes to keep him safe. Do you understand me?"

"Yes, I do," said Simpson with conviction. "That's why I apologized."

"How would you like it if I followed you around to bleed your assets dry?"

"That depends on how many Americans had been murdered," Jay said looking around. "You're not America's savior, despite what you may think."

"Fuck you, Simpson. I'm the one who ID'd this guy when no one else could. It's not my reputation that's up for debate here."

"Agreed." Simpson threw his hands up in appeasement. "I only meant we should work together on this. If this guy is Arazi's son...."

"How much did Longer tell you?"

"Enough to connect a few dots. This isn't a turf war, Marshall. We need to find this guy. Everybody's in."

"Stop using my name," hissed Luke. "In fact, why don't you stop talking."

Jay laughed. "I can help you. I've got more resources at my disposal than you could possibly use."

"The CIA to the fucking rescue," said Tommy sarcastically.

"I'm not sharing my asset," Luke said with a note of finality.

"Fine." Jay wasn't fazed by Luke's underlying threat of violence. "But I do need to know what he tells you."

Luke studied him for a moment. Reaching into his pocket he pulled out his key card with their hotel name printed on it. He handed it to Simpson. "Room 608. Knock seven times."

"Gotcha, Arrow," said Tommy in his ear, confirming he heard the instructions.

Jay Simpson took it and winked at Luke then disappeared down the alley without turning around. As soon as he was out of sight, Luke wheeled and headed back to the shopping district.

"Wizard?"

"Yeah, Arrow."

"I want everything relating to my target sanitized. Understand? Wiped from the face of the earth. Database searches. Even Yelp reviews. Clear?"

"I'm all over it."

"Do it before the spook gets there."

"Roger. You can find your way back?"

"Yep."

Luke meandered the market in a circuitous route, now hypersensitive to the actions of everyone around him.

After a half-hour, his earbud transmitted Tommy awkwardly introducing himself to the CIA agent. Luke made a few more turns.

Satisfied he was clear, Luke found a public restroom and ducked into an empty stall. He waited until the only other patron left before he spoke.

"I'm gonna be out of range for about an hour," he said before pinching the short wire to draw the earbud out.

"What? What do you mean...." Tommy's voice faded as he yanked it out, flung it into the toilet, and flushed it. Then he took out his phone's SIM card and stashed it in a separate pocket, so Tommy, or anyone else, couldn't track his location.

Luke left the stall and washed his hands as another shopper walked in. Then he walked out into the warm night.

It wouldn't take much to reveal his asset. Even the background noise of a coffee house, and Simpson would be able to piece together who Luke had seen. The spook was on a need-to-know basis tonight, and Luke would decide what he needed to know.

If Simpson didn't like it, he could find Arazi on his own.

8

———

Luke dreaded coming back to this part of the world, but this time felt very different. No desert was visible in the urban cosmopolitan riot of flashing colors and shiny skyscrapers.

The only sand he encountered was the hotel beach with the warm Persian Gulf lapping at his feet.

This trip downrange felt more like a vacation. He and Tommy landed two days before and spent the next forty-eight hours in a luxury hotel room tracking down their target.

Tommy's performance cemented Luke's decision to keep him along for the ride. It would have taken Luke weeks to find the target, not hours.

Luke paused in a breezeway with a soaring arched ceiling and leaned against a pillar between booths selling cheese pizza and kebabs. He had a clear view of the entrance to the Al-Abib coffee house.

Ibrahim Mahmoud was now Ibrahim Samim, at least in the Department of Traffic driver database. He owned the coffee shop and was a respected pillar of the community, just as he had been in Iraq.

Once a doctor in a small village outside Mosul, Ibrahim's

family lived there until it was destroyed during the war. They moved into the city where it was safer if there was such a thing in those days.

American forces had made a concerted effort to contact and recruit doctors in the area. Sadam's elite had the resources for the rare luxury of private family medical care. It was a strategy aimed directly at the insurgent leadership.

Luke first met him in a firefight. The doctor was on his way home from a house call when he found himself pinned between insurgents and American soldiers duking it out in a Mosul alley.

Luke delivered him safely home and secured the cooperation, and friendship, of the best-connected man in the northern provinces.

The Egyptian-educated doctor liked to know and had amassed a Holmesian-esque army of gutter rat kids that gleaned information from every source imaginable in the greater Mosul area.

Sure enough, it had been Ibrahim to which Nasir's mother and uncle came after the boy was wounded in a bomb-making snafu.

Under the guise of making house calls on the convalescing youngster, Ibrahim gathered valuable information needed for the successful raid on Arazi's compound. Arazi never suspected him.

In return for his cooperation, Ibrahim demanded relocation for his entire family. After the big fish was reeled in, Command was happy to comply.

Luke volunteered to see Ibrahim and his family safely out of Iraq. Jammed into a rusty van to avoid attention, Ibrahim couldn't stop talking once he found out Luke played shortstop at Westpoint. Ibrahim had a fascination bordering on obsession with baseball.

Ibrahim had given up medicine and now practiced his

love of conversation as the owner of a small but popular coffee shop. In the mornings old men would gather and talk politics and current events, just like the old days.

Later in the day, drawn by the novelty of traditional Turkish coffee service, the young people showed up and the talk became pop culture references, soccer, and Twitter. As always, Ibrahim had his finger on the pulse of his community.

Satisfied everything was calm, Luke backtracked and entered a service alley. He stopped at the back door of the suite housing the coffee shop, propped wide open. He smelled strong coffee and heard clinking china.

Luke peered inside and saw four cooks and three servers scurrying around the modern kitchen equipped with stainless steel counters. An open fire burned in a brick hearth and copper pots with long ornate handles sat directly on the coals, the way the traditional drink had been brewed for centuries. Ibrahim was a slave to the details, his greatest strength.

In the main dining room, visible through a hanging curtain of beads, Luke could see and hear a healthy crowd of coffee drinkers cheering a soccer match on TV.

Luke slipped into the kitchen and scanned the faces hoping he would recognize the man after all these years. He nodded at a young man loading a tray with coffee and said in Arabic, "Pardon, where can I find Ibrahim? I have some documents from his attorney."

Instead of answering, the rushed waiter pointed to a swinging stainless steel door off the kitchen.

Luke thanked him and pushed through the door into a storage room with shelves piled with boxes and plastic-wrapped supplies. The aroma of coffee in the small space was strong enough to give Luke a burst of energy.

On the opposite side of the room was a more traditional

wooden door with a window carved into it mimicking the curved dome of a traditional Mosque. Gentle light glowed behind it.

Luke peered through the glass. Behind a narrow desk, an old man sat writing in a bound ledger. He wore the traditional Kuwaiti kandura, a long white tunic with a banded collar that buttoned around the neck and a red ghutra headpiece secured with a black cord. His long white beard brushed the desk as he bent over his book.

Luke rapped on the door.

"Enter, friend," came booming Arabic.

Luke turned the handle and pushed the door in. He stepped into a lavishly furnished office resplendent with bright Persian rugs, paintings of horses in the desert, and two overstuffed chairs. East was easily identifiable by two ornate but worn prayer rugs pointing toward the left wall.

"Yes. What is it?" The old man did not look up from his book.

"Hello, Ibrahim." Luke spoke in English, causing the man to stiffen as he looked up.

Surprise, then fear, passed over his face before Luke saw recognition. The old man stood slowly to his feet and rounded the desk.

Luke stood still, unsure of how he would be greeted after all these years.

A wide smile split Ibrahim's lips revealing coffee-stained teeth. The old man threw his arms wide and grabbed Luke in unrestrained joy. A few hard slaps on the back and Ibrahim released him.

"Lucas Campbell, it is an honor to see you again," the old man continued in English.

"You too, old friend."

Ibrahim gestured at the two chairs. As Luke moved to

them, Ibrahim poked his head out the door and yelled loudly in Arabic.

Someone answered him through the stockroom door and Luke heard him ask for coffee. Then he dropped stiffly into the chair next to Luke. Only when the old man sat did Luke sit down.

"You have been very busy, Lucas. Imagine my surprise last year when I turned the television on and saw your handsome face flashed all over the screen."

Ibrahim wagged a finger at him. "Did you tire of destabilizing your own country and come to destabilize mine again?"

The jab eased Luke's anxiety. He laughed. "Your old country didn't need my help. And I like your new one."

"Yes. 'Tis nice here. Peaceful."

"How are you, Ibrahim? You don't move around so well these days."

He waved a hand. "Old men do not move around so well, Lucas. But my children are grown with families of their own and my wife doesn't nag me anymore, so life is good." He grinned.

"How is Bushra?"

"She is with Allah now."

"I'm sorry. How long has it been?"

Luke felt a pang of sadness as he remembered Ibrahim's sweet wife. She had been kind to a weary, bloodied soldier when she had every right to hate him. She fretted over Luke as much as her own children. Ibrahim had a decidedly Western way of bluffing through his grief. Luke knew he missed her.

"Three years now." Ibrahim pointed an arthritic finger at Luke. "But you also look older than when we last met, Lucas."

"You can call me Luke. You know my real name now."

"Yes." Ibrahim brought his fingertips together in thought. "As do your enemies, if they were paying attention."

Ibrahim nailed it. At the time, Luke had been too consumed with his own agenda to think about the unstable mixture of a high-profile case and his spec-ops background. Overnight he went from being a ghost to having his own Wikipedia page. But it was too late to worry about that now.

"Some of them *were* paying attention, Ibrahim. That's why I'm here."

They broke off speaking as a waiter came in balancing two blue and red painted cups and saucers on a copper tray. He placed the coffee on the table that stood between the chairs.

"Thank you, Aabir," said Ibrahim.

The young man nodded and left. Luke picked up the saucer closest to him and looked at the steaming, frothy brown liquid. He took a sip. It scalded his tongue, but the sweet strong coffee was delicious. He set the cup and saucer down.

"It is good, yes?"

"Best I've ever had," said Luke with a smile.

Ibrahim smiled as he sipped. "You did not come for the coffee, I think. Or for my spirited company as much as I would like to think it."

"Unfortunately no, Ibrahim." There was a tense silence for a moment. "I'm here about Mahmoud al-Din Arazi."

Ibrahim lowered his cup to his saucer and set it on the table, suddenly tense. "What of him, Lucas? I thought that matter was concluded many years ago."

"I need to know what happened to his son after the raid."

His body might be breaking down, but the old man's

brown eyes had lost none of their steel. "Why are you asking about Nasir? After all this time."

"I think he is behind the Europe attacks. His revenge on me for killing his father."

Ibrahim looked thoughtful for a long time before speaking. "The prevailing theory is that Nasir was killed by the same man that killed his father."

"Nasir was alive when I left that compound." Luke leveled a burning gaze at Ibrahim. "I can get local propaganda anywhere. That's why I came to you. I need the truth."

"Yes, I know." Ibrahim smiled and began to sip coffee again.

"I saw him, Ibrahim, on a camera in Rome. The video was taken about a month ago." He told the old man about the bombing and the man in the camera with the same eyebrow scarring as Nasir.

Ibrahim's brow furrowed as he sipped.

Luke leaned forward. "I know you heard what *really* happened to him."

Ibrahim studied Luke over his coffee cup. "I have heard rumors of al-Din Arazi sightings in Syria. I know this to be impossible because I know that you killed him. When Lucas Campbell aims, he does not miss."

"Nasir did look a lot like his father," muttered Luke. "You've heard he's been to Syria?"

"Only rumors. Not proof."

"Still listening to the world whisper, I see." Luke looked around. "I haven't seen any desert rats run in and out," said Luke referring to his underage intelligence network.

"They are only allowed to come in the morning." Ibrahim shrugged like it was no big deal. "Many people depend on me for information," he said. "I do not want to disappoint them."

It was no secret the old man craved influence. He fed off it. And knowledge was influence that could be wielded to great effect, especially from a man as intuitive as Ibrahim.

"Why was he in Syria? We don't think he's connected to ISIL." Luke resumed sipping his coffee.

"I do not know."

"Did he go to Syria after the war?"

"Yes. Nasir spent a couple of years with a relative after his father and mother died, then made his way to Jordan. He found a job as a kitchen boy in a hotel. After some months he caught the eye of a visiting Saudi, who was impressed by the boy's work ethic, or perhaps the Prince just liked him, I don't know.

"Whatever the case, Nasir joined the Prince's entourage. All of this I know only because I have recently become acquainted with one of Nasir's distant cousins."

Luke leaned in. "Is this cousin too distant for any recent news?"

Ibrahim smiled at Luke. "Nasir has been back to Iraq in the past year. Iraq, Syria, and Belgium according to my source."

"Belgium? Why would he go to Belgium?"

"He was looking for someone."

Luke waited, silently chafing at the delay as Ibrahim finished his coffee.

"There is an arms dealer in Brussels. He is used by many of the jihadists that have taken refuge there."

"Name?"

Ibrahim shook his head. "That I do not know, Lucas."

"So he's after weapons. Why Belgium? There are plenty of weapons in Iran and Syria. I'm sure there's no shortage of bomb material either."

"Then perhaps he is after something different."

Luke grabbed his cup. The coffee had cooled enough for Luke to drain the sweet liquid.

Lost in thought, he forgot that coffee grounds settled at the bottom of the cup and tipped it all the way back. He choked back a cough when the fine grounds dumped into his mouth. Instead of being rude and spitting them out, Luke pulled a face and swallowed them.

Ibrahim laughed then grew serious. "Sometimes you must let the answer dictate the question, Lucas."

Luke looked at Ibrahim. "I don't suppose you know what that answer is?"

Ibrahim shook his head. "I am sorry. I have no contacts in Belgium."

Luke shook his head. "Don't be sorry, old friend. As usual, you are the one with the answers. Once again, you shine light onto my path." He rose to leave.

Ibrahim did the same, although slower. "Luke Marshall, you must be careful."

Luke stopped dead at the sound of his real name from the man's lips. It sounded wrong.

"If it is Nasir al-Din Arazi, then you are not dealing with the same type of jihadist you Americans are used to dealing with."

Luke nodded his head in agreement as Ibrahim continued. "If he is like his father, he will be very brutal indeed. Brutal and smart."

They fell silent, both remembering too well the innocent Iraqi citizens and American soldiers alike slain by the elder Arazi. Now his son carried on the family legacy.

"Thank you, Ibrahim. Blessings on you and your family."

The old man threw his arms wide and embraced Luke. "Be careful, my friend."

Thirty minutes later, Luke knocked on his hotel room door. The handle turned and it swung open. Simpson stood in the doorway, a scowl on his face.

Luke pushed past him and walked to one of the two king beds to pull his boots off.

Simpson bolted the door behind him and turned, still miffed.

"What the hell, man?" Tommy threw up his hands from the desk on the other side of the room.

Tommy's mobile TOC had cords and wires sticking out in every direction. It came with a beautiful view of the water, but that wasn't soothing the angry nerd. "Where's your earpiece?"

"In the shitter. Hope you brought a spare," Luke said.

Jay eyed him without saying anything.

Luke ignored Jay and spoke to Tommy. "Tommy, I want tickets on the next flight to Brussels."

"Okay." Tommy didn't ask any follow-up questions.

"What's in Brussels?" Jay asked for him.

"Apparently Arazi has made contact with an arms dealer in Brussels. He's the go-to guy for the extremists that have taken up refuge there."

The displeasure melted from Jay's face at the news. "Probably Kirill Kazlov. Or Boris Suminski, depending on who you talk to," said Jay.

Luke looked at him, incredulous, one boot in his hand. "How the fuck do you know that?"

Jay looked smug again. "He's a Georgian native who carved a niche supplying the new version of jihad in Europe. Part of the cache for the Paris attack was sourced from him. He's well known to us and Interpol."

Furious, Luke overhand threw his boot at the wall. It hit

with a loud thump and fell. "So you just leave him in business?"

"Kazlov is very, ah, flexible with information depending on how it benefits him. We received some of our best intelligence about terror cells in Europe from him, and he leaked the home address of the mastermind of the Paris attack to Interpol."

Jay leaned against the wall and crossed his arms as he continued. "Don't be so judgmental, Marshall. At least fifty men like him are waiting to take his place. Most of whom would not be so accommodating."

Luke could feel the bile rising in his throat. His distaste for the flexible morality of Simpson's world had not faded over the years. The false truths and the half lies take a toll on the conscience. A man should say what he means and shut up.

"I need to know where to find him," Luke said, yanking off his other boot and standing to take off his shirt. He needed a shower.

"You want me to share CIA assets, but you're not willing to share DIA assets?"

"He's not a DIA asset," growled Luke. "You probably don't understand this word, but he's a friend."

"I understand that word gets people killed."

"Arazi's been to Syria in the last year as well." Luke turned his back on the men to strip off his shirt. "We need to find out why."

"I'm on it," said Tommy.

"I have contacts in Syria if you need them. Despite your reluctance to do the same, all you have to do is ask."

"Thanks," Luke said grudgingly. "We can discuss it on the way to Brussels."

"Sorry, my man. You're on your own."

"You're leaving?" Tommy sounded surprised.

Jay winked at him. "This isn't my only op, kid, and Brussels isn't my turf. I got a problem I gotta go deal with. Besides, you and the old guy have it under control. I'll be in touch."

Luke watched Jay pull on his ridiculous linen jacket. He had to admit the spook was being very forthcoming with his information. No doubt Frank's extensive connections at Langley greased wheels.

"We appreciate the help," said Luke.

"Just following orders," answered Jay, confirming Luke's suspicions.

"So, two tickets to Belgium and one to...?" asked Tommy looking at Jay.

Jay clapped Tommy hard on the shoulder making him wince. "I only roll private jets, kid."

Tommy rubbed his shoulder as Jay gave Luke an enthusiastic thumbs up. "Keep me posted. The kid knows how to get me."

Luke nodded without a word. Jay unbolted the door and walked out.

9

———

Rue de Pavillon
Brussels, Belgium
March 23
1722 Hours Local Time

"Does the GRU know you're smuggling this shit out of Russia?"

No doubt prompted by Simpson, Frank had given Luke strict orders not to physically harm Kirill Kaslov. But Kaslov didn't know that. This slimy little man thought he was going to get a beat down unless he gave up what Luke wanted.

Luke was off to a good start. Kaslov looked terrified.

"I am not smuggling it out of Russia. I am importing it *to* Russia. For my customers," Kaslov insisted.

The short, rotund man waddled rather than walked. Curly black hair covered every inch of his body and tufted out the collar of his silk shirt. A love of rich food and wine strained the buttons of his expensive pants.

"You can't...beat brow me like this. I'm too valuable to American intelligence operations." His accent was thick, but his English was perfect. "Russian intelligence doesn't care about me anyway."

"Okay, first of all, it's browbeat. If you're gonna use American euphemisms, do it right. And, so we're clear, it's not your *brow* I'm going to beat," Luke said menacingly.

Jay offered to have a meeting arranged with the arms dealer, but Luke declined. He knew better than to be indebted to men like Simpson.

Besides, schmoozing this tiny Baltic cretin was not Luke's game plan.

Tommy easily found Kirill Kaslov's current outfit in the Belgium capital. Not that he was hard to find. He advertised the art and antiquities business that was a front for his more lucrative pursuits.

Simpson's assessment, however, was accurate. This pit stain of a human being began negotiating the second Luke kicked his door in. Kaslov had distilled fence straddling to an art form finer than the stolen masterpieces he fenced.

Kirill Kaslov outfitted an ISIL cell in Brussels that later carried out the deadliest terror attack ever on French soil. The explosives came from a different source, but the guns came from Kaslov.

True to character, the Georgian then turned around and fed information to Interpol and the French Police about the location of the cell's leader resulting in his arrest in Brussels. Kaslov's timely cooperation netted him a hundred thousand euros for the bounty on the terrorist.

Luke wasn't playing that game.

Kaslov looked up at him unsure if the American looming over him was joking. No one talked to him that way. He stood and drew his fat frame up to its full five foot, five inches.

"What would they do to you if they knew you snitched

to Interpol? Might hurt business if you're on the wrong end of jihad. They might turn those guns at you."

Luke had been authorized to offer money in return for the information he was after. Or a favor from the American government, if that was more palatable for Kaslov.

Luke chose a third option; the only one he could stomach.

He leaned against one of the large wooden packing crates that littered the renovated third floor of the old warehouse.

On one end of the huge room, a desk sat on a luxurious rug in front of an enormous fireplace flanked by custom-built bookshelves. Crates occupied the rest of the open floor. They were marked 'Fragile'. Luke knew some contained weapons, some art.

Kaslov swallowed hard and his eyes flicked to his shattered door as he inched his way toward his desk.

Luke let him go and picked up an unframed oil on canvas. Luke knew nothing about art, but the white wigged man on the painted canvas looked legit and very expensive.

"Listen up, you hairy asshole. You sell guns to murderers who kill innocent people. That makes you the bad guy, no matter what friends you've made."

"I have been given personal assurances direct from the station chie...."

Luke fought the urge to throw him to the ground. Instead, he studied the painting. "Do I look like the CIA station chief to you? Answer my question. "Nasir al-Din Arazi. Did he come to see you?"

"I need to make a phone call." Kaslov had made it to his desk and reached for the phone.

Luke dropped the canvas and covered the ground to Kaslov's desk before he could get the receiver to his ear.

Luke's hand cut a wide swath across the desk sending a stack of papers and the phone flying off the desktop.

The fat man froze where he stood.

"Nasir al-Din Arazi. Did he come to see you?" Luke asked again with his hands on the desk and his gaze boring into Kaslov.

"Who?"

"That's not going to work," Luke growled and moved around the desk.

With a shaky hand, Kaslov reached under his desk and pressed a button.

"They're not coming," Luke said.

The two security blobs employed by Kaslov were lying on the rubble-strewn second floor, zipped tied, and gagged with their own neckties. Kaslov's mouth moved, but he couldn't get any air over his vocal cords. His eyes were wide with fear.

"If you want to keep selling to the highest bidder, you have to survive me. Understand? Nasir al-Din Arazi. Did he come to see you?" Luke spoke through gritted teeth.

Kaslov pumped his head up and down so fast his chins jiggled. Without his security, Kaslov offered little resistance. Simpson was right, he was easy to control. Anyone else would not be as compliant.

Luke took a step back to give the man some breathing room. He stooped over and picked up the painting that he dropped earlier and pulled a knife from his pocket. It was a basic three-inch folding blade, but the second he held it to the canvas, it caused Kaslov more panic than when Luke kicked in the front door.

"I...I don't know this Arazi," blurted out Kaslov.

"You don't need to know him, Boris." Luke smiled when the man flinched at his real name.

"He's missing half an eyebrow." Luke tapped the knife

blade above his left eye. "And scars in his hairline." Luke tapped his temple. "I'm sure you noticed that. Probably looking for bomb materials."

"Isn't that a question for your CIA?" Kaslov sneered, "I don't deal in materials. They know that."

It took every bit of self-control Luke possessed not to choke this tiny clown out of his penny loafers. "Then why did he come here?" Luke played a gut feeling.

Kaslov hesitated, eyeing the knife in Luke's hand. Sweat darkened his collar despite the cool spring afternoon.

Luke moved the blade closer to the painting and selected a spot right across the painted man's throat. He put the tip of the blade to the canvass and tensed to push it through.

"That is a Jacq...NO," Kaslov lunged forward as he saw Luke move. "You American donkey. Fine."

Luke pulled the blade back and look expectantly at Kaslov who hurried on.

"A man by the name of Sergio Arenas came to me. He had the," Kaslov swirled his index finger in a spiral over his eye and temple, "the, the eyebrow."

"When?"

"Four or five months ago. I'm not sure. It's been a while."

Luke lowered the knife. "What did he want?"

"He didn't want material. Not exactly." Kaslov squinted at Luke. "He wanted the bomb maker."

Luke cocked his head to the side confused by the man's choice of words. "*The* bomb maker? There's only one?"

"Only one that can do what he wanted."

"Which is?"

"Plans. I believe you call it a custom job." Kaslov's mouth cracked into a smile. "What? You were not expecting me to say that?"

"He knows how to make a bomb. He's already done it three times very effectively. Why does he need plans?"

"This man is not really a bomb maker. He is more of a bomb designer, you might say. This Arenas, he wanted very specific plans. You have to make it yourself."

"These 'plans', are there many of them?"

Kaslov shrugged. "They are a...what do you say... novelty? The kind of trinket a violent mind likes to possess. They have never been used successfully as far as I know."

Luke's upper lip curled at Kaslov's philosophy but couldn't disagree with it.

"Plans, okay. But the hard part is putting it together. Assembling the bomb is what takes expertise. Arazi knows this firsthand. It's why he's got a jacked-up eyebrow."

Kaslov bent forward, suddenly eager to talk as though the subject fascinated him.

"It is not the job of a bomb to be complicated. I have seen the bomb maker's work. It is a true work of art. Eh," Kaslov waved dismissively. "It's not like he needs the money. It is a hobby for him. An obsession really. Custom plans, straight to your email. For a price of course."

"Easy to get through airport security," said Luke.

"Kaslov nodded. "Especially if you hide them between some naked pictures of a pretty girl. Security does not go through everyone's cell phone. Technology has made it easy to hide what you do not want the world to see."

"Where would they get the components to build it?"

Kaslov shrugged. "That is the problem of the buyer."

"And who is this budding designer?"

Kaslov hesitated. "I didn't catch who you work for."

"I didn't say."

"I like to know who I'm dealing wi...." The little man scrambled back behind his desk as Luke chucked the painting across the room and advanced on him.

Luke stabbed the tip of his knife into the smooth shiny wood of the desk. The tip sunk in and the knife stood straight up quivering.

"The only deal you're making right now is for your life, Kaslov. Tell me who he is, or I'll kill you. This is the only deal you'll get from me."

The little man let out a squeak of fear. "Taras...Taras Ivanov," he panted as Luke pulled the knife out and ran his thumb along the razor-sharp edge.

Luke propped one leg up on the desk as Kaslov delicately brushed off his expensive jacket trying once more to look incensed instead of afraid.

"Where is he?"

"He has a penthouse in the Palace Hotel in Kyiv. He owns a string of, uh, businesses in Kyiv that are very profitable from illegal forms of...uh...commerce. The local police are probably familiar with him since they are probably on his payroll to look the other way about the drugs and prostitution. I would avoid them if I were you."

Kirill shuffled nervously behind the desk and it occurred to Luke that he might be looking for a weapon.

Luke stood and immediately Kaslov threw up his hands and froze. He then proceeded to act like he was insulted by Luke's continued presence.

"I've told you all I know. I have nothing else on Ivanov, he's known to me by reputation only."

"You've been very helpful, Mr. Kaslov," said Luke standing, grateful he could finally leave.

Kaslov spun his chair around to put it between him and Luke. "Of course the world revolves around you Americans," Kaslov sneered from behind his cover. "I am very busy you know. Why can't you Americans not bother me at the same time?"

Luke froze mid-rise.

This time Kaslov vomited out the words before Luke could advance on him.

"You are the second today to ask about Taras Ivanov. The others were here a few hours ago. I supposed you are looking for the uranium too?"

Luke took a step toward Kaslov. "The what now?"

The color drained from the man's ruddy face. "Two Americans came asking about some Cold War uranium that went missing fifteen years ago. I knew of it, but I don't know where it is."

Kaslov had the chair in a death grip. He would tell Luke anything to make him leave.

"And they wanted to know about Arazi? Arenas?"

Kaslov shook his head. "No. They never said that name. They asked for Ivanov. I assume they think he has the uranium."

"What fucking uranium?" Luke said it through gritted teeth.

"I don't know. I don't know." Kaslov cowered away from Luke. "I thought it was a myth. Buried treasure nonsense."

"Still think that?" Luke eased up. He believed the sweating man.

Kaslov shook his head vigorously.

"And this Ivanov, you think he has the uranium?"

"It would make sense that he might have it," admitted Kaslov. "Or know where it is. The woman was more interested in his money. Typical woman."

He nervously chuckled at his own joke, then grew serious when he saw Luke scowl.

"Why was she asking about Ivanov's money?" Luke did not like where this conversation had arrived.

The fat man shrugged. "She is not wrong about it. Money speaks."

"You said there were two of them."

"The man wouldn't tell me who he worked for either, but he is definitely an agent like you."

Luke didn't bother to correct him. "What did they look like?"

"He had dark skin. Hispanic perhaps. She had brown hair and seemed very desperate. Beware the desperate man, but a desperate woman? Run away as fast as you can." He laughed nervously.

Luke didn't laugh. "Did they want anything else?"

Kaslov shook his head.

Luke sensed he had gotten everything usable from the man. At least without breaking Frank's edict to leave the man's face intact. He straightened and turned to leave, then looked over his shoulder. "But Ivanov might know where this uranium is?"

"In Ukraine, that is always possible."

Luke strode the length of the room and out the broken door. He took the winding stairs two at a time and hopped over the guards still lying bound on the second-floor landing. The final flight of stairs led out to the street through a shuttered storefront.

He made sure he pulled the front door tight before stepping out onto the Rue de Pavillon. Breaking into a brisk walk, he pulled out his cell phone and dialed Tommy. He told Tommy what he'd learned and instructed him to start gathering a dossier on Taras Ivanov.

In the time it took Kaslov to stutter that sentence, everything changed.

It was no coincidence that someone wanted Ivanov for a bomb and uranium. If Ivanov had the uranium, then that was what Arazi was after, not just a bomb.

And if Arazi was after missing uranium, he was going to detonate a dirty bomb. On US soil if he could find a way.

The game just changed. Luke needed to get back to the embassy. He needed a secure phone to talk to Frank. Frank would need to bring more resources and assets to bear based on this new information. Frank also needed to find out why no one but the bad guys seemed to know about missing uranium.

By the time he made it to the next block, Luke hung up with Tommy and slipped his phone into his pocket. He had a long way to walk and every street in this city looked the same.

Long rows of connected multi-storied apartment buildings grew more dilapidated the further they stretched from the affluent city center. Two old women sitting on the cracked sidewalk in kitchen chairs eyed Luke suspiciously as he passed.

Ahead a lone woman walked toward him, her hands stuffed in her pockets and shoulders hunched against the cold. She wore ripped-up black jeans and an oversized sweater. She wouldn't have drawn his glance a second time, but her boots were wrong.

The black combat boots she wore were scuffed and worn. Not exactly the kind of punishment they get hanging out at cafes and street corners.

Her gaze flitted to him and she looked away, the way women do when they see a strange man. But it was where her eyes went that caught his attention. In a move so slight he nearly missed it, her eyes flicked to the third floor of the building he'd just left.

They passed and Luke almost convinced himself he imagined it when he looked back at her. She was glancing over her shoulder at him. As soon as he looked she turned away.

He slowed and turned his head to watch her out of the corner of his eye. She kept an easy pace to the corner. Then she shot a glance in his direction before turning left onto Rue Vanderlinden, away from Kaslov.

The second she rounded the corner, Luke spun and jogged after her to get a visual. She'd been close enough to see him leave that building. Why would she care? She probably didn't. He was going to give her another look to prove to himself he was overreacting.

Luke peeked around the corner and swore under his breath. She was already three blocks ahead, her sweater flapping in the wind as she sprinted away.

10

Luke rounded the corner and broke into a run. The woman glanced over her shoulder then sped up heading toward the train station.

At the intersection of Rue Vanderlinden and Rue des Palais, she sprinted across the three-way intersection without looking, narrowly missing the grill of a white Mercedes Sprinter van. On the other side of the street, she ducked right and crossed another small street to Rue d'Aerschot.

Ahead was a five-foot retaining wall with a weedy berm that rose twenty feet. The light rails that serviced the city's public trains were on the other side. She had to turn left or right.

She went left. Luke went after her, cursing himself for not letting Tommy mic him. He'd refused, wanting to be the only one in his head. Tommy with an eye in the skies over Brussels would be helpful right now. Instead, he had to chase her down on his own.

This had to be the woman that came to see Kaslov earlier. That fact that she ran confirmed it, but why was she alone? Luke glanced around. Where was her partner?

Pain spiked up his left hamstring. He'd been out of the game for a long time, and he could feel the rust on his bones as he ran. Judging by her speed and agility she wasn't quite as rusty.

At the Rue d'Aerschot, he tore around the corner only to see that she'd gained half a block on him. She was northbound back to the Gare du Nord train station and the red light district where he'd gotten off to find Kaslov.

Luke sped up as he ran down the Rue d'Aerschot toward the train station with the berm on his right. Graffitied storefronts lined the street to his left. The ones that weren't shuttered were occupied with scantily clad women trying to set a hook in the mostly tourist foot traffic.

Luke gradually closed in on his prey. She was quick, but he was catching up.

She shoved past a group of young men. Her dark hair whipped as she turned to get eyes on her pursuer. Then she ducked through a bright purple door with a red neon heart hanging above.

By the time Luke made it to the brothel door, the group of young men had picked themselves up off the sidewalk speaking rapid Japanese.

Luke barreled into them knocking two of them down again and slammed open the purple door. The brothel was beginning to buzz for the night.

Inside, Luke slowed to make sure she hadn't set an ambush. Black lights illuminated the room making everything glow blue.

A beefy security guard appeared in the hallway, alerted by the woman who just charged through. The guard challenged Luke first in Flemish, then French, and finally in broken English.

Before he finished speaking Luke lowered his shoulder and plowed into the guard slamming him into a console table. The table splintered spilling an ugly vase of plastic roses and a ceramic dish of condoms. The guard's head bounced off the floor and he didn't move.

Luke jumped up and stepped into the doorless entry of a large room with assorted couches and divans. Women in various states of undress milled around serving glasses of liquor to the lounging patrons. She wasn't there.

A door slammed upstairs, and Luke tore up the stairwell. At the top, he paused in the hall that led toward the front of the building. The doors were all shut, but the light was better up here. He studied each of the locks for tampering.

A man yelled from the bedroom at the end of the hall. Luke ran to the door and saw that the wood by the deadlock was splintered. He pushed it open and saw the woman disappear over a small ledge outside the window.

A naked woman was already trying to close the window against the chilly spring air. Luke shoved her aside and threw the sash open again as the naked man started yelling for a bouncer.

Luke leaned over the wrought iron railing and looked down at the street he just left. She had dropped to the concrete sidewalk beside the group of tourists she already plowed into. They scattered in fear.

When she saw him looking down at her, she took off down the street.

Trying to spare his joints, Luke hopped over the railing and hung from it before he dropped the remaining six feet to the pavement and ran after her.

As they neared the train station entrance, Luke figured she would duck inside and try to lose him among the platform crowd, or the pedestrian tunnel to the other side.

Before they reached the entrance, she darted across the street and ran toward a high safety fence blocking off a crumbling flight of stairs. She scaled it effortlessly despite sprinting for more than a mile and ran up the embankment.

He cleared the chain link with a little more effort. Luke felt his muscles start to burn. By the time he made it to the top of the hill, he lost some of the ground he had gained.

The tracks were ahead, and he saw her drop lightly down the five-foot drop to the gravel rail bed.

The woman turned to see him clear the top of the steps. They were so close he could tell her eyes were green. She whipped around and bolted across the two parallel tracks as an incoming train slowed to enter the station.

Luke dropped to the rail bed as she darted around the front of the train. The conductor blared the horn at her, but she didn't flinch.

It was a short local train. Luke paused to allow it to pass then ran to the back. By the time he rounded the last car, Luke saw a leg flip over another chain link fence on the far side.

Privacy webbing hid whatever was behind, but Luke didn't slow down as he jumped up and climbed over. He dropped lightly to the ground and twisted, looking for his target. Nothing moved.

Graffiti sprawled over every inch on this side of the fence. The gravel lot was filled with old rail cars in various states of decay. The only light came from a weak streetlamp in the far corner of the lot. It cast deep shadows as the last daylight faded.

Luke stood still and listened. A low rustle of gravel made him turn. Ahead next to a pile of rusting axles stacked eight high he saw a quick movement.

"Who are you?" Luke spoke in English. "I know you went to see Kaslov. Let's talk. Maybe we can do business," he lied.

He moved quickly to the pile of train axles and rounded it. She was gone.

Something flashed on his left. His hand went numb and he whirled to face his attacker relieved he hadn't lost her. His relief didn't last long.

She backed up two steps once she landed her kick, but showed no signs of backing down further. She moved lightly on the balls of her feet. Hooded eyes locked onto his chest avoiding his face, not from shyness as he assumed earlier, but a skilled tactical awareness. A face only intimidates, hands kill.

"Who are you?" Luke said.

"Why are you following me?" Her accent was definitely American.

"You know why."

"I'm going to give you one chance to leave," she said, finally meeting his eyes.

"I'm not leaving until you tell me why you're talking to an arms dealer."

Her face showed no emotion and she began to circle.

Luke rolled his shoulders loosening for a fight. Before he could settle into a stance, she rushed, a heel aimed at his face. He blocked it, but it had the intended effect of distracting him. She slipped into the shadows again.

So that's how they would settle this. Guerrilla style.

Luke righted himself. He too picked a shadow and began to stalk her around the rusty train skeletons. Her soft footfalls moved in a large circle around him. She was done running.

Luke rounded a pile of crushed cars and crouched as he heard gravel crunch on the other side. He tucked into a corner of stacked train doors and let her circle back around.

She was hunting for him, quiet, quick. He let her close the distance.

When she was five feet away he lunged and grabbed her around the chest crushing her arms in a bear hug. She snapped her head back but connected with nothing. He had control of her for the moment.

Luke intended to interrogate her this way if that's what it took. He didn't have anything to tie her hands.

Pain shooting up his instep interrupted his thoughts of how to secure her.

Her foot slammed into his leg and raked down his shin to his foot. At the same time, the pain shot up his right leg his arms melted upward. She chicken winged her elbows and his grip loosened.

Going limp, she fell to all fours and aimed a donkey kick at his crotch.

Luke snatched her ankle. His hand closed around the boot speeding toward his crotch and he yanked it to the side.

He felt a tug and realized too late she had used his iron grip as a fulcrum to pull herself up to a handstand. Her free leg came over his occupied hands aimed at his face.

He shoved her leg hard and managed to keep the boot connecting with his temple to a glancing blow. They both fell and he heard her grunt as she hit the ground hard.

Luke jumped up already on guard, but she left him no ground. By the time he made it to his feet, she was attacking. Her hands moved so fast he could barely see them in the dim light.

She fought like a cornered animal. All he could do was block. If she landed a blow, it was lights out for him. She hit hard.

Luke saw her wind up for a backhand. His hand shot out and caught her wrist like a line drive. He twisted her arm so hard she had no choice but to obediently bend over or take a broken elbow.

"Who are you? Answer me." Luke commanded again, trying to hide how hard he was breathing.

Instead of answering, her head went toward the ground and he felt her center of balance shift to her other foot. He twisted harder. She cried out in pain as her arm bent the wrong way.

Luke's gaze dropped and he saw her free hand reaching toward her boot. Metal scraped against hard plastic as her hand came up skimming her boot. Her body hid the hand, but Luke recognized the movement. She had a knife.

Luke gave a vicious twist on her wrist and yanked so hard she went reeling across the gravel. She tucked her shoulder and rolled, easily landing in a crouch twenty feet away.

He could see her more easily now. She had landed in the weak pool of light from the lone streetlamp. She held her throbbing arm close to her ribs. The other hand flicked quickly then settled by her side.

That's when he saw it. When she moved, the dim light glinted on a metal dagger between her fingers. She moved it like it was just another appendage and settled it in a backhand grip. The original black powder coat had been worn off the blade and the wicked point. The woman flexed the arm he almost broke, trying to regain full motion.

Luke knew her gaze was focused on his body, reading him, but he couldn't tear his eyes off the dagger. They were moving so fast, there had been no time for Frank to get him weapons in country. He would have loved to shoot her.

He jerked his attention back to her right hand. In seconds, she could bury that thing hilt deep in his hide.

The woman didn't seem worried about escape. She wasn't cornered anymore. She had a clear shot to the back gate, but she stayed to fight. Now she seemed intent on teaching him a lesson. The metal tip of her dagger drummed her thigh, unconsciously, waiting for action.

When he first saw her, he thought she was afraid. That assessment had evolved several times over the past few minutes from afraid to guilty to desperate. As he readied himself for the attack, he knew he faced a seasoned fighter.

The game just changed again.

With catlike grace, she lunged at him and slashed the blade across her body aiming for his chest. Luke jumped back, but she attacked again and again. Each time, Luke took a quick stride back and to the same side, expertly side-stepping the relentless offense.

The woman made one more lunge. This time when he sidestepped, she changed direction in mid-air slashing the dagger around backhanded. She took the bait.

He easily caught her wrist and stopped the blade before it touched him. But she recovered fast. Before he could clamp down, she yanked her hand back, sliding through his grasp leaving a small cut on his wrist.

She left her chest wide open. Luke drove the heel of his palm into her breastbone. The knife clinked on the gravel and he heard the air leave her lungs with a soft 'uumph'. She dropped to the ground and rolled away.

Luke didn't give her a chance to recover. It was his turn to go on the offensive. Before she stopped rolling he was on top of her, straddling her, pinning her arms to her chest. He felt her legs writhe and kick as she struggled to break his hold.

Luke leaned forward needing his full weight to keep her arms down. Just when he thought he had control, he didn't.

Her left leg came up and swept in front of his face and hooked around his neck. Her thigh flexed and pushed his head to the side. His body followed. At the same time, she twisted in the opposite direction and tore her arms apart, breaking his grip.

Her body bucked underneath him, throwing him up enough for her to scoot from under him and create distance. Her eyes were wild now as she faced him again. She barely got out of that one.

Luke jumped to his feet ready to attack again. He heard someone running.

"Enough, Maze." A man's voice cut through the dark, and Luke whipped toward it, pivoting to take on two assailants.

The man came from behind the rusted pile of train doors they had been grappling beside. At the man's command, the woman obeyed and stepped back. She didn't look any calmer, but her body loosened from its coiled stance.

Luke's gaze flicked between the two of them. The new guy didn't look like he was going to join in the fight. He was calm, unlike the woman whose chest was heaving from exertion. Her gaze shifted to the new guy.

He turned from her and addressed Luke. "Mr. Marshall, I think we need to talk."

11

"Mr. Marshall, my name is Adrian Romero. I work for the Department of Energy. I see you've already met Maisie Sheppard." He gestured to the smudge of blood on Luke's wrist.

Luke looked at her. She glared back, a wild look still in her eyes.

Satisfied the woman wasn't going to charge again, Luke turned his back to her and studied the man. He was taller than Luke and smartly dressed in a gray corduroy jacket with a black t-shirt and blue jeans.

"I apologize for that, Mr. Marshall, but we're here on," he paused and looked around the rail yard, "business of a delicate nature."

So Kaslov told him the truth. They were looking for uranium.

"What business is that? If you know who I am, then you know who I work for," Luke said. "My clearance is higher than yours."

"Not on this it isn't," the woman said.

Romero looked annoyed. "Neither is yours," he said

quietly to her before turning back to Luke. "I know you're investigating the America tourist bombings."

"Yes." Luke didn't offer any more information.

"I got an interesting call a few minutes ago from my office." Romero glanced around again. "Let's go somewhere more secure. We need to talk."

Tommy was tracking his cell phone from back at the embassy. Luke was supposed to take a different route back rather than get back on the train. After Kuwait, they were both on high alert. The nerd would have known something was up when he saw Luke's signal sprinting through the streets of the red-light district. He didn't know yet that Luke was the one in pursuit this time. He must have alerted Frank immediately.

Luke followed the pair through the gate. As they walked toward the Gard du Nord train station entrance, Luke made sure the woman stayed in front of him.

At the crosswalk, Romero hailed a cab and the trio piled in, the woman jammed in the middle. She crowded Romero trying to pull away from Luke. Suited him.

After Romero gave an address to the driver, they began to whisper so the cabby couldn't hear.

Luke could hear them just fine.

"Why did you go back?" Romero sounded irritated.

"He wasn't telling us everything. I thought if I was alone, I could get more information out of him."

"You mean beat it out of him," Romero said, his voice flat.

She shifted next to Luke. Her glance flitted toward him but she avoided eye contact. "Not unless I needed to," she mumbled.

"Maze, you have to stay with me. Don't make me regret bringing you in on this."

"But you *did* bring me in." Her answer was defensive, but

the way she talked to the DOE Agent struck Luke as respect-ful. Reverent even. These two had a history. Fucking perfect.

Luke's phone buzzed in his pocket. He fished it out and tilted the screen away from his seat partners.

"You OK?" It was a text from Tommy.

Luke tapped a quick message back telling Tommy he was fine and would be gone a while longer. Tommy already knew who he was with. The nerd would keep tabs on his location.

"Ok," was the reply.

Luke opened a customized audio recorder app Tommy put on his phone and texted 'recording' so Tommy could listen in.

After they passed downtown, they took the second right off a massive roundabout. Four blocks later they stopped in front of a multi-storied building indistinguishable from a thousand others in the city.

Romero paid the cabbie and got out first, then Maisie. Luke followed. In silence, they trudged up two flights of stairs to an apartment door. Romero punched a code into the door keypad and entered.

The flat was clean and sparsely furnished. Sterile white tile continued through the open kitchen into a living room. In the living room, a blue Ikea couch and two cheap armchairs grouped around a small flat-screen TV.

Without a word, Romero crossed the room and yanked back the curtains. He examined the lock on the window, then checked the second window. Satisfied they were secure, he disappeared down the short hall to check the rest of the flat.

Luke took his phone out of his cargo pants pocket like he was checking a text. He saw the audio recorder timer still ticking and slid the phone into his breast pocket.

In the kitchen, the woman eyed him suspiciously as she

filled an electric tea kettle with shaky hands. Luke couldn't place her ethnicity. She had light olive skin, dark brown hair, and those blazing green eyes. She could have been from Eastern or Western Europe, or anywhere in the Americas. The only thing readily apparent about her was her resolve to kick his ass in that train yard.

She put the kettle on its base and clicked it on. Except for the icy glare she returned when Luke looked at her, she acted like everything was normal. She acted like they weren't chasing around a psychotic murderer trying to procure nuclear material.

Soon Romero came back into the living room and shed his jacket. "DOE doesn't have many safe houses these days," he said. "This is a random online vacation rental. It's easy enough to pose as a couple on vacation. Our security is keeping it low key."

He fell onto the couch and rested both elbows on the back of the couch and sighed like it had been a long day. "Or at least we were keeping it low key." He glanced at the kitchen.

After the cool spring night, the flat felt warm. Luke took off his jacket and noticed a rip in the cheap fabric. He'd bought it off a store rack when they arrived and realized it was much colder in Brussels than Kuwait. The only coat he owned didn't survive the foot chase.

He dropped it on a chair and sat down in the other. Unlike Romero's relaxed pose, Luke sat forward with his elbows propped on his knees.

"Maze, can you throw me a bottle of water?" Adrian called to the woman.

Luke heard the refrigerator door open and a plastic bottle came sailing over the kitchen island. Romero snatched it out of the air and twisted the top off. She didn't offer Luke any.

"You want one?" Romero held his up.

He appeared not to notice the withering looks traveling between Luke and his female companion. Or ignored them. Luke couldn't tell yet.

"No, thanks," Luke answered turning his attention back to the relaxed DOE agent. "Who exactly is looking for you?"

Adrian grinned sheepishly. "I don't think anyone is, to be honest." He pointed at Luke with his bottle. "It does seem, however, that we are here to see the same person. What do want from Suminski?"

"I know him as Kirill Kaslov. I think my suspect came to him. For bomb components, I thought, but now it sounds like he's after bomb plans."

Adrian raised an eyebrow. "Who's your suspect?"

"Nasir al-Din Arazi."

Romero looked thoughtful then shook his head. "Never heard of him."

Luke was done with chit-chat. "But you've heard of Taras Ivanov."

Romero straightened and leaned forward. "Yes."

From the corner of his eye, Luke saw the woman freeze, listening. "Kaslov gave you the same information then," Luke said.

"What do you want from him?" Adrian sat back.

"According to Kaslov, he's a theoretical bomb designer. If Ivanov drew up plans for him and I get my hands on them, it might narrow down his target list."

Luke saw Romero readjust on the couch. The information seemed to shake the DOE agent.

"I didn't know he existed, but Kaslov said you asked for him by name." Luke stopped and let the sentence hang.

Adrian breathed out heavily. "Yes. I went to Suminski to find Ivanov. I think he might know the location of...." Adrian trailed off looking at the woman again. Not for confirmation.

Luke got the distinct feeling he was gauging her reaction.

She propped her elbows on the countertop, a steaming mug between her hands. Her expression was hard, but Luke saw the slight head shake she gave Romero.

Romero considered for a second and then continued anyway. "The location of some highly enriched uranium that went missing several years ago. Out of the blue, mention of it showed up online several months ago. There were details in an email that no one should know about."

Luke's stomach felt cold. Not just uranium. Weapons-grade uranium. "Tell me about it," said Luke sharply. "How much? And what is 'several years ago'?"

"You didn't seem surprised when I told you who I worked for," Romero hedged.

Luke shrugged. "There's been a lot of nuclear activity in this part of the world since the Cold War. I know the DOE keeps tabs on it to a much higher degree than other intel outfits."

Luke noted that Romero kept saying 'I'. He didn't seem to include the woman as part of his op. At least not officially. It made her presence problematic, beyond the fact that Luke simply didn't trust her.

Adrian Romero studied Luke for a moment. "What I'm about to tell you is classified. It would cause a lot of powerful people heartburn if it gets out."

"I'm comfortable with that."

Adrian laughed. "That's what I hear." Then he grew serious. "In the mid-nineties, the Department of Energy and the government of the newly independent Ukraine collaborated on a nuclear disarmament project. The mission was to transfer a large cache of uranium from Ukraine to the States. At the time, Ukraine lacked the operational capacity to dispose of it.

"We had five tons of the purest batch of atomic material ever recorded outside of Russia proper. Ninety to ninety-three percent uranium - 239. Enough to develop dozens of nuclear weapons.

"The project was code named Orchid. It was the kick-off attempt to control the stockpiles of nuclear material left after the Soviet Union collapsed. Back then the worry was rogue states in the early stages of nuclear arms development. Today the use for that kind of material has expanded." He looked appraisingly at Luke. "Limited only by imagination, it would seem."

In the kitchen, Maisie snorted. "And the size of your bank account."

Romero ignored her and continued. "Project Orchid was spearheaded by John Bressler and Charles Sheppard. The two of them were the best agents in the field at the time. Maybe ever. Charles trained me. I was a new agent at the time."

Luke cocked his head. "Charles Sheppard?" Her last name.

"Her father." Adrian nodded to Maisie.

In the kitchen, Maisie pushed off her elbows, suddenly stiff. Her face looked so pained Luke almost felt bad. She mastered herself quickly, and again the DOE agent ignored her palpable discomfort. The vibe between these two was weird.

Adrian continued. "The packing teams packed 259 barrels with 8 pancakes each," Adrian made a six-inch circle with his hands, "separately packaged in lead-walled containers. The barrels were loaded onto four different ships bound for the US.

"Our cover story was that the barrels were crude oil samples to be tested for refinement potential. It was a free for all on Ukrainian oil at the time, so the cover was perfect.

Orchid was immediately declassified and became the standard in nuclear non-proliferation participation."

Adrian leaned forward and rested his elbows on his knees. "Except for a few operational hiccups, it was an unqualified success. Or so we thought. In '02 I discovered some of the U went missing during transport and no one knew."

"Then how do you know it was during transport? How did no one notice?" Luke felt the questions bubbling up.

The woman had forgotten her cup of tea. She stood like a statue in the kitchen, listening. Adrian paid her no attention, but Luke was acutely aware of her presence.

Adrian gazed toward the window not seeing anything. "I've asked myself that every day for fifteen years." He cleared his throat.

"In May of '02, I went to see Charles in Prague. He never came back to the states after he retired, so I went to pay him a farewell visit. I found Charles in his flat. He'd shot himself." Sadness clouded Romero's face.

He sighed deeply and continued. "That's when it all fell apart. I found a newspaper clipping in Sheppard's apartment about a car crash that killed John Bressler, three days before. The newspaper said the brake lines had been cut. Charles' suicide raised a lot of questions.

"The DOE said nothing officially, but I started investigating. Quietly." Adrian glanced up at Luke with a hard look. "It wasn't long before I found a serious problem in the Orchid project file."

Luke jumped up and started to pace. Adrian was about to give him the rest of the story, but it didn't really matter. There was loose radioactive material out there, and it looked for all the world that Arazi knew about it. He needed to get back to the embassy. He needed to think. Instead, he contained his burst of energy by pacing while Romero talked.

"There were four different manifests, one for each of the ships we contracted. The first ship carried 71 barrels, the next carried 64, then 56, and the last 68. For mission integrity, we compartmentalized the entire operation. There were three packing teams at Ulba. Each did their thing, packed up and left before the next team came in. The Ukrainian transport crews were hired separately and thought they were loading barrels of oil.

"Stateside, we had four different transport crews, all DOE guys. No one in the Ukraine government was privy to the stateside transport op, and the only ones that knew the entire op, including the total amount of U, were Charles, John, myself, and a select few agency supervisors.

"The third manifest, for 56 barrels, was missing the embossed US customs stamp from Norfolk Harbor. I interviewed the transport crew, and they all recounted 47 barrels. Every single one of them said 47. Mr. Marshall, I helped load those barrels onto the ship in Odessa. There were 56."

"It can't be that easy to dupe a bunch of DOE agents transporting nuclear material," Luke said.

"It's not. Per DOE regs, the transport team leaders have to make sure the paperwork is complete and correct before they take possession. Also per DOE regs, all project files have to stay together. Loose paperwork is grounds for review. The teams would not have taken possession without a complete case file, including orders that matched the manifests. Team leader signatures were all there except for the third shipment. He swears up and down he signed one for 47 barrels. I believed him. I still do."

Adrian stretched out his back and finally glanced toward the kitchen before he continued. "The third ship was delayed in Odessa for mechanical reasons, and it threw off the stateside transport schedule. The Ukrainian government wouldn't release the payload without the paperwork; they were having a hard time letting go of socialist bureaucratic tendencies, so we'd load one ship and fly the intact file across the Atlantic to meet the arriving ship and transport teams.

"The third ship wasn't repaired until a week and a half after the fourth ship had departed. We figured I had enough time to load the final ship and still fly over in time to meet Charles with the file for both arrivals.

"When I got to Norfolk, the third ship with 56 barrels berthed and the shipment had already left the shipyard only hours before I got there. Charles told me our supervisor had approved transport on just the manifest and the orders because of the mechanical snafu. I was a new agent. I didn't even think to question Charles.

"During my investigation, the transport team said Charles had all of the appropriate paperwork including orders that matched a 47 barrel manifest. They also said he had the complete case file." Adrian leaned forward and rubbed his face. "He couldn't have. I didn't get there until after that transport left. I had the file."

"So there was a fake copy," muttered Luke. "How original."

"Complete with an authentic manifest and authentic orders," said Adrian. "The transport team wouldn't have been fooled by anything else. The manifest for 47 barrels and the marching orders were nowhere to be found."

"Where was the partner during all of this?" Luke looked at Maisie. He still didn't know why she was here. She didn't look at him.

"Back at the warehouse overseeing cleanup. He was responsible for the packing and cleanup ops. Charles and I ran both sides of transport op."

"Sounds like you think Sheppard was behind it." Luke said it loudly to make sure the woman heard. The fact that he even had to say it pissed him off. Romero had a blind spot. Luke knew a thing or two about that. "Did Sheppard have the kind of pull it would take to get a fake set of orders generated?"

Adrian shook his head. "Someone else typing that up would have asked too many questions. I think he made them himself." Romero paused picking his words carefully. "Mr. Marshall, Charles signed for the manifests for customs in Norfolk. There's no way he would have missed that. He knew how many barrels were on each ship."

"So the second file fooled the transport team, then the correct forms were put into the real file and submitted? And everyone overlooked the missing customs seal." Luke made sure he had it right.

Adrian nodded. "John, Charles, and I all signed off on it after submitting our reports. Then it went into secure file storage. We were busy toasting our success. I missed it. I assumed Bressler missed it too. Now I'm not so sure."

"Did anyone else look at the file?"

"Yeah, the chain of command signed off, but bureaucrats never notice stuff like that."

"So now you think they were working together," said Luke already knowing the answer. "He would have needed a second person."

Romero nodded. "Exactly couldn't have gotten those barrels off and still have been in Norfolk to receive. The ship's captain had to sign off on both manifests. His signature is on the 56 barrel manifest from Odessa. It would have to be on the 47 barrel manifest in Norfolk as well to fool the transport team. Those guys are sharp."

"I assume you spoke to the captain."

"He died later that week. His crew found him floating in

a Norfolk International Terminal berth three mornings after the ship docked. His blood alcohol concentration was over point three oh. Celebrated his profit a little too hard I guess."

"And you're sure Sheppard killed himself?"

"I was for a long time. Now I'm not sure of anything anymore. I never thought he would do that, but then I was wrong about a lot of things."

"You don't ever really know somebody," Luke said looking at Maisie.

She gave him a caustic smile.

Luke sighed, feeling suddenly tired. He trudged back to the chair and dropped into it. "Tell me about the partner. What was his name? Breightling?"

"Bressler." The word was barely a murmur when Maisie said it, but it raised the hairs on the back of Luke's neck. He looked back at her. Her green eyes were dark and locked onto Adrian.

Romero didn't skip a beat. "After I found the newspaper clippings by Charles' body, I went to the crash scene in the Carpathian Mountains. The police report said the break lines appeared to have been cut. The body was burned beyond recognition. Three molars were the only thing identifiable. This happened three days before Charles killed himself. No way that's a coincidence."

"No," agreed Luke.

"I thought maybe they had teamed up and something went sour. It looked like Charles killed him then killed himself. All that changed six months ago when a source informed me that Bressler is alive."

"A source?" Luke didn't like the sound of it.

"I've been putting out feelers for the last fifteen years. I couldn't advertise the missing uranium so I went after information on Bressler hoping it would lead to the U. I got lucky. One finally turned productive." Adrian shrugged.

"My team turned the flat and the Prague field office upside down in '02. We didn't find the second file. I think Bressler faked his death to disappear. If he did, he's got the file, and probably the U. A lot of time has passed."

"The pressure is off and he's ready to make some money." Luke finished Adrian's thought.

Adrian nodded. "We," he threw a thumb in the woman's direction, "think he may have wholesaled it to Ivanov. Ivanov would have plenty of buyers on a waitlist, including your guy. I'm out of time, Mr. Marshall. We both are. We have to find the product."

Luke huffed at the word 'product'. "Tell me what happens if Arazi detonates a dirty bomb. How is this uranium different from any other nuclear waste?"

"It's a common misconception that dirty bombs kill by radiation. The product is in a solid state. It's soft metal basically. It is radioactive, but at a much lower level than when it's heated. So low in fact that it's not readily absorbed through the skin. For short exposure periods, you can handle it with latex gloves. If you disburse the product it will emit radioactivity, but it dissipates quickly. Too quickly to do any large-scale damage."

Luke screwed up his forehead. "You're telling me it's not dangerous?"

"No, that's not what I'm saying. The real danger is the heavy metal particles being ingested. The product acts like a toxin. If you ingest it, you'll get sick. You might die. The digestive system absorbs most of it to excrete, so survival is a toss-up if you swallow it.

"If you inhale it, however, it's a vastly different outcome. Small particles easily cross the blood barrier in the lungs and attach to blood molecules. From there it can deposit into any organ tissue. And quickly. Even at low doses, your cancer risk skyrockets. Higher doses can cause large scale organ failure within days. With a product this pure, a couple of breaths would be a lethal dose."

Luke blew out a breath and raked his fingers through his hair. "Is this common knowledge?"

Adrian threw his hands up looking defeated. "It wasn't twenty years ago. Today you can Google it."

Then Arazi knew it. He was after a specific type of bomb to disburse it. Shit.

"Where did the barrels go missing?" Luke already had a bad feeling about the answer.

"I have no idea where it was offloaded. It would be a hell of a lot easier to hide it in Ukraine than on US soil. And easier to move later. Or it could have been taken somewhere along the way. There's a lot of real estate along the Med Sea route. Romania, Bulgaria. Libya, God forbid."

"Fuck. How many people know about this?"

"In a post 9/11 world, this kind of information is dangerous. We had to keep it quiet. Only four people knew. Me, the direct supervisor on Project Orchid, Richard Fienne, who's now the Secretary of Energy. Fienne's direct boss, and the then Secretary of Energy, George Price who died three years ago. Six total if you count Sheppard and Bressler."

"Six?" Luke looked over at Maisie. At his question, she looked up.

"She makes seven," Romero admitted following Luke's gaze.

Adrian's expression softened. "Maisie's mom died when she was nine. Charles couldn't bear to be away from her, so when he took over the European Regional Field Office in Prague, she went with him.

"Charles was a talented agent, but he didn't know how to separate work and home life. Maisie was on a first name basis with more covert agents than an average operative. She's here at my request. She was the one who suggested that Ivanov might have the U."

Luke shook his head. The Department of Energy contracted the daughter of an American traitor because she knew her father's assets. Now he really had seen it all.

Romero hurried on sensing Luke's apprehension. "If Bressler sold, or is trying to sell, Ivanov's our man. He's the big kahuna in charge of the Kiev underworld. If it goes down in that part of the world, he knows about it. We needed an invitation from Kaslov. Otherwise, we'd never get close to Ivanov. He calls it an 'introduction'. He won't speak to anyone without it."

Luke's eyes narrowed. Kaslov left that part out. He turned to Maisie. "Is Ivanov one of your dad's lackeys too?"

"No. He was a KGB operative then. I only knew him by reputation."

"KGB?"

"He tells everyone he's Ukrainian, but he's Russian." Adrian spoke for her.

"Your father dabbled in a lot of Russian politics, did he?" Luke challenged Maisie again.

"He worked in post Cold War Soviet Bloc countries. What do you think?" She glared at Luke.

Luke turned back to Adrian. "You trust Kaslov?"

This time Maisie answered in loud voice. "Yes. Him I know. He owed my father his life several times over."

"That doesn't mean much to men like Kaslov," said Luke.

"I trust *her*," Adrian interjected. "I never would have known Kaslov's connection to Ivanov without her. This is very hard for her, but she's here."

The woman looked emotional at his words for a split second before she remembered herself and her expression turned back to stone. Luke saw the knuckles on her clenched hands turn as white as the countertop, but her face stayed relaxed.

Romero stretched and yawned. Eager to get going, Luke took it as a signal to leave. He stood and grabbed his jacket. "Thank you for the information," he said in a tight voice. "I'll be in touch."

12

———

American Embassy
Brussels, Belgium
March 23
2230 Hours Local Time

"Nada." Tommy leaned back in his seat. "Sergio Arenas was a mid level computer engineer at a banking firm in Madrid. Government records say he was born in Spain and lived his whole life there, except from 2011 to 2016 when he attended school in London. No presence on social media. He's a nobody."

"Those records can be faked or altered?"

"Hell yeah, they can, but it gives us jack. We need that name to pop on flight manifests or credit card transactions, but that trail went dark over a year ago. If it does show up, it's because he wants it to be seen. He's too smart for anything else."

Luke's hope that learning Arazi's alias would spawn leads had been dashed. "What about Ivanov?"

"That guy is definitely a somebody. Taras Ivanov is the deadliest agent in KGB history." Tommy's fingers slid up and down the mouse pad of his laptop making the screen jump up and down.

He read the rundown sent by Frank's team. "He's suspected of over a hundred assassinations, and that's just what's been documented. And, unsurprising, his weapon of choice was small-scale explosive devices."

Tommy clicked on the photo of a mangled body sprawled on the floor of a destroyed Russian apartment. "This guy is bad news. Now you say he's moved into bomb making?"

"Designing. Sounds like he's done getting his hands dirty." Luke sat slung back in his chair, his head back and eyes closed. His hand rested next to the desk phone ready to snatch it up when it rang.

After leaving Romero and the woman, Luke took a meandering route back to the embassy until he was sure he didn't have a shadow. His simple identify-and-get-out assignment had ballooned into a mess and he was getting tired of being followed.

Immediately upon returning to the vacant embassy office that had been home for the last two days, Luke phoned Frank. Over the secure line, Luke told him about the misplaced radioactive material and a not-quite conventional bomb to disperse it.

Frank's tone had flipped from measured to military. Once again he became the brash, elemental Colonel Luke remembered from the sandbox. He ordered Luke to wait with Tommy while he made phones ring all over Washington. Luke situated himself by the phone while Tommy read him everything Frank's superstar team dug up. They did a very thorough job, which annoyed Luke.

Tommy whistled. "This is insane. They like this guy for the assassination of Alexander Valeriy Menshikov who, at the time, was the deadliest assassin on the Russian mob scene. Ivanov is a butcher and a very effective one. Got run out of the motherland despite earning the coveted 'thief in law' status. Looks like some hot water with the Russian Federation in 2008. Now he runs most of the organized crime in the greater Kiev area. This guy's got real mobster chops."

Luke drummed the desktop with his fingers. "What kind of hot water?"

Tommy shook his head. "Not sure, but there's a five million dollar bounty on his head. He certainly pissed somebody off."

"No idea what it was?"

"Doesn't say. Probably slept with the President's side piece." Tommy laughed at his own joke.

"You got what you need? How long?" Luke pressed him. He knew the nerd would breach Ivanov's entire online life. How long he'd have to wait was the question.

"I'm working on it." For the first time, Tommy sounded exasperated with Luke's impatience. "Magic ain't easy, you know."

Luke rolled his eyes but relented. He pushed out of his chair as his thoughts swung to the woman.

Kaslov said she'd been particularly interested in Ivanov's money, then she tried to see him a second time. That woman was not looking for a sugar daddy. What was she looking for? "What do we know about the woman?"

The nerd's face lit up. "Thought you'd never ask. I Googled her fine ass the second I heard her name."

Luke stepped over his rumpled sleeping bag and approached the window. "Googled?"

Tommy chuckled. "My version of it. Eh, okay most of it came from the team. Anyway, your girlfriend's got an interesting past."

Luke suppressed a glare and studied the skyline instead.

Cities look better at night. From the tenth floor window, the lights of downtown Brussels rose like a giant beacon. Sparkling city lights radiated out from it.

He felt bad not joking with Tommy, but nothing about that woman was funny.

Tommy cleared his throat and switched to a professional tone like he was back with the team in that stuffy conference room. Luke felt worse.

"Lillian Maisie Sheppard is the only child of Charles Sheppard and Hannah Mizrahi Sheppard. Mom is from Tel Aviv. Mom had dual American and Israeli citizenship. She does too. In '03, about a year after her father died, she went back to Israel. She'd been living in NYC at the time."

"Why?"

"Not entirely sure. She bounced around to several community colleges in '02, then got rejected from Texas A&M. She tried to enlist in the Marine Corps and the Army but was denied enlistment both times due to health reasons, but it doesn't say what. Probably diagnosed with having a vagina." Tommy snorted as he laughed.

Luke looked at him, unamused.

Tommy cleared his throat and continued. "Actually, she was flagged by the CIA. Probably the real reason she was denied enlistment. That blows."

Luke turned back to the window as Tommy hurried on. "Daddy was from Houston, and the rest of his family is dead. She didn't have much to take her back to Texas, I guess. Her maternal grandparents were in Tel Aviv. Makes sense she would go back there."

"Are they still alive?"

"Uhh," Tommy scrolled down reading. "No, grandpa died in '05 and G-ma in 2012."

"Military?"

"Yup. IDF from '03 to '13. Well over the mandatory two

year stint. Oh wow, it says she possibly served in Sayeret Matkal. Don't know where they got that information. Women aren't allowed in most IDF spec-ops units."

"Not officially, anyway. It explains a few things," Luke said thinking of the way she fought. "Mossad?"

"No idea. Can't confirm it or rule it out."

"Isn't that a confirmation in itself?"

"Not with those guys. Mossad is completely black and Israeli spec-ops isn't much looser."

"How often are you requested to research Israeli special forces?"

"You'd be surprised," Tommy said grinning.

"You're the wizard." Luke wiggled his fingers in the air. "Can't you do the magic and get her service records?"

"No. I'm not doing that."

Luke turned as Tommy flat out refused his request.

Tommy looked at Luke like he'd lost it. "I'd need a team, and about eight damn years to get it done. And that's if there is even a spec-ops electronic record, which I'm not sure there is. Not even trying."

Luke didn't press. If Tommy said it couldn't be done, it couldn't be done. "Any chance she's still working for them?"

"I seriously doubt it. Her enlistment lapsed in 2013, and it looks like it might have ended badly. Her passport has been red-flagged if she enters Israel. She's not wanted, but somebody wants to know if she comes back. Looks like she doused that bridge in gas and torched it."

Luke thought for a moment. "What are the odds she's got Mossad contacts." It was more statement than question.

"We should operate under the assumption that she does. Man, that's hot," Tommy said, his scrolling halted on a picture of Maisie Sheppard in desert brown BDUs and a tight sand-colored t-shirt.

She had one foot propped up on a crate, a slung M4

carbine cradled in the crook of her arm. Tendrils of dark hair escaped her braid and curled across her face, lit by golden late afternoon sun. "She can kick my ass any time."

Luke walked to Tommy and looked over his shoulder. She was much younger then. Too young for the hardness he saw in her eyes.

"So she's helping the DOE guy find this uranium?" Tommy started scrolling again, but the other photos were only home candids of a much younger Maisie.

"Helping might be too strong of a word," said Luke. "And Romero?"

"He's legit. A senior agent at the DOE. He's got commendation after commendation, but he never rose through the ranks, just agent. Status quo kinda guy."

The phone on the desk rang and Luke snatched it up.

Frank started talking without a greeting. "You're going to Kiev. I'm sending new IDs and paperwork to the embassy."

"Yes, sir." A smile pulled on the corners of Luke's mouth.

Frank had forgotten Luke volunteered for this. The old war dog ordered him around like it was twenty years ago. It felt familiar, comfortable. Luke hated to admit it but having something to distract from the constant thoughts of Tully was a relief.

Frank continued barking orders. "Finding that uranium is now your primary directive. If we don't find that uranium we will burn, Marshall. Maybe literally. I'll let Arazi detonate a hundred IEDs before I let him get his grubby jihadist paws on easily disbursed radioactive material."

"Yes Sir," Luke said again. His smile prodded a suspicious look from Tommy.

"I've talked to the Secretary of Energy, the CIA Director, and Brandis and we're all in agreement. You have a lead. You're going to follow it. Tomorrow the four of you report to the DOE field office in Kiev and meet with the chief of station."

The smile slid from Luke's face. "The four of us?"

Colonel Longer ignored him and plowed on. "At the earliest possible, you are to snatch this ruskie asshole and interrogate him. I want to know what Taras Ivanov knows. If you're as good as you used to be you'll end up finding Arazi too. Time to brush the dust off."

"Sir, that's not a good idea."

"Why not?"

"I don't trust the woman."

Frank didn't miss a beat. "You don't have to. You're not working with her. You're working with Agent Romero, and if he feels he needs her then we don't have the luxury of cutting her out. The stakes are too high."

"She could be an operational threat," Luke argued.

"I know." For the first time, Frank's voice dipped to a hush. "If she becomes a problem, take care of the problem."

"Sir?" Luke couldn't believe what he was hearing.

"You heard me," said Frank, his voice grave. "You have authorization to do whatever is needed to preserve the integrity of the mission. Whatever is needed."

Luke paused for a moment. This thing had snowballed on him. "Understood."

"If the team digs up anything else, you'll be the first to know."

"Alright, Sir."

"Luke."

"Yes Sir?"

"Be careful."

Luke hung up with Frank and sat in the dark office for a few minutes. Luke didn't mind Adrian Romero tagging along. He disagreed with Tommy's status quo assessment. The guy seemed sharp and driven, even obsessed. Only an obsession to find the uranium could make a man give up a promising career to stay with this shit case for so long. To Luke, that had clear value in a high-stakes environment.

Sheppard presented a problem. She was the daughter of a traitor and abandoned not one, but two countries. Still, even with a traitor as a father, she could still be an asset. He could believe that.

What bothered him about Maisie Sheppard was how cool she tried to play it. She'd been betrayed by her own blood, but she was calm and controlled.

That he couldn't believe.

13

DOE Safe House
Kiev, Ukraine
March 24
1130 Hours Local Time

Maisie's hands slammed into faded green carpet as she did a pushup. Pulling her legs into a crouch, she exploded into a jump.

She'd rather be sprinting up and down the stairwell to burn off the frustration, but a run-in with the stalled, violent youths roaming this high-rise Kiev tenement would not be low key. Burpees in the safe house was what she got.

If depression had an address it would be this crumbling dump on the North side of the city. She longed for the endless sun and blue water of the African coast. At least the flat was clean and warm.

And it had coffee. After twenty more, Maisie decided she'd had enough and went to the adjoining kitchen. The high-end coffee machine stood in stark contrast against the ancient appliances and bubbling linoleum.

Rooting around in the cabinets, she found the coffee and

started the pot brewing. Then she went back to the living room where Tommy was fighting a losing battle with his awkwardness.

Sitting on the couch buried behind a laptop and a chaotic nest of equipment was the brains of Marshall's outfit. Tommy typed furiously to avoid eye contact. To make matters worse for him, she wore only shorts and a sports bra.

Falling to the floor, Maisie did fifty pushups directly in front of him before sitting on the pea green carpet to catch her breath. She stared openly at Tommy for a moment, a smile playing around her lips.

"Who was it?"

"Who was what?" He looked up, confused.

"Who did you hack to end up with this shit assignment? You should be at some private company with four screens, organic matcha green tea, and one of those carpal tunnel mouse pads or whatever. But here you are, in paradise." She waved around the dismal flat.

At the look on his face, she laughed out loud.

"They *did* bust you, didn't they? I was just kidding. They got lucky and caught you hacking into some corporation's server plantation, didn't they? Suddenly you're working to stay out of jail by stopping the indigenous black hats from doing exactly what you used to do."

"That's not how it works."

Maisie smiled at him. She liked this kid. "Really? Not at all?"

"Not most of the time," he answered, visibly wilting.

"Was it Anonymous? Sony? The FBI hack? Wiki leaks? Did you hack a cartel boss's Insta page and post granny porn? What?"

"No. None of that. I'm just really good at what I do."

"Kid, everybody here is good at what they do. The thing

is, even if you're the best, you don't end up here without," she cocked her head, "motivation."

Tommy shook his head, but she saw a little smile break on his face. "It was a hobby that turned into a career."

"Yeah, okay." She screwed her left eye into an exaggerated conspiratorial wink.

It seemed to break the ice. Tommy smiled. "What is your skill set?"

"Having the wrong daddy, apparently."

Tommy finally laughed. "And you're giving me shit for not answering questions?"

"I just crack heads, kid. I'm nothing special." Maisie picked at the carpet. "Not really complicated. You and Adrian are the brains. Me and Marshall, we're the instruments. The hands-on crew."

"Tip of the spear?"

Her eyebrow flew up. Mouse Pad must have seen history on her. "Something like that," was all she offered.

The coffee machine beeped that the coffee was done.

"You want some?" Maisie jumped to her feet and walked to the kitchen.

"That'd be rad," he said. "Is there sugar?"

Maisie rifled through the cabinets and refrigerator. "Yup. And milk."

"Just sugar, please. A lot of it."

Maisie poured two mugs. Into one cup, she dumped a large amount of sugar. She went back to the living room and nudged a router aside to make room for Tommy's mug on the end table.

"Thank you," he said.

"Sure." Maisie sat in the chair opposite the couch. "What are you doing?"

"Running encryption protocols on Ivanov's firewall."

"Ahh." She nodded then shook her head. "What does that mean?"

"Getting into his server was easy. But his IT guy knows what he's doing. There are layers of pixelated encryption attached to each document, e-mail or account statement and such. So even if you make it into the server, you have to un-pixelate any image you want to see.

"It gets even crazier because you can write multiple pixelation algorithms and rotate them through. Un-pixelating one doc doesn't mean you get everything. It's new and it's very good."

"Wow. But you've gotten through a couple layers of...whatever?"

"Yeah. I'm working on a master algorithm that will interpret the pixelation rotation rate. It's hard because the algorithms are rotating before I can fully map them, so I have to backtrack every time it rotates through. But if this works, I'll own them."

"Damn, Mouse Pad. That's impressive."

"It's taking longer than I thought. I don't think I'll have anything by the time they get Ivanov to the...," he paused, "welcome shack."

Maisie snorted with laughter. The men had left two hours before to set up Ivanov's interrogation sight at an abandoned farmhouse that Marshall dubbed 'The Welcome Shack'. The plan was to snatch the Russian from underneath his bodyguards at the club the next night.

Then a quick trip to the 'Welcome Shack' to see what he knew.

The men had left her and Mouse Pad at the derelict housing project with the baggage.

Tommy gave a sheepish grin and reached for his coffee mug.

"What I've gotten so far are some bank account e-statements. They're all for legitimate businesses, like the hotel he owns. There's a lot of cash there, but nothing that would put him on the Forbes list. Either he's hiding his money or he's broke."

"He ain't broke," Maisie said.

At her confident tone, Tommy studied her. "Yeah, that's what I'm thinking. So where's his money?"

Maisie took another sip and avoided Tommy's eyes. "That's the question, isn't it?"

It was *the* question. The only question she was here to answer. Adrian and Marshall could worry about the HEU and the little terrorist asshole.

"Can I ask you something?" Tommy took a sip of coffee.

"Sure."

"You think they're actually gonna be able to snatch Ivanov? This guy's got like twenty men on body security payroll alone. I'm willing to bet they're muscle-bound fart-plugs, just like him."

She laughed. "Eh, those guys aren't usually all that tough. They're muscle and no brain. Marshall seems to think they can."

"I'm not so sure about that. Rumor is when Ivanov was younger he fought wild animals gladiator style, with nothing more than a knife to prove how strong he was. I think this guy is trouble."

"That's a load of horseshit meant to intimidate." Maisie caught Tommy's gaze. "Don't worry about it, kid. You're not responsible for how this turns out. Remember that."

Tommy thought for a minute then nodded. "Give me your cell phone," he said. "I put an app on Luke's and Adrian's phones that shows me everyone's location. It looks like some rando Japanese game. I use it all the time and no one has any idea it's a tracking app. I'll show you how to use it."

Maisie picked at the armchair fabric. "I, uh. I don't have one."

"You don't have a cell phone?" Tommy gawped like she just said she ate raw cats. "How do you survive without a cell phone?"

"I don't really have anyone to call." She grimaced to make it seem funny. Or less pathetic.

"Oh, okay." Tommy dropped the topic.

The next three hours went by in awkward silence. Maisie prowled from room to room checking the windows in between rounds of sit-ups, push-ups, and pull-ups on a particularly stout closet rod.

Except for trips to the coffee machine and the bathroom, Tommy stayed on his laptop.

By four o'clock Maisie's stomach was growling and she went to the kitchen to dig through it for anything edible. She had one cabinet open when the front doorknob jingled.

Glancing around she spotted a knife block with black-handled kitchen knives. She pulled out the largest one. The blade was dull and rusty. With a huff, she threw it down and slid her dagger out of her boot. The deadbolt rotated and the door swung open.

Maisie clicked the dagger back into its scabbard and straightened.

Marshall led the way, his eyes already on her, narrow with suspicion as she straightened from re-sheathing her dagger. She met his gaze without looking away.

Adrian followed behind Marshall talking to the most average-looking man Maisie had ever seen. He had hazel eyes and a salt-and-pepper mustache. He carried a black canvas bag and she wouldn't have looked at him twice on the street.

Then she spotted what she really wanted to see; Adrian's

hands clasping plastic bags with styrofoam take-out containers. Food was here.

Marshall finally stopped glaring at her and breezed into the living room. "You got the uplink ready?" He addressed Tommy in a grumpy tone.

Maisie's lip involuntarily twitched in anger.

"Almost," replied Tommy with an edge to his voice. "It's not like I had a time frame to work with. You didn't tell me when you'd be back. And it's not like I don't have anything else to do right now."

Maisie couldn't help a smile. Mouse Pad didn't have time for Marshall's curmudgeon act either.

Luke mumbled something in apology and stalked off to the bathroom.

Adrian approached Maisie and gestured to the new guy. "Maisie, this is Leo Turner, DOE Station Chief in Kiev."

Leo grasped her hand in a firm shake. "Nice to meet you, Miss Sheppard." A quick nod then he followed Adrian into the living room to meet Tommy.

Maisie pulled two sodas from the fridge, grabbed the food bag, and headed to the living room. She didn't know what they brought, but it smelled fried.

She put a styrofoam container next to Tommy's seat and set a Coke on top of it. He now had his head stuck behind a small flatscreen TV with a camera attached.

"Here's your food," she said.

"Thankth," he said, a tiny screwdriver in his mouth.

Adrian and Leo moved to the kitchen for a hushed conversation. Maisie took a spot on the floor and sat crossed-legged, leaning against the half wall separating the kitchen and living room. She opened her container and looked down at fried sausages and a heap of golden fries. She stuffed three fries into her mouth as Marshall came into the living room.

He went to Tommy keeping his voice low and started asking about the aging equipment Leo had sourced for them to broadcast Ivanov's interrogation to Frank and his team.

Maisie watched Marshall with hooded eyes, but he was nice this time. He must have gone to the bathroom to pull the stick out of his ass.

Adrian finished his conversation with Leo in the kitchen and Maisie heard the balcony door open and shut. Leo stepped out for a cigarette. Adrian walked into the living room and headed for the back bedroom.

Maisie sat her food down so quickly french fries went spilling over the edge. When she caught up to him, Adrian was opening the bedroom door, a phone at his ear. Before he could close the door, she wedged her foot in and forced it open.

"Adrian, I need to talk to you."

"I'll call you back," Adrian muttered into the phone. He pressed 'end call' and tossed it on the bed. "About what?"

"Tomorrow night. You and Marshall are going in without me? What am I doing? Holding the door?" Maisie shoved her way into the bedroom.

"Maisie." Instead of recoiling, Adrian gently laid his hands on her shoulders sending a chill down her spine. "Ivanov might know who you are."

"Oh, that matters now? Until Marshall showed up, the original plan was for me to lure him away so I could talk to him. It didn't seem to matter then."

"We had no choice when it was the two of us. The plan has changed and I need you in the car."

Maisie could feel her face heating up. "You need me in the car? You came to me for help and now you need me in the car? Why are you pushing me out on this?"

"Why are you so dead set on going in, Maisie?" Adrian's voice was soft, unfazed by her anger.

Sudden fear startled her. Maybe she hadn't misdirected him as skillfully as she thought. She took a step back.

Adrian's eyes narrowed as he watched her demeanor change. In a cool voice, he said, "You're staying with Tommy and Leo. You're responsible for their six. And ours when we bring Ivanov out."

"So I *am* holding the door."

"I'm sorry, Maze." Adrian turned and reached for the phone on the bed.

Without another word she left the bedroom and closed the door, her head buzzing. It was all falling apart. If the Russian made it to the welcome shack, she would never get what she came for.

Did Adrian know how desperate she was to stop them from taking Ivanov? Was he on to her?

Marshall showing up in Brussels was the worst luck. She was a hair's breadth away from failing. Again.

Keeping her breath even, she threw out a hand and dragged it down the wall so she didn't have to look where she was going. She needed to think.

At the open doorway to the living room, she staggered when the wall suddenly ended. She righted herself, but not before she noticed Tommy glance up at her.

She hurried down the hall to the second bedroom. The men all agreed the woman would get the remaining room. At least she could regroup in private.

Her hand was on the pitted doorknob when she heard rustling behind her. She whipped around.

Tommy stood in the hallway, insecurity etched on his face. He held something out.

"You can use this one."

He held out a black smartphone. "You know...if you

want. For the op...or whatever. My number's in there. And Marshall's. It's encrypted and spoofed. I'm the only one who can track it." His face went red. "Call if you need anything... or...whatever."

Maisie looked down at the second-hand phone he'd placed in her hand. Suddenly her eyes felt hot and her anger at Adrian evaporated in the face of this offer of friendship. An offer she'd not had in years.

She cleared the lump from her throat and nodded enthusiastically trying to cover her emotion.

"I will. Thanks, Tommy."

Twenty minutes later they were all gathered in the living room.

"Cool," Tommy said and sat down. He grabbed his food and twisted the cap off his Coke.

Marshall dragged a chair from the kitchen, flipped it around, and straddled it. Leo leaned against the wall by the balcony door where he just finished his third cigarette.

"Alright. Let's get started," said Adrian. The TV flickered to life. Tommy handed Adrian his laptop who set it on the small console. Tommy had gotten the old tech to play with his new tech, but his laptop was tethered to the ancient TV by a three-foot cord.

"This is our target," Adrian said as a man in a ridiculous three-piece pin-stripe suit appeared on the screen. "Taras Ivanov is former KGB turned Russian mobster now operating in Ukraine."

The man on the screen looked in his early sixties. From the lines on his face, his hair should have been graying, but vanity and hair dye kept it a youthful black. He had a barrel chest and appeared fit for his age.

"This is a current pic. Leo got this shot yesterday once he

knew we were coming. Leo is familiar with Ivanov and this region in general." Adrian gestured to Leo who nodded.

Maisie crammed more fries into her mouth then remembered something. She set her food down and went to the fridge. God bless Americans in Europe. They were the only ones able to find ketchup. She sat back down and squeezed some on her fries. The bottle made a loud thbbbbt sound.

Marshall glanced over his shoulder, but he didn't look at her. Tommy did. She offered him the bottle, but he shook his head. She jerked her head at Luke and winked at Tommy. Then she squirted the bottle again.

Thbbbbt.

They shared a silent laugh when Marshall's eyes pinched shut in annoyance.

Good ol' Adrian didn't skip a beat. Never was one to pick up on her attempts at humor. Attempts at anything for that matter. She had to be direct and straightforward with Adrian or he missed it. A personality trait she decided to exploit the day he showed up in Mombasa.

Adrian leaned over and hit the arrow button to advance the photos. "Ivanov's organization is responsible for roughly sixty-five percent of prostitution, gambling, and drugs in Kiev and surrounding areas. Even the gangs pay him to operate in the city. For reasons we don't know, he's banned from Russia so now he's here."

He took a sip from a bottle of water before continuing. "We're hoping to glean some information from him about the location of the missing uranium, and maybe the terrorist behind the European attacks."

Maisie's eyes flicked to Leo looking for a reaction. His face gave away nothing. Adrian must have briefed him on the U.

"Our roads intersected," Adrian motioned to Luke,

"when, according to Boris Suminski, we found out he's also in the business of concept bombs."

Leo straightened. "Concept bombs? What on earth are those?"

"Plans basically," answered Adrian.

"Oh yeah, plans," Leo said. "Everybody knows he sells those. Overly complicated from what I hear. I just thought it was a racket. There's no way anyone could build one." He looked around, doubt on his face. "Right?"

"If you get the plans into the right hands, you could," said Maisie. She saw Luke glance over his shoulder again.

"According to Suminski, he was contacted by this man." Adrian leaned over and tapped the keyboard once. The surveillance photo of Marshall's terrorist in Rome came up.

Maisie squinted at the screen. He looked young.

"Based on our timeline, if he hired Ivanov, he probably already has the plans. It's very worrying that we're here to see the same man about missing uranium."

Maisie swallowed a mouthful. "That the only picture?"

Tommy answered her. "Yes. And we only have that one because he wanted us to."

Adrian pointed to Leo. "Anyway, if any U has been moved through this region, there's a good chance Ivanov will know about it. Leo's been keeping loose tabs on Ivanov for years. His habits are pretty stable. He goes to the Crescent disco club every night at nine. He owns it and he likes to do business there."

"We just call it the club," Tommy grinned at him.

"Right," Adrian said without a smile.

"You're just going to walk in there and take him?" Leo sounded skeptical.

"He drinks like a fish, so he'll have to take a piss at some point." Adrian advanced two slides. "According to the blueprints you gave us, there's a choke point here," he pointed at the screen, "before you get to the VIP bathroom."

"How many go with him?" Marshall's head came and he finally looked interested in the conversation.

"He takes four," said Leo, making Maisie wonder how many nights he'd spent in that club.

"He takes four men with him to the john? What is he afraid of?" Tommy scoffed.

Leo shrugged. "Assassins, Interpol, random American agents who show up to snatch him. He's not wrong to be paranoid." Leo turned to Adrian. "That still leaves the issue of getting him out to the car."

"We'll take out his thugs. I doubt he'll put up much of a fight with a gun jammed into his kidneys," Luke said. "Does he have a driver? Chase car?"

"Yeah, one of each," said Leo.

"Plus club security," said Luke.

"Piece of cake," said Leo sarcastically.

"Tommy got us a VIP booth near his," Adrian pointed to Tommy who nodded. "That will get us close enough to watch him. Leo, you and Tommy will stage with the car one block away on Kostolna Street. You know it?"

Leo nodded. "We can handle the car." He motioned at Tommy who looked nervous but nodded.

"We'll bring him out the side entrance. You pick us up here," Adrian pointed again, "at the rear of the alley. The front of the alley is the front of the club. If we have to go caveman on him, I don't want to carry an unconscious gangster past the entry line."

"That's through the kitchen," Luke said in a low voice. "Kitchens have a lot of weapons."

Adrian nodded. "I know, but it's that or the front door. We'll make it quick. Alright, Leo is going to shadow him tonight and during the day tomorrow to make sure he doesn't deviate from his schedule. Luke and I will finish up at the house tomorrow. Everybody get some rest. Tomorrow's gonna be a long day."

Adrian abruptly turned and walked to the hall pulling a buzzing phone from his pocket.

15

———————

DOE Safe House
Kiev, Ukraine
March 25
1500 Hours Local Time

Luke ignored the heavy breathing behind him as he unzipped the black canvas bag of weapons that Leo had sourced for the op that night. The pittance of firepower he managed to scrape together was disappointing, but sorting it out would at least pass the time.

The woman chose a different method of killing time. She ran around the apartment in a tank top and booty shorts like a fitness enthusiast having a psychotic break. Right now, she was doing pull-ups on the bar inside the empty coat closet. Her back flexed and she grunted trying to get one last rep.

"I can't believe that thing holds you up," Luke said dryly.

She dropped and rounded her shoulders to stretch out her back. "In Soviet Russia, closet rod break you," she said in a Russian accent.

Across the room, Tommy laughed. He sat in his usual

139

spot surrounded by his equipment and multiple cups of cold coffee. Sheppard and the nerd seemed to be on good terms.

It annoyed Luke that he had to fend off a smile. "Shut up, weird science, or I'll unplug you," he said, trying to sound lighthearted.

"Was that a jo...did you just make a joke?" Sheppard lightly tapped her temple like she was knocking water out of her ear. Tommy laughed again. Then she fell to the floor and started doing push-ups.

"You probably shouldn't put your face too close to that carpet," Tommy said, his eyes never leaving his screen.

She banged out twenty-five pushups before she spoke. "Got to," she panted. "Can't leave the flat."

Luke ripped three handguns out of the bag a little harder than he meant to. She was right about that. He was wired and desperately needed a release. When he did finally get to blow off some steam, Ivanov would bear the brunt of it.

He slammed a box of ammo onto the vinyl tabletop, then slowly unwrapped his clenched fist from around it. After several deep breaths, he serenely pulled four more boxes of ammo, three smoke grenades, one flash bang and several feet of nylon rope, and a few dull knives out of the bag.

It wasn't much. A Beretta 92SB that had seen better days, a Smith and Wesson model 60 with a cracked wooden grip, and Sig P228 with one mag. It would have to do.

Luke started thumbing ammo into the spare magazines, thinking about calling Frank to see what he could get his hands on. He dismissed the idea quickly; they only had five hours before go. He was just going to have to improvise.

Minutes later he had the weapons loaded snug in their second hand holsters and arranged neatly on the tabletop.

Luke was mediocre at interrogations to begin with and he knew it. Not his strength. He'd have to get resourceful with Ivanov.

Looking at his pitiful armory, the hesitancy he'd had about teaming up with Romero bloomed into regret. Next time he would go to Frank for some real firepower and bypass these small-time spooks and their empty weapons lockers. He almost wished Simpson would show up again.

In the living room, Maisie jumped up off the floor and wiped at beads of sweat from her face. Luke could feel her eyes on him, then fall to the guns on the table. He didn't want to give her one. He didn't trust her, but she was going to be in the car with Tommy and they needed protection.

He met her gaze without blinking, then picked up the Smith and Wesson. Walking into the living room he handed it to her.

"Ah, I was hoping I'd get the peashooter. I like knowing I'll be able to fend off stray cats should the need arise," Maisie said.

Luke turned back toward her, his temper flaring at her sarcastic tone. Then he saw her amused smile and realized she was poking the bear. He choked back his anger, surprised by it.

She had done nothing to make him hate her, other than be an insufferable asshole. But he couldn't cast any stones into that puddle and he damn well knew it.

"You can give it back if you want." Luke kept his voice measured.

"No, I'll keep it." She flipped the wheel open and checked the load. Snapping it shut with a flick of her wrist, she smiled. "I hate cats."

Luke turned around. Let her play her little games.

"Luke, you'll want to see this." Tommy beckoned from the couch.

"Show me." Luke strolled to him and bent over to see the screen.

"Okay, not to brag but I have full access to Ivanov's servers."

"You can brag." Luke grinned. The nerd was good.

"He banks here locally with Universal Bank. Not unusual. It's easy to access money in and out, right? Even mobsters need banking services, but there are a lot of transactions, both credit and debit. This seems very business-oriented to me. He's storing his net worth elsewhere, but some of these transactions are very informative."

Luke scooted a blinking box over so he could sit on the end table next to Tommy.

About six months ago, Ivanov received a wire for twenty grand from this numbered account. There have been about fourteen of that exact same deposit amount over the last four years. On the same dates, large-format emails were sent out."

"Bomb plans?"

"Probably. These outgoing emails were wiped from the server after *exactly*," Tommy emphasized the word, "twenty-four hours. Only the deletion record remains. My bot hasn't made it through everything yet, but so far nothing else has been handled with that kind of precision."

"So the money is the trail."

"Always," said Tommy.

"Any deposits from last year?"

"Four. All from numbered accounts."

"Swiss?"

"Three were Swiss. One is Syrian. Or their version of it. Luke, I don't think Ivanov has the uranium. Adrian said that would fetch about five million. There's nothing approaching that here."

Luke scowled. "This is probably a stupid question, but is there any way to trace the money backwards?"

"Maybe. There might be a back door through Ivanov's banking system. I'm still working on it. It's not exactly," Tommy's eyes darted to the woman. "Legal. Anyway, I'm not super confident I can pull it off. I wouldn't count on it too much."

Luke felt his phone buzz in his pocket. He pulled it out and saw a long string of numbers that he didn't recognize. Mashing the answer button he put it to his ear. "Hello?"

Someone breathed on the other end. He stood bolt upright forgetting about the equipment scattered on the table. "Who is this?"

Tommy looked up.

"Mr. Marshall." The voice on the line was smooth with the faintest trace of an accent.

"Nasir."

Tommy's hand flew to the side table and he cleared a wide swath of camera equipment he had wired for Ivanov's interrogation. His fingers whizzed over his laptop keys. Luke hit the speaker button so he could pull the phone from his ear and set it on the end table Tommy just swiped clean. Tommy leaned over for the number on the screen and went to work.

"Nasir al-Din Arazi, I presume," Luke said.

A pause. "Yes, Mr. Marshall."

"And how can I help you today, Nasir?" Luke knelt by the table and planted his hands on it bowing his head. He fought to keep calm. Tommy needed time to work.

Silent seconds ticked by. "Do you remember me?"

"Barely," said Luke coldly.

"I remember you."

"I bet you do," said Luke.

"It is very difficult to get the attention of a man like you."

"Well, you have it now."

"Yes. I've learned violent men like you only pay attention when someone else speaks the same language of violence. It was a painful lesson to learn, but a necessary one."

"Really? It should have been obvious for someone with a father like yours."

"Are you proud of killing my parents?" Nasir's voice was soft but inscrutable.

Tommy looked up from his screen to watch Luke.

Luke paused. His heart raced and he felt adrenaline kicking in. It felt obvious next to Arazi's calm voice. He'd called to fluster Luke, throw him off balance. There could be no other reason for it. Luke was not going to give him what he wanted.

He took one deep breath. His voice was low and even when he spoke. "No. But the mission was just."

"As is mine."

"What is your mission, Nasir? Killing your way to me? Is that your Jihad?"

"Jihad is for simplistic racist zealots who can't fathom a larger picture. I'm not a terrorist. I do not care about politics or policy."

"Just good old fashion revenge then."

"You talk as though it wasn't revenge that brought you and your countrymen to my doorstep, but it was. Not a lofty ideal. Revenge. People died that did not deserve to. You called your mission just because you are blind to any truth you did not invent."

"Open my eyes, Nasir," said Luke.

"The world is groaning under the weight of injustice. We cannot undo it. All we can do is answer it. The strong have a duty to do so, or else we will all be consumed."

"Very poetic, Arazi. No one is better at justifying what he does than a murderer."

"I could not agree more. You taught me that."

Luke froze as the words punched him in the stomach. Arazi didn't miss his hesitation.

"The only difference between us is that I don't pretend my mission is heroic. What is the saying, 'it is what it is'? If injustice can only be answered by injustice, I cannot change that. I no more chose my mission than you did the night you killed my family, Luke Marshall. It was chosen for me. And, like you, I will see it done."

Luke cringed at hearing his real name from the man's lips. "Cowards call everything an 'injustice'. What a fucking broken record. If you want revenge, come and get it. I'll meet you anywhere, anytime. I give you my word I'll come alone."

"Your word?" Laughter came from the speaker. "I know them thar Americans don't fight fair there, slugger." Arazi exaggerated a twangy southern accent. Then he dropped it. "I know you are after the Russian. You may think you can stop me, but you will fail. In the end, justice always prevails. Another lesson from my fine teacher."

Nasir sounded like he was winding the conversation down. Luke looked at Tommy. Tommy gave him a thumbs up accompanied by a scowl.

"You know what, Nasir? Maybe you're right. Maybe we are the same, but there's one difference. I don't hide behind unarmed civilians."

"Yes, but I am alone. Any courage I possess doesn't come from the army behind me. Till we meet again, Luke Marshall." The line went dead.

"Did you get it?" Luke fired at Tommy.

Tommy nodded with a grim look on his face. "Oh, I got it. A prepaid calling card from a major European carrier. Went to a switchboard. Probably used a prepaid phone too. It's untraceable. He could have been calling from next door for all I know."

Luke expected that. Nasir was too smart for anything else. Luke was getting too close and Nasir wanted to throw him off. Coldness settled in Luke's stomach. How could Nasir know how close he was to anything?

"How did he get my number?" Luke's voice was low.

Tommy's face hardened at the question. "He can't. Our phones are spoofed. Any calls we make bounce around from server to server online. There's no way to find your number unless...."

Luke slammed his fist down on the table. "Unless someone gave it to him."

"Shit," said Tommy.

"Why does he want revenge on you?" Her voice was soft.

Luke stiffened. He'd forgotten she was in the room. She'd heard every word.

An hour later Luke turned off the shower and stepped from the rust-stained enamel onto the threadbare bath rug. He toweled off and wiped the steam from the sink mirror. He'd trimmed his beard two days before and decided it was still passably neat. He'd only just gotten his towel tucked around his midsection when Sheppard barged into the bathroom.

"I'm not done," he said.

"You look done," she said, not hiding her eyes moving up and down his body.

Months of lugging hundred-pound sacks of coffee beans up and down the pier had packed muscle on his chest and arms and shaved his body fat to a level he hadn't seen since his twenties. His deep tan ended in a strip of pale skin just above the low-slung towel.

She winked at him and pulled her shirt over her head revealing a sweat-soaked sports bra. Luke could see why

Tommy had been so uncomfortable around her. That kind of brash confidence was unusual. Or fake.

As she reached into the shower to turn on the water, Luke saw a thin silvery scar curve from her shoulder blade down her right side. Only a razor sharp blade would make such a clean incision. It must have gone deep.

When her shorts hit the floor it was his turn to admire the view. Her skimpy thong revealed a fit body. It also revealed a scarred over bullet wound on her lower back and a fresh, pink scar on the back of her thigh.

It unsettled him to see battle scars on a woman's body. Women were supposed to be a soft, soothing touch after the battle; tender that balanced aggression. This woman was none of those things, and it threw her out of step with the world she lived in.

He felt a spike of pity for her. There were plenty of damaged men like him, but women like her were scarce. Alone without a brotherhood to legitimize them.

Scars like that could twist a soul into something unrecognizable. Adrian was blind to that because of their past. Luke didn't blame him. He couldn't judge a man for making the same mistakes he did.

"Tommy said you were Delta," she said, eyeing him. "Is that why you get the urge to control everything?"

Luke, however, would not be making that mistake again. "You might have Romero fooled, but not me."

"That's kinda rude."

"Why do you care about finding uranium you supposedly never knew about in the first place?" He didn't have time for games.

Her eyes narrowed at the word 'supposedly' but Luke pushed on. "You smell like ulterior motive to me."

"Well, I am about to take a shower."

Luke's face darkened. "No facts. Just jokes."

She tilted her head and gave him a cryptic smiled. "There are no facts. Only interpretations. Usually the wrong ones."

He turned his back on her and ran a comb through his hair. "Those days are long gone. I just want to finish this so I can get back to a simpler life. Away from all this."

A soft hand grazed down his forearm. She was close. Very close. Steam from the shower swirled around them as she ran a finger over his tattoo.

"A simple life? You tattoo your body with old Bill's most ambiguous play and say you want a simple life?"

"And you quote Nietzsche to justify being deceitful."

She held onto his arm and they looked at each other for a moment.

"I don't believe you, Luke Marshall." Her voice was low. "You knew what you signed up for. Then and now. You keep coming back for it. A simple life is there for the taking, but people like you and me? We never take it. Why don't we?" She finished in a whisper.

Luke said nothing. How many times had he told himself the same thing? That he was trying to walk away. The truth was he didn't know what else to do. He had chosen to attend West Point. He volunteered for special forces, and he volunteered to join the 75th.

Back then his choices had a purpose. Now, even when he couldn't remember what that purpose was, he couldn't walk away.

Her hand tightened around his wrist. "Because without this, we don't exist. This is all we get."

Luke leaned in closer and whispered, "You don't know anything about me."

A pleading look took over her face. "I know that you hate this, but here you are. I know that much. We're both here to do something we don't want to do. We're not that different, despite what you think."

Her sudden sincerity caught him off guard as did the urge to touch her. Instead, he pulled his hand away.

Despite her practiced seduction technique, it felt like Adrian Romero had staked a claim to that particular piece of well-formed ass. This was just another ploy to misdirect him. He didn't believe anything coming out of her mouth.

Luke turned and walked out of the bathroom.

16

———

"Is this going to be a problem?"

Luke turned to Adrian after the umpteenth glare Sheppard shot at her old boyfriend. She sat across from them, her jaw flexing as her teeth ground down on a soggy toothpick.

The three of them sat in the back of the stretch limo with Leo and Tommy in the front playing their roles.

Sheppard's efforts to convince the DOE agent failed. She had been sullen since Adrian refused to let her come into the club on the off chance the Russian would recognize her.

Not that it mattered. On Frank's orders, Luke assumed control of the op largely taking Adrian's say out of it. She was shady and she wasn't coming in. The DOE agent agreed. His tagalong didn't.

To be fair she wasn't just angry about car sitting. Leo, as it turned out, was a bit of a dog and procured the skimpiest dress Luke had ever seen for Sheppard to wear. Even at the correct size, it left a trifling amount to the imagination, but she pulled it off.

It was creepy how good she looked in a dress picked out

by an old man. She looked like a rock star. A pissed-off rock star who was staying in the car.

Adrian watched her cinching down the belt of a black coat she stole from his suitcase. "No. It won't be." Without missing a beat he turned to watch the scene outside.

The night was starting to heat up. It was ten-thirty by the time Leo pulled the limo to the curb. A long line of eager revelers snaked from the entrance down the stairs and along the sidewalk by a velvet rope. Dull thumping from inside reached them half a block away.

She looked at Luke. For a moment Luke thought she was going to start arguing with him instead of Adrian. Unlike Adrian, Luke actually paid attention to her so he could watch her. Half the time Adrian acted like she wasn't there.

Instead, she flopped back against the seat, resignation replacing rage. She was playing it cool again. Mistrust stirred in Luke when the hothead said nothing.

"Two minutes," said Tommy. Their limo moved forward as one ahead pulled away.

Luke checked his pockets one last time to make sure he'd grabbed the wallet with his fake ID, and his leg for the several stout zip ties hidden in his sock. He stashed his gun under the seat. Adrian followed suit.

"Short Bus, you got us?" Luke said in a low voice.

Tommy snorted at the code name Luke picked for him. "I've got you, Mustang. GPS and comms. Try not to flush it down the toilet this time."

Luke grinned. His heart pumped faster and the heady rush came strong and welcomed. Sheppard wasn't wrong. Just like his days as an operator, the high was intoxicating.

"Viper, you copy?" Tommy said.

"Copy," said Adrian.

"Mercedes?" Tommy waited. "Mercedes, you copy?"

Sheppard spat her toothpick onto the floorboard. "What difference does it make?"

"I'll take that as a yes," said Tommy. "And last but not least. Cadi, you copy?"

"I copy you," said Leo right beside him.

"Alright. Mustang and Viper you are set up in VIP booth #4. That's a five thousand-dollar bottle service, by the way. I hope you appreciate the sacrifice Mercedes and I are making by staying in the car. You need anything else?"

"Nope. Let's get this show on the road," said Luke.

Leo pulled the car to a stop and Tommy hopped out and ran around to open the door like the fake valet he was playing. Adrian exited first and buttoned his tailored jacket. Luke followed and gazed up the imposing marble stairs.

An old Soviet government building now housed the trendy Crescent Club. The grand portico was held aloft by two-story fluted columns lit bright white. Between the columns, long blue banners hung to the ground. In the center, over the front door, an eight-foot neon blue crescent moon was the only indicator of the nightclub's name.

At the top of the stairs, past the long line, a much shorter line formed. Luke took the stairs two at a time toward the VIP entrance, Adrian right behind him. At the top, Luke gave the woman their reservation and complied when a beefy security guard ordered him to spread his arms for a pat down. Luke used the time to count security.

Two at the VIP entrance included the one frisking Adrian. Six on the main entrance working the large crowd. They were searching the men but letting the women through.

Luke glanced down the stairs. Leo pulled away to stage one block away. They were a go. A pulsing concussion of bass hit Luke as the double metal entry doors opened to admit them. The party was full steam inside. A lingerie-clad hostess led them through the crowd.

The main floor of the nightclub was the massive two-story lobby. The dance floor occupied the first floor of the atrium next to a stage where the DJ and strobe apparatus were set up.

More columns supported a wide covered hall on both levels around the perimeter. The center atrium was open all the way to the glass ceiling one hundred feet above.

They followed the hostess to a wide carpeted staircase and up to the second level where the private booths lined the second-floor gallery. Halfway down, they climbed three more stairs into their private booth. Their booth was surrounded on three sides with tufted leather seats and a low lit private bar on the fourth wall. It also had a commanding view of the dance floor below, the front entrance and, more importantly, Ivanov's private corner booth.

Another lingerie-clad waitress appeared and took their drink orders. As she plunked ice cubes into highball glasses, Adrian leaned in and said something in her ear that Luke couldn't hear.

She smiled and nodded. Adrian plopped down on the bench across from Luke and raised his hands as if to say, "What do you think?"

"You did good, Short Bus." Luke spoke at a normal level. No one would hear him over the music.

"My ability to set up a premier techno club experience is the reason I'm so highly sought after in some circles," said Tommy.

Luke suppressed a smile. He picked a spot that would allow him to see Ivanov's now empty booth and took a seat. He hated these places. The noise was suffocating. He reached up to loosen his tie and remembered he wasn't wearing one.

It was unlikely Arazi would be at the club, but after the phone call earlier, Luke couldn't help searching every face that passed. He needed to relax. The waitress handed him two fingers of whiskey and he downed half in one gulp.

Adrian didn't seem to hate nightclubs as much as Luke. His face lit up when six young, beautiful Ukrainian women filtered into their booth talking and laughing as they swayed to the music. They must be what Romero 'ordered'.

Luke prayed Ivanov would show up before long. The first drink went down too fast. He got up to pour another intent on sipping it when a blond and a brunette made their way over to him and pulled him back down talking in broken English. More whisky appeared in his glass.

Minutes later through the cleavage surrounding him, Luke saw him.

Ivanov emerged from the staircase, his entourage in tow. The short stout Russian wore a bespoke suit and led a gaggle of hot women to his private booth. The entourage ended with a few assorted men and a posse of burly guards.

Ivanov's booth was twice the size of all the others with plenty of room for the half naked women to dance. A gold-plated handrail completed his opulent oasis.

Luke caught Adrian's eye and they shared a faint nod. They had agreed to wait thirty minutes before approaching him to give the illusion they were there to party. Luke tried to feign interest in the girls and realized his glass was empty again. He set it down. No more liquor.

Luke brought his hand up to his mouth and fake coughed. "The mark is in the building."

He was grateful the obnoxious music was only assaulting one ear. Tommy had the foresight to bring tiny noise-canceling earpieces, only slightly bulkier than the one he flushed down the toilet, so they could hear each other in the loud environment.

Tommy didn't answer. Luke sighed and leaned back trying to look like was enjoying the show, a little peeved that Tommy hadn't acknowledged him. Then his earpiece squawked to life.

Tommy sounded breathless. "Uh, Mustang. We got a problem."

17

———

Crescent Night Club, Lypky
Kiev, Ukraine
March 25
2322 Hours Local Time

Luke's anger mounted with every passing second. He almost bought that bullshit in the safe house bathroom.

Tommy's shaky voice saying that woman just shoved a gun in his face was all the information Luke needed. The urge to choke out Adrian's little doxy right there on the club floor overwhelmed him but he fought the urge. He would deal with her when Ivanov was safely in hand.

Luke shoved two women off his lap so he could shed his jacket. He rolled up his sleeves as he studied the pulsing crowd then looked to Ivanov. The mobster was busy with the swelling crowd at his booth.

By the time his eyes moved back to the atrium, Luke saw her emerge from the staircase onto their level. Now she sauntered down the gallery like she owned the place, and it was working. Every man in her general area looked.

He kicked Adrian in the shin and jerked his head in her

direction. Luke saw his eyes bounce around the crowd then narrow as he found her. His lips went thin with repressed rage.

Luke might not have to kill her himself.

With a start, he realized her trajectory had her passing Ivanov's booth before theirs. Anger seared through him when he realized it was her plan the whole time. He threw a blond out of his way to get to Adrian.

"She's going to his booth. What is she doing?"

"I don't know," said Romero, his face tight.

They watched as Sheppard stopped in front of the mobster's booth and leaned suggestively against the railing.

In spite of his anger, it impressed Luke how easily she slipped in and out of a character. A practiced liar.

It was working on Ivanov. She looked no better than the hundreds of other scantily clad women that night, but her outrageous brashness oozed sex appeal. The five men nearest her fell victim and vied to chat her up.

Luke and Adrian watched as she reached out and gently parted the obedient men obstructing Ivanov's view. She was there to catch Ivanov's attention, and catch it she did.

The Russian's gaze fell on her, and he waved off the tattooed thug trying to conduct some seedy business transaction. A burly bodyguard grabbed the man and ejected him from the booth while another approached Sheppard. She smiled and took the arm he offered. She said something in his ear and Luke saw him blush.

Luke didn't bother covering his mouth. "Short Bus, is she mic'd?"

"Negative. She took it out."

"Shit. Viper, keep your head on a swivel. She's going in."

"I see it." Adrian's teeth clicked as his jaw clenched.

Everyone in Ivanov's booth turned to look at Maisie. The girls were sullen and the men gawked. The wildly confident look on her face never faltered. It looked borderline maniacal.

Ivanov looked her over then smiled. He patted the leather beside him and Sheppard sat, crossed her exposed legs, and leaned in to place her lips by his ear.

Ivanov motioned for a drink which was promptly delivered to Maisie. Then he snapped his fingers at a guard who dispersed the remaining line. The Russian was done with business for the evening. Whatever that woman came for, she was about to get it.

Luke struggled to keep his rage in check, racking his brain for a way to salvage their objective. Then he saw Sheppard clutch her seat and rock back and forth. She'd lost the self-assured look and Ivanov's expression had turned from hungry to brutal.

Something was wrong.

Ivanov munched a piece of ice from his drink as Maisie staggered to her feet and dropped her glass. She threw up a weak hand to knock the guard that grabbed her shoulders then collapsed.

Before the bodyguard caught her, Luke was on his feet mirrored by Adrian. Someone screamed as four men barged into their booth. Not club security. Luke expected to take six of Ivanov's men, but all of the known muscle were with him. The four men bearing down were new information.

Ivanov knew they were coming.

Luke dropped the first guy with a fist to the face. Blood squirted from his nose. He hit the floor and lay still.

Another man bore down on him. No one had a gun. They must have assumed they didn't need them. They thought wrong.

Luke deflected his wild haymaker and drove a palm into the man's throat. He felt windpipe crunch under his hand.

Before the man hit the floor, Luke spun and clamped a

figure-four chokehold on one of the two men assaulting Adrian. The man let go of Romero. He couldn't break Luke's hold and gradually the flailing lessened until the man slumped over. Luke let him slide to the ground.

Romero was jammed in the corner by the last thug. Adrian held him off but wasn't making much progress. Luke reached out and yanked the man back by his collar while sticking out his foot. The thug flew backward and hit the floor so hard it stunned him. Luke didn't give him a chance to stand up. In an instant, Luke was on him raining down blows on his face.

As soon as he felt the man weaken, Luke flipped him over and pulled out the flex cuffs intended for Ivanov. After he secured the man's hands behind him, he jumped up and looked down the gallery. Everyone was still partying. The strobes and throbbing music covered the noise of the struggle.

But Ivanov's booth was empty. Luke's eyes flew around the scene. A straight-line motion through the pulsing dance crowd on the first floor caught his attention. He saw a body-guard carrying Maisie's limp form past the stage.

They were going out through the kitchen.

Back on their level, three of Ivanov's remaining body-guards who had stayed behind were shoving their way toward Luke and Adrian. Luke vaulted over the low booth wall with Adrian close behind. The men sprinted around the gallery to the stairs, trying to put as many club-goers between them and the bodyguards as possible. They didn't have time to fight right now.

Luke took the stairs down three at a time. He sprinted past the stage toward the kitchen. Screams behind made him turn. The men chasing them plowed through a group of dancing patrons. They had guns and were waving them around for everyone to see.

Luke shouldered through the swinging doors into the large industrial kitchen. "Short Bus, which way did they go? Short Bus, you copy?"

No answer. The heavy concrete building was blocking the signal down here. Luke shoved a white-coated cook out of his way and sprinted through the kitchen as the kitchen doors slammed open behind him. The drywall ahead exploded as two slugs buried themselves in the wall.

Screams and crashes echoed in the kitchen as the employees dove under the stainless steel prep counters.

Luke and Adrian reached the exit and tumbled into the alley. To their left, the sidewalk in front of the club was still lined with people. To the right, fifty yards down, an iron gate creaked on its hinges.

Beyond it, Luke saw the taillights of a black Range Rover as it squealed away from the curb. He barreled down the alley and through the gate trying to get a glimpse of the tag. He got the first five digits before it sped out of view.

U5748.

It would be enough for Tommy. With a satellite feed, Tommy could track that vehicle to Timbuktu. "Short Bus," Luke hissed as they ran. "Do you copy?"

A gunshot rang out in the alley behind them. The men ducked.

"This way," Luke said to Romero and went left down the street. Their limo was a right turn, but they needed to lose these guys. Luke wasn't about to lead them to Tommy and Leo.

Luke felt a hand swat his arm. Adrian pointed to an unlit construction site ahead. A flimsy eight foot chain link surrounded the skeleton building and pyramids of construction materials. The men scaled the fence and melted into the darkness.

A loud crash sounded beside Luke making him spin around.

"Shit," Romero whispered, righting himself after nearly tumbling over single stacked bricks.

"What the fuck?" Luke growled at him. His night vision was still sharp from the low-lit club. It was dark but the piles of construction materials were dimly backlit by the street-lamp on the sidewalk. This guy had turned into a liability.

Half a block away, one of the four men chasing them flung orders in rapid Russian.

"Here they come," said Luke, grim.

"Split up," whispered Adrian.

That was a terrible idea. Romero almost got his ass kicked back in the club, and now he clumsily revealed their location. Too late to argue now. Romero disappeared into the dark. Luke ducked into a room outlined by metal studs and squeezed through the other side.

Ahead he saw a skeleton staircase. At the bottom sat a saw table with various lengths of two-by-fours piled on it. The one on top was roughly the length of a regulation bat. He tucked it under his arm then ran quietly up the stairs. At the top, he peered down trying to locate his opponents. Three shadows were coming over the fence.

Luke tucked in behind an elevator shaft at the top of the stairs. When he heard boots scuff on the concrete below, he clapped his two-by-four against the cinder block.

Voices hissed and seconds later boots thudded on the stairs. Sounded like two coming up.

Romero was going to have to handle the last one on his own.

Luke waited until they were close then stepped out and swung his lumber like he used to swing at a two-seam fast-ball. The first man to the top didn't utter a sound when the two-by-four collapsed his face. The second man up the stairs dodged his partner's limp body and let him roll down the stairs.

The second man leaped the last two stairs. He was smarter and moved to the middle of the room placing himself in the cover of darkness.

Staying in the deep shadows, Luke stepped away from his cinder block cover. The movement alerted the man who swung around, searching. Luke could barely see the extended arm, but he knew the man had a gun.

He flung the two-by-four at the man who grunted when it made contact. It didn't hurt him, but it did the job. The man swung his gun hand away from Luke.

Luke slammed into him, one arm wrapping around his throat, the other hand around the gun. As he landed on top of the man, he wrenched the gun away.

The Russian's free hand made contact with the side of Luke's head. Luke slung the gun into the darkness and tried to wrestle the man into a rear choke hold, but he was strong. Luke squeezed the man's neck hard. A hard hit caught him on the crown of his head causing him to lose his grip. He rolled away to put some distance between them.

Luke made it to his feet then felt his back leg slip into a hole. He threw himself forward barely avoiding a fall. He glanced down.

A dumpster sat fourteen feet beneath to catch construction debris. Even in the darkness, Luke could see backlit lengths of jagged rebar and concrete chunks.

He moved left keeping the hole on his side. No sooner had he started moving than man was on him. This dude was fast and rained down blows like a prize fighter.

Luke bladed himself and the blow glanced off his chest. After deflecting three more punches, he took an uppercut to the solar plexus.

The Russian squared himself for another blow. Confident from his success, he slowed to build up steam for a more powerful hit.

It was all the time Luke needed. Bending over, he caught the man at the knee and yanked upward. The man slammed into the plywood next to the yawning gap in the floor. Luke twisted his foot and the Russian tumbled over the edge.

The man managed to grab the ledge to keep from falling. He held on by his fingertips.

"Where are they taking her?" Luke knelt to talk, trying to get the wind back in his lungs.

The man whined in Russian.

"What?" Luke grabbed the man's wrist, upsetting the delicate balance holding him up.

The bodyguard slipped lower. "Nyet," he pleaded.

"Where are they taking her?" Luke asked again.

Downstairs he heard yelling and then several pops of gunfire. He hoped Romero was faring better than he did in the club. Another yell and a final shot sounded below.

Luke looked back at the man. "Where?"

"He will kill me if I say this to you." The man's broken English dissolved into panicked Russian.

"You knew we were coming here."

The man whimpered again. "Yes," he wheezed. "Taras knew."

"How?" Luke gripped his wrist tighter.

"I don't know. A phone call. No," the man panted as he slipped again. "Please, no. I don't know from who the call."

Luke couldn't believe what he was hearing. "I don't believe you." He moved like was going to throw him down, making rapid Russian come out again.

"English."

"I am just bodyguard. They don't tell me all business."

"When? When did you find out?"

"Yesterday. He got call yesterday. We were to take the girl and kill rest of you."

"The rest of us?" Fear spiked in Luke's gut.

"Yes."

With a flick of his wrist, Luke twisted the man's wrist breaking his hold. Pitched screaming suddenly stopped in a sickening thud. He looked down and saw rebar poking through the dead man's chest. He squared himself to the staircase as footsteps pounded on it.

Adrian came into sight breathing heavily. He moved slowly, recovering from the exertion, but otherwise seemed unharmed. He had a gun in his hand that he'd taken from one of his attackers.

"We have to get back to the car. Now." Luke walked to him. "Are you hurt?"

"No."

"Let's go."

"But they took her," Adrian argued.

"We're going to make sure the rest of our team is safe and regroup at the safe house. There's nowhere on this planet Tommy can't track them down." Luke was already halfway down the stairs.

Adrian tucked the gun into his waistband and followed. In the distance, sirens sounded. Locals had heard Adrian's shots and alerted police. They hopped the fence and settled into a jog for the three blocks to the limo.

Two minutes later they turned onto Kostolna Street and saw the limo idling by the curb. The second he cleared the corner, Luke kicked into a sprint, his stomach churning. The driver's door sat ajar in the cold spring night. As he drew close, he saw the arm hanging limp, holding the door open.

Luke came up on the limo so fast he slammed his palms into the hood to stop his forward motion. Through the window he saw Leonard Turner slumped in the driver's seat, his window spider webbed by a single bullet hole. A large red wound opened on the left side of his face.

They were ambushed from behind.

He couldn't breathe as he looked to the other side of the seat. He slammed both fists on the hood of the car again denting the metal.

By the time Adrian caught up, Luke made it to the passenger door and yanked it open. He had to throw out his hand to keep Tommy's limp body from falling onto the pavement.

Tommy's head lolled to the side as Luke pulled him onto the sidewalk. A curtain of crimson blood oozed from the deep slice across Tommy's throat.

Luke knelt by Tommy's body and hung his head. The sirens grew louder.

"We need to go," Adrian said from across the seat. He was leaning over Leo, taking Leo's credentials, gun, and earpiece. "Half of the cops in this city are on Ivanov's payroll. They cannot find us here."

Luke gently pulled off Tommy's headset. Tommy's laptop had fallen to the floorboard still open. Luke snapped it shut and stuffed it, and every piece of loose equipment he could see, into the blood-spattered bag on the floorboard.

"HQ will make sure they're taken care of." Adrian now spoke through the open privacy screen. He had moved to the back of the limo to wipe the interior of prints.

Luke reached down and shut Tommy's eyes. Then with a massive effort, he took the rag Adrian offered him, wiped his own prints from the door handle, and followed Adrian into the dark.

When this was over, whoever sold them out was going to get a bullet in his, or her, head.

18

Crescent Night Club
Kiev, Ukraine
March 25
2322 Hours Local Time

How adorable. She'd slipped through more Palestinian checkpoints than she had fingers to count on, but Marshall thought Tommy and Leo could stop her.

And now this Ukrainian Betty Boop thought she was slick.

Maisie told Ivanov she represented a wealthy Russian who needed to outsource a sensitive contract job. It seemed like he bought it, but when Maisie saw the Ukrainian porn star wannabe pull that vial from her bra and lace her drink, Maisie knew things had gone sideways.

Her plan was to beat the boys to the mob boss, seduce and lure him into a dark corner, and have their conversation. Now she had to wing it.

Maisie smiled and took the nasty fruity drink. She pretended to sip and flicked the excess off her lips. If Ivanov was trying to drug her, he didn't plan to kill her. Yet.

Adrian and Marshall locked onto her the second she walked in. She hoped they picked up on this development too. No time to warn them. Somebody sold them out.

She shook her head. It was probably ketamine in her drink, so Maisie timed her reaction appropriately.

Rising she staggered forward, her sky-high heels making it easy to feign instability. Cold vodka and ice splashed her leg as her drink hit the floor. Strong arms cinched around her waist and she went limp, feigning a drugged daze so she could keep her eyes slit.

Somebody yelled "Go, go, go," in Russian.

Ivanov just sent his goons after the boys. They would have to handle their business.

The mobster's lips skimmed Maisie's ear. "Now you come with me," he said in accented English.

The burly bodyguard snatched her up like she weighed ten pounds. He carried her quickly through the crowd banging her head and feet into drunk revelers. One shoe slid off.

Ivanov would take her to a secluded place to interrogate her. He bought her act so maybe she could salvage this. Had Ivanov not sent all but two of his goons after the guys, she would be in hot water. These two jokers, however, she could twist with her eyes closed.

The fluffy goon grunted with effort as they descended the stairs. She counted every time her head hit something as they barreled through the crowd. She was going to pay back every last bruise when she fake woke up.

Her thoughts jerked away for a split second. She kind of deserved this. Tommy was the only person who was kind to her, and twenty minutes ago she threatened him then ran off.

Surely he knew she was bluffing, but the look on his face

made her stomach hurt. She just had to get through this then she would make it up to him.

They entered the kitchen and the staff went about their business despite the limp woman being carried through. Damn Ukrainians partied hard.

Through the next door, Maisie realized they were in the alley where they planned to take Ivanov. Ironic. A short bumpy run later she was shoved in the back seat of an SUV. Ivanov climbed in beside her and pulled her head onto his lap, stroking her hair. Her skin crawled at his touch.

She couldn't stifle a reaction so she improvised. Moaning, she flopped over to face away from him. The ketamine should have knocked her out cold, but they didn't seem to know that.

The car ride was short. Minutes later she was stuffed into the back of an idling helicopter.

A short flight later, Maisie found herself in the back seat of a much smaller car. This time she had the seat to herself.

Carefully she opened her eyes. She couldn't see anything except her guards in the front and a bright moonlit night. The headlights of another car shined in the rearview. Ivanov better be riding in that car.

Minutes ticked by until finally, they stopped by a tall building sitting silent and gray in the bright moonlight. The car headlights were the only artificial light. No street lights, no windows, no lit cigarettes. Not a single light burned anywhere.

When the driver snapped off the headlights the darkness felt physically heavy. It was the eeriest place she'd ever felt. Even midnight in the Negev wasn't this ominous.

Maisie opened her eyes trying to take in her surroundings. All she could see was the tall building outlined in moonlight.

The men stepped out and clicked on flashlights.

"Take her up. Get her ready. I'll be up in a moment." Ivanov's voice came from behind. He spoke Russian to the men, then switched back to English.

Maisie realized he was on the phone, but his voice was so low she couldn't hear what he said.

"Da," said the taller of her guards. He turned to his partner. "Carry her, you lazy donkey. Don't drag her through this shit."

A moment later her head bounced off his shoulder and her other shoe fell off. They headed into the building. When his flashlight slashed across the landscape, Maisie couldn't stop the surprised jerk as she saw their destination. Her goon paused, decided it was a twitch, and kept going.

The building was from a horror movie, abandoned for ages. Grass grew waist high along the broken cement sidewalk. The building had no front door.

Maisie's dread grew as they climbed one flight of stairs and started down a long hall. The flashlights cut through a forsaken landscape.

Open doors ticked by, their insides long exposed to the elements by gaping, glassless windows. Every wall and ceiling peeled in jagged strips. Even in the cone of light, everything was dull gray.

As the men walked down the hallway Maisie saw a single tiny shoe flash in the light. Then it disappeared into darkness. This building died a long time ago.

Winging it didn't seem like a good idea anymore.

At the end of the hall, they entered the last door. Maisie saw an 80's era kitchen. It was an apartment building before it was abandoned. This particular apartment had been reclaimed, but not for habitation.

Plywood covered the windows, caulked on the edges so no light would escape. In the corner, a small generator hummed powering two high-wattage construction lights that both illuminated and heated the space.

A few chairs were grouped around a plywood and sawhorse table covered with an assortment of construction tools. The tools were stained with a deep reddish-brown goo.

The lights illuminated an upside-down U-shaped contraption of welded steel. Nylon straps hung from the top crossbar.

She wasn't going in that thing. No more winging it.

In one fluid movement, Maisie ran her hand around her guard's thick midsection and pulled his gun from its holster. He didn't have time to react before her elbow slammed into the base of his neck, dropping him to the floor. Maisie arched her back and landed softly on her bare feet.

The other guy was adjusting the straps when his friend hit the ground with a poof of dust. When he saw her standing, he fumbled for his beltline. Maisie already had a bead on his chest.

"You want to die here?" Maisie spoke in perfect Russian. "In this place?"

His arm went limp.

"Move." She waived her muzzle toward the kitchen.

He obeyed. Maisie snatched a pair of flex cuffs from the plywood table and followed with her gun aimed at the back of his neck.

"Put your hands behind your back or you won't have a throat anymore," Maisie ordered.

She cinched the flex cuffs around his wrists. Then she slammed the butt of the UDAV 9mm into his temple and he slumped to the floor. Patting down his unconscious body, she found car keys, a backup gun, and two knives. She took all of it.

In the living room, she cuffed the first goon and stashed

the weapons out of sight behind the kitchen door, dumping her UDAV in favor of SR-1 Vector from the second goon's waistline.

From the table, she dragged a cracked pleather chair to the middle of the room. A seat for Ivanov. Then she pushed herself against the wall behind the front door and waited.

Soon she heard footsteps in the hall. Ivanov walked fast, expecting to come in and see his target spread eagle and ready to talk.

The door swung open and the Russian entered followed by an ugly, hollowed-out old man. Probably his driver.

Taras Ivanov crossed the threshold and his eyes fell on his unconscious goon, then flicked to the kitchen where he saw feet. The older man drew down.

Maisie slammed the door closed behind them causing them to whirl. She brought the Vector up and pulled the trigger. The driver fell, a single round through his right eyeball. She stepped out of the shadow.

Ivanov looked at her, in her torn dress and bare feet, more in amazement than fear.

"Hello, Taras. Have a minute?" She spoke in English.

"How did you...."

"Have a seat." With her muzzle, she pointed to the chair now facing the blinding light.

"I know who you are," he said, walking to the chair. He eased into it unconcerned that three of his men were down. The gangster was ice cold.

"Is that so?" She secured his hands with a pair of flex cuffs. Then she ran her hand around his waist checking for a weapon.

"I don't carry a gun, malyshka," he said.

She took his cell phone and powered it down.

Ivanov eyed her with satisfaction. "You are the American traitor's daughter."

"And how do you know that? You didn't know my old man."

"No need. He vas, who do you say? Legend?"

"Okay," she gave a sarcastic laugh. "Fuck you, buddy. Let's talk about how you knew I'd be at the club tonight?"

He shrugged. "I have sources."

She stepped from behind the blinding light to stand in front of him. "Not sources like that you don't."

He glared at her, no longer impressed. "Don't pretend to understand how the vorld works, malyshka. Let the men handle business."

Maisie walked over to the table and picked up a screwdriver that had been sharpened to a lethal point. Dark brown gunk peeled off the tip in curly flakes. Blood.

She walked back to him. "Okay, I believe you."

His lip curled as he looked at her. "Why are you still here? You took out my men. Why are you not running away?"

Maisie laughed. "If you think I run, then you don't know who I am."

She studied him for a moment. "I need something. I tried to bring my request to you like a professional when your concubine drugged me."

"You vant something from me?" Ivanov's accent deepened as he started to laugh.

"I don't want a favor, idiot. Everyone knows you don't do favors. And you and I both know I can't torture it out of you."

"Vat then? A deal? I vill not help your government."

"I'm not American anymore."

"I think you are vorking for them."

She leaned in and tapped the screwdriver on his cheek. "So do they."

Ivanov studied her for a moment before answering. "Vhat is it that you vant?"

"I want to see the Banker."

He looked surprised. Then suspicious. "Who?"

"Cut the shit, Taras. I know you're a client. The only way to find him is by arrangement. A system you stole from him, no doubt. Set up the meeting."

"You can't possibly know that. The clients are never listed. Never known."

She smiled at him. "I have sources."

Ivanov frowned. "But you have no money. Certainly not enough to go to the Banker."

"That's not your most pressing concern is it, Taras? You should worry more about keeping twenty-twenty in both eyes." She rapped the screwdriver against his temple making him flinch. "All you have to do is get word to him. I require nothing else."

"Vhat makes you think he vill see you? He declines almost every referral."

"Will you do it?"

"You are very strange to do this," he said, switching to Russian. He was calling her bluff.

"Not as strange as bringing me to Chernobyl to torture me," she answered in Russian, then she switched to English. "It's fucking weird, dude."

"Vhat do I get in return?" Ivanov fired back.

"In return, I don't kill you."

"That doesn't seem like good deal. I risk losing my account."

Maisie shrugged. "That's the deal."

"I have better idea," he said, smiling. Again he seemed unworried about being tied up in a torture dungeon with a poker next to his eyeball.

Too late Maisie realized her mistake. She hadn't checked

for a dedicated tracker. She forced his head toward his knees and checked his collar. Nothing. She yanked up his cuffed hands and saw the thin wire with a small node protruding from his expensive suit sleeve.

The cavalry was coming.

A split second later the door splintered as a boot came through it. Maisie dragged the chair around to put Ivanov between her and his response team. Three men piled through the door with their guns drawn. She'd left hers on the torture table.

These guys were younger and stouter than the geezer driver. And unlike her two goons, who were thick around the middle, these dudes weren't wheezing after a run up the stairs.

She held the screwdriver low to shield the fact it wasn't a firearm. The three of them locked eyes for an eternal second.

Then Maisie dove for the kitchen doorway. She tucked her shoulder and rolled to change direction, putting herself behind the stout concrete block wall as the room lit up with gunfire.

Something burned her arm and chunks of concrete peppered her as she rolled over something hard and lumpy. Her stash of weapons. She pushed her back to the cinderblock wall and fished through the pile pulling out a OTs-27 Berdysh.

"Don't kill her," Ivanov screamed to be heard over the din. The firing stopped. "I need her alive. Get over here. Cut me loose."

Maisie heard a knife click open as she looked down at her arm. A line of bright red blood ran above her elbow. It was just a graze but it stung like hell. Glass from a broken tumbler scattered over the floor. She picked two pieces out of her left foot.

Ivanov called out. "I like your style, Maisie Sheppard. You have earned a few minutes of my time. Maybe we can do business, malyshka."

Leading with the gun, she peeked around the corner. Ivanov stood rubbing the welts on his wrists. His bodyguards flanked him, but their guns were lowered.

Ducking back behind the wall, Maisie ejected the magazine and checked her rounds. Five, and one in the chamber. "Why do you want me alive?" She slammed it back into the gun.

"I think you did not come without something to barter, eh malyshka? A girl as smart as you knows better. I think maybe ve can help each other."

Crouching, she readied herself for the pain when she put her full weight on her torn up feet. In a smooth motion, she straightened and pointed her gun.

Ivanov's men reacted by raising theirs, but Ivanov put his hands out and spoke calmly. Reluctantly they lowered their guns.

Suppressing a limp, Maisie stepped out.

Ivanov's eyes flicked to the bloody footprints she left behind. He motioned to his unconscious men and dead driver. "Vas that necessary?"

"Was that?" She nodded at the straps hanging from the steel bar.

Ivanov threw back his head and laughed. "You are a she-bear, malyshka. I give you that."

Maisie leaned against the wall and raised her foot while keeping her gun on his men. She picked more shards of glass out of her sole and tried not to wince.

Ivanov's gaze never left her. "You vant a referral to the Banker? I can do that." Ivanov cocked his head. "He is a vell connected man, but I did not know he dabbled in nuclear material."

"He doesn't." Maisie cut him off. How the hell did Ivanov know so much?

"Then why do you vant to meet him?"

"That's my business."

Ivanov shrugged. "Fine. It will be done."

"Thank you."

"Do not thank me. Remember this is not a favor, Miss Sheppard. What is my payment?"

"What do you want?" Maisie put her foot down and immediately felt a shard she missed.

"I vant the uranium everyone is seeking. You know vhere it is, no?"

So that's what he intended to extract from her. He didn't know the location either.

Maisie shook her head. "No. We don't know where it is."

"I don't believe you. Why else vould you be with two American agents?"

"I am looking for a person, not uranium."

"Then you have nothing of value. You should have said you knew. That was your power." Ivanov gestured loosely toward her, indicating his bodyguards to shoot her.

The closest one was fast. Maisie saw him move and the next thing she knew a gun was pointed at her face. Then three.

She was hobbled, weakened, and exhausted. And about to rot in this radioactive wasteland.

"Wait," she blurted. "I can get you back into Russia."

Ivanov's eyes narrowed trying to figure out her play. He was shrewd and smart, and he forced her hand. And he knew it.

The guns pointed at her lowered. It was too late to go back now, so she pressed on. "You know who my father was. I can get you back into Russia."

Ivanov leaned forward, listening.

"I have a name. A name the Kremlin would very much love to have."

Ivanov had a hard time hiding his delight. "This for a referral? We make deal."

Maisie collected herself enough to sound sarcastic. "Calm down, Tolstoy. I also want the plans you gave the little desert rat." She needed to go back to Adrian with something or Marshall might kill her for that little stunt in the club.

Ivanov's brow furrowed. "That is not possible."

"Like hell, it's not."

"I have broken no laws and I do not discuss my clients. I do not know where or if he intends to use it. That is not my business."

"Whatever helps you sleep at night, dick. If those plans kill Americans, they'll come after you with both barrels."

"I am not a terrorist."

"You think that will matter?"

Ivanov weighed her words for a moment. "I'm not giving my plans. That is my offer. If you do not like, you can try to shoot your vay out, malyshka."

Maisie didn't need to weigh her options. He had her backed into a corner. "Fine. I need the referral. As soon as I meet the Banker, you'll have your name. And your life back."

He studied her for a moment. "Vould you like some shoes?" Ivanov gestured to a pile of men's shoes in the corner.

Unlike the moldy shoes in the hallway, these were new. The former belongings of Ivanov's interrogative targets. "You can buy some better shoes in Venice."

She nodded at him knowingly and accepted the too-big boots Ivanov handed her.

He broke into a wide grin and brushed past her into the

kitchen. From the freezer, he pulled out a bottle of vodka. "A drink to complete our business?"

She nodded and accepted the bottle, letting the icy liquor dull the pain.

In sultry Russian Ivanov asked, "Perhaps we can go someplace more comfortable to celebrate our agreement?"

Maisie shook her head. Selling her soul was nothing to celebrate, and his hands would not touch her again. "I have to get back to my keepers. I know it will take a few hours and I need my passport."

"Alright, Maisie Sheppard," Ivanov said, "but remember our terms. The Banker meets few of his referrals. I vant it understood now, that our deal stands even if he refuses to see you."

Maisie looked grim as she handed Ivanov the bottle. "He'll see me."

19

DOE Safe House
Kiev, Ukraine
March 26
0604 Hours Local Time

Luke looked down at his bloody knuckles then at the hole in the drywall. Punch after punch he punished the wall because he couldn't punish himself. The pain in his hands finally brought him back to his senses.

Slamming his knuckles into the wall one last time, he rested his head on the scuffed paint trying to corral his raging mind into something that resembled thought.

He never left a man behind. Never. Tonight he left Tommy in the street like a dead dog.

The men split up after they left the car. Adrian went to clear the field office of any sensitive information and arrange a team to take care of the bodies.

Luke went back to the safe house to call Frank. He delivered the partial tag so they could attempt to track the woman's location. Luke didn't think Adrian could deliver anything. He wasn't even sure he trusted the DOE agent anymore.

As far as they knew Sheppard had betrayed them to Ivanov. She was the most likely candidate.

An hour later, Frank hadn't called back. Luke paced around the apartment punching holes in whatever was in front of him.

Luke realized he was violently thirsty and stalked into the kitchen for water. As he passed the table, he kicked something hard. Tommy's bag of equipment. He'd thrown it on the floor when he got back and forgot about it.

The urge to kick it around the room hit him. Instead, he took a deep breath, picked it up, and set it on the table. After a slow steadying drink of water, Luke turned and unzipped it.

Tommy's silver laptop sat on top, smears of blood by the screen latch. Luke pulled it out. He saw more smears on the sides from bloody hands picking it up.

Taking a deep breath, Luke opened the laptop and felt the air punched from his lungs. Tommy must have been alive for a few moments after they slit his throat. A bloody word was swiped across the 19-inch screen in shaky scrawl.

k@la$htar

Luke straightened and raked his hands through his hair. The rage gurgling up threatened to overwhelm him. He left the table and returned to the wall he'd just beaten into submission.

This time he forced himself to gently place his palms against it and practiced tactical breathing. *Four in. Four hold. Four out. Four hold. Four in...*

Emotion held no value right now.

He opened his eyes when he felt his racing heart rate slow. It spiked again as he realized something. Why would

Tommy write his password on the screen as he lay dying? There was something Tommy wanted him to know.

Luke went back to the laptop and sat in front of it. He drew his finger across the mouse pad and the screen sprang to life with Dungeons and Dragons dork stuff all over the screensaver. A password prompt appeared, partially obscured by blood. Luke typed in the password and hit enter.

More nerd wallpaper and a bunch of icons with techie labels appeared. With a lump in his throat, Luke ran his hand across the screen to clear it of Tommy's blood. It took several passes before he wiped enough blood off to see the screen.

In the top right corner, conspicuously away from all the others, Luke saw a file icon titled 'Asa Hussan'. He clicked on it and a standard DIA intelligence brief document popped up onscreen.

It was empty except for the narrative section which contained only a bullet point list. Judging from missing words and spelling errors, it appeared to be typed in a hurry.

1. Ivanob receive 20K pymt from Syrian version of numbered account. Just a bozo online account with no names, hackable. Accessed encrypted metadata.

2. Account had 5 mil balance late last year. Entire balance withdrawn November last year and account closed.

3. Bank stores information on closed accounts in a separate server ecosystem that has more metadata attached to it than the open account – for regulatory audit. Recovered all available electronic fingerprints associated with this account.

4. Account associated originated at branch in Hama, Syria.

5. E-mail account was attached. No VPN on IP account. Silly goose.

6. quick search shows other electronic uses of that IP address include chatroom visits to monitored chat sites. Chat threads posted by user IP add solicited donations over the past year for daddy dearest of one Asa Hassan who needed surgery in the US.

7. Nine months later, around the time the account was emptied and closed, one last post stated that a miracle had been performed, praise Allah. The IP address still active, no more posts. Should probably send flowers.

Luke pulled out his phone and dialed Frank for the second time that night. As it rang, he noticed how bloody his hands were. He tucked the phone between his ear and shoulder and went to the sink to scrub away Tommy's blood.

"What've you got?" Frank got right down to business.

"I found something on Tommy's laptop. I'm not really sure if it's anything. Tommy told me he was working on something before he died, but he didn't have anything to report then."

"What is it?"

"Some background on the account that paid Ivanov for the bomb and possibly for the U. Your team needs to look at it. If Tommy found it, there will be value in it."

"I agree, Son."

"I'm sending it to you from Tommy's logon."

"Alright, Son. I'll get them right on it."

"Frank, you know the name Asa Hussan?"

The line went silent.

"Frank?"

"Where did you hear that name?"

"Tommy found a chat room thread soliciting donations for the father of an Asa Hussan. Tommy seemed to think it was sketchy."

"He changed it decades before the Iraq war, and decades before your bomber was born, but Asa Hussan was al-Din Arazi's real name."

"Shit."

"Sounds like Tommy found something real."

The front door flew open and Adrian came in, a bag over his shoulder. "I think I found her. Rolling in five."

Luke muttered into the phone so Adrian couldn't hear. "Sending the brief now. If I find anything else, I'll send it."

"We're on it, son." Frank hung up.

Luke grabbed a towel and wiped his hands. He quickly sent the brief from Tommy's email and clicked the laptop shut.

Adrian dumped the bag on the living room end table and pulled out ancient body armor and two more small firearms – the rest of the DOE Kiev office's meager weapons locker.

Adrian called out to Luke, "You coming? Whoah."

Luke had moved to the living room swiftly and silently. By the time Adrian called out to him, he stood beside the DOE agent already getting in his space.

It satisfied Luke to see the man startled. "That was quick. You were supposed to be seeing to the bodies."

"It's done. A team is on a jet headed this way. The bodies will be on the plane by tonight and the local case closed." Adrian sounded clipped as he eyed Luke. Then his gaze flicked over the damage Luke inflicted on the walls.

Luke bristled at his matter-of-fact tone. "What the fuck happened out there?"

"What do you mean?" The DOE guy had the audacity to look confused at Luke's question.

Anger seared across Luke. He planted both hands in Romero's chest and shoved him against the wall.

"Answer the question. What the fuck was she doing?

Sheppard's off the reservation and there's no way you didn't see this coming. Now Tommy's dead. You better start talking, because if they don't kill her, I will."

Romero open his mouth, then decided against what he was going to say. His shoulders slumped. "I need her help to find Bressler."

"Open your eyes. She's not helping you," roared Luke in his face.

"No one knew her father like she did. Not even me. If anyone can find Bressler it's her."

Luke thumped Romero's chest and stepped away. "You need to get your house in order, Romero. She's running circles around you."

Adrian straightened his shirt looking defeated. "I know. It's my fault. I was trying to give her some closure, but I don't think that's going to be possible."

"And when she finds this Bressler, what then? How badly does she want to hide her father's role in this? Enough to make the file disappear?"

"I don't know."

"Bullshit," Luke fired back. "What has she ever done to make you trust her so much?"

Adrian studied Luke carefully then looked away. "Nothing," he conceded.

Luke's head buzzed with everything that had gone wrong and could still go wrong while this limp noodle gave his girlfriend 'closure'. Women were major league champs at sniffing out weakness in men and this bitch was team captain.

"How did you find her?"

Adrian adjusted the straps on his body armor. "The partial tag you got matched a vehicle in Ivanov's fleet. Headquarters linked with a satellite feed that had coverage in this area. The car went to the airport then they took a chopper to a small airstrip north of the city. They lost feed after that, but there's only one place to go in that direction."

Luke looked at him suspiciously waiting for the answer.

"Pripyat."

"What the fuck is Pripyat?"

"It's an abandoned town inside the Chernobyl exclusion zone. Disaster tourism is the only thing that goes on up there now."

"Obviously not the only thing. Is it radioactive?"

"Radiation levels are tolerable for a few hours in most areas. Enclosed places like the hospital and the graveyard register dangerous levels of radiation, but buildings open to the elements have far lower levels. That's probably where he's got her. In one of the abandoned office or apartment buildings."

Adrian rummaged in the bag and tossed Luke a small pager-like device. "Here's a personal radiation detector. Anything above 2sv and we need to move. We'll be safe enough in most outdoor places for a short period of time."

"I'm assuming there are government patrols. Any chance they're not on Ivanov's payroll?" Luke slipped the PRD into his pocket.

"Yes to the first. No to the second," said Adrian.

The second ballistic vest was way too small, but Luke grabbed it anyway. Better than nothing. What he wouldn't give for a MK18 CQBR. All the heat he brought to this party was a 9mm Beretta with a single backup magazine.

His time with this shit show was drawing to an end. Tommy gave him a far better lead to follow than a shady operator and this guilty conscience Casanova. Luke wanted nothing more than to wash his hands of this, but he wasn't about to let Romero walk into a hornet's nest alone.

Out of habit, Luke checked his weapon once more, then walked to the living room where Romero was on the phone.

Adrian hung up and turned to Luke. "I got a chopper standing by at the airport."

"How do we find her?"

"There's no power, so we'll be able to pick up any light sources. Shouldn't be too hard, but it may take a little searching."

"Okay." Luke shoved his gun into its leather holster. "Sure we don't need suits?" He didn't want to glow when he got back.

"Just don't lick anything, you'll be fine." Adrian grinned. "And throw your shoes away after."

Someone banged loudly on the door. Instinctively Luke drew his weapon and crouched, pointing his muzzle down the hall at the front door.

Adrian drew his own gun and tiptoed down the hall hugging the wall to avoid Luke's line of fire. At the door, he stretched his neck and peered through the peephole.

Luke heard him gasp, "Maze."

Adrian reached for the door handle and turned it.

"No," hissed Luke. They had no eyes on the other side of the door. Anyone could be out there standing out of sight. He jumped up and fast walked down the hall.

Adrian ignored him and yanked the door open. Sheppard stood in the doorway, disheveled, dirty, and bloody, swaying on her feet. Romero reached out and pulled her inside.

Luke brushed past them into the breezeway, his trigger finger taunt. He scanned left then whirled right. Empty. She was alone. Backing into the apartment, he bolted the door but he didn't holster his gun.

In the kitchen, Adrian settled Sheppard into a kitchen chair and pressed a dish towel to a gash still oozing from her arm.

Luke followed slowly, tapping his index finger on the trigger guard as he studied her. Her dress was torn and she looked like she'd been rolling around in a fire pit. A haunted look pulled on her face. When he rushed down the hallway and pushed a gun in her chest she hadn't reacted. Probably an act.

"Maisie." Adrian gently pulled on her chin to make her look at him. "What happened to you? Where were you?"

She shuddered. "I think...I think maybe it was Pripyat."

Adrian nodded. "What did they want?"

Her forehead furrowed and she shook her head. "I don't know."

"Bullshit," said Luke, loudly.

Maisie's eyes flew to Luke, then to Adrian to see if he believed her. "I heard them talk about the U, Adrian. It didn't sound like they know where it is. They were going to interrogate me about it, but I didn't give them a chance."

"So you overpowered, what six, seven armed men? And drugged no less. Impressive." Luke's voice dripped with doubt. He put his gun back into its holster.

At his challenge, Sheppard glared at Luke. "Did I mess up your dramatic rescue?" Then she dropped her head like it was too heavy to hold up. "I've fought my way out of worse," she sighed.

"How did you get back? That site's at least sixty miles away," Luke said. If she expected sympathy, she was barking up the wrong tree.

"I stole their car." She smiled weakly at Adrian. "They took me out in a chopper. I had to drive back."

Adrian smiled and lifted the towel off her arm. The oozing had stopped. "I'm gonna find you a blanket," he said brushing her hair out of her face.

When he left Luke moved in front of her. He towered over her. "Were you followed here?"

"No."

"How can you be sure?"

She looked up at him, defiant. "Because they're all dead.

Luke knelt in front of her. He rested his arm on the table and leaned in to get in her face. "What did they really want?"

For the first time since he met her, Sheppard looked afraid. "They knew we were looking for the U. Somebody blew us."

She leaned away causing Luke to lean in more. "No shit, Sheppard. You didn't answer my question."

"I told you. They're trying to find the U."

"They knew everything about us, including our plans last night." Luke slammed his fist on the table making Sheppard jump. "They would've known we didn't have the location of the uranium."

Her eyes grew wide. "Unless whoever sold us out thought I knew where it was."

She sounded sincere which made Luke furious.

"And do you?" His voice was low and menacing.

"No. I told you. I don't know anything about it. Who would do this?"

"Well now, that's the question isn't it." He stood, once again towering over her. "One that you can rest assured I will get answered. And when I do...," Luke let the rest of the sentence hang.

"Why don't you just get it over with?" She raised her head and met his burning stare. "I know there's a standing kill order on my head," she whispered. "There's no one here to stop you."

They both fell silent as Adrian came back in with a blanket that he wrapped around her filthy shoulders. She tugged it closer, shivering, still watching Luke. Adrian's eyes narrowed as he looked between them.

Luke's phone buzzed. It was Frank so he left to speak in private. As he walked away, he heard her ask where Tommy was, and Adrian's muttered answer.

"What?" Sheppard shouted.

Luke closed the bedroom door against the sound of her arguing with Adrian that Tommy couldn't be dead. It was the most emotion she'd shown since she got back. Probably a lie too.

Luke put the phone to his ear.

Frank spoke loudly over the ruckus of yelling and phones ringing in the background.

"We can't replicate any of what Tommy found on the bank account, but we got on that chat room. The donations for this Asa Hussan's were to be sent from a local Imam in Hama through several hawala brokers that we monitor. Old school, Luke, the way they used to finance terrorism. We have our finger on a few. It's not much to go on but I have sources with HUMINT in the area. We're all over that mosque to see if we find anyone of any interest."

"Alright. We're gonna keep pulling on this thread. Keep me in the loop."

"What's the next move, Luke?"

"I'm staying here until Tommy is on his way home."

"Is that wise?"

"I'm not leaving him. When he's on his way home, this little side mission is done. This place was a dead end. The DOE is a dead end. Get me something." Luke really meant 'she' was a dead end, but Romero put up with it. Luke was done wasting time.

"Alright, sit tight till we have something actionable."

"Frank, can you do one more thing for me?"

"Name it."

"Tommy had all of Ivanov's personal information. I'm sending it. Check incoming and outgoing phone calls and location data on all his phones. I want to know who he talked to and met with yesterday. Get me a name. After I find Arazi, I'm going to handle this. You can tell Tommy's family that."

"You'll have it the minute I do."

Luke mashed the end call button, grabbed his bag, and walked out of the bedroom.

Adrian and Sheppard had moved to the couch. Adrian's arm was around her as she sat in stunned silence, tear trails streaking down her dirty face.

Without a word, Luke crossed to the corner, set his bag down, and started cramming Tommy's electronic equipment into the blood stained duffel. He glanced at Sheppard and saw her watching him with a pleading look. Luke felt the fury build again.

At least she had the good sense to stay quiet. Had she uttered a single syllable he might have shot her on the spot. How fucking dare she mourn Tommy. She was supposed to have Tommy's six. Even if she wasn't the rat that sold them out to Ivanov, a big if, she left the car. She left Tommy to die.

Silence settled over them for a long minute. Luke's intention to leave hung thick like smoke.

Adrian stood and approached Luke. "Apparently under stress, one of the guards let it slip that Ivanov keeps a residence in Venice. We're gonna try to find it. See what we can get."

"Good luck with that," growled Luke.

"You're not coming then." It was a statement.

Luke hesitated for a moment, then shook his head. "I'm going to find Arazi." Luke said nothing about the Syria connection that Tommy found. She was listening.

Adrian stuck out his hand.

Luke shook it. "Watch your back." He looked pointedly at Sheppard.

She had her face in her hands.

Adrian nodded. "I know. I'm going to finish this."

Luke grabbed both bags and walked out of the apartment.

20

———

Grand Canal
Venice, Italy
March 26
1850 Hours Local Time

"How would your wife feel if she knew you were in Venice with an old girlfriend?" Maisie smiled at Adrian.

He sat beside her on the rear seat of the water taxi. Cold wind blew down the Grand Canal and sent tendrils of hair flying. She looked away to let the wind clear the hair from her face, and to take in the sight.

On both sides ornate windows from every age of history piled on top of each other, their walls gilded by the setting sun. The wide canal churned with rotor wash from boats of every size and shape. Clusters of gondola fleets bobbed in the choppy water by the stone breakwaters, and small watercraft darted in and out of smaller secondary canals.

Adrian's eyes narrowed at her dig for personal information. "I'm divorced."

"Oh, good."

"What the hell, Maisie?"

"I meant good for her." She laughed.

Adrian smiled reluctantly.

She knew that would get her desired response. An unexpected wave of sadness washed over her. After tonight she would never see him again.

"Maze," Adrian's voice was soft. "I'm sorry about everything. I wish you knew how sorry I am that your father did this to you."

"He wasn't responsible for everything," she said, holding Adrian's gaze.

"Don't do that, Maze. You left for Israel on your own."

"If I'd stayed in America my employment options would have been flipping burgers."

"Maisie...."

"I was blacklisted by my own government. Every application I submitted ended in rejection. Retribution for something I didn't do."

"Every military application, Maze." Adrian shot back. "They flagged your intel profile, that's all. You knew you would endure some scrutiny as the child of a rogue cold war operative, but that was it. So what if you couldn't enlist."

There was so much she wanted to say, but she held it to, "I shouldn't have had a 'profile'".

"That's bullshit and you know it, Maze." Adrian refused to field her excuses, but he looked sad too. "Hate me if you want, but you don't get to blame your choices on me. Leaving was your decision. Yours. I wanted you with me."

She looked back at the ancient city gliding by. Her father brought her to Venice on business trips so many times. The brackish smell of the water brought back memories of gelato and walks that lasted all day.

Those tiny alleys were so tangled that no accurate map existed. Solving the mystery of the next turn and getting gloriously lost both captivated and frightened a lonely teenager.

The old city hadn't lost her magic. Memories of happier times came flooding back. How appropriate that she would find him here. Her thumb absent-mindedly rubbed the scrolled ridges on her locket.

She jerked in surprise when Adrian brushed the hair out of her face. A familiar thrill shot through her body as his fingers lingered and traced the outline of her jaw.

Back when life wasn't so hard, he touched her hair constantly, twirling it around his fingers. It was so hard to remember what happiness felt like, but here in this place, when he touched her, it came easier.

"It was never supposed to be this way," he said.

"What?"

"You and me, Maze."

She squeezed her eyes shut. This was the part she was terrible at. Talking. Maybe if she was better at it, they would be married with 2.7 kids. It was all she'd ever wanted.

"It's going to be alright, baby." The warm hand skimming her cheek slid to the back of her neck. His grasp felt hungry like he wanted to pull her closer but resisted in the public setting.

Her eyes flew open and a white-hot spike tore through her body confusing her. Was it desire or fear? Fear that she might lose her resolve because she still wanted him so much.

Maisie Sheppard had been a willful, defiant child. A headache to her teachers and a rebel on the playground. Always the one to ask why when everyone else blindly obeyed. When everyone else asked permission, she did as she wanted; a trait she'd carried into adulthood. But from day one she'd had trouble telling Adrian Romero no.

This time 'no' was her only choice, but she had to keep

him on the hook for a few more hours. She needed to be careful. Even now, after all that happened, she felt pulled back in.

The loudspeaker announced their arrival at the San Angelo water taxi stop, saving her from having to speak. The driver maneuvered the floating bus alongside the limestone jetty as Adrian and Maisie grabbed their bags and joined the line waiting to disembark.

They strode across the wide avenue along the main canal to a narrow alley. Ahead the neon sign of a local restaurant hung over several unoccupied tables that took up most of the alley. After another hundred feet, the alley ended in a large square spreading out in front of them. A large church with a plain facade presided over the campi, and a boarded-up stone well marked the center.

Here, away from the heavily touristed parts of the city, the plaza meandered with unhurried local time. A scarfed old lady sat on a bench watching three young boys kick a soccer ball around. Their shouts and laughter rang off the walls of the square.

"There." Adrian pointed across the square. A limestone mansion with peaked gothic windows sat on the other side of the quiet campi. These days it was a hotel.

They crossed to it and shouldered open the heavy wooden door into a stone hall. At the desk, Adrian spoke to the attendant as Maisie surveyed the expansive common area.

The vaulted stone ceiling rose forty feet overhead. Thin, uncomfortable-looking chairs were scattered around in groups. Maybe tonight they could sit and talk over a drink before everything ended.

Adrian handed her a heavy old-fashioned key on a red plastic fob. Without a word, he grabbed her bag and led the way back down the hall to yet another stone passageway.

Adrian stopped at his door. Maisie walked two doors down to #13.

She insisted they book separate rooms. Adrian hadn't argued. Maisie put her key into the lock.

"Don't forget your bag."

She glanced back at Adrian holding out her duffel. She pulled her key out and walked over to him. As soon as she reached him, her bag hit the floor and his wrist wrapped firmly around hers.

"It wasn't your fault." He'd been waiting for her to get close again to continue their conversation from the water taxi.

Maisie studied the stone floor.

"Tell me you know it isn't your fault."

She didn't want this. Not now. Her eyes stung and she squeezed them shut afraid tears would make an appearance. Instead, goosebumps erupted over her body as his hands snaked around her neck and gently turned her face up. Before she knew it her body brushed against his.

No, they were just supposed to talk. She pulled away, but he held on.

"Maisie. Baby, look at me."

She felt his breath on her face as he spoke. Her eyes flew open and Adrian's big brown eyes swam into view.

"I should have made you say it years ago. Say it to me. Tell me."

She reached up and gently hooked her hands onto his forearms as a hot tear broke loose.

"Say it to me, Maze," he repeated.

She swallowed hard to get her voice to work. "It doesn't matter."

"It's all that matters." His thumbs encircled her jaw and he brought her face closer. "I let you carry it alone, while I ran from it like a coward. I should have been beside you instead of hiding. I made you feel like it was your fault."

They were both betrayed, but Adrian felt like he was the one needing forgiveness.

Maisie swallowed hard. If Adrian knew what she had done, what she was about to do, he wouldn't ask for forgiveness. He would make her beg for it.

His lips grazed hers and the ache between her legs made her want to beg for something else. So much time had passed and she still had no defense against him. She opened her lips just enough to invite him closer.

Adrian's lips smashed down hard and hungry. They broke apart and fumbled trying to get the door open and their bags inside.

She barely shut the door when Adrian yanked her around and slammed her into the heavy wood. Fumbling for his shirt hem, she yanked it over his head. Then she pulled her shirt off, impatient to feel his skin on hers.

His hands skimmed down her neck and chest, then wrapped strong around her. He pulled her to the bed and pushed her onto it.

They made love over and over until long after the dinner hour was over. Fifteen years of hunger to sate in a single night. Three hours later they collapsed from exhaustion. Maisie burrowed into Adrian's chest listening to his heartbeat as he drifted to sleep.

When this was over she would tell him everything. It wouldn't be tangled in bed together, or over a glass of wine, after tonight she could never see him again, but she would find a way to tell him that she was sorry she spent so many years hating him, and that like him, she only did what she had to do.

It was time to go.

In Adrian's ear she whispered, "I'm going to take a shower."

"Mmmm," he murmured and rolled over settling into a pillow.

She slipped out of bed and pulled her clothes on. He would stay like that until morning. She grabbed her bag and went to her room.

Maisie's room sat on the front side of the old mansion facing the campi. That would make things easier. She dropped her bag and bolted the door.

Crossing to the window she flung open the shutters. The boys were still out there kicking the soccer ball and laughing, despite the darkness. She looked down. An easy eight-foot drop.

From her bag, she pulled out black jeans and a tight black turtleneck. In the bathroom, she freshened up and changed clothes. Checking her reflection in the mirror, Maisie wished she had a little makeup. Then she slipped on her boots and strapped her dagger sheath into them.

It didn't matter what she looked like. It would make no difference to the man she came to see.

She turned the shower on full blast and closed the bathroom door on it.

She didn't have long. Soon Adrian would find out what happened in Kiev and come looking for her. When he did, she had to be gone.

Time to get what she came for.

21

The cool spring air had coaxed a thick fog from the warm water of the lagoon. It enveloped the city, making every stone dark with moisture. Even the many lights of Saint Mark's Square four blocks behind her barely cut through the mist.

Maisie hurried along a wide avenue with the San Marco lagoon on her right side, away from Saint Mark's Square. Ahead warm yellow light spilled onto the gray night from a shop window facing the water.

As she passed the window piled with leather carnival masks and leather-bound books, she slowed down. In the dismal night, the light looked like warmth and she wanted to linger in it, but she had to keep moving. As she passed, everything plunged once again into a dark haze. Maisie shivered.

A block later, she turned left into a dark alley leaving behind the wide-open space for the claustrophobic jumble of the city streets. Soon she emerged into another campi, marked by another boarded well and the ever-present church. On the far side, Maisie spotted a small clothing shop with racks of clothes outside a half-closed grate. No one was around it.

When she got closer, Maisie saw a long gray tulle skirt poufing out from the last rack. She grabbed it without slowing down. In the next alley, she slipped the elastic waist over her jeans to alter her appearance. The best she could do right now.

Maisie didn't know where she was going, only where she needed to end up. With the help of the stolen skirt and some dark shadows, she could pass for a theatre patron, her destination. She shivered again wishing she had stolen a jacket instead.

She couldn't help looking behind her. Adrian wasn't following her, but he would be soon. Every minute he slept increased her time cushion. She moved faster.

Every few blocks Maisie spotted what she was looking for, an arrow painted on crumbling stucco pointing the way to Teatro La Fenice. Every time she saw it, she made the turn and checked behind her.

After crossing what seemed like a hundred bridges and canals, her narrow alley opened to a small campi sitting adjacent to a much larger one. The small square contained a cafe with a few people inside.

Beyond it, the lights and noise of the large plaza blazed through a wide break in the medieval houses. Edging around the dark campi, she made her way toward the light to check out the scene.

None of the elegantly dressed and elaborately masqued theatergoers seemed bothered that it was freezing, and too late in the year for Carnevale. They laughed, drank, and danced in the glow of the square while they waited for the intermission to end.

Maisie sidled up to a vendor cart selling cheap Chinese-made paper-mâché masques and swiped one while the attendant was busy texting. Pulling it down over her face, she made her way through the tipsy revelers to the circular stone well. This well was ornate carved marble, not the rough-hewn stone of the more humble campi.

She hoisted herself up and sat on the edge of the well and took in the scene. The grand, columned Teatro La Fenice dominated the campi. Lifting her mask for an unobstructed view of the sparkling white building with a history of spontaneously combusting every hundred years or so. La Fenice had risen from the ashes as many times as she had.

Something moved in the shadows in a side alley. A man in dark clothing stepped into the light and looked directly at her. A shorter man stood behind him. They withdrew back into the darkness.

Maisie jumped off the well and followed them pushing past a tipsy couple messing around in the alley. She saw a movement ahead and ran to it.

The passageway ended at a broad canal. She ripped off her mask and looked left. Nothing. To her right, the street ended where the broad canal met another narrow canal. Houses lined the walk.

At the dead end, the tall man stood at the top of three massive stone steps leading to the water and a tied-off speed boat.

"Do not move," said a heavily accented voice behind her.

Maisie skidded to a stop. The short guy hid in the shadow at the corner waiting for her to run by.

A beefy hand wrapped around her bicep. Her first instinct was to drop and spin on him, but she stayed still. She asked to be here.

His other hand began to move over her body. She forced herself to remain still as he patted her down.

"Where is your weapon?"

"Why?"

"We were told to check you for weapons."

Maisie smiled despite herself. She turned to face the bear of a man that just released her. He had thick hair on his massive forearms. "He has nothing to fear from me. He told you who I am?"

"Yes. He did." The short guy said in a deep baritone. "Probably why he said not to trust you."

I deserve that.

Reaching down she pulled the dagger in its sheath from her boot and handed it to him.

"Anything else?"

She shook her head.

"Do not move," said another voice in an accent Maisie had not heard for years. He was Czech. The tall partner had walked up behind her and pulled her hands behind her back. She didn't resist as cold steel clamped around her wrists. He took her masque.

They led her to the boat and sat her down. The tall one pulled a piece of black fabric from his jacket.

"I am sorry to do this," said the big guy as he slipped the blindfold over her face. He tied it clumsily and apologized again when it pulled her hair.

His speech was slow and gave him a meek demeanor that clashed with his hulking size. It was like he switched voices with his short partner.

When he was done, he slipped her masque over the blindfold and sat next to her. Even if they passed a patrol, no one would know she was bound and blind.

Maisie didn't struggle or protest. She would be treated no differently than any other of the Banker's clients who were lucky enough for a face-to-face.

The engine made a guttural sound, and water churned behind them. The boat lurched forward and swung right.

They were moving fast, the driver skillfully navigating the narrow channels.

Minutes later the engine noise stopped bouncing off close buildings. They'd made it to a larger canal or the lagoon.

The driver gave it more gas and the boat shot forward. Maisie shivered as cold air whipped around her. She felt movement next to her, and a moment later a jacket draped over her shoulders.

"Better?" The big guy yelled to be heard over the wind whipping around them. "Are your cuffs too tight? I can loosen if they are too tight." He was clearly the nicer of the two.

Maisie smiled in his direction. "I'm fine, thank you."

She didn't tell him the most useless piece of equipment was the blindfold. Even with GPS coordinates, she would never have found their destination in this bewildering place.

Soon the boat slowed and swerved left then right. They were headed back into the maze of canals. Maisie counted six more sharp turns, each with reduced speed. The engine noise grew louder as the canals narrowed into the interior of the city.

The driver cut the engine and the boat bumped to a stop. Shoes clicked on stone. Maisie heard a door creak open.

"Stand up, please," said the big guy. He gently pulled her to her feet and led her to the side of the boat. Strong arms from above yanked her up and she felt slick, moss-covered stone beneath her feet.

Hands guided her five steps away from the water. The rusty hinges creaked again. The door slammed shut and the sound reverberated through the cavernous space they now stood in. A faint ripple of water echoed in the empty space. The hem of her skirt was soaked.

It smelled like an aquarium. She just walked through the water door of whatever Venetian home they were at. Made sense. It would be hard to take a blindfolded, cuffed woman through the front door. Even the notoriously private people of Venice were bound to notice.

The flimsy elastic on her cheap mask snapped as it was yanked off. Then the blindfold came off. Maisie blinked as her eyes adjusted to the dim light.

They stood in a two-story foyer. The floor was tiled with black and white checked marble, each tile at least three feet square. A half-inch of water rippled across the marble swaying tufts of fluffy green algae around their feet.

The deep turquoise water door behind them faded to rotting brown at the bottom. A half-circle of filigreed wrought iron topped the door. During the day the stairwell was lit by daylight from a gothic window above the water door. At night the only light came from a gas lantern on the wall.

A staircase rose to the second floor with a carved stone balustrade that ran up the stairs and around a walkway overlooking the space. The walls were red flaking stucco.

For the first time, Maisie saw her escorts. The tall one had blunt features that contrasted oddly next to light blue eyes. His nose was crooked from repeated breaking, and his right ear was a misshapen cauliflower mess. He smiled shyly at her just like she thought he would. She smiled back and he looked down.

The little guy was short, muscled, and bald. He scowled a lot but seemed more stiff than mean, maybe. She wasn't about to test that theory. He took her cuffs off then jerked his head toward the staircase.

"Time to go."

Hesitating, she placed a hand on the stone banister. A firm hand between her shoulder blades propelled her firmly upward. She pulled her skirt up and climbed the stairs as slowly as the hand on her back would let her.

In a heartbeat she had committed treason to get here, now she was dragging her feet. The urge to run overwhelmed her. Seeing him after all these years scared her more than anything she'd ever faced.

But she deserved whatever waited for her on the other side of those doors. Her fate was her own fault, no turning back now.

On the landing, they faced a wide wooden door with the same arches as the balustrade. Unlike the neglected water entrance, however, this door was a deep cherry wood heavily shellacked against the damp.

The short guy reached around her for the iron door handle. The well-oiled hinges did not protest, and the heavy door swung open to reveal an interior much different than the spooky foyer.

Glossy parquet floors stretched across a large room strategically interrupted by plush Persian rugs. Three distinct groups of chairs and sofas made the cavernous space more intimate. The last sat in front of a fireplace so large her tallest escort could walk in and not stoop. A fire roared inside, glinting off the gilded rococo mirror above the imposing mantel.

Original rough-hewn timbers lined the fifteen-foot ceilings. Paintings in gilded frames covered the walls. Floor-to-ceiling plated windows at the far end of the room looked out to the Grand Canal. The dome lights of the Basilica of Santa Maria della Salute were just visible through the foggy night.

Maisie forgot to move. The hand on her back pushed her out of the doorway and she tripped over her skirt as she stepped forward.

No lamplight illuminated the dark room. Light from the

fire cast onto a man sitting in a chair looking out the windows. Standing next to him, looking directly at her, was a thirty-something bearded man. His chin was high and his manner icy.

Another shove made her realize she had stopped again. The hand on her back kept pushing until she was far enough in that he could close the door. Again she nearly tripped over her bedraggled hem.

As Maisie righted herself, the seated man raised his hand ever so slightly and pointed toward the roaring fire. That's when she saw it.

Distracted by the opulence of the room and her own fear, she missed the wheelchair. The aide pushed it toward the fire.

Then she heard a voice she hadn't heard in fifteen years.

"Hello, Maisie."

22

Sestieri San Marco
Venice, Italy
March 26
1150 Hours Local Time

"Alexei," Maisie breathed. Her knees felt wobbly and she took a stutter step trying to steady herself.

"Who is Alexei?" The short bodyguard turned to his tall partner.

The younger man pushing the wheelchair stopped his face a mask of suspicion. "And who are you?" He called across the space between them. His English was perfect, his accent German.

Alexei reached back and patted his forearm saying something in German.

"I don't care," the younger man fumed, refusing to be calmed. "She shouldn't call you by that name."

"It's alright, Nico." Alexei switched to English. "Please show her in." He took over wheeling his own chair as the younger man stalked over to Maisie.

As Nico approached, the two men behind her split and

posted up in separate corners. "May I take your coat," Nico said coldly, sizing up her disheveled appearance, and her boots peeking out from underneath a sopping hem.

Maisie started when Nico demanded the coat her tall escort had given her. Her attention had been locked onto the efforts of the feeble man moving from the wheelchair to the sofa. She shrugged off the jacket, but let it fall to the floor before Nico could grab it.

Alexei's legs didn't seem to work, and his arms weren't much stronger. He fell onto the sofa and labored to right himself. He was formal and cold as he spoke. "This is Nico, my assistant. You have already met Max and Timo."

Maisie heard the tremble.

She couldn't stand it anymore. Maisie sprinted for the sofa. Timo and Max lurched forward, but they backed down when Alexei raised his hand.

By the time she threw herself down in front of the sofa, tears stung her eyes.

"Alexei, what have they done to you?" She reached for his hands but recoiled when he pulled away. Instead, she kneeled before him, head bowed like a contrite sinner.

"I go by Philipp now. Philipp Kaufmann, but then that is who you asked to meet, is it not?

It surprised Maisie when she laughed. "Still changing your name every chance you get."

A smile cracked his solemn face. "Maisie Sheppard. Still throwing everything into chaos because of some damned fool notion."

Maisie looked up. He was reaching out to her. She wrapped her hands around his and rose to sit on the sofa.

Alexei was two years younger than her, but in the firelight, he looked ten years older. Suffering and pain had etched deep lines on his face. His blond hair had gone gray. The only thing the same were his sharp blue eyes.

"Why are you in a wheelchair, Alexei?"

"Philipp," he corrected her.

She smiled sadly. "Not to me."

Her childhood had been lonely. Charles had regular operations that took him to places she could not follow, so she stayed home with a nanny or, when she was older, alone. The bright spot of those empty days was Alexei Kovalcik.

They met in primary school and bonded over their inability to make friends with normal kids. Maisie's unrelenting audacity drove her fellow students away. Alexei was quiet and withdrawn, but two years ahead of his grade. The day she punched a bully for pushing him on the playground they became inseparable.

Maisie always told him the kids were mean because they were afraid of someone so smart. She'd said it to make him feel better, but it turned out Alexei had an IQ of 170 and spoke five languages fluently, with a decent command of six more.

She taught the genius boy how to be a tough talker, and he taught her how to tame her runaway mind and focus. They honed each other's skills as they roamed the streets of Prague.

"Multiple sclerosis," he said. "I was diagnosed eight years ago. It attacked my lower spine with a fervor. The doctors have managed to slow the disease, but the damage is done."

"Eight years?"

Nico returned with tea service and put it down too hard on the marble-topped coffee table, glaring at Maisie now crowding her childhood friend. Alexei thanked him as he began pouring.

Nico handed Alexei a delicate china cup and saucer, then Maisie. She sat back realizing how cold she was and took a tiny sip. The warmth of the tea and fire made her shiver violently. Her entire body felt icy.

"Nico has been with me for seven of them. I wouldn't have survived without him. Much less thrived." Alexei motioned around at the opulent drawing room they sat in. "He is a large factor in my success."

Nico looked happy.

Maisie shivered again. She put her tea down so she didn't spill it on the custom brocade sofa. "I'm so sorry, Lexei. I...I didn't come back. You asked me to and I...I didn't know." Her shoulders pinched together as she hunched in shame.

"You were fighting your own battles, Maisie. No one knows that better than me."

"It doesn't matter. We should have been together. And it was my fault we weren't. I should have been with you, not running away. I should have been with the people I loved."

"Most of the people you loved abandoned you. You were protecting yourself before it happened again."

"You never abandoned me." She looked pointedly at Alexei.

He smiled softly and she felt the pinch in her shoulders release. With steadier hands she picked up her cup and took another sip. The fire and the tea warmed her from the outside in.

She looked around the room. "You're not kidding about thriving. You are the only name in private untraceable banking services."

"Oh, there are others." Alexei looked a little bashful. Just like she remembered.

She smirked. "Not with your reputation."

He waved her off.

"You always said you'd get out of there. Make a name for yourself. Now look at you." She gestured around the room.

"Yes, I did."

"You were the smart one."

Alexei held up his saucer as Nico draped a heavy throw over his knees. "And you were the brave one."

"No. I was the stupid one. It's clear which is more lucrative." She leaned back taking another deep breath savoring the familiar peace she had around this man.

"You were always in trouble but that doesn't mean you were always wrong," said Alexei. "You defended me in school more times than I can count. Remember the tubby boy that pushed me into a puddle?" Alexei leaned forward ever so slightly and chuckled. "You forced him to eat mud, do you remember?"

She leaned in the rest of the way and touched her forehead to his, like a thousand times before. A lump blocked a laugh and she swallowed to clear it. "That little shit had it coming."

Alexei threw his head back and laughed, making Nico size Maisie up jealously.

Maisie looked at Nico and smiled warmly, flustering him. He cleared his throat and rearranged the perfect tea tray.

Alexei grew serious. "But I think this time you are the one in trouble. Yes?"

Maisie's smile faltered.

"You are here about your father."

The damn lump blocked her throat again. He called her on it. She abandoned her best friend to the world so she could run from her own pain and came back only when she needed something.

His forehead wrinkled. "We were together, do you remember? The day you heard your father was dead."

She nodded. They'd been on a long weekend in the south of France when she got the phone call.

"I knew that day you would never be the same. That look on your face. And I'm looking at the same expression again."

"Lexei...I...."

He waved her off and set his teacup down. "I am glad you came to me, Maisie. I will help you in any way that I can."

"Alexei...," she stammered before finding her voice. "He's alive, Lexei. John Bressler is alive."

He didn't seem surprised. "I'd heard that as well."

The room contracted around her as she processed what she heard. "You knew?"

Alexei calmly nodded. "I've followed your case with some interest these past years. Mostly because of what it did to you," he said with a little smile. "I followed you too, although you moved around every few months."

"Then you know why I'm here. I have to find him, Lexei."

"I know." Alexei's voice was soft.

A sudden surge of anger and adrenaline hit. She jumped and raised her hands like she was about to fight some unseen figure in front of her. Catching herself, she clenched them instead and held them rigid at her side while she gazed into the fire.

"He set up dad, Lexei." Her voice cracked. "Dad was innocent. That bastard killed him then framed him, and now he's selling the uranium."

Alexei's voice was soothing. "Maisie. Are you sure you want to pursue this?"

She turned to face him, calmer. The urge to fight something had passed. "How can I walk away?"

"You must be sure about this. You know what kind of men our fathers were, and John Bressler was much the same. Keep digging and you may unearth things about your father that you cannot forgive."

"How can you say that? If Bressler is alive, I have to find him. They accused my father of murdering him. No one else seems to care, so I'll be the one to make him pay for it."

"Kill him, you mean."

"No."

Her decisive tone made Alexei cock his head. Nico's cup stopped midway to his mouth.

"When I find Bressler, I'll find the file. I will give it, and that murdering bastard, to Adrian and clear my father's name. Death is too easy for him. He will live out his days with his sins on his own head, not my father's."

"Adrian? Adrian Romero?"

She nodded.

"Is he in Venice?"

"Yes."

In their respective corners, Max and Timo shifted uncomfortably. Timo, the big one, went to every window and door making sure they were locked.

"Maisie." Alexei sounded reproachful, like a father scolding a child.

"He doesn't know about you. He has no idea where you are," she hurried on.

Alexei's voice grew softer. "Why did you bring him here, Maisie?"

Maisie's voice sounded small. She messed up. "I didn't have a choice. I did what I had to do...after I arranged this meeting, I needed him. He had my passport. I had to string him along. If I'd left him he would have followed me, and I couldn't have kept you a secret."

"He's looking for you then."

She shook her head. "He thinks I'm in my room. He won't look for me until morning. I'll be long gone by then."

"You shouldn't have brought him here," said Alexei, but he relaxed back on the sofa.

Maisie sat beside him again. "I'm sorry, Lexei."

Without hesitation, he wrapped his arm around her shoulders. She buried her face in the crook of his neck.

His grip was weaker than it used to be. Every time she broke up with a boyfriend or got into a fight, or both, Alexei was there to catch her. As long as he was in her life she had never been alone. Another wave of guilt washed over her.

For his part, it didn't seem like even a weekend had passed. He stroked her hair like he always had. It soothed her like it always did.

"I have lost more sleep over what happened to you than anything else in my life, including my own illness." He twisted to look at her. "I worried for you, Maisie, not something as silly as your father's reputation. And yet I know that is the reason you avoided me all these years."

She looked up at him, tears rimming her eyes. He could still read her every thought.

"You should have known that would not matter to me."

She bowed her head. "I'm so sorry."

He put a thumb on her chin and pressed gently. "You were forgiven the moment I knew you were coming. You were right to think I would help you. I will always help you."

"Forgiven?" Nico sniffed. "I've never seen him do, what do you call it, a wheelie in that chair before." He tried to sound disapproving but failed to convince.

Maisie offered him a conciliatory smile, then turned back to Alexei. "Yes, I knew you would help me. You are the only one in this world I trust. Everyone else can burn."

"Everyone? My Maisie always stood up for the weak." Alexei gazed at her with an eyebrow lifted.

"People change," she answered sadly.

"Yes, I suppose they do," he said.

Maisie reached for her cup and sat back. Fresh tea and Alexei's favorite colorful French macarons kept appearing on the coffee table, and the fire kept roaring, stoked periodically by Nico. They talked for hours, as though nothing had ever passed between them.

She'd never tell snooty Nico, but this was the best tea she ever tasted.

"What will you do when this is all over?" Alexei asked.

She smiled, her head laid back on the headrest. "I haven't thought about it. Maybe something where I don't have to fight Russian mob bosses."

"Yes, I hope that too," said Alexei. He sounded tired.

With a start, Maisie lifted her head and realized the sky over the city had turned pink and blue. It was five AM.

She sighed deeply. Leaving sounded like torture. She wanted it to stay like this forever.

Alexei was thinking the same thing. "You'll come back to me? After you get back from Budapest?"

She sat bolt upright. "From where?"

Alexei wasn't looking at her. He was looking at a very smug Nico sitting in the armchair across from them.

"You talked about him all the time, did you know that? Your father." Alexei focused on her again. "When we were kids, he was all you ever talked about, especially when he was gone. It used to make you so angry that he wouldn't take you, even though it was dangerous." Alexei laughed softly.

Maisie nodded impatiently, no longer in the mood to reminisce.

"When I heard that John Bressler was alive, I had Nico look into it. Nico here is a sleuth extraordinaire." Alexei reached over and clasped his hand.

Nico laid his hand over Alexei's frail one and they shared a warm knowing smile.

"One of his great strengths." Alexei turned back to Maisie. "We backtracked all the way to Prague. Bressler had no family so it was unlikely he would return to America.

And it is much easier to blend in when you speak the language and know local customs." said Alexei. "So we...."

Maisie interrupted. "You found him?"

"Everyone has to pay medical bills if they're not really dead," said Nico cryptically. "If you narrow down a geographical area and a gender and age, add in facial recognition, it's not really that hard."

Her eyes flicked back and forth between the men. She forgot. Bressler had type 1 diabetes.

"That must have taken ages."

Nico shrugged, but Alexei answered. "Not so long. Like I said, he is extraordinarily good at what he does."

Overwhelming shame threatened again. What had she ever done to deserve a friend like this?

"Why would you do that?" She kept her voice soft so they couldn't hear the tremble.

"Do you not know?" Alexei turned to her. "He destroyed someone I love and I am a man of resources. I am not a violent man, but he was going to pay."

A leather-bound notebook appeared on Alexei's lap and Nico sat back down. Alexei flipped through it and ripped out a page with a handwritten address.

"Lexei," breathed Maisie gazing at the piece of paper. "How can I ever repay you?"

"I have some ideas," said Alexei with a little smile.

She tore her eyes away from the neat script. "Anything."

"Come back to me. I miss you. And you have skills that Max and Timo lack. Skills that a man in my line of work can use."

Maisie slid off the couch and fell to her knees in front of him. "Then you have them. Forever."

Alexei stifled a groan as he shifted in his seat. "Nico, when the boys get back, have them take Maisie to...."

Her head snapped up on high alert. She hadn't realized Max and Timo left. "Where did they go?"

"I sent them to check on your Adrian. To make sure he wasn't nosing around since you brought him to our doorstep," Nico sniffed at her. "They'll be back presently."

Her eyes flew back to Alexei. "He won't find you. I swear."

"I know. But I've held you up for longer than is prudent. Go and finish what you started so you can come back to me."

She nodded and rose to her feet.

"Nico, please show Maisie to a guest room where she can freshen up. Please provide her with anything that she needs. There is ample cash and supplies in the safe."

Nico nodded curtly and stood. "This way." He walked fast toward a mahogany paneled staircase.

Maisie gave Alexei a quick peck. "I'll see you soon." Then she was on Nico's heels.

Deep, soft pile carpeted the upstairs hall. Nico pushed open the second door and ushered Maisie into a small but luxuriously furnished room. Luxury linens cocooned the bed and the ensuite bathroom was pink marble. A far cry from her dingy flat in Mombasa. She became painfully aware of her untidy appearance.

Nico deposited two fluffy white towels on the bed as she gazed at the opulent room. This was a guest room.

"There are toiletries in the bath, including a comb." Nico eyed her hair, frizzy from her nighttime boat ride. "I will be back with cash and other items. I'm sorry, but there isn't time for another passport. You'll have to use your own. Agent Romero will be able to track you, but I suspect it will take him longer than it would take me. If you move quickly, he shouldn't be able to catch up. If there's anything else, please let me know." He turned to leave.

"Thank you, Nico." Maisie's voice was soft.

"You're most welcome," he said formally over his shoulder.

"Not for this."

Nico stopped short and looked back.

She stood by the bed, a towel on her arm watching the shadows outside the window disappear.

"I love him like a brother, Nico, but I didn't treat him like one." She finally met his eyes. "So what I mean is, thank you for taking care of him all these years."

Nico's blue eyes went wide with surprise and looked misty.

She felt awkward and hurried on. "It should have been me, but you did what I couldn't do. I am in your debt."

He nodded curtly to compose himself. After blinking several times he settled on a husky, "You're welcome," and left.

The top drawer of the bathroom vanity revealed an assortment of decidedly feminine toiletries along with makeup. It was a well-stocked guest bathroom for a recluse who never entertained. Probably put there in case she ever came to see him.

Maisie pushed the thought away. She scrubbed and moisturized her face and put on mascara. Combing her unruly hair, she corralled it into some semblance of a braid. Then she stepped back and looked at herself in the mirror.

If she kept her head down, she could pass for a harried traveler. It would be enough to get through train station security screenings. A change of clothes and a hat would help.

Someone pounded at the door.

"Miss Sheppard," Nico called. "Miss Sheppard."

"Come in."

"Does he have a way to track you?"

Maisie's heart sped up. Adrian. She shook her head. "I have a phone, but I took out the sim card. I don't know what else he has access to."

Nico nodded, keeping his anger in check. Instead of raging, he became businesslike and efficient.

"Where is he?"

Nico threw something on the bed. "I'm not sure, but Max and Timo have seen him in this sestieri. He must have realized you were gone before you expected him to."

She nodded. Time to go.

"Take that." Nico motioned to the bed. "Philipp told me to give them to you."

She turned and saw the two items he deposited on the bed. A small leather cross body bag and, she squinted. A Kimber Warrior SOC in thigh rig holster. Not exactly her trusted Colt 1911, but it would do nicely. She pulled it out. It felt good in her hand.

Impressed, she looked at Nico. "You *are* good."

He was already in the hall. "Yes. Now follow me."

They headed away from the main staircase. Maisie hopped along behind him trying to get the holster buckled and situated beneath her tulle skirt.

"There should be sufficient cash in the satchel and some prepaid credit cards. Remember, you need to move fast. Stay in one place too long and Agent Romero will catch up. If you end up in custody, there is little we can do for you. Understand?"

"Yes," she answered. That was an understatement.

At the end of the hall, Nico pushed a pane of ornate paneled wood on the wall. A hidden door opened under his hand revealing a narrow spiral staircase.

"School children run over these houses every day like a damned herd of elephants," Nico said as they climbed.

They stepped into a steeply pitched attic room with

heavy beams. Out the large round window, Maisie could see their roof connected to the endless roofs of other Venetian homes.

"There is a path. You can see it" Nico crossed to the window. "I don't know where it leads. Be cautious, though. It is covered by water collection reservoirs and laundry lines."

He unlatched the window and swung it open. "Some people like to put their undergarments on display for the world to see, I suppose," he said decisively as though it was a pressing topic.

Moments later Maisie sat on the sill, pulling her skirt through the window. The path ran four feet below her, a silver thread through black tar.

"Keep the Basilica on your left," Nico instructed her. "You can make it a long distance before you have to find a way down. And lose that hideous skirt when you can."

She smiled. "Thank you."

Nico nodded and Maisie dropped to the roof. Without a glance back she turned and ran across the rooftops.

23

———

Al Nawforaa Coffee Shop
Hama, Syria
March 26
1420 Hours Local Time

Too old to fight in the war, the old men drank tea and talked about it instead. They grouped around small tables on the wide sidewalk lining the busy street. Fighting had died down in the region, so everyone was out and about making up for lost time. It wouldn't be long before bullets started flying again.

Auto traffic was slow along the congested route. Hooded, masked housewives and pedestrians wove in and out of traffic using the pitted street as their personal sidewalk giving no attention to the blaring horns. The fastest things moving were motorbikes zigzagging through the mass of people.

Nasir stood at the corner looking past the shops and cafes. Ahead, in the only slice of shade on the sidewalk, he saw a man sitting at a table surrounded by other old men in deep discussion. The old man picked up a teacup and sipped, unbothered by the chaos around him.

Even as a boy, al-Nujaifi seemed old. As Nasir studied his gray hair and deep wrinkles, he was acutely aware of the time that had passed. At twenty-seven, Nasir was in the prime of his life. Al-Nujaifi had grown old.

Abdul-Malik Amjad al-Nujaifi was once his father's most trusted friend in the days before the Americans invaded Iraq. A lifetime ago.

With a final look around Nasir nervously adjusted the backpack over his right shoulder and stepped out, melting into the throng of people moving down the road.

Nasir dipped his head as a patrol rumbled by. The last thing he needed now was trouble in Syria. He wished the rebels luck against the pig of a president, but they probably wouldn't be so understanding of him and why he was there.

They were simple soldiers, high on the promise of a victory they would never achieve. And even if they did, they would produce yet another failed Islamic nation adding to the list of reasons the West laughed at them.

It was dangerous coming here. When he'd contacted the American to transfer money for payment on the uranium, he was told Marshall was closing in. How much of it was true, Nasir didn't know.

One thing he knew for sure. Time was growing small.

The fifty-caliber truck mounted technical rig rumbled over the potholes and past him. Nasir slowed and stopped a few feet away from the table where al-Nujaifi sat.

Al-Nujaifi finished his tea while absently scanning the crowd. When his eyes passed over Nasir, he calmly nodded once.

Nasir turned and walked to the next street corner and lounged against the wall, waiting. Moments later the old man excused himself from the group. As al-Nujaifi approached him, Nasir stepped out from the cinderblock building.

Al-Nujaifi stopped and the two generations of men embraced.

"Nasir, my boy. You are alive." He patted Nasir on the back roughly. "When you came to me last year, I did not think I would see you again. But it seems you have had success in your endeavors."

"Yes, Alim. Thanks to you." Nasir planted a kiss on his forehead in a show of respect.

Al-Nujaifi nodded and beckoned for Nasir to follow him. Five minutes later, they sat on a broken park bench by the river bank.

Nasir came for the final piece of the puzzle. A piece he could only get in person. He couldn't risk the Americans intercepting an email or any other form of electronic correspondence. This he had to do in person.

And he owed his father's old friend a final thank you. He had not been close to al-Nujaifi as a boy, but things were different now. The only thing in the world that mattered to him would be a success because of al-Nujaifi's expertise. Justice would never be served without his help. Nasir might even muster a traditional blessing. It would be insincere, but the old man deserved to hear it nonetheless.

The old man sunned himself on the park bench as untroubled as the tranquil river flowing behind him.

Nasir turned to him. "Peace be upon you," he said.

"And upon you, my child," answered al-Nujaifi. "Are all the arrangements made?"

"All but one, Alim."

Without another word, the old man reached into his pocket and pulled out a scrap of paper folded in half. "They are already working on the device. Assuming you have been able to procure your fuel, everything should be on schedule."

"They have the," Nasir paused unsure if his question would be disrespectful, "capability to build according to the plans?"

The man looked at him shrewdly, making him nervous. If he refused to give Nasir that scrap of paper, Nasir would have to kill him. He didn't want that.

Instead, al-Nujaifi lifted an eyebrow in amusement. "You young ones don't have the faith that we used to. I suppose that is to be expected."

Nasir bowed his head to show deference. "Forgive me, Alim. I did not mean disrespect."

"And that is why I did not feel disrespected." Al-Nujaifi held out the scrap of paper. "Their address is just outside the city. You will have to arrange transport. They will assist you, but they will not be seen in public places with you for operational security reasons."

Nasir nodded and took the paper. "My family would never see justice without you, Alim. Now they will rest easy. May Allah bless you."

"And you, my child. May you find the peace you so desperately seek."

Nasir stood and kissed the old man's forehead. Then he turned and walked away, the piece of paper securely in his pocket.

He'd traveled thousands of miles for a two-minute conversation, and now he must travel those miles again. Nasir crossed the street and turned left, continuing a few more blocks, forgetting to look around him.

Nasir didn't notice a young man across the street watching him. He didn't notice the man follow as he walked the five blocks and got into a rental car and drove away. He didn't see the young man dial a number on his cell phone and put it to his ear as he disappeared into the crowded street.

24

Hotel Dyukovskiy Bar, Batyyeva Hora
Kiev, Ukraine
March 27
2000 Hours Local Time

Luke pushed his hamburger away. It was half finished but he couldn't stomach any more food. Ukrainian beer on the other hand wasn't half bad. He drained his bottle contemplating another.

Twisting his neck, Luke performed his periodic scan of the hotel lobby from his corner bar stool. This time he saw what he was looking for.

A blond man in laughably stylish clothes sauntered through the door and stood looking around. The men locked eyes and Jay Simpson started toward him.

Luke turned back to his beer. He said nothing as Simpson approached and slapped him hard on the back.

Jay pulled out the stool beside him and motioned to the bartender for a beer. "You sure have good taste, Marshall." Jay motioned to the shabby hotel lobby.

When Luke didn't answer, Jay's voice grew soft. "I'm

sorry, Luke. I liked Tommy. He was a good man. A good agent."

"Is the team here?"

Jay threw up two fingers at the bartender asking for two beers. "There's two teams actually. Longer refused to let those DOE hoes touch Tommy. He wasn't happy with a liaison so now there's a DIA team pissing off the energy guys." Jay chuckled.

Jay fell silent as the bartender delivered both beers then retreated back to his corner and his paperback.

"Tommy will be on a transport plane in less than an hour. He'll be at Andrews by morning." Jay handed Luke a bottle and held his out. "To Tommy."

Luke took it, clinked Jay's bottle, and chugged it. "Something tells me you're not here to oversee Tommy's transport," growled Luke.

Jay grinned at him. "You've made some impressive headway since Kuwait."

Even though he was relieved to see the spook, Luke scowled. "What's the Company paying you for? I keep doing all your work."

Jay clapped him on the back again. "Don't worry, Marshall. They're not paying that much, but I got this round."

"So you need my help. That's when I usually catch you following me around."

Jay laughed. "It's the other way around this time, brother. You need my help."

"Oh my god." Luke coughed into his beer. "You're Frank's connection in Syria."

"So far you've been the superstar. Now it's my time to shine," Jay said, grinning.

Luke swung his head to look at Simpson trying to tell if he was kidding or not. For once, Simpson looked dead serious.

Luke looked away. "I tried partnering up and it was a fucking disaster."

"You don't have much choice right now. This got decided above our pay grade. Unless you have assets in country who can avoid the rebels and Assad's men, you're screwed. And I happen to know Frank has none of those things."

Luke's head snapped toward Jay. "They found him?"

Jay gave him a smirk. "That was a good catch finding those deposits in Ivanov's account."

"Tommy caught it. Not me."

"And he'll get the credit for it. Looks for all the world that Arazi is working with his father's old money man."

"Al-Nujaifi," Luke breathed.

"That's him. He goes by the name Mohammad Aamir now, but it's definitely him. And my asset knows right where he lives. Apparently, he's well known and respected in those parts."

Luke turned back to his beer, his heart racing. That son of a bitch did it. Tommy may have just saved them all.

"As of five pm today, I'm your tour guide to hell and back again." Jay threw a Hryvnia five on the counter and stood. "And you're wrong about one thing," he said, buttoning his jacket. "I did come to make sure Tommy gets on that transport. That job is done. Now I have to get you to the ops brief in Turkey."

Luke squeezed his eyes shut. He'd broken his own rule and now Tommy was dead. Placing even a small amount of trust in the unproven Marrero was the dumbest thing he'd ever done. But Jay was right. Any mission into Syria without a guide was suicide. The spook's direct communication with Frank made it a little easier to swallow.

Luke drained his beer. "Getting in is easy. Getting out is the bitch."

"Piece of cake," Jay said, his characteristic grin back in place. "Chop chop. Longer's waiting on us."

Luke grabbed his bag and followed Jay.

Twenty minutes later jet engines whined higher as the men climbed the gangway to the Learjet. He stopped on the top stair and looked across the tarmac.

Three hundred yards away an unmarked brown cargo transport plane waited with the tail ramp down. Plain-clothed men were unloading two long unmarked metal boxes from a white Mercedes van.

They wheeled one box to the waiting aircraft. Tommy died for his country and he was being smuggled out in a box marked as engine parts instead of under a flag.

The fire in Luke's stomach kindled again and felt torn down the middle.

Tommy was dead, betrayed, but Luke had work to do before he could kill the Judas responsible for his death.

Luke ducked through the open jet door and dropped his bag. He sank into one of the leather bucket seats as Jay headed to the cockpit. He hadn't slept in thirty-six hours and he was starting to feel it.

The engines pitched higher as Jay emerged from the cockpit. The spook took the seat across from him and buckled his seatbelt as the jet lurched forward. Once they were in the air, the seatbelt sign went dark.

Jay popped out of his chair and headed to the small galley between the cabin and the cockpit. He leaned over and opened the small refrigerator and called out to Luke. "Water?"

"Yeah," said Luke. He sat staring out the window at the light blinking on the wingtip.

Jay sat back down across from him with a tired groan and handed him a plastic bottle.

"Tell me about Maisie Sheppard," said Jay.

Luke's eyes went to the spook. "Since when do you care about her?"

"Since this morning when a deep-cover CIA asset at the Kremlin went dark. A man by the name of Iliya Utkin. An absolute intelligence juggernaut since the late eighties. Our best source out of the Big Red House since....ever probably."

Luke's stomach twisted. "And now you're asking about her."

"In the last few hours, my agency alone has had two in-country assets 'robbed'," Jay threw up air quotes, "and killed. They've got Utkin and he talked. We had to yank everybody out of Moscow. We're flying blind at the Kremlin."

"And...," Jay trailed off.

Luke cursed in a whisper.

"Not two hours after our man goes dark, Taras Ivanov shows up for a meet and greet with the damned president of Russia himself. Who might know about a dirty bomb plot on American soil."

"How would Sheppard know about a CIA deep-cover asset?" Luke asked.

"Her father got his start with the Agency. Some light reading revealed that Charles Sheppard worked several ops with Utkin back in the late 8os. Sheppard had a background in physics and got headhunted by the DOE. That's how he ended up chasing down nukes behind the iron curtain."

Luke twisted his neck, trying to process this new information.

"If I'm not wrong, you and that DOE schmuck were following Sheppard around precisely because she knows more about her father's work than she should. It's not a leap to assume that she knew about our Kremlin asset from way back in the day, although he was probably less valuable back then."

Before he knew it, Luke was pacing in the narrow aisle.

That's why she went to see Boris. She needed to find Ivanov, not to find out about the highly enriched uranium, Ivanov didn't have it and she damn well knew it, but because she had something to sell.

Or was she buying?

Luke turned. "And you're sure it was Ivanov in Russia?"

"Oh yeah," said Simpson. "Modern technology doesn't lie. Is she after the uranium?"

Luke shook his head. "I don't think she gives a shit about it."

Jay shrugged. "It's worth millions, but okay."

"No, this is personal for her," muttered Luke, pausing to lean on the table.

She was trying to find Bressler. And Adrian knew it.

Luke wondered why he didn't see it earlier. He could never get the hang of women. What Romero said he was after and what he really wanted were two different things. And he clearly knew how to push that woman's buttons. So Bressler had the U.

Unless Bressler is clean.

Luke stood stock straight at the thought. People who steal millions of dollars worth of uranium want the cash in their hands, not the U. He hadn't sold it in fifteen years. He still had the file too it would seem.

Like everyone else, Luke assumed the man that disappeared was the guilty one. Admitting it to himself now made it sound silly. That wasn't always true.

Maisie Sheppard may have played him, but she hadn't betrayed him. She didn't know it was coming. She hadn't sabotaged their comms either. Luke remembered it clearly now, his conversation with Tommy after Sheppard left the limo. Besides, now he knew the deal she made with Ivanov, and she didn't need to kill Tommy or Leo to do it.

"You alright, Buddy?" Jay watched him.

Luke suddenly remembered the spook was next to him. He plopped down in the other bucket seat. He wasn't going to discuss it in front of Jay and risked the traitor being snatched up before he meted out justice for Tommy.

All he said was, "I think there's a rat in the silos."

Jay shifted uncomfortably in his seat. "Yeah, that's been punted around for a while. That whole Orchid mess was a raging success for two decades until all of a sudden it wasn't. Even my IQ is high enough to know that's some grade-A bullshit."

Luke's voice dropped. "Mark my words, it's the same person that sold us out to Ivanov, and I swear on Tommy's grave I will find out who it is."

"Judging from the two goons you killed, I have no doubt," Jay said, raising an eyebrow. "But that's for later. You need to clear your mind. I need you here with me, brother."

Luke's gaze bore into Jay. "Two? You mean three."

Surprise showed on Jay's face. "How 'bout that," he said in a whisper.

"It's fucking Romero, that lying sack of shit," hissed Luke.

"But no low level officer could offer a juicy steak like that," Jay said. Then he added, "Unless he was authorized to."

Heat rose into Luke's face as he thought about what he was going to do after he neutralized the uranium. God help Adrian Romero.

"Exactly," was all he said.

Luke felt a spike of concern for the woman he'd spent the last few days hating. She better know what the hell she was doing.

Jay groaned as he stood and stretched. "Get some sleep. It's going to be a long night."

Luke nodded and Jay walked into the aft cabin and shut the door.

Two hours later, a familiar oppressive dry heat roiled into the jet cabin as the pilot opened the door. He was back in the sandbox. Luke glanced at the closed cabin door in the rear of the plane. It was still shut. Jay could find his own way around. Luke grabbed his bag and headed down the gangway.

The Incirlik Air Base in Adana, Turkey was quiet at two in the morning. It had been a while since he was there, but Luke recognized the older end of the multi-national base where they stashed the 39th Air Base Support Wing. Not much down here, but a line of hardened aircraft hangars at the end of the runway and two plain cinder block buildings.

Ten feet from the bottom step, a sand brown four-seater utility vehicle sat idling. In the driver seat, Comb Over waved at him. Unlike his polished appearance in Arlington, he looked scuffed up. He looked a little tougher that way.

Luke approached him and stuck out his hand. He didn't have the energy to be shitty. "Chad, right?" If Frank trusted him enough to make him the advance team, then Luke could too.

Surprise flickered across Comb Over's face when Luke said his real name. "Yeah. Good to see you upright, sir." Chad eyed the scratches around Luke's cheekbone.

Luke threw his bag in the back and climbed in next to Chad. "Is Frank here yet?"

Chad shook his head and cranked the souped-up golf cart. "No. He had a few wheels to grease in DC. He should be airborne by now though."

"Has anyone notified Tommy's family yet?"

Chad eyed Luke for a moment. "Not yet. Colonel wants to keep a lid on it for now. It would be hard to keep the Syria op under wraps if his death gets out. Powerful people tend to ask a lot of questions."

Luke nodded.

Chad put the four-seater in drive and gunned it. At the end of the tarmac, he whipped the wheel right and they raced down a black top road behind the aircraft hangars.

Eight-foot chain link fence topped with spiraled barbed wire encircled the base. Floodlights pointed out into the surrounding darkness, and dated cameras were mounted on poles every hundred yards. Two Turkish soldiers with German Shepherds patrolled the fence line. No one else was around.

Their destination was a set of beige three-story cinder block buildings at the end of the road. Chad brought the utility to a screeching halt at an unmarked door.

"This cluster and those hangers belong to us." Chad gestured to the cinder block buildings and the four hangers they just passed. American IDs will get you into any of those buildings." He handed Luke a lanyard and ID card and climbed out of the cart.

Luke grabbed his bag and followed.

Chad pointed behind him at the smallest of the four hangers. "Briefing is in there at 1900. Chow Hall is next door. This is the bunkhouse." He started toward the larger build-ing. "I suggest you use the time to catch up on sleep."

The plain brown entry door opened as they approached. A very young soldier with MP insignia held it for them and nodded to Chad as he led the way through.

On the third floor, Chad stopped by yet another brown door. "Here you go. Bathroom is at the other end of the hall. Be in the hanger at nineteen hundred."

Luke nodded, flipped on the light and closed the door behind him.

The room was warm. Against the far cinder block wall were two sets of metal bunk beds. The lower beds each had a folded set of sheets, a brown blanket and a lumpy pillow. A desk and chair completed the stark room.

Luke slung his bag on the chair and spied an ancient fan sitting on the desk. He plugged it in and sighed in relief when it ground to life.

Ignoring the sheets, Luke spread the blanket over the plastic mattress and plopped down fully clothed. He set his watch alarm, doubting that he would sleep.

Ten hours later, his alarm went off. Luke sat straight up narrowly missing the metal bars above him. His mind slogged through the jet lag trying to recall where he was.

Thirty minutes later he was showered, dressed and every remnant that he ever slept in the bunkhouse was stashed in his bag.

Luke opened the door intending to go to the dining hall to find some food. His eyes ran over the tarmac and the runway shimmering in the late afternoon heat. In the gaping open door of the nearest hangar, Luke saw Frank Longer standing with his arms crossed gazing over the runway, no one around him.

He knew the salty Colonel was saying his version of a prayer, his old habit on the eve of battle.

25

Sestieri San Marco
Venice, Italy
March 28
0547 Hours Local Time

Maisie ran flat out over the rooftops staying close to the window overhangs. Some roofs were flat, while others forced her to slow down to navigate the steeply pitched angles. Low fog still blanketed the city, but the sun was beginning to burn it off revealing the highest spires, domes first.

Not that fog hid her. If Adrian had a drone feed he could see through it. She glanced up and kept moving. She knew the DOE was so embarrassed by the Orchid mess that they would try to keep it quiet, even within the agency.

And, hopefully, she had a few more hours before the entire U.S. Government found out what she did and began their own manhunt.

In the early morning quiet, all Maisie could hear was her own thudding feet and heavy breathing. Its rhythm matched the steam puffing out of her mouth into the cold air.

She vaulted over a three-foot ledge marking the wall between two homes and drew a deep breath. The cold air burned her nose and lungs but it felt good.

She slowed to catch her breath. Alexei was far enough away now that she could slow down. She had no idea where she was in the city, but a broad street ran in front of the houses she now ran on. Time to find a way down. There were no roof access doors near so she kept going.

Sixty feet ahead she saw the rooftop drop away. A canal cut between the houses. It looked narrow enough to jump. Maisie tightened the bag straps, drew a deep breath, and took off running as fast as she could.

Her foot hit the ledge, and she sprung off of it kicking into the air. Not until she was airborne did she realize she miscalculated the canal's width.

The roof of the house she aimed for had a decorative overhang that sloped down. The actual roof ledge was another five feet out. She wasn't going to make it.

She slammed into the overhang and began to slide down the slick tiles. Scrambling, she managed to catch her foot on a wrought iron flower hanger before she plunged over the side.

The canal flowed three stories down, and she was fully visible to the wide street she had been parallel to. Her hidden passageway lay one story up some very slick terra-cotta roof tiles. She scrambled up the roof keeping her weight evenly distributed to get enough friction. It worked, but the tiles shifted and cracked beneath her making a terrible racket.

"MAISIE."

Her head snapped right when she heard him yell her

name. On the arched bridge that spanned the canal she just jumped stood Adrian with his cell phone out.

Shit.

There was no way he happened to be right where she performed a flying circus show, especially after she told him their mark was on the other side of town. He tracked her.

Maisie threw herself into the upward scramble. Her sleeves tore as she reached the roof ledge and heaved herself over it. She slammed into the gritty tar-papered roof, banging her head and ripping her skirt on a ventilation pipe that stuck out of the roof.

She pushed herself to her feet and ducked under a bank of wires. He would be on her soon. How was he tracking her?

Reaching back she grabbed the skirt waist and yanked it so hard the fabric ripped. She drew her dagger and sliced through the tulle opening it enough to get it off.

She started a fast walk while she ran her fingers over the seams of her shirt. Nothing. She rolled down the waistline of her pants. Swearing, she patted her pockets. Nothing.

Resheathing the dagger, her eyes fell on her boots. She stopped and bent her left leg to search the sole. There it was.

Wedged deep into the seam between the heel and the tread was a tiny microchip, just visible.

Maisie's lip curled as she scratched it out with her nail and tossed it over the ledge into the canal. Then she drew the Kimber and double checked that a round was chambered. Adrian wasn't stopping her.

Holstering the gun, she looked around. He would be on her any minute now. His little amateur tracker must have been defeated by the city's heavy buildings so close together. Otherwise, he would have found her already. Alexei was safe.

She needed to move.

Maisie took off running again, but the flatter roofs had given way to wicked angles. She slowed down after losing her footing several times.

Six houses behind, she heard a rattle then a roof access door splintered as someone kicked it. Adrian appeared in the doorway. He didn't have his gun out.

She needed to get off the roof. Up here she had one path. Down there she had thousands to lose herself in. She looked around and saw nothing. Venetians weren't big on fire escapes.

She saw it a split second before she jumped over. Another canal. Her feet dug into the tar as her path suddenly came to an end at a chasm. A wide canal flowed below her. Adrian bore down behind her.

There was no way she could jump it. A balcony caught her attention. It was four windows over and one floor down. She started picking her way along the edge.

She couldn't climb down, but if she got directly over it, she could jump and catch it. If she fell, she would fall five stories onto limestone.

Her other option was jumping into the canal, but she had to choose before she left the rooftop.

The ledge gave way to an eave pitched almost straight down. Exhaust pipes and jagged pieces of clay tile stuck up out of it. The window was right below her now.

A shout behind her made her jerk and she wobbled on the narrow ledge as she turned to see how close he was. A loose tile gave way underneath her foot, sending it, and her, sliding down the eave.

Her clothing ripped as she careened down the steep roof on her back. She threw out her hand and grabbed a thin vent pipe praying it would hold her weight. It squeaked loudly but held. Her momentum flipped her onto her side, she kicked out a leg to flip onto her belly, looking back up at the roofline.

Snatching the Kimber she thrust it upward, aiming at the roofline.

Seconds later Adrian's head appeared. Maisie adjusted her aim.

Adrian still didn't have a gun drawn. Neither did he look surprised to see her clinging to a pipe pointing one at him.

He wasn't just calm. He was cold.

"Did you get what you came for?" Adrian stepped up onto the ledge and looked down at her. He fully exposed himself, daring her to shoot.

She held her gun on him but didn't answer.

"By the way. Your check to Ivanov cleared. They found Utkin's body in the Moskva River."

"I don't expect you to understand," she said.

"Well, there's not much to understand about selling state secrets."

"I have to do this."

"Why is that, Maisie?"

"Because no one else will."

Adrian knelt on the ledge and looked out over the city as though contemplating what to have for breakfast. "Your father's not innocent, Maisie. You're throwing your life away chasing a narrative you made up in your head."

Maisie said nothing. Adrian knew her true motivation from the very beginning. He'd probably counted on that desire to clear her father's name as motivation to find the file.

She felt her face get hot but remembered that she'd done the same to him. They were both liars and deserved whatever they got.

"And one more thing, Princess. If you think I don't have the stomach to pull the trigger with you in my sights, you're dead wrong. So you better shoot me, because the next time I see you, I will kill you."

Maisie decided and released the metal piping and slipped over the edge. As soon as she cleared the eave, she kicked the wall as hard as she could. It propelled her over the sidewalk and she slammed into the water, narrowly missing the stone. Twisting around, she expelled all the air from her lungs and let herself sink. Then she swam as hard as she could under the surface.

Sneaking a look in the murky water, Maisie could only tell where the shadow ended and the morning light hit the canal. She kicked hard for the sunlit water until spots dotted her vision.

Surfacing, she gulped in air unable to keep quiet. The spots cleared from her vision and she holstered her gun before she accidentally shot herself. At the edge of the canal ahead she saw a deserted boat landing and two gondolas bobbing in the water.

She swam to it and hunkered down in the cutout of the stairs, half of her body still in the cold water, and looked back up the canal. The roof was out of sight so he couldn't see her. She climbed out of the water and into the frigid air.

Walking around soaking wet would be conspicuous enough without a holster strapped to her thigh. She shivered as she fumbled with the buckles on her thigh rig. She shoved the gun into her bag. The holster plopped onto the surface of the water and sank.

Now she shivered so hard her back hurt. She needed to get out of these wet clothes. Three blocks later she spotted a young woman unlocking the door to a small clothing shop. The grates were still down and the lights off. Poor girl was the first to arrive that morning.

The girl opened her mouth to scream as she saw the soaking wet woman advance on her with a gun drawn, but

Maisie put a finger to her lips and the girl choked down her scream.

Once she shoved the woman inside the store, Maisie took the girl's cell phone and apologized in broken Italian while stuffing her into a closet. Someone would find her soon.

Maisie grabbed some dry clothes off the rack and held them up to see what would fit. She stripped off her soaking wet shirt and wiggled into an olive green t-shirt. Brown leggings and an oversized shawl made her look like a grunge hipster. She kept her boots even though they squished water.

She tucked her wet hair under a military-style hat and smeared on some deep purple lipstick. She grabbed a bright pink souvenir sweatshirt and a ball cap and stuffed them into her bag in case she needed a wardrobe change later.

Five minutes later she stepped back out onto the street and shoved her wet clothes into a garbage bin. She pulled her hat low and set out for the train station.

Time to bring Bressler back from the dead.

26

Incirlik Air Base, hangar 4
Adana, Turkey
March 28
1900 Hours Local Time

The makeshift tactical operations center was in a nondescript empty office in hangar 4. Inside, Comb Over and another woman Luke had never seen before were fidgeting around a folding table with three laptops and a phone wired directly into the ceiling.

Jay was already there, talking to a man Luke didn't know. He nodded at the older man and approached Luke. He had dark circles under his eyes but still managed to be irritatingly peppy. "Get some sleep?"

Luke nodded. "Doesn't look like you did."

Jay slapped him on the back. "Superheroes don't need sleep."

"I wouldn't know."

"Ya'll ready?" Frank positioned himself in the center of the large room.

Chad and the woman took a seat in front of the laptops.

Luke grabbed a chair from the corner and flipped it around to sit on it backwards. Jay lounged on the edge of an empty table.

"Alright, this is the mark." Frank pointed to a large monitor that Chad had keyed up a photograph on.

An aging man dressed in traditional Arab garb popped up on the screen as Frank continued. "His real name is Abdul-Malik Amjad al-Nujaifi. The ten of hearts. He's one of six that we confirmed fled to Syria in the early days of the Iraqi insurgency.

In his new life, Al-Nujaifi pretends to be an Afghan national under the alias Mohammad Aamir. A cover he's kept to this day. He settled in Hama just outside of Dier ez-Zur, where he's been for the last ten years.

Chad spoke. "Here's a more current photo."

He tapped on the keyboard and a grainy picture popped up. It had been taken from a distance and showed a man with two children in hand, and a woman dressed head to toe in a black Burkhas following behind. The scene looked urban with multi-story buildings all around. "This was nine months ago in Hama."

Frank nodded. "We assumed he'd retired from Jihad and was living the family life. He hasn't taken an active role in the Syrian conflict. He's got a reputation around town as the guy to help wealthier, and I use that word loosely, Syrians hide their money from the government. That's how Tommy found him."

Frank paused and cleared his throat before he continued. "Tommy found the money trail, we just had to put the pieces together. And thanks to a CIA asset in country," Frank indicated Jay, "we now know his address in Hama."

"And we also know that Arazi has been to see him within the last week," said the other man that Luke didn't know.

Extending an arm toward him, Frank said, "Marshall, this is Dan Dinsmore of the CIA Istanbul field office."

Luke nodded as Frank continued.

"Unfortunately for us, Al-Nujaifi also has extensive contacts inside the US. He has since the early days. He was suspected of setting up, read financing, sleeper cells in the US in the early days of the Iraq war, but that fell off the radar when he did. If Arazi is using this guy, it probably means an attack on US soil. We may be in some deep shit here."

Luke closed his eyes briefly trying to comprehend the brewing storm and his own involvement in setting Arazi in motion.

Alright." Frank pointed at a satellite image Chad pulled up. It was a satellite map of the Syrian and Turkey coasts with three red arrows.

"This op has been designated Intercept. Any communication will go by that language. It goes without saying this is the worst option we have but stopping an attack on US soil is paramount."

Frank motioned at Dinsmore. "Dan and I will be running the TOC from here. Chad and Melanie are manning comms and information services. There's a helo waiting to take you to Karatas and a DEVGRU boat team standing by for incursion."

Luke looked over at Jay in time to see him grimace. Yeah, he didn't love the water either.

"You'll infil by water just outside Jableh, Syria, roughly eighty miles away," continued Frank pointing to one of the red arrows. "At which point the boat team will retreat two and a half miles off the coast. The roundtrip to Hama and back should take three hours, four max. I want you two back on the boats by oh five hundred at the absolute latest. Rally is the same as the drop off, with an alternate north of the refinery in Baniyas."

Frank pointed at Jay. "Confirming your guide says in-country time should take no more than three hours, four max?"

"Yeah."

"He's assuming there are no surprises which there probably will be. The area between the coast and Hama is heavily al-Nusra, our old al-Qaeda buddies. They're receiving aid from the Saudis, so you might also run up on some Saudi forces. The Saudis deny that they're in Syria," Frank said. "But then, so do we."

Jay chuckled. Luke never took his eyes off Frank.

"Most of the proposed route is under Asssad's control," Frank said. "The rebel controlled pockets change almost daily."

Frank's gaze bore into Luke. "I don't really have to tell you this, but if you run into ISIL on the way, you'll probably lose your head, and not in a figurative sort of way. If the Syrian rebels get you, you might survive, but not before they trot your hostage video all over the internet."

Then he scorched Jay with his gaze. "And if you get picked up by Assad's forces, it's my neck. So, don't get caught. Get in. Get what you need. And get the fuck out."

"You got secondary exfil points?" Luke's mind processed all the things that could go wrong and at what points along the route.

With a glance at a very stiff Dinsmore, Frank nodded. "In the event of an unforeseen fuckstorm, there are two emergency exfil routes. And when I say emergency, I mean that in the strictest sense of the word, Marshall.

One is north to the Turkish border. They'll be pissed, but we can smooth it over with them easier than we can with Lebanon, which is your second option. Both are terrible options because first, you're gonna be smack in the middle of this shithole and so far from either border you'll have to cross a lot of shark infested water.

"Then there's the matter of the border crossing itself. We can assist your crossing at the Turkish border, we cannot at the Lebanese border. Assuming you make it across, there will be no help for you until you make it to the embassy in Beirut. So just make it back to the beach and we won't have a problem."

"The POTUS and JSOC have been briefed. The infil and exfil are to be completely dark."

Frank looked at Luke. "Even the success of the mission is subservient to that condition. That is a direct order from the top. Understood? This is an incursion and will be viewed as such if it is known."

Luke and Jay both nodded.

Frank clapped his hands together once. "Grab your gear and let's get this nightmare over with."

Chad waived them over to where he stood by two bags, one small one large.

"Mr. Simpson, you'll be carrying the credentials of a Canadian photojournalist," said Chad as Jay flipped through his wallet.

Chad held a black portfolio wallet out to Luke. "Mr. Marshall, you are a Spanish reporter."

Luke opened it and flipped past his own face staring up at him from the visa page. For the next six hours, his name was Marc Bautista from Barcelona. The authentic passport contained entry and exit stamps to a dozen countries including the one they were about to enter illegally. There was no exit stamp.

Tucked inside was a paper ticket for a Delta flight into the Airport Martyr Basil al-Assad International coming from London, as well as a Spanish-issued ID, credit cards, receipts, and a few Indian rupees and Syrian pounds.

"I don't speak Spanish," said Luke.

"That's okay," Chad said. "Neither do they. If you have to speak, use English with an accent other than British. It'll be good enough."

"Great," said Luke.

"Your official story is that you are a reporter-photographer team, freelancing for the BBC office out of Mumbai." Chad pulled open the first bag made of tan canvas.

It contained a laptop, several well-worn notebooks, and camera equipment. "It's all very basic. If anyone looks through it, they'll find a bunch of pictures and rough drafts of generic magazine articles. Very sanitary. It also contains a change of clothes for each of you once you're on the beach."

"And this bag," Chad ripped open the larger bag made of black canvas, "This is a little 'oh shit' bag for you. Hope you don't need it."

Pulling it open, Luke saw two identical FDE H&K MP7s with mounted pressure switch flashlights. The stocks were collapsed and each had a 20-round magazine to fit in the bag. He felt even better when he saw six additional 40-round mags.

A set of twin H&K USP .45 Tactical pistols were holstered on two bare bones riggers belts. The belts contained nothing else but four taco pouches carrying two MP7 mags, and two .45 mags each. Two slimline CRYE plate carriers peeked from beneath the guns.

Luke nodded at Chad while he nosed through the bag. Finally, some real firepower.

"Here." Melanie stepped over and handed Luke and Jay each an abnormally large phone. "It's a satellite phone. If it falls into the wrong hands all the numbers are legit except the contact marked 'office'. That will ring here. Chad or I will answer the phone as the BBC Mumbai office. Frank and Dan will be right beside us."

Jay took the camera bag and stuffed his identification and sat phone into it. "Is that how we're getting out?"

Chad nodded. "Once you guys leave the fast boats this is your only communication with us. When you're ready for extraction, call the office. Just remember they need time to move in from their hold point, so plan accordingly. We're gonna have you up on a drone feed the whole time you're in country."

"Anything else?" Chad asked Frank then pointed to Dan. Both men shook their heads.

"Chopper leaves in ten," said Chad.

Luke zipped up the gun bag and wrestled it into the waterproof cover that Melanie handed him. Beside him, Jay did the same with the camera bag.

Luke slung his pack over his shoulder, his mind already shutting down focus on everything except the task at hand. He felt Frank's hand on his back.

Luke turned.

"Tommy's home," Frank said. "Brandis is going to see his family as soon as you're safely back."

Luke nodded once then followed Jay out the door.

Twenty minutes later, Luke ducked under the rotor wash and tugged at the wet suit he'd donned on the helo ride from Incirlik. It was binding around his crotch, reminding him why he didn't join the Navy.

The boat team was almost invisible on the dark shoreline, every piece of gear as black as the night around them. The only thing marking their position was the glint of the helo's landing light on their wet helmets. Two hard sided swift boats bobbed in the surf.

Luke and Jay shouldered their bags and jogged over the deserted rocky beach.

At the edge of the water, a tall hulk of a man stepped forward and extended his hand to Luke. "Lieutenant Marshall. Captain Ryan. Welcome back to the suck."

Luke shook his hand.

Ryan nodded, all business now. "You two are in the lead boat with me." He pointed to the one on the left.

Luke waded into the water after him and hurled his bag into the boat. Reaching over the heavy rubber he grabbed an integrated handhold and hoisted himself in.

He lifted Jay's bag as it crept above the surf and tossed it next to his. Luke turned to see Jay struggling to get over the side. He caught the spook's waistline and heaved him into the boat. Jay landed on the floorboard panting.

"You good?"

"I'm good. I don't do boats," Simpson said.

"Let me guess. Just yachts?" Luke grinned at Jay then gave Ryan a thumbs up.

The team leader made a lasso motion with his index finger, and two men on each boat pulled themselves aboard while the rest began to push.

When they were chest high in the rough water, the rest of the boat crew boarded with effortless precision, and the high-powered props fired up.

Jay staggered to the side and sat clutching the handhold as the skipper pushed the throttle and the boat launched forward. In seconds, both craft were at a cruising speed of 80 knots.

Luke made his way over to Jay and sat beside him, ducking to stay out of the wind and spray rushing over them. He wasn't a big fan of the open ocean either, but the salty air whipping around him wasn't entirely unpleasant. And the spook hadn't puked yet. So far so good.

After ninety minutes, the engines pitched into a lower

gear. All around him the sound of metal on metal pinged softly as the team conducted last minute weapons checks.

The skipper held up two fingers to Ryan who turned to Luke and did the same.

Two minutes.

Luke checked his wrist mounted GPS. They were nearing the coordinates for the drop off. Everything was on schedule. He gave Ryan the 'okay' signal with his index and thumb touching.

Roger that.

Luke picked up both bags as Ryan helped up an unsteady Jay. Ryan gave Jay a questioning 'okay' gesture. Jay returned it, although his signal lacked the frogman's snap.

Luke handed Jay's bag to him and slung his own over his left shoulder. He grabbed the rail and straddled it awaiting Ryan's signal.

Jay stiffly slung his own pack and copied Luke, hunching as the surf grew rougher near the shoreline. Even in the dark, he looked green.

Suddenly the engine cut out and Luke felt them drift. Ryan reached to his chest and clicked his radio. Luke couldn't hear what he said over the waves, but every one of the SEALs flipped down NVGs and raised their weapons in perfect unison. All trained at the dark shoreline.

A hard tap on Luke's shoulder told him it was time. He brought his leg over the side and slipped into warm water up to his chest. Salty spray splashed his face as he pumped his legs and paddled with his free hand toward the beach.

Behind him, Simpson struggled but kept up. Soon the water lapped around their waists and their feet had more purchase in the soft sand.

Luke glanced back at the waves but the frogmen had already melted into the night. They were on their own.

When they reached shore, the men sprinted to a low

growing shrub field that lined the beach. Making their way up the shoreline they spotted a break in the shrubs that led to a small grove of olive trees. It offered better concealment than the shrubs.

Luke threw his bag down and unzipped his wetsuit. "You good, Simpson?"

"Fuck me," Jay answered. But he sounded more like himself so Luke took it as an affirmative.

Quickly they changed into dry clothes and buried their wetsuits under a large rock. It was straight into the water when they got back.

Luke's costume was khaki tactical pants, a green long sleeve, and a vest. He felt reasonably at home in the casual garb.

Jay changed into similar khakis and a blue shirt but with a pocketed vest befitting an international photographer.

Luke opened his duffel and pulled out a riggers belt. He press checked the USP, then holstered it and took off all the taco pouches to make it more concealable. Then he buckled it around his waistline and pulled his shirt over it.

He tossed the second belt to Jay who followed suit as Luke double checked the MP7s. Dumping the extra taco pouches in the bag, he zipped it up.

They slung their bags again and made their way toward the M1 that led into Jableh.

After a few hundred yards, Luke consulted his GPS. As soon as he did, Jay punched his arm.

"This is it," Jay hissed.

They knelt behind some bramble and looked across the street at an abandoned, burned out gas station. A single light in the parking lot still worked. In the weak light, Luke saw an old pay phone still standing. The parking lot was empty.

"He should be here by now," muttered Jay.

Luke looked both ways down the road. Nothing. He turned to Simpson. "You trust your guy?"

Jay nodded looking around. "He's a Kurd posing as a Sunni in Damascus. Assad imprisoned his father for speaking out against the regime, and ISIL killed his mother and little brother in the north. He hates both sides equally. I trust him. Plus he's getting a lot of money."

Luke scowled but said nothing. Then they both looked down the road. Thumping music reached them and grew louder by the second. Laying prone, they flattened themselves into the rocky sand so a vehicle passing by couldn't see them.

Soon headlights rounded a turn and raced toward them. A gray older model Russian Lada pulled into the gas station and screeched to a halt by the pay phone. Nobody got out.

"Is it him?" Luke's voice was low.

"I don't know. He didn't know what he'd be driving. He had to steal a car."

They watch for a few minutes listening to the music thump from their shallow ditch on the other side of the road.

Ignoring his pistol, Luke rolled to his side and gingerly unzipped the duffle. If Jay was wrong, they were going to need some real lead.

Jay squinted at a young man now playing drums on the steering wheel singing loudly. "Yeah, it's him." He grabbed his bag. "I think."

"Seriously?"

"I'll do the talking," said Jay.

"I'll do the shooting," Luke shot back.

"Trust me. How many nonofficial cover ops have you run?"

"Not a damn one. How many gunfights have you been in?"

Jay grinned and stepped onto the road heading for the car. "Not a damn one."

Luke followed him scanning both ways for threats, his hand stuffed in the duffel clutching an MP7.

It was oddly quiet, even for the rural location. The locals didn't want to be out at night, afraid of what lurked in the darkness.

Luke hung back as Jay approached the driver from behind. Music still thumped from the car hiding, Luke hoped, their footsteps.

Thirty feet from the car, the driver door flew open, and Jay stepped back in surprise. Luke yanked out the four-six in one smooth move. He had it on target by the time Jay called out in Arabic.

27

———

Jahbleh Agricultural Area
Central Coast of Syria
March 28
2100 Hours Local Time

A young man popped out of the driver seat with his arms held wide. His short black hair was curly and he wore jeans, an old Adidas jacket, and a broad grin.

"Hello, friend," the young man called out too loud. He embraced Jay. "You are alright, friend?" He couldn't stop patting Jay on the back.

"I am," said Jay. He turned and gave Luke a thumbs up. Jay tossed his duffle in the back seat and walked around to the front passenger seat as the young man slid in behind the wheel.

Luke slowly clicked the safety on and dropped the rifle back into the bag. His duffel went next to Jay's and he took what was left of the tiny back seat. Soon they were on the road.

Jay twisted in his seat. "Marc, this is Zarif."

"Hello," said the driver in English with a heavy accent. He waved at the back seat. "Nice to meet you."

"Hi," said Luke.

As Jay and Zarif chatted in Arabic, Luke watched out the window as fruit and nut tree groves gave way to bleak sandy desert. As they headed inland, the water sources that fed most of Syria's agricultural efforts tapered off. There was nothing out here but rocks, blood, and death.

Luke listened as Zarif told Jay that he had seen Mohammad Aamir, as he knew the target, that morning going into his residence. His excitement at their mission struck Luke as genuine. He had his doubts, but Jay beamed at Zarif like a proud father.

The beat up car protested as Zarif pushed faster than he should have in a car that probably hadn't had its oil changed in years, but Zarif didn't seem to notice. Jay grilled him about the meeting between Aamir and a young man.

Apparently, Jay had Zarif watching the old hawk since before he showed up in Kiev. Zarif had watched from a coffee shop across the road from the main open air shopping center in Hama. The old man had talked to a much younger man on a park bench. He couldn't hear what they were saying, but he noticed the younger man's lack of beard and his strange eyebrow. The two had embraced before parting. The entire meeting only took about five minutes. That was two days ago.

For the last twenty minutes, they'd been on the highway alone. As they grew closer to Hama, they passed a few vehicles, including two military trucks mounted with .50 cal machine guns. Luke's phone buzzed in his bag and he dug it out. The 'office' was calling.

He punched the answer button. "Go."

Chad was on the other end. "You have a checkpoint about five miles ahead going into town."

"You know who it is?"

"No. It's not on the official list. Must have been set up tonight."

"Alright, we'll handle it. Thanks." Luke hung up. "Check point ahead," he said to the front seat.

Five minutes later floodlights lit up the road with the makeshift barricade blocking it. A truck mounted .50 cal sat pointed toward Hama. Ahead, a flashlight moved up and down signaling them to stop.

"It looks like Syrian army," said Jay squinting through the windshield. "We're heading into ISIL held territory. These aren't unusual." He tried to sound nonchalant, but Luke heard the stress in his voice.

Jay looked at the driver who had started to sweat. "It's just a checkpoint," he coached Zarif. "You're from Damascus and translating for a couple of journalists. We practiced for this."

Zarif nodded and wiped his palms on his jacket. He slowed and nosed the car up to the barricade.

Luke pulled out his passport, ready to bust out his best Spanish accent should he need to. He made sure the gun bag was under Jay's decoy bag and pulled his shirt further over the H&K.

A guard wearing the Syrian army uniform shined his flashlight into the car. Zarif cut the engine and rolled down the window.

"Marhaba," he greeted the soldier.

"Where are you going?" asked the soldier.

"To Hama. They are journalists," said Zarif, thumbing at his passengers. Another soldier carrying an AK-47 strolled around the car peering in the windows.

"Papers," demanded the soldier.

Luke held his passport out and Zarif grabbed it and Jay's and handed them over.

Luke plastered an overly friendly smile on his face to appear cooperative and confused by the language.

In the front seat, Jay assumed the same pandering look. It seemed to work on the younger, less jaded, soldier. He went to the makeshift guard shack to call Syrian customs to confirm their passports.

An older soldier sauntered around the car with a scowl on his face. He motioned for Jay to roll down his window. He began talking to them in rapid Arabic checking for a glimmer of recognition. It clearly wasn't his first day on the job.

Jay played his part flawlessly. Half nervous and half afraid he shook his head and put his hands up. "I'm sorry. Do...do you speak English? I have an interpreter." He motioned to Zarif.

Luke rested his right hand lightly on his thigh next to the gun on his hip with a smile still on his face.

"Why are here?" The soldier switched immediately to broken English.

With a sudden Minnesota inflection and a bunch of 'eh's', Jay told him they were here to cover the war, and that Zarif was a local from Damascus hired by BBC to drive and translate.

Zarif offered the soldier a folded wad of papers. The man let out a sigh of annoyance at Jay's story. No doubt he'd seen a flood of Western journalists all coming into the area to earn awards and pats on the back for covering the plight of Syria.

In an irritated voice, the soldier told them they were headed into ISIL controlled territory, and beyond the checkpoint they could not guarantee their safety.

At the same time, the young soldier came back with their passports and handed them to Zarif. Everything checked out.

"What can I say?" Zarif threw up his hands speaking in Arabic. "Europeans need to feel better about their shitty lives."

That earned him a laugh from both guards.

"I do not recommend going to Hama," the young soldier told Zarif. "The city fell to the rebels three months ago. If they stop you and find out you are in the President's service, they will kill you and take these two." He indicated Jay and Luke.

Zarif cranked the car. "Then I will tell them I am a servant of ISIL, and they are covering God's work in action." He shrugged and forced a laugh. "It might work."

The older soldier didn't laugh but waved his hand and the reflective arm swung up to let them pass. Zarif gave a small salute as he pulled slowly through the checkpoint. Then he hit the gas and the car jumped forward.

Oxygen flooded Luke's brain as he started breathing again.

Jay laughed. "I'm impressed, Zarif. You're quick on your feet."

Zarif looked at him confused. "But I am sitting."

Jay chuckled. "Sorry. It means you think fast."

Zarif beamed. "Good enough to be CIA agent?"

"Close, kid. Damn close."

The lights of Hama shone in the darkness ahead. It was still ten miles to Syria's fourth largest city now teeming with sworn enemies of the United States. Fighting had lapsed in this area over the last three months, moving to points further north. Still, anything could happen in ten miles.

Every time they saw headlights they held their breath for the time it took a beat up sedan or pickup to pass. Only one decrepit, military green Datsun passed them, carrying three men with AKs. The rebels wore ragged clothes instead of uniforms and seemed to take no notice of the old car puttering by.

Fifteen minutes later, they entered the city. Luke could see it was larger than the lights suggested. Power was spotty in the region and only a fraction of the powered lights remaining worked. Many only had electricity during the day, if they had it at all. Piles of debris and rubble lay everywhere he looked.

Soon the residential neighborhoods gave way to warehouses, shops, and two industrial plants sitting on the banks of the Orontes River flowing through Hama.

Zarif rounded a three lane traffic circle, and they entered a relatively well lit stretch of road. Only half of the street lamps were out. Here the buildings looked old, some ancient.

Next to the river, aqueducts built by the Byzantine Empire still cast shadows in the weak light. The stone viaducts once carried water to thousands of people and terminated in massive, wooden water wheels.

Built in the twelfth century the water wheels, called Norias, still turned in the river's current as they had for five hundred years. Luke heard their mournful creaks as they drove by.

On the opposite bank, the curved roofs of the Grand Mosque curved into the sky. It was easy to see the gold roof and spiked spinnerets. The mosque was the best lit place in town. Not a single light out.

Luke snapped back to attention when he heard Zarif curse. Ahead a truck mounted with a .50 cal machine gun lumbered down the road, patrolling. They were the only idiots out in this part of town, which no doubt had a curfew.

Zarif killed the headlights and swerved into an empty lot along the banks of the river. In the days when tourists actually came to Syria, they could park here and walk up and down the banks of the river, dining on local food, taking in the ancient wonders. It sat empty now except for weeds and a few old cars.

The car rattled as Zarif slammed it into park and cut the engine. Luke already had his MP7 pulled out of the bag. He swapped out the 20-round mag for a 40, extended the stock, then slung the rifle. He offered the other rifle to Jay who shook his head.

Jay also shook his head at the plate carrier Luke held out. He was afraid a random onlooker would get spooked and sound the alarm. Luke shoved it toward him again, harder. The dark would cover them and the citizens of Hama were accustomed to seeing it anyway.

Jay reluctantly velcroed it on.

"Ready?" Jay looked at Zarif then Luke.

Zarif nodded, looking nervous.

"Ready," Luke said.

All three men rolled out into the cool night air and eased the doors closed behind them.

Zarif took the lead and darted between two cars and sprinted to the edge of the parking lot with Luke and Jay right behind him. They threw themselves behind a window-less shack as the patrol stopped. Its spotlight flicked over the cars in the parking lot.

Moments later the truck started moving again. The men ran behind a row of storefronts with metal grating over the windows. Then they darted across the street away from the river and into the labyrinth of cinder block buildings.

This neighborhood had narrow streets lined with three and four story residential buildings. Streetlights were sparse. The dark was better cover, but here there were more eyes to see them.

Three streets merged at the next intersection. Zarif stopped and pressed himself against the corner, looking down the widest of the three streets. Luke checked behind them. Clear.

Luke heard Jay whispering to Zarif. He turned to see the spook crouched next to the young man. Even in the dark, Luke could sense the indecision coming from the front of the group.

He didn't like this at all. They had to keep moving to stay off the X. Every second was a second closer to being captured. Luke readjusted his grip on the MP7 but kept it tucked to his side.

This wasn't the first time his back had been pushed against concrete pitted with bullet holes. But back then, he had full combat gear, an elite team of warriors, and air support. Now he had James Bond and a local squirter.

They were dead if they stayed out here much longer. That patrol wasn't the only one.

Luke heard Jay asking what landmarks were on al-Nujaifi's street. Perfect. Zarif wasn't scared. He fucking forgot where they were going.

Zarif's head jerked up at one of Jay's prompts.

"Wait here," Zarif hissed and took off into the darkness before Jay could grab him.

Luke moved to follow him. He wasn't letting that little weasel out of his sight. Jay threw out a hand to stop him.

"What are you doing? He's hanging us out to dry."

"No," insisted Jay, but the strain was evident in his voice. "He's coming back."

"You fucking sure about that?" Not caring anymore if anyone saw, Luke shouldered his rifle.

"No guns. Keep it down."

"Fuck off," whispered Luke. If he was going to die, he would go down fighting. It would be a short fight if a .50 cal came to play, but a fight nevertheless.

Jay stopped arguing and Luke saw the spook's hand

hover over his own handgun. He strained his eyes in the direction Zarif disappeared.

Luke pivoted to cover the remaining two streets so Jay could focus on his flighty asset.

On the third floor of a building two hundred feet behind, a match flared as someone lit a smoke. The glowing end of the cigarette burned brighter as its owner took a long drag. It was still, its owner unalarmed. In the distance, a dog fight broke out.

This was taking too long. Luke looked around for a place to shelter in case they needed to get off the street fast.

As if answering his thought, the rumble of a vehicle reached them. Headlights illuminated the intersection behind them as a patrol approached.

Luke thumbed his safety off.

Here we go.

28

Csúszdapark, Gellért Hill
Budapest, Hungary
March 28
0800 Hours Local Time

Charles Sheppard lay buried in a potter's field outside Prague, disgraced, while John Bressler played chess like a retired gentleman of leisure, very much alive. Only now he went by the name Joszef Bárány.

Maisie tucked her jacket tighter around her and pulled her hat further down over her eyes. She pretended to read a book on a park bench two hundred yards from where Bressler played chess every morning.

She had to concentrate to keep up the appearance of a relaxed reader. The urge to fidget nearly overwhelmed her. All these years and he was three hundred feet away. The hat over her face was unnecessary. He wouldn't know her. But she remembered every feature of his, even if they were now wrinkled with age.

Everyone in the neighborhood was out on the beautiful spring morning. The flush of light green on the trees radiated the bright morning sun. Laughter came from the nearby playground full of children too young to join their siblings at school.

After faking his death, Bressler fled to Hungary and married a Hungarian woman. They had two sons and eventually settled in Budapest.

Bressler now sat at a bank of tables with old men like him. They all bent over their game boards, serious expressions on their faces. Every one of them showed up precisely at eight o'clock and, after a brief greeting, sat down to play.

John Joseph Bressler was the most serious among them. Ever the strategist. The son of a Polish Jew who immigrated to America, he graduated from college in '73 with a degree in aeronautical engineering. But instead of working in the field, he'd joined the Army and did a stint in Vietnam.

After the war, he got a job with the young Department of Energy. Covert roles agreed with him, and he quickly developed a reputation as an effective and tenacious agent.

John Bressler didn't watch history on TV. He lived among it. He watched the wall fall in Berlin and stood beside Maisie's father as the Russian army retreated out of Prague.

For ten years he and Charles operated in Western Europe. At first trading in nuclear secrets, then ferreting out stockpiles of nuclear material the collapsing Soviet Union left in its wake.

Russian nuclear activity outside the motherland had been the highest in Ukraine, and the newly elected Ukrainian president was eager to curry favor with the Americans. When the request for a 'clean' came from on high, he and Charles cooked up Project Orchid and set their sights on the big fish. Then he framed Charles Sheppard for treason, killed him, and disappeared.

Maisie suppressed the burning itch to shoot him where he sat. She flipped an unread page and waited.

Two hours later, the man now calling himself Joszef Bárány rose from his bench, said goodbye and tucked his newspaper under his arm. In no particular hurry, he wound his way down toward the river. Maisie followed from a comfortable distance.

Bressler made his way to a coffee house a mile away and whiled away another hour talking to more old men while Maisie simmered in a cafe on the other side of the street. She'd waited for this moment for fifteen years. A few more minutes meant nothing.

The information she got from Nico was that he played chess in the park in the mornings and that his kids went to a nearby school. She didn't have time to do proper surveillance on him, so she was going to have to wing it.

Through the cafe window, she saw him reach into his pocket and pull out a gold-wrapped hard caramel. She could taste its syrupy sweetness. She'd eaten more of them than she could remember.

In 2002, while coming home from a three-day nuclear non-proliferation summit, John Bressler's car careened over a rocky cliff in the Carpathian Mountains. Three days later Adrian called her to say he found her father's body in his Prague flat, dead by his own hand.

Like an innocent child, she believed it. Until she stood over her father's empty easy chair three weeks later. His body was gone, and the apartment had been viciously tossed by the investigating agents looking for more evidence of treason.

The books she and her father had read together lay in a jumble on the shelves, her father's collection of vinyl records tossed onto the floor. And six of those gold wrappers from an upended waste basket by the couch where John Bressler sat every time he visited her father.

Every Saturday for her entire life, they had cleaned the house from top to bottom on Saturday mornings. A tradition maniacally enforced by her mother and continued out of reverence after she died. Even now, any cleaning Maisie did to her current living arrangements happened on Saturday morning.

Her father died on a Monday. Those wrappers had been put there in the three days before he died. Bressler had been there within the last two days. How could he have died three days earlier?

They asked her nothing, and she said nothing. They quickly finished their sham investigation and hastily labeled Charles a traitor. They made up their minds about Charles Sheppard's guilt. A silly little girl talking about candy wrappers wouldn't dissuade them.

Adrian had been no better. He had been like a son to Charles, and he just accepted the lies that Bressler planted like everyone else.

The man inside that cafe had taken everything from her. She watched Bressler pull on his wool overcoat that looked like a holdover from the 80s, far too old-fashioned for the modern sensibilities of Budapest. Her father's killer had turned into just another old man who couldn't let go of the past.

His success would soon be over. In the next few hours, everyone including Adrian would know the truth. John Bressler would be exposed for the traitor he was.

She wanted to kill him so much she could taste the bile rise in her throat. But killing him would be cheating herself out of witnessing his abject humiliation. His second-chance family would now experience what she felt. No, she would make him tell her where the file was, then leave him trussed for Adrian to find.

Bressler drained his cup and threw a few forint coins on the table. He left the café and started walking again.

Maisie followed fifty yards back. Every so often he would look around. He didn't appear nervous, still Maisie ducked into a storefront and took off her tan jacket. She fell back in behind him, grateful the lunch crowd was growing.

Bressler followed the switchback down the hill past the Citadella until the road intersected with the wide river avenue that curved around the banks of the Danube. Soon he turned onto a narrow cobblestone path wedged between ivy-covered stone walls that ran up a steep hill.

The alley was far too narrow to avoid being seen, so she hung back at the bottom of the hill. Moments later, she peeked around the corner and saw that the path was clear. She sprinted to the top.

At the first turn off, she peered around the corner and saw a quiet street with row houses. No Bressler. She sprinted uphill to the next opening in the stone wall. Another narrow street cut into the hill with well-appointed modern row homes overlooking the river and the Liberty Bridge.

Bressler stood at the row house on the far end of the street. He was pushing a key into the lock of the sleek birch wooden door.

As soon as he disappeared through it, Maisie took off in a dead run. She shoved her foot between the door and the jamb before it clicked shut. Pivoting, she rammed her shoulder into the wood and pulled out the gun Nico gave her.

Bressler stumbled into the foyer as the door hit his back. By the time he righted himself and turned, she had her gun aimed at his face.

"John Bressler."

The keys in Bressler's hand hit the wooden floor with a clatter. He squinted at her for a moment before he recognized her. "Maisie Sheppard. Is that you?"

She pushed the muzzle of the Kimber into his throat and flipped his coat back, checking his waistline.

"I don't carry a weapon."

"You should," she said. She grabbed his coat lapel and swung him around to march him into the great room ahead. "You had to know this day was coming."

"Please not here," he said in a hoarse whisper.

His fear gave her a thrill of pleasure. It didn't last long. As soon as she shoved him into the great room, a boy of about ten rushed up to Bressler speaking in rapid Hungarian. Proudly he held up a piece of schoolwork for his father to inspect until he saw the strange woman standing behind. The little boy stared at Maisie with his mouth slack.

Shit. The kids were home from school.

Maisie immediately tucked her gun into her pocket and hid her body behind Bressler's hoping the boy hadn't seen it. A second boy, younger than the first, sat at the table with a large hunk of bread in his hand.

Behind the little boy, the dining room picture window had a breathtaking view of the Cathedral. The house was modern and sleek with stylish furniture and well-tended house plants occupying every available corner. A delicious smell wafted in the air and half-filled bowls of goulash and the crusty remains of a loaf of bread littered the table.

It was the very picture of domestic bliss. Her father's killer had the life she wanted while she scraped her way through life, abandoned and alone.

"Joszef?" A pretty woman of about forty-five, with dark hair and pale skin stood in the kitchen doorway.

Instinctively, Maisie pivoted so the woman was in front

of her. The whole damn family was home. The kids were supposed to be at school.

"It's alright, Irenka," Bressler told her, patting the air with his hand to calm her.

Irenka didn't buy it. She stood frozen in place, her eyes flicking from Maisie to her husband reading their body language. The oldest boy backed up to his mother and she wrapped her arms protectively around his shoulders.

"It's alright," John said again. He mustered a stiff smile for his wife and oldest son. "Irenka, dove, this is," he paused, "Anna, the daughter of an old friend. Anna, my family," he finished gesturing to them.

Maisie made a slight adjustment when she realized the youngest was watching her gun hand jammed into her pocket. A glimpse of black was visible above the hem.

"The three of you finish lunch without me. I need to have a few words with Anna." He looked at his wife. "It will be okay," he insisted as Irenka looked like she was about to argue.

Bressler looked over his shoulder at Maisie. He held his hand out motioning toward a hall off of the dining room. "This way," he said.

Maisie let Bressler lead the way. They entered a small office with the same stunning view as the dining room.

"I work from home," he told her, not really expecting an answer. He put his back to her. "You can work from anywhere these days," Bressler said, thoughtfully.

Maisie shut the door behind them. "And *as* anyone, it would appear," she answered as she threw the lock and pulled her gun back out.

Bressler turned his back on her and walked to the window. He clasped his hands behind his back and gazed out. They both knew he was too old to be effective against her.

She didn't need the gun. Unlike him, she had not grown soft and fat from comfort and love. A difficult life had kept her body and mind hard. Occasionally, in brief moments like this one, it seemed more gift than curse.

"You know why I'm here," she said, not willing to wait any longer.

"Yes. But I never expected it to be you that showed up, Maisie."

"After what you did it was only ever going to be me." The menace in her voice made him turn to face her, his face still inscrutable.

His mustache and hair were still dark. He must color it, she decided. Side effects of a younger wife. He looked much like he did when she knew him in better times but with deeper lines on his face.

"After what I did," he repeated softly.

Maisie's gun hand twitched with rage.

Then he held her gaze with the audacity to look fatherly. "I never knew what happened to you, but I prayed you were okay." He sounded wistful and sad.

Maisie felt her face heat up, and her gun hand twitched again. "You killed Dad. Why would you care what happened to me, old man?"

John Bressler remained facing her, but she heard him sign and saw his shoulders drop. He said nothing.

"Enough," Maisie hissed. "Where is the second file? I know you have it."

29

"Is that what you came here for?"

"Yes."

"And what then? What will you do with it?"

"Give it to Adrian so he can parade you through the streets in leg irons like the traitor you are."

"If they told you what I suspect they told you, you have every right to feel that way."

"The fuck does that mean?"

"They told you my car was found before your father died. Three days in fact."

Maisie's gun dipped. "Fuck you," she breathed.

"The Romanian Police found my car the day after your father died. Because that's when I put it there. You can check the official police record. Older reports are not online and are likely still accurate for that reason."

"That sounds right," Maisie said coldly. "You killed him then faked your death to escape."

"I didn't kill your father, Maisie. I was helping him undo a terrible mistake. It wasn't until after Charles turned up dead that I faked my death. The same man that killed him would have killed me too."

He met her eyes once more. "You and I both know Charles would never kill himself. Perhaps I know it better than you because I know how much he loved you."

Maisie's head suddenly felt thick, like it was filled with cotton. She didn't understand. "Wha...," was all she could stammer out.

"Your father called me three days before he died. He sounded afraid and begged me to come. So I did. You are right about that, Maisie. He gave me the file and asked me to keep it hidden and safe."

"You took it." She shook her head. "You took it and killed him before he could expose you."

"No, Maisie." Bressler looked sad. "I didn't kill Charles. Someone at the Agency did, but it wasn't me."

"You're a liar." She pointed a shaking gun at his face.

"They were coming for it. He gave the file to me to keep the uranium out of the wrong hands. They were going to sell it."

"Who was going to sell it?"

Bressler hesitated. "I have my suspicions, but I don't know every player."

She shook her head. "That makes no sense. If you weren't involved why would he give it to you? Why didn't he just expose them?"

Bressler's eyes dropped to the locket around her neck. He thought for a long time before answering. "Things had changed, Maisie." He watched her face.

"I don't underst...what?"

"Your mother's cancer put him in terrible debt. In a weak moment, he decided to take the easy way out. Your father wasn't a bad man, Maisie. He was tempted and he caved to it. But everything changed when the towers fell. Terrorism had de-evolved to brutal simplicity. Uranium that pure in the wrong hands meant thousands of people dead. He couldn't go through with it."

"Go through with what?" Maisie flinched like she was being pelted with hailstones. She couldn't comprehend what she heard.

"Your father contracted with the Russian mercenaries. In exchange for a portion, they agreed to do the job. They posed as a substitute Ukrainian loading team on the last voyage. They took a portion for themselves as payment. The rest they took to an unknown location."

"No." She shook her head and backed up as though distance would make it less terrifying.

"Your father altered the file to get the payload through customs and hid the real one. He held it for five years. But by then the world had changed. Everything changed. The profit was no longer worth destroying the world you were about to enter as a young woman. You were all he thought about, Maisie. You are the one that changed his mind."

"YOU'RE LYING," she screamed at him. She turned the gun sideways and stabbed it toward him, her finger inching toward the trigger.

This wasn't right. Her entire life - every mission, every workout, every gritty day training in the desert, every sacrifice - it had all been so she could look her father's killer in the eye as he begged for mercy. He was lying.

Bressler's eyes went misty. "I wish to God I was." He turned and moved slowly to the desk in the corner.

"I'll give you the file, Maisie. It's yours to do with as you please. You can give it up and expose the truth or keep it a secret. I see now that I should have done this a long time ago. It was never my choice to make. It was always yours."

"Why...why is it my choice?" Her voice sounded weak in her own ears. Movement startled her and she shifted to cover him.

From the top desk drawer, Bressler retrieved a small key then turned to a painting on the wall behind the desk. The key unlocked a hinge and the painting swung open. A small safe nestled between the studs behind it. Bressler spun the dial left, then right, then left and opened the door.

From inside he pulled a faded green folder with 'Top Secret' stamped across the top, above the blue, green, and gold emblem of the Department of Energy. The paper layered inside looked crinkled and yellowed. He placed it on the desk.

Instead of reaching for the prize, she kept her gun trained on him. She didn't fear him. She'd learned to trust her instincts and there was no deceit in his behavior. Only defeat. But she feared what he had to say. "Who killed Dad?"

He studied her face. "Are you sure you want to know?"

"Lie to me and I will make you beg for death," she answered.

Bressler reached out and flipped the folder open. The first page was typewritten on yellowed paper. All but a few words had been redacted with a black marker to mimic the real file. The next few pages were the same.

He stopped on a document that had been light blue long ago. The corners were faded to a dull yellow and the ship logo of the NorthEastern Logistics Corporation was stamped on the top. The top right corner of the page had a thin rectangle cut from it.

"This was the real manifest. The coordinates were written in the corner for the mercenary team to deliver the barrels to. They were all killed in '03. I have no idea what happened to their portion."

Shaking, she took a step in.

At the bottom, she saw her father's signature on the authorization line accepting custody of forty-seven barrels of crude oil from the shipping company.

Her vision blurred and she suddenly felt like she was drowning. She heard gasping and realized it was her. Her lungs refused to take in oxygen. Her gun arm fell limp to her side.

Maisie managed to suck in a breath, but her chest tightened and pain spiked up her back. On the next line down, authorizing transfer of a payload of fifty-eight barrels in Odessa was the neat script of Adrian Romero.

"I'm sorry, my dear. I am so very sorry. The third ship didn't have a mechanical failure. It was sabotaged. Charles was supposed to sign for all four shipments on both ends, but the delay meant he wouldn't be in Norfolk to accept the first three. I offered to oversee loading, but Charles insisted Adrian could handle it. I went back to the warehouse to assume control of the clean-up crew. I thought it odd that he would let a trainee do that, but things were going so smoothly that I agreed."

Maisie's head whirled and she didn't realize she had staggered until her back slammed into a narrow console table. She slid to her knees.

In one instant, her reason for living shriveled on the desk alongside a child's belief in her father. His handwriting on the falsified manifest marked him as the traitor they all said he was. Not only him but the man she once thought she would marry.

Forgetting to drop the gun, she hunched over and grabbed her hair, trying desperately to stop her heart from beating out of her chest.

"Do you know what I've done," she croaked out. What I did to find you?"

"No," Bressler answered softly. "But I know how very much like Charles you are. I know you would turn the world backward to accomplish your mission."

Maisie felt numb. "I've done worse than that."

Bressler said nothing. He looked out the window giving her grief some privacy. "You did what you had to. We all did."

A calm suddenly washed over her. The same feeling that came before a mission, the night before a battle. Calm that shouldn't exist between falling mortars. Her mission had not changed. Only the target.

And he was on his way here right now.

Slow and controlled, Maisie rose to her feet. She gazed out at the panoramic scene and spoke softly. "You have to come forward. You have to testify against Adrian. This is your chance to make this right."

"No."

She turned on him, anger flashing across her face. "What do you mean, 'no'?"

"You have what you need in the file. You don't need me."

"I'm a traitor now too, John. I turned in a high-level American spy to find you. He's dead and I'm probably already on a wanted poster. They'll throw me in prison for the rest of my life. They'll never believe that you're alive. If you don't come forward, Adrian will keep hunting you. Your family too. He can't let you run around with the truth."

"My family is why I can't come forward. Do you think a junior agent like Adrian Romero got that file into the vault without anyone asking questions? Every operational file was vetted by four different department heads. A discrepancy between the transport team's report and the in-country teams would be noticed. No rookie agent could have maneuvered around that." Bressler paused and rubbed his forehead.

"Someone with serious pull got that file through the chain of command. Whoever it was, if they had that much power back then, I can only imagine their status now. If I come forward, we would be dead in a week. My family is only safe if I remain dead."

Maisie stared at him speechless for a moment. Bressler was right. The set up in Kiev. Someone with serious rank would have had to make that deal with Ivanov. Someone sitting behind a desk at the DOE had Tommy's blood on their hands.

"Take the file to the CIA, not the Department of Energy. Keep it out of their hands completely."

"It's the CIA that wants to lynch me," said Maisie.

"Listen. It's not my place to tell you what to do, and I'm in no position to judge no matter what you decide, but I am not coming forward." He nodded his head to the wall separating them from Irenka and the boys. "What I do is not for me."

He picked up the file and held it out to her.

Maisie looked at it without moving as though she was trying to decide if she wanted it or not.

"If you don't take it, I'm going to mail it parcel post to the CIA and let it go where it may. I'm done carrying it." He nudged it in her direction again.

Maisie looked out the large window. The early afternoon sunshine glinted off the river. It was beautiful. Beauty was not part of her world right now, but maybe it could be. Her mind went to Alexei, and she realized she too had a family now. A family to go home to.

Her shoulders rose as she took a deep breath. If she finished this, then she had a chance to make her life beautiful too.

"What are you going to do?" Bressler spoke softly.

She crossed the room and took the file. "Do you keep a bug-out bag?"

"Yes."

"You need to leave now. I used my ID for the train ticket

here so my passport would be scanned. Adrian isn't far behind me."

"You led him here on purpose?" Bressler recoiled.

"I came here to do one of two things. Kill you or have you arrested. Now I'm going with plan C. It's time for you to go. If he finds you, he'll kill you. All of you." She motioned to the kitchen.

Without another word, Bressler hurried to the door and called Irenka. Maisie heard them speaking rushed Hungarian and Irenka shuffled down the hall, calling to the boys. Then he went back to the safe and took out a zippered leather pouch. He rifled through it and pulled out four passports. Maisie saw several thick wads of American dollars.

Minutes later, John and his family were gathered in the living room in coats, each holding a small bag. The boys and Irenka looked terrified. Bressler's mouth was pressed into a thin line.

Maisie looked at Bressler. "I swear to you, no one will come after you."

John took a step forward and laid a hand on her shoulder. "You need to leave too, Maisie. You have the file. You'll have better odds if you run."

She looked at him, her face hard. "I'm done running."

30

Bab Qibli District
Hama, Syria
March 28
2253 Hours Local Time

The cone of headlights widened as the patrol neared them. They could go straight or turn right, but they couldn't go back. Luke twisted to aim at the approaching patrol, while Jay still peered into the darkness after Zarif.

The earlier patrol vehicle was quiet. This one had a faulty muffler, so Luke knew there were at least two in this area.

They needed to find cover so he could call the office. Maybe the drone feed picked up wherever Zarif had fucked off to. There was a chance they could still piece together a location on this al-Asshole.

Time to make a decision. It didn't look like Jay was going to make one.

Luke knelt on the broken concrete and scanned 180 degrees. The street to the right was darker. Entryways and alleys cut off from it.

He clasped Jay hard on the shoulder and chopped his support hand in the direction he wanted to go.

The spook shook his head. "Wait," he hissed back.

The headlights and the roar of the unmuffled engine had almost reached the corner a block behind them. As the nose of the truck came into view the street was suddenly filled with the roar of the exhaust echoing unchecked down the street. If the patrol looked left they would see them.

Luke had a fistful of Jay's shirt, about to force him to cover when Zarif's wide eyes appeared in the castoff light. "This way."

They slipped around the corner and followed him. Luke heard the unmuffled engine get quieter. It sounded like they continued straight ahead. He exhaled.

All hesitation from Zarif evaporated. The trio didn't dart from shadow to shadow. Now they were in a full sprint.

Three turns and they ran down a street with wide sidewalks that were mostly intact. The buildings on both sides of the street also lacked much of the damage scarring the rest of the town. The nice part of town.

Halfway down the street, Zarif ducked into a doorless stairwell and ran up one flight of stairs. Jay and Luke followed and nearly plowed into him on the second landing.

Zarif stopped and pointed at the second of the two peeling doors on that floor. Neither had a number, but he pointed at the door on the right with confidence that even convinced Luke.

A match flared in the darkness and Zarif held it up. A short black mark had been scratched across the wall above the door. Zarif left it there after he followed al-Nujaifi back, in case he forgot which of the identical buildings he lived in. Just as Jay had instructed him to.

Gently, Jay tried the knob. Locked.

Luke pivoted to cover high and low as Jay knelt next to

the door and began to pick the lock. There was no deadbolt. The doorknob was already so loose that it would have yielded under a light kick, but stealth was preferable. A few moments later, the door inched open under Jay's hand.

Luke planted a hand on Zarif's chest and gently pushed him against the wall as Jay stood and drew his gun. Luke moved to the opposite side of the door. His thumb hovered over the pressure switch of the flashlight mounted on the rail.

They had no schematics, so the layout would be a surprise. They pulled ski masks over their faces. Luke gave a single nod indicating he was ready. Jay placed a hand on the door and pushed. It swung open.

Luke went first, his weapon at the ready. He veered right and drove into the back corner. It took less than a second to clear the room.

This room was probably the largest room in the apartment. Overlapping brightly colored rugs carpeted the floor from wall to wall. A ragged sofa sat against one wall, and the rest of the floor space was taken up by big pillows. An ancient TV with rabbit ears sat on a metal cart by the window on the front side of the building.

A doorless opening led to a tiny kitchen with ancient appliances and plywood countertops. A small hallway ran off the back of the kitchen.

Luke rounded the room and met Jay against the inner doorway. His muzzle leading the way, Luke pushed through the kitchen and into the hall.

He tested the knob of the first door. It turned under his hand. Carefully he eased it open. Hooking his index finger over the flashlight lens, Luke pushed the pressure switch, and dampened light exposed the room.

Nestled on thick blankets on the floor were three small

forms and one adult sized. According to Zarif's intel, al-Nujaifi had two wives and three children. Luke clicked off his light and pulled the sling around so the rifle rested on his back.

His light was replaced by Jay's flashlight which he handed to Zarif standing in the doorway. Zarif resisted a little, so Jay grabbed his hand, put the flashlight in it and pointed it at the ceiling so he wouldn't blind them.

Luke was already at the largest sleeping form. She stirred. She woke to the zip of flex cuffs being tightened around her wrists. Her eyes widened and she opened her mouth to scream, but Luke stuffed a headscarf in her mouth and she made a choking noise instead.

Luke grabbed both shoulders and lifted her to her feet. "Get the kids," he said and shuffled her forcefully out to the living room.

The three young children of about seven or eight had begun stirring. Unlike the terrified woman, they were confused about the strange men in their house. They looked at Jay curiously.

He put a finger to his lips to tell them to be quiet. The little boys mimicked him, putting a finger to their mouths. The youngest, a girl, just looked at him. Jay picked her up and shooed the boys out.

In the living room, Luke positioned the woman on the floor in front of the TV. Jay deposited the children next to her. At the sight of the gagged woman, the little girl began to cry.

They left Zarif to watch them as they went back to the second door. On the other side, al-Nujaifi slept with his second wife. Luke pushed open the unlocked door and shined his light full in the face of the man he came to find.

The second the light hit him, the man woke. He propped

up on one elbow squinting into the bright light. Luke recognized the distinctive mole on the right side of this nose. He was nearing seventy now, his beard mostly white.

The second wife, younger and prettier than the first, raised her head and shielded her eyes from the light.

"We have your children," said Luke in Arabic. "Do not make a sound."

The woman gave a panicked whimper.

"Who are you?" The man demanded.

"Up," commanded Luke.

The man hesitated, shielding his face from the light.

"Get up," Luke ordered the man again, this time in English. He saw the man stiffen.

Jay holstered his gun. He grabbed the man and yanked him up. The old man knew he was no match for Jay so he didn't resist. He stumbled when his loose pants twisted around his legs. Jay righted him by sheer force and shoved him toward the door. The woman was still frozen in place.

Keeping the rifle trained on her in case there were weapons nearby, Luke moved to her and grabbed her arm in a crushing grip. She tensed like she was about to resist.

"Do not fight and you and your children will be safe," Luke said in rusty Arabic.

She stood. Luke guided her into the living room, rifle trained on her back. She faltered when she saw Jay and Zarif in ski masks and the rest of her family on the floor.

Luke dropped his weapon long enough to flex cuff her hands. "Sit," he ordered.

She obeyed.

Luke yanked the old man over to the couch and shoved him down. The women shrieked and began crying. The oldest son, maybe nine, looked up at Jay standing near the women with his gun at his side.

Zarif had backed into a corner with hunched shoulders and a pained expression.

"You checked the sofa?" Luke asked Jay in English, his eyes never leaving the man.

"Yes."

A mixture of fascination and disgust replaced the surprise on al-Nujaifi's face. He raised his chin higher and spoke in English. "I know who you are."

"Good. Then you know what I want." Luke faced him.

A smile split al-Nujaifi's lips revealing yellow gappy teeth. "So, I am finally paid a visit by the Butcher of Mosul."

"Tell me what I need to know and your family will not be hurt." Luke spoke in Arabic so there would be no chance of him misunderstanding.

"You expect me to believe what you say?"

Luke grabbed the USP from his waistband and dug the muzzle deep into the man's temple, driving his head back into the sofa. "I don't give a fuck what you believe, old man. I'm not promising you your life. Only theirs."

The man raised his hands slowly to indicate compliance.

Luke backed off a little. "The son of Hussam al-Din Arazi. Nasir. You saw him two days ago."

After a pause, the man nodded. Luke pulled the gun back and allowed the man to raise his head.

"Why? What did he want?"

"He said you would come. And he said you have become an old man like me. He was right."

Luke ignored him. "I know you financed him. And others. But he didn't need to come here for the money. What did he come to you for?"

Luke's teeth ground as the man's face turned to a controlled calm.

"Zarif, wait outside," Jay said.

The door opened and softly closed. Zarif couldn't get out of there fast enough.

"Nasir wanted me to tell you everything so that I would live. But I think dying is better than helping you."

Al-Nujaifi's jaw jutted out in defiance. "Your sin has come full circle. You killed a father in front of his son and now you must do it again. And then you will unleash two more sons. Do not blame me that things are as they are. You have done this with your arrogant violence."

"What about all the innocent people Nasir is going to kill? Do they deserve to pay for my arrogance?"

"Yes."

"So he did talk to you about his plans."

A surprised look crossed the man's face before he could squelch it.

Luke straightened and stood by al-Nujaifi with his gun at his side. "Last chance. What did you give him?" Luke's voice was calm and low.

Al-Nujaifi glared at him.

The stock of Luke's rifle collided with the man's forehead. The skin split and a gush of blood ran down his cheek.

At the smell of blood, long repressed memories bulldozed back into Luke's consciousness. He smelled blood, but what he remembered was the grit. Sand and fucking blood. For five godforsaken tours, he never saw one without the other.

This man financed some of the biggest players in the Iraq insurgence. The same extremists who had killed half his team, and a host of other Americans. Soldiers. Sons. Daughters.

Luke felt sick, but he knew it wasn't this man, or even

what he'd done. It was his own actions, and what he had to do, that made him want to throw up.

They were running out of time. He spoke in slow Arabic so everyone would understand. "Then you can pick who you want to die first."

Al-Nujaifi raised his head and looked at his captors. "You lie. Americans do not have the stomach."

Luke went to the cowering women and children. He grabbed the oldest boy by his arm and dragged him to the couch. The little boy struggled but had no chance against Luke's powerful grip. He slung the boy onto his father's lap.

Al-Nujaifi swung his bound arms up over his son's head and settled them around the boy who hid his face.

Ignoring his churning stomach, Luke kept his voice calm. If the old man thought Luke was bluffing, a lot of people would die. Luke pointed his rifle at the back of the boy's head and said, "If you think that, then you know nothing about me."

The women and the boy begin to wail. The little girl just sat in her mother's lap watching.

"You would kill a child?"

"How many children is Nasir going to kill?" Luke hissed at him. "How many Kurd babies have your al-Nusra filth killed since this fucking ridiculous war started? Tell me, old man, how many tears did you cry for them?"

The man squeezed his arms tighter around the boy.

Luke knelt on one knee so that he was eye level with the former al-Qaeda honcho. It sounded like someone else's voice talking. It felt like someone else's hand clutching the gun now pressed to the little boy's head. It couldn't be him. He could never do something like this.

Luke could only manage a whisper. "You say you know me. Then you know what I will do for my country. And I swear by Allah, if you don't tell me what I want to know, I will end your lineage tonight."

"You are a monster," choked out al-Nujaifi. "A monster."

In the moment it took for al-Nujaifi to say the words, Luke knew the truth of it. Any hero inside him died in the desert. It died with Tully. Now he was just a desperate man. And desperate men become monsters.

"It takes a monster to stop a monster." His muzzle pressed harder into the boy's scalp.

"No stop, I beg you. Colorado. He is going to Colorado." The words rushed out of the old man like air out of a punctured balloon. "He needed supplies. And a place to work."

"Where in Colorado?" Luke moved his muzzle away from the boy's head. The small movement prodded even more information out of the man.

"Denver."

So Arazi was going after Luke's hometown. "And who did you put him in touch with?"

"Damia Ayad and Abdul Basir."

Off to the side, Jay pulled out a scrap of paper and started writing.

"Where in Denver?" Luke asked.

The man shook his head. "I don't know. I swear. I swear." He brought his hands up as Luke's gun inched up again. "We don't give each other addresses. Just sectors. Electronic communication only."

"What is his target?"

"He didn't tell me."

Luke's muzzle dipped toward the boy again making the man throw up his bound hands pleading. His own sobs mingled with the crying of the children. "I swear to you. I swear to you I do not know. He did not tell me because he knew you would come." Al-Nujaifi lifted a bloody, wet face toward Luke, looking for mercy.

Jay approached and grabbed the boy from al-Nujaifi's lap and deposited him back to the oldest wife who clung to him. Then he nodded to Luke.

Then Luke pointed his rifle at the man, his index finger tightening. Justice for his dead men was a trigger pull away, but he hesitated. After what he'd just done to that poor child, Luke wasn't sure he had it in him to kill an unarmed man, whatever he had done in the past.

Shuffling sounded behind him and Jay swore. A little figure ran by Luke and jumped on the couch. The little girl rushed to her father. She climbed into his lap and threw her arms around his neck.

It felt like ice water had dumped directly into his bloodstream and Luke's rifle dropped, his arms limp. Luke took a step back and stumbled over a pillow. He couldn't do it. Turns out the monster didn't have any teeth.

Al-Nujaifi eyed Luke through slits. He read Luke's hesitation and hope that he might survive the night bloomed. Gently he set the little girl back on the floor and prodded her back to the women.

Luke pulled a pillowcase over his head and flex cuffed his feet as well. Jay did the same to the women. Jay nodded at Luke with a hard look, and Luke stepped into the stairwell. As his boots hit the concrete, he heard a gun report. The women began wailing again.

Luke turned, his eyes wide as Jay stepped through the door and closed it.

"The fuck was that?" Luke challenged him.

"I got my own set of orders, brother." Jay was all business. "We need to move."

Jay hooked Zarif's shaking arm and pulled him down the stairs. Luke followed.

Luke fell behind so Jay wouldn't see his chest heaving with emotion and the jerky movement of his legs. He wouldn't have heard a bomb go off over the buzzing in his ears. He forced himself to focus on tactical breathing trying to control his pounding heart and clear his head.

Soon the buzzing stopped and his heart rate slowed enough to focus on the task at hand. Getting out.

Five minutes later they were back at the car and a panting Zarif fired it up. Luke climbed in the back seat and pulled the equipment bag from the floorboard. He loaded the remaining pouches back onto his belt. Out of habit, Luke ejected the clip from his MP7, checked it, reinserted it, and seated the round.

As soon as Zarif pulled onto the road, Luke took the satellite phone out of his pocket and dialed the office. It took a few seconds for the phone to connect. When it did, Luke heard it ring once before someone picked up.

"Thank you for calling BBC Mumbai. How may I direct your call?" The woman's voice had a smooth British accent.

"The Editor, please," Luke said.

"One moment please."

A moment later Luke heard the Colonel's voice come on the line. "Grim, what's your status?"

"Eagle, we're done and heading to the rally point," Luke answered.

"Uh, Grim, there's a problem with that."

"What?"

"That checkpoint you hit on the way in. Did the soldier make a phone call checking your IDs?"

"Yeah, we told them we were coming from Damascus."

"Well, they must have followed up with their customs people to confirm your story and didn't like the answer. We're tracking military craft in the water from the port in Latakia. Four total gunboats ranging all the way down the coast to the refinery. Floats one and two have had to drop back. We're also monitoring ground activity near Aleppo."

"What about the secondary rally?"

"Grim, we can't get you out by sea."

"Shit."

"Can you make it to the Turkish border?"

"Hold on. Zarif, what are the chances of getting to the Turkish border?"

"What's wrong?" Simpson twisted around.

"Water exfil is a bust. Syrian army is onto us."

"Shit," Jay turned back around. "If that's true, you can bet their little spies have leaked it to the rebels."

"Yes," Frank said on the other end of the line overhearing Jay.

"Zarif?" Jay prodded the driver.

Zarif shook his head. "I don't think it's good. Too many rebels between here and the border. It would be entire day before we reach Aleppo. We would need to find a place to hide for the day."

"Fuck that," said Luke. "I'm not staying in this country another day. What about Lebanon?"

"There will be fewer rebels, but I don't know about getting across."

"I guess a Lebanese jail is better than a Syrian beheading," Luke said into the phone.

"That's the spirit," Frank answered. "The last information we got is that Syrian forces control it. It's moot anyway since they're after you too. Just go around."

"Affirmative. I've got some headlines for you, Eagle." Luke snapped several times at Jay to get his attention.

"Go."

Jay dug the scrap of paper out of his pocket and passed it to Luke who relayed the names they got from al-Nujaifi. Luke didn't like giving it over the phone, but if they didn't make it out of Syria, Frank needed the information.

"Something tells me the JTTF will be familiar with these guys," Frank answered. "I'll pass it along."

"Sounds like they might be building the bomb in the house. Make sure nobody rushes in. They could scare him off, or worse, burn the casserole."

"What's the plan, son?"

"Ride fast. Shoot straight."

"I'm keeping this line open. And the bird's still got you. Good luck."

"Thanks."

The phone went dead. Jay looked back at him. "So the beach is fucked, I take it."

Luke nodded. "The government got wind of us and deployed boats along the coast and forces in the north. We have to head south."

Zarif looked at Jay, worry etched on his face.

Jay clapped him on the shoulder. "Looks like you're going to America sooner than you thought, friend."

Zarif smiled. Jay had promised to bring him to America and get him into school when his undercover usefulness ran its course. "America, here I come," he said with a wide grin, his thumb and pinky finger in the air.

Instead of taking the 56 back to the coast, the way they came in, Zarif took the exit onto the M5 and headed south. The interstate-like road leads through the war torn Homs and into the southern city of Damascus. It was forty-five kilometers to Homs and another ninety to Damascus.

Once they reached Damascus, they would cut east across the mountains into Lebanon and go as far as they could before ditching the car. They'd cross on foot from there and hope they didn't get picked up.

It sucked, but it was their best option. They would be on foot over the more desolate parts of the border but going directly through a border checkpoint was out of the question.

If the Syrian side was controlled by the government, they would have already been alert to the two supposed journalists and their guide. They wouldn't make it out of the country. If the rebels had control, who they pretended to be wouldn't matter.

Luke passed Jay the other MP7 and a couple of extra mags. Then he put the two 20-round mags in the left cargo pocket of his pants.

"Can you make it to the border without refueling?" Jay asked Zarif, loading his rifle.

"Oh yes. I can get you all the way to Iraq on this tank of petrol." Zarif patted the faded dash.

"I'm not going back to Iraq," growled Luke.

"That is good," said Jay ignoring Luke. "We'll steal another ride on the other side. That should get us to Beirut and we're home free. Easy peasy."

"What is peasy?" Zarif sounded confused.

"Lemon squeasy." Jay grinned at his young protege. "You're gonna have to learn the lingo, Zarif. We Americans love our slang."

"Easy squeasy." Zarif grinned at Jay.

Luke watched out the window as the desert sped by. Zarif was driving like a bat out of hell, but he liked it. The faster they drove, the faster they got out.

Thirty minutes later they passed through Homs. This city was a flash point of activity over the last few years and they expected trouble. But the mortar-pitted bypass was empty. No one stopped or challenged them.

Instead of relaxing Luke, it put every sense on high alert. He clutched and unclutched the rifle, his eyes darting to every shadow, every building. It was calm.

Another hour and they saw jagged mountains rise in the

distance backlit by the lights of Damascus, Syria's largest city, nestled in their foothills.

From twenty miles out, the city of Damascus looked more sprawling metropolis than bombed-out suburb like Homs. But as they got closer, the ancient city too bore the scars of war. Every few miles an entire building had been reduced to rubble.

Zarif exited onto a four-lane bypass that led around the city. As they passed a burned-out car, they saw a Syrian army patrol approaching from the other direction.

Jay and Luke slid into the hot vibrating floorboards as the patrol passed by, eyeing Zarif. He waved at them with a big smile and they kept moving. Residents on their way to work routinely ignored the curfew.

The men stayed low as Zarif made his way through town. As soon as they were south of the city limits Luke and Jay sat up. Ahead Luke saw the blue road sign for the road that would take them to Lebanon. Sixty kilometers to go.

Zarif cursed in a whisper.

Luke's eyes snapped down the road to Lebanon. Half a mile down, powerful spotlights lit up the desert for three hundred feet in every direction. An entire convoy blocked both lanes of the road. A spotlight roved up and down the rocky terrain, and two more were trained down the roadway in each direction.

"Keep going south," Luke commanded him.

"But that is the only way to anti-Lebanon," Zarif protested, referring to the mountains and the pass that separated the two countries. Their way out.

"Do not turn onto that road," Luke said.

Zarif drove past the exit still heading south. The spotlights faded behind them. In five minutes they were in darkness again.

"They must have figured we'd try to make it to the border," said Jay who was checking his weapon again.

"This is your house," Luke said to Jay. "Is there another way out?"

"The Golan."

"We can't go to the Golan. They already said they're out."

"We are going to Israel?" Zarif sounded more nervous than he did staring down Syrian soldiers.

"No," Luke answered. "Israel doesn't do anything they don't want to do. And they don't want us there."

"They'll let us through, right?" Jay tried to sound jovial and dismissive. It came out wrong so he stuck to sounding rational. "We were going to sneak across the Lebanese border. We'll just sneak across the Israeli border. They catch us, ID us, we get our pee-pees slapped and go home. Not so bad."

"You don't sneak across the Israeli border, Simpson. You get shot sneaking across the Israeli border. Let me call...."

A hail of bullets ripped through the driver's side door shattering the window. Bright flood lights on an armored personnel carrier flipped on lighting up the car. They had been approaching from the south, completely blacked out, no doubt alerted by the roadblock.

Luke saw Zarif jerk, and the car lurched off the road as Zarif held onto the wheel and slumped to the right. The car slowed as it bounced over rocks and dug into the sand.

"They made us," yelled Jay as he lunged for the wheel pushing Zarif's limp body aside. He got the vehicle under control and his own foot on the gas pedal and managed to get them back on the blacktop. They flew by the armored truck with men pouring out of it. "Marshall...."

He was cut off by another hail of bullets pounding the trunk. Luke felt a round punch through the seat padding next to his shoulder and saw it bury in the front seat. Jay lost control and the car careened off the road. It bounced violently over the edge of the pavement back onto the desert floor.

It was dark. Very dark. The only light came from the spotlight mounted on the APC now bearing down on them.

"Jay," Luke hissed. "Simpson."

There was no answer.

31

———

17 Bérc Street
Budapest, Hungary
March 28
1147 Hours Local Time

Maisie sat in a dining chair facing the front entrance, absentmindedly running her fingertips over the gold locket around her neck. She opened it and looked at the tiny memory of her family, maybe for the last time.

Adrian was on his way and she was going to kill him if he didn't kill her first. She ran her fingers over the worn picture like she had a thousand times before. The photo had a line down the middle from years of her fingers brushing it.

Now as her fingers ran over it, she realized it wasn't a line. It was a ridge. Maisie scraped her nail over it to be sure it wasn't just an old fold as she had always assumed. Sure enough, her nail caught on something.

Heart pounding, she ripped it over her head and pried open the gold rim holding the photo in place. The crusted edges stuck to the metal as she tried to pry it off without damaging it.

When she finally got it off, a thin strip of paper folded in half sat underneath. Blue like the missing edge of the shipping manifest. She scraped it out and gingerly opened it.

A handwritten set of coordinates was visible in perfect ink. Protected from the elements, the paper and the handwriting had not faded. The ink was still dark. She fell back against the chair.

Her father sent her the location of the uranium before he died. In the locket. All these years she had been the only living soul who had the location and she never knew it. Tears sprung up when she realized she didn't know if Charles sent it to her because she would do the right thing, or as a gift to sell and reap the reward he never did.

She didn't know anything about the man that raised her. And, it seemed, he knew very little of her.

Clearly, she didn't know anything about Adrian either.

Maisie blinked to clear her eyes and placed the photo back into the locket and the coordinates on top. She snapped it shut, and draped it around her neck once more, tucking it into her collar.

Then she waited.

An hour later, the door creaked open. Maisie waited, silent, as he stood by the door listening. It opened further and she saw his mop of brown hair first. Then those brown eyes. The same eyes she thought her children would have.

She stood, placing the table between her and the door. The file sat on the table in front of her. Without a word she watched him enter from the foyer, gun drawn.

"Hello, Adrian."

Romero swept the room with his weapon and advanced into the dining area. His eyes flicked down the hallway looking for Bressler.

"It's just us," said Maisie.

"Where is he?" Adrian spoke as he continued to check corners.

"Dead," she lied, dipping her head toward the hall. "In the bedroom. That is what you wanted, isn't it?"

Adrian's eyes narrowed, but he lowered his weapon.

"That. And this." She picked up the file and tossed it to his side of the table making the breadcrumbs jump on the birch surface. She watched as her calm unnerved him, and it gave her strength to tamp down the rage.

Adrian's gun jumped to her chest as she moved to the side of the table. He eyed her with suspicion.

"It doesn't have what you want." Her mouth turned up in a sad smile.

Adrian's face hardened. "You shouldn't have read the file, baby."

"Why not?"

"There are things I was trying to protect you from."

"Protect? Is that what you call it?" Maisie's finger traced a circle over the table. "I know why Dad did it. Why did you?"

"Come on, Maze. Babe, you can't still be this naive. You're still going on about good and evil. Black and white. The world doesn't work like that."

"Then educate me."

With an exasperated huff, Adrian lowered his gun. Then he gave a little laugh.

"Your father talked me into it. That's the funny part. I didn't want to do it at first, but I wanted to make a good impression, and the money was promising. He needed me to pull it off and he knew I had a soft spot for you. It was all for you, Maze. For your future."

Maisie stayed silent. Adrian seemed like he wanted to keep talking.

"We agreed to wait five years. To let everything cool

down. Five years later, he grows a fucking conscience after 9-11. After years of risk, I don't get a payday.

"But you had the mercenaries' portion? You took it from them after you killed them, right? That's what Marshall's terrorist is after."

Adrian's eyes grew wide. He didn't expect her to know that information.

"You could have lived like a king the rest of your life off just the merc's portion. Why did you want me to...." Maisie trailed off. She looked at Adrian, the truth dawning on her.

She threw her head back and laughed. "You did sell it. You didn't wait five years, you started taking orders right away, didn't you? Boy, I bet they're tired of waiting. The merc's portion wasn't going to satisfy demand, was it?"

Something else occurred to her. "There never was any 'source'. You always knew Bressler was alive, you just couldn't find him. Then your emails with Arazi got intercepted by hackers, you donkey. It all makes sense now. What else would make you desperate enough to come to me."

"*I'm* getting tired of waiting," he hissed. "I want what's mine."

"How much did Arazi pay you? Does it cover the deposits you took on the rest?"

He glared at her. "Five. Enough to disappear if I can't deliver the rest." Anger twisted his face. "Exactly what moral high ground are you condemning me from, babe? After that little deal you made."

"I don't know about moral high ground, but I do know you shouldn't sell merchandise you don't have."

"Your father was a master of fucking with people. I just never thought he would do it to me. Turns out there was no one he wouldn't screw over."

Maisie watched him from under hooded eyes. She had been entranced by this man since the first day her father spoke so glowingly of him. She'd loved him since the day she met him.

Now he stood in front of her whining like a spoiled child. There was no love when she looked at him now. Only disgust.

"Dad deserved to die," Maisie said softly, surprised at the conviction in her own voice. She didn't intend to mislead Adrian, but it was clear that her demeanor had sparked hope of winning her over.

Adrian's tone changed from hard to supplicating. "I didn't want to torture him. I...I couldn't," said Adrian.

"Yes. That would have left a lot of messy questions. Much easier to shoot him and stage it as a suicide."

"That's...that's why I came to you, Maze. All those years of looking for Bressler and coming up empty handed. I knew you'd never turn up a chance to go after him and let's face it, you're better than me, Maze. I don't mind admitting it. And damned if you aren't every bit as tenacious as your old man. You didn't disappoint."

"If that's true, then I'm the only one in my life who doesn't disappoint."

"Maisie," Adrian said softly, "don't talk like that."

It struck her as odd when his soft voice had no effect on her. He used it now because it had always worked. Even if its only purpose had been to soften and control her, it always worked.

Now, it made her skin crawl. And he was beginning to circle the table.

"I loved you," Adrian said, his brown eyes wide, gazing at her. Any hope of winning her over was fading as her face remained motionless. He tried again. "I still love you."

Maisie's stomach flopped. The words made her sick. He begged with that tired bullshit like it would still work. For the first time in her life, she was in control while he crumbled. It felt good.

"If that ever was true, the girl you loved is dead. I buried her long ago."

Adrian shifted, anger building on his face.

She reached over and picked up a bottle of rubbing alcohol and a matchbook she staged on the table. "We can burn it together. Everyone thinks Dad was guilty anyway. Why hand them the proof?"

"Not yet." His gun hand came up. "I'm taking the coordinates."

"I told you. They're not in the file."

"Show me."

She flipped open to the manifest with the missing corner. Adrian drew near making sure to keep his gun at least an arm's length away.

"Shit. Where are they?" He frantically flipped through the pages before swinging his gun at her face. "Where the fuck are they?"

She shrugged. "They were cut out a long time ago. Probably before Bressler ever got it."

Adrian let out a stream of profanity as he realized his mentor had screwed with him yet again. First Bressler, now this. Double protection against him finding the uranium.

Maisie felt a stir of pride for her father. He screwed up but damned if he didn't patch up the leaks. If Charles Sheppard didn't want it found, it would never be found.

Adrian pounded his fist on the table, shouting, "Where is it?"

"If I knew I wouldn't be here. I thought Dad was innocent, remember? Remember the real reason you came to me? All those years, you knew I blamed Bressler."

Adrian considered her words for a moment, then he took the rubbing alcohol she held out to him. Without looking away, he squeezed it over the paper until the bottle was empty. He tossed it aside.

She pinched the matchbook and pulled the match through. The flare at her fingertips flickered until she lowered it to the alcohol-soaked paper. As soon as it touched, flames erupted and licked as high as the chandelier.

"Who contacted Ivanov? I know it wasn't you."

The hunger on Adrian's face as he watched the burning file dissolved into fury. His brown eyes grew dark.

"Who else were you and Dad working with?"

Adrian sent the butt of his gun at her jaw.

Maisie leaned back narrowly avoiding it, but in a flash Adrian righted himself and brought the gun to bear. He'd never been much of a fighter, and he knew it. And given the revelations of the last few minutes, there was zero chance he was going to fight fair. Anything coming from him was coming at her sideways.

Maisie only had time to twist to the side as she saw Adrian's finger flex on the trigger. She felt the concussion from the barrel close to her face. The muzzle blast made her ears ring. The wall behind her exploded in a cloud of dust.

Clarity flooded over Maisie. He hadn't shot her. He was trying to get close enough to incapacitate her so he could interrogate her about the coordinates. His mistake. He should just shoot her.

"Where's your gun, Maze? I know you have one. You might want to get it." Adrian advanced on her, confident he had stunned her enough to get close. He pressed his hot muzzle to her temple.

She smiled. "I gave it to Bressler in case he ran into you."

Adrian's gaze flicked to the hallway as he comprehended what she said.

Quick and smooth, she grabbed his gun with her left

hand and drove her right hand under it snapping it up and back. His grip broke and the gun stayed in her hand.

She straightened. Still holding his gun, she drove her right hand in for a fast jab at his nose.

In a single fluid motion, she sent her left elbow into his solar plexus while releasing his wrist. Her arm scooped underneath and she slammed her elbow into his, bending his arm and entire torso backward. All she had to do was push and Adrian stumbled two steps before he fell over the chair she sat in moments before.

Calmly she walked to the opposite side of the table. Before she reached it, she had his Sig field stripped. Meeting his eyes across the blazing table, she tossed the pieces into the fire.

No guns. This was personal.

"You have fucked everything up," he said standing. "Why can't you just play along? Help me find it. I'll give you your father's cut, then you can fuck off to wherever your little heart desires."

"I'm not helping you anymore."

"You never were helping me, Maisie." Adrian paced on his side of the table like a caged animal. "You were helping yourself and we both know it. But you can help me now and get well paid."

Maisie planted herself, still, on the opposite side of the blaze from his fevered twitching. She held her chin up, her eyes clear and hard.

"Fuck you, Romero."

The rage that clouded his face she'd never seen before, but it seemed like second nature now that her eyes were open.

But it wasn't second nature. His good guy character was his disguise. The real Adrian stood before her in a murderous rage.

He grabbed the edge of the table that had not yet caught fire and flipped it so hard the legs went airborne before the flaming top hit the wooden floor.

Maisie backpedaled as sparks and floating ash obscured her vision. She couldn't see, but she heard him moving.

She hadn't yet blinked the ash out of her eyes when he hit her. Her shoulder slammed into the floor and he landed on top of her. He flipped her onto her back and dropped to his knees straddling her. Strong hands closed around her throat and crushed down.

Adrian lowered his face to hers. "How are we going to do this, Maze? Tell me where your asshole dad hid it. Don't waste my time telling me you don't know. If anyone can figure him out, you can."

His desperation was her balm. He couldn't conjure up the uranium he needed to save his own skin.

Not her problem.

Maisie folded her hands together on her stomach and drove them up through his arms, not stopping until her hands were over her own head. Air flooded her lungs as he lost his grip and his hands ripped off her neck. Adrian collapsed onto her.

She wrapped her left arm around his neck, holding him to her chest. Breaking her legs free, she wrapped them around his waist.

Metal tinged on hard plastic as her right index finger caught the groove ring of her dagger. She drew it out and drove it hilt deep on his right side below his armpit. She twisted the blade, then bucked her hips rolling him off of her.

Adrian rolled twice then came to a stop. Maisie jumped up, watching.

Adrian staggered to his feet. His knees wobbled then collapsed. He slammed face first into the floor.

Maisie walked to him and rolled him over with the toe of her boot. "I know where the uranium is," Maisie said, looking down at him. She patted her chest where the locket lay against her skin. "Dad told me."

Adrian's eyes grew wide and he clutched at his chest. The hold she'd torn in his lung gurgled and bubbled as he gasped for air.

"Now you tell me something." She knelt beside him. "Who sold us to Ivanov?"

Panic grew on his face as he struggled to breathe. She must have nicked something else. There wasn't much time left.

She leaned in, placing her face next to his. "Tell me."

It was too late. Adrian Romero's eyes emptied and his head rolled to the side. She'd have to find out the hard way.

Maisie rose to her feet and stood looking coldly down at his body. Then she resheathed her dagger.

One minute later Maisie pulled the front door closed behind her, her jacket buttoned down and hair smoothed.

There was no need to clean the scene. The fire would do most of it for her. Adrian's burned body would be identified and she would be named as a suspect in his death.

She turned right and took the wide winding street down the hill instead of the alley stairs. The wail of fire trucks sounded from far off. Someone in the neighborhood saw the smoke. When she reached the bottom of the hill, the firetrucks screamed by as she walked, unhurried, down the sidewalk.

Maisie turned left when she came to the Liberty Bridge. Under the first tower, Maisie stopped and leaned against the railing to catch her breath. The bridge was crowded with tourists and locals alike, all out to soak up the beautiful day. She pulled out the phone Nico gave her and dialed as she looked out over the city.

"Allo?"

"Nico, did you find him?"

"He's in St. Petersburg. Would you like me to send the jet?"

"Yes. I'm going to need it for a while. There is something I need to do after I visit Ivanov. Thank you, Nico. You're the best."

"Yes, I know," he said.

She smiled and hung up.

In the middle of the bridge, she stopped and looked out over the rippling surface of the river. She'd sealed her fate and going back to her old life wasn't an option. Not that she wanted to go back. She was a bad guy now, a fugitive.

Strange peace washed over her. A sense of purpose was better than pining over a life she would never have. She straightened and with one last look back at the plume of smoke on the hill she turned and melted into the crowd.

32

———

Seventeen kilometers south of Damascus, Syria
March 29
0217 Hours Local Time

Luke didn't wait for the car to stop. He kicked open his door and rolled out, his clothes and skin tearing on the jagged rocks littering the desert floor. The vehicle's front tire caught in a rut and jerked to a stop.

He ran to the passenger side and knelt in the sand. "Simpson," Luke called in a harsh whisper through the shattered window. "You still with me, buddy?"

"Yup." Jay's voice was hoarse.

Luke didn't know how badly Jay was hit, but he didn't have time to check. "You gonna sissy out on me, frat boy?"

"You'd like that wouldn't you," Jay coughed out.

Luke grinned. "Alright, get your shit together. Contact at our eight o'clock. Seventy-five yards out."

"How many?" Came Jay's strained reply.

"Six."

Their own spotlight backlit the approaching idiots. Luke

could make out every single one of them, and the AKs they carried.

"That shouldn't be too hard," Jay wheezed.

"Think you can put some cover fire down? I'm going around front." Luke heard a toggle click.

A groan. "Yup, I can do that."

"Sixty seconds and we're out of here. On my mark."

"Roger that, Grim."

Luke made his way to the front of the vehicle and crouched next to the front tire. Heat rolled off the engine warming him in the cool desert night.

Luke steadied his barrel on the rusty bumper and snagged one of the men in his sights. He waited. They were still fifty yards out. Let them think everyone in the car was dead.

Their noise discipline sucked. The men were geeked up and stomping the ground like a herd of wild ponies. Luke could have hit them blindfolded. Thirty feet out they slowed down and showed the first sign of caution.

Luke held his breath and waited until they got within thirty feet. "Are they dead?" Someone spoke in Arabic.

Luke pulled the trigger and the man in his sights fell. Snapping his sights left, he dropped another.

"Now," Luke yelled at Jay.

Jay's MP7 came up through the busted driver's window using Zarif's lifeless body as a prop. Jay wasn't aiming, but the men scattered, opening fire wildly in the direction of the car.

Every instinct told Luke to duck behind the car, to put some metal between him and the rounds whizzing past. But with Simpson hurt, he couldn't afford to get pinned down. The only way out now was brutal offense.

He ducked his head out for a look. The men cowered on the sand, still backlit by their own spotlight.

Luke crouched and darted in a straight line perpendicular to the car, the only place the cone of light did not reach. He made it to the darkness by the time the men picked themselves off the ground.

Three men broke right together. One straggler went left around the front of the car.

Simpson stopped firing. Probably reloading.

Out here, the darkness seemed darker next to the blazing cone of light. Luke froze in a combat crouch. He could make out more than their outlines in the light. They were not wearing uniforms. The roadblock was not Syrian forces like they thought.

They were fighting Syrian rebels, or more likely, the third side of the war, highly motivated ISIL insurgents. ISIL had spies everywhere in the Syrian government. If the government knew about them, ISIL knew. Two Americans would be a juicy prize.

Luke kept his aim on the three men in case they collected themselves enough to return fire at the car before Jay could reload. To his credit, Simpson got that bitch reloaded in record time.

When Jay started firing out the window again, Luke sprinted across the desert until he had flanked the men.

Luke had sights on target as soon as the stock hit his shoulder. He let a short volley loose and the coward that was hanging back died. He toggled to full auto and walked at the two men still focused on Jay's cover fire. They didn't realize their partner was down.

Luke drove in hard dumping his mag. The second man fell and didn't move. The third stumbled but did not go down. Luke thumbed the magazine release and the empty clip dropped into the sand.

He combat loaded a new one and the hammer slammed

down on a fresh round. Another short volley and the man went down and didn't move. One left.

Several rounds puffed up sand at his feet. Luke sent a spray of bullets in the shooter's direction and darted into the darkness to get off the X.

The last man standing finally smartened up and receded to the cover of darkness. Except he continued to fire in the direction he'd last seen Luke, giving away his position.

Jay stopped firing. Sand swirled in the light and it fell quiet.

Luke never took his eyes off the mark. His support hand skimmed the hot rail of his rifle and found the pressure switch.

It wouldn't be long until reinforcements arrived. Before they engaged the car, the transport probably radioed to the roadblock that they spotted them.

Rocks clinked together as someone kicked them.

Luke raised his MP7 in the direction of the sound. He fired a short volley and immediately broke right in a fast walk, watching.

The answer came quick. Luke saw the man's face in the muzzle flash. He pushed the pressure switch and one thousand lumens shined into the man's eyes as Luke dumped the second mag until it was dry.

His opponent dropped his gun, but still stood, swaying on his feet. Luke let the rifle drop and transitioned to his USP.

By the time the rifle jerked on the end of its sling, the sixth tango lay dead from a single .45 round to the head.

Luke sprinted to the driver's side and ripped the door open. On the passenger side, Jay slumped against his door, a cherry red stain spreading on his lower back beneath the bottom edge of his plate carrier. His eyes looked glazed.

Luke pulled Zarif out onto the sand and knelt beside

him. He closed the young man's eyes and rested a hand on his forehead. "Thank you, Friend," he whispered in Arabic.

Luke reloaded the rifle with his last magazine, then unslung it and stashed it where he could reach it. Sliding behind the wheel he cut the headlights and threw the car into drive swerving back onto the road.

The white lines on the road were just reflective enough to keep him on the pavement. Behind them, headlights blazed but pulled over by the dead rebels. They didn't see the blacked out car speeding south.

Luke fished his phone out and dialed the office. He cursed as the phone took its time connecting to the satellite.

"Thank you for calling BBC Mum..."

"Eagle," Luke yelled into the phone.

"One moment."

"Grim. Status?" Frank's voice came over the line.

"Were fucked, Eagle. That's our status. ISIL was waiting for us."

"Any casualties?"

"Our guide is KIA. Vista is wounded and I'm headed to the promised land."

"Negative."

"Fuck negative. In about two minutes they're gonna know I'm headed south. I can't go any other direction. Make it happen."

Luke heard the Colonel cover the receiver and say something.

"How many men are on the Syrian side of that border?" Luke asked.

"You can't shoot your way across if that's what you're asking."

"Can't I?"

"You'll be able to count the RPGs as they fly in and

bomb your ass back to the stone age. And that's if Israel misses you with a drone. Which they won't."

"We both know there's another way in. Make it happen. I know you've got the contacts." Luke gritted his teeth as he spoke.

Beside him, Simpson was fading. Any route other than the border crossing was rough mountainous terrain. Jay couldn't walk. Luke would have to carry him.

"Stand by." Frank's voice had an edge to it, something that rarely happened.

Luke set the phone down between his thighs and pulled Jay back from the dash. He tried to assess where Jay was hit and look for the tale-tell gurgling that signaled his lungs were taking on fluid. He didn't hear it, but that didn't mean much.

After several minutes, the curves became sharper and the front end pitched upward. Luke flipped on the head-lights as they headed into the mountains. He began to feel uneasy about how long Frank was taking to get back to him.

The Israeli Defense Force had a heavy presence in the hotly disputed Golan Heights region, a vulnerable spot for them. This wasn't their fight, and it would bring down more grief on them than two lousy Americans were worth. Luke couldn't blame them for not wanting to get involved.

"Grim. Grim." Luke heard the phone squawk. Frank was yelling into it.

He picked it up. "Go."

"Proceed two miles on your route. On the right side of the road there is an unmarked cut off that leads to an old trail. It's not marked so watch carefully. Follow that road about two and a half miles. It ends in the middle of an abandoned herder's village.

From there, proceed to coordinates I'm about to send you. That's the border. It should put you far enough away from the crossing that foot patrols will be minimal. When you get there, if you're challenged, answer 'there is no God but Jehovah'."

Luke pressed his lips together. That was the rockiest, most unforgiving terrain in the region. He looked over at Jay who was trying valiantly to stay upright. "Okay."

"Sun comes up in three hours, Grim."

"See you on the other side," said Luke. He hit the end call button and dropped it on the seat.

He reached over and clapped Jay hard on the shoulder. "Stay awake, frat boy," he said loudly. Jay stirred and tried to lift himself upright in the seat. He sank against the door with a moan.

Soon Luke saw the lights of the border crossing light up the sky. Even from ten miles away, they blazed bright.

Luke turned his attention back to the road. As it curved higher and higher into the hills, shrubs and trees grew more dense. He kept his eyes trained on the side of the road.

After another minute, his headlights disappeared for a split second into the dense shrubbery. Luke hit the brakes and threw out a hand to keep Jay from pitching forward. He swung off the road, grateful the hill rose up to shield his bouncing headlights. Anyone at the checkpoint watching through binos would have seen them.

It wasn't a road. It wasn't even a trail. A pitted, uneven goat path cut into the side of the mountain. The car creaked and rattled as Luke pushed it as hard as he dared with the steep drop off on the right.

Twenty minutes later, he saw cement slabs with spiky weeds mounding around them. A few more minutes and the remains of a four house town appeared. The only building still intact was an old barn, leaning at a precarious angle. Luke drove into it.

He killed the engine and cut the lights. He only allowed

himself one deep breath before he clicked on his flashlight and got to work.

The barn, although rotting, was relatively clear of debris. He got out and found a level space before pulling Jay out of the passenger seat and ripping his plate carrier off and his shirt open. Luke retrieved the trauma kit from the gear bag, then turned his flashlight on Jay's chest.

Simpson had been hit twice, once high through the right shoulder. That round passed all the way through. The bleeding had nearly stopped.

Luke rolled him over and saw the entry wound on his lower back. That round was still inside him. The rounds had slowed passing through the car, probably the only thing that spared him.

Luke put his ear to Jay's back. There was no bubbling or gurgling so his lungs were intact and his heart wasn't hit, but the wound still bled freely.

"This might hurt a little." Luke ripped open a pack of Quick Clot with his teeth. Using his shirt tail he wiped away the blood from Jay's skin. Then he pressed the bandage down hard on the hole in his back.

Jay jerked and moaned.

Luke wound a bandage around Jay's midsection. It was crude, but it was the best he could do right now.

He left Jay moaning on the ground and went to the car. He wiped the interior of fingerprints and blood and put all of the remaining ammo into his pockets.

Everything else, including Jay's guns he put into the gear bags. He hauled the bags to the ledge that dropped off the goat path and chucked them over the cliff. The car keys followed the bags to the bottom.

Luke checked the sat phone and set his wrist mounted GPS for the coordinates Frank sent, then powered the phone down. He slung his rifle securely so it wouldn't swing.

Then he looped a piece of parachute cord around his flashlight, lashing it to his chest so that his shirt covered most of the lens. The result was a small amount of light illuminating a tiny patch at his feet. It would be difficult to spot from a distance but still provide light.

He took a couple of deep breaths and stretched out his back. Eight miles of difficult terrain left to cover with a hundred and eighty pounds of dead weight.

When Luke slung Jay over his shoulders, the spook groaned then lapsed back into unconsciousness.

The GPS led directly up the hill, but that wasn't going to happen. Even without Simpson on his back, the huge boulders and dense prickly vegetation made a straight path impossible.

He angled up the hill picking his way left or right depending on which way looked least likely to break his ankle. By the time he reached the top of the hill, sweat poured into his eyes despite the cool night.

Luke took his time going down the ravine on the other side. Rocks and dirt gave way under his boots and his feet constantly slipped, straining his already tired muscles. By the time he crossed a washout at the bottom and started making his way up the other side, Luke started to zone out.

It was dangerous, he could miss a step in the dark, or fail to hear something around him, but the pain was setting in. Jay grew heavier by the minute. Luke let his mind wander as he put one foot in front of the other. Anywhere else to forget how much it hurt.

He walked up and down hill and ravine, one after the other, only pausing to check his GPS. Two and a half hours later his foot rolled on a loose rock and pain spiked up his shin.

He went down to one knee and eased Jay to the ground. His ankle throbbed, so he took a moment to flex it and walk gingerly in a circle. The pain subsided after a moment and he checked his GPS again. Two miles to go.

Considering the terrain and his burden, he'd made good time on the last six miles, but he needed to pick it up. Sunset was an hour away.

As he heaved Jay back onto his shoulders, his flashlight flickered. His ankle throbbed but he picked up his pace making sure to pay more attention to his feet.

Thirty minutes later his flashlight flickered again and died. Luke checked his GPS. They were three hundred yards from their destination. Safety was three football fields away across an open field and dawn was breaking over the mountain ridge.

Luke paused in a grove of trees and lowered Jay to the ground. They were on a plateau of some kind, the ground level. Exactly the place a patrol might be. From cover, he scanned the open field and the trees on the other side.

GPS said straight across the field.

Luke adjusted his rifle for easier access and listened. Nothing.

He checked Jay's pulse. It was faint. With one more glance around, he loaded Simpson and moved out. One foot in front of the other until he hit the tree line on the other side.

His GPS buzzed telling him he had arrived at his destination. Luke looked around.

Nothing.

He lowered Jay to the ground and pulled out his phone to call Frank. He needed a new set of coordinates.

A twig cracked to his right and he heard a voice. "Halt," a man said in Arabic with a strange accent. "If you move you will die."

Slowly Luke raised his hands. In English he answered, "There is no God but Jehovah."

33

―――――

7 Kilometers East of Dan, Israel
Northern Golan Heights
March 29
0518 Hours Local Time

"Do not move," came the answer in English. "What is your name?"

"There is no God but Jehovah," Luke repeated.

The same voice muttered Hebrew into a radio. Luke couldn't hear the reply. The unseen man wore a headset.

Seconds later, a man in dark brown camouflage tactical gear stepped out of the shadows pointing a heavily modified M16 CAR15 at Luke's face. Rustling meadow grass told Luke the soldier was not alone.

"Follow me," he said in accented English as his five teammates appeared in a bristling semi-circle around Luke, their rifles trained on him.

None of the men offered to take the unconscious man from Luke, and he didn't ask. He was grateful they hadn't shot him on sight, advanced warning or not. Israel didn't employ 'ask first' techniques.

Without another word, the man turned and passed through the stand of trees they had been hiding in. There was no trail, but he walked confidently downhill picking a path through the rocks and shrubs.

Luke followed, stooping a little more with each step. The sun crested the horizon by the time several open back jeeps and a pickup came into view. They were parked on a sheep trail much like the one he'd taken across the mountainside a few hours earlier.

The leader said something to a soldier walking beside Luke as they approached the vehicles. He'd grown more and more impatient at Luke's slow place.

Luke felt Simpson's weight lift off of him. Two of them grabbed Jay, and with surprising gentleness, laid him in the bed of the pickup and put a blanket under his head to protect from the bouncing on the bumpy path. Then they put one on top of him.

Luke hauled himself up into the bed of the truck and groaned as he eased himself down and leaned against the side.

The soldiers slammed the tailgate and tires spun on loose dirt as the convoy took off down the road. Luke figured they were under orders to take the two Americans directly to Haifa and get them on the first aircraft Frank could get there.

The sky was lighting up quickly now. Luke could see Jay, gray and ashen. By some miracle he still had a faint pulse, but if he didn't get medical attention soon, the CIA agent was going to die

Luke looked into the cabin of the pickup. The man in the passenger seat had a rifle slung to his chest and wore sunglasses.

This man wasn't with the team that picked up Luke and Jay. He'd been waiting at the trucks, clearly the one giving orders. He sat upright and rigid in the seat with one foot propped up on the dust covered dashboard.

He munched a toothpick in his teeth while he looked straight ahead, not glancing into the bed of the truck at the men. His uniform didn't fit him well. Luke suspected he was Mossad.

The convoy made a hard right turn and Luke felt the tires glide over smooth asphalt. As soon as they hit the pavement, the two young soldiers riding beside him sprang to life. Bags with clear fluid, gauze, and assorted medical supplies came out of a sack.

Luke made himself small in the corner so they could triage his fading partner.

They drove for almost an hour on a deserted backroad, before hitting a larger highway for a while. Before long they turned down an unmarked paved lane. It led to a small but well maintained airstrip cutting through an olive grove. The airstrip ended in more olive trees that went on as far as Luke could see.

Brakes squeaked as they ground to a halt beside a hangar. Luke jumped over the side to get out of the way of the two medics loading Jay onto an improvised stretcher.

A white unmarked jet sat on the tarmac in front of the hangar with the cabin door open, the engines idling. Luke took out his satellite phone to call the Colonel.

The second he hit call, Luke looked up and saw Frank Longer step out of the jet. He put the phone in his pocket and jogged over to him.

Frank's hand closed around his in a strong grip and he gave Luke a hard slap on the back. "Glad you're okay, you slippery son of a bitch."

Luke gave him a tired smile. "Sir, we're gonna need another jet."

"You're never happy, are you?" Frank yelled above the engine noise.

"Simpson needs a hospital ASAP and I have to get to Denver."

Frank nodded. He already made that assessment when he stepped out and saw how badly injured Jay was. He stepped back in to speak to the pilot.

Luke was keenly aware of the Israeli commander standing beside him. He glared at the Israeli who was thoroughly unfazed by it. This man didn't bluster. He had an intense confidence and gruff manner that exuded an aura of strength, although he said next to nothing. He was the kind of man that menaced without even speaking.

Frank popped back out of the jet and hurried down the steps to let the men get Jay's stretcher onboard. With his phone still by his ear, Frank turned to the man by Luke.

"Moshe, let your people know we have another jet inbound. It should only be about twenty minutes away."

Moshe gave a single nod and beckoned a soldier with a single wave. The gangway rose and Jay's plane turned to taxi down the runway. Two minutes later the light aircraft shot forward and lifted off before it reached the middle of the runway bound for Landstuhl Medical Center in Germany.

Frank walked to the tree line, in deep conversation. The morning became still again. Luke watched Moshe stand next to him not saying a word. He didn't acknowledge Luke, but Luke knew he wanted the troublesome Americans off his turf ASAP.

Luke jumped as the phone in his pocket buzzed. It wasn't the satellite phone. It was the phone he hadn't used since Tommy died. He pulled it out and looked at the caller ID. He couldn't hide the surprise on his face.

Moshe's eyes fell to Luke's screen, then narrowed with suspicion.

Luke's finger hovered over the green circle before he hit it. He put it to his ear. "You're still alive I see."

The line was quiet for a moment. "You too."

"Talk to me, Sheppard. What happened?"

"Adrian's dead," said Maisie.

"Are you alright?"

"Ivanov is dead too. I made sure he knew it was for killing Tommy."

"What have you done, Sheppard?" Luke turned away so Moshe wouldn't overhear.

"Marshall, I...."

He heard a car door slam and she said, "*Aeroport*." She spoke in Russian. Then she came back on the line. "Do you know his target?"

"Denver, somewhere."

"Luke," her voice was pitchy now like she was having trouble controlling it, "the uranium is in America. It's already there. It's always been there. Arazi just has a small amount. It's a separate portion that was given to the mercs working with my father. The rest is still missing, but what he has is enough to do a lot of damage. Luke, Adrian sold it to him. He was working with my father." Her voice trembled again.

Luke felt like someone punched him in the gut. "And the file?"

"Gone. But I have something for you. Under, uh duress, Ivanov told me the bomb is designed to fit into a soda machine or a snack machine. Arazi requested it specifically for a vending machine. It's big enough that he would have to remove the mechanism. The machine won't work. I don't know if that helps."

Luke straightened at this news. This he could use. His elation was short lived.

"Luke, he came to Ivanov over six months ago. He's been

planning this for a while. That bomb could go off any minute."

"I know. Where are you?" From the corner of his eye, Luke saw Moshe watching him.

"Maisie, where are you?"

"You know I can't tell you that."

"You're not done yet. You were supposed to find the uranium."

"That's not my job anymore."

"You help me stop Arazi and find the uranium. We'll negotiate immunity."

Luke watched Moshe's eyes harden.

"You don't understand, do you?" Maisie sounded calm now, resolute. "There is no proof that Adrian was ever involved. They're going to accuse me of his murder too. Every lie he ever spread remains."

"We'll work something out."

"There's nothing to work out, Marshall. But it's okay."

"No, it's not okay," he yelled into the phone.

"I'll help you however I can. But I won't come in."

"Maisie...."

"Take care of yourself, Luke."

"Maisie. Shep...," Luke yelled into the phone, but she had already hung up. He tried dialing her back but it went to voicemail.

"Fuck," he said softly.

The whine of another jet on approach filled the air. A shiny blue Embraer Legacy 500 bore down on the landing strip as Luke stood fuming at the phone in his hand.

Luke looked up at Moshe. The Israeli's eyes had not left him since he answered the phone.

"You know Maisie Sheppard," said Luke. It was a statement.

Tommy was right again. She did have high Mossad contacts.

Moshe didn't move. Then, slowly, he gave an almost imperceptible nod.

"I know she's not my enemy, but I'm still having trouble trusting her," said Luke.

Moshe studied Luke for a moment, chomping on the toothpick. Then he spit it out. "I have trusted her with my life before and I would again."

Luke may have questioned her loyalty, but he didn't question the Israeli's assessment. Coming from a man like Moshe, it was high praise.

Moshe took out another toothpick and stuck it between his teeth. "Is she safe?"

The plane touched down with a squeak of rubber and a rush of noise. Luke waited until it taxied to a stop by the hangar.

"She's gotten herself into some trouble, but I think she'll be okay."

The Israeli nodded and extended his hand with the first smile that Luke had seen. "Yes, that sounds like her. Good luck, Mr. Marshall."

Luke shook his hand firmly.

Frank reappeared his phone still in hand. He clasped Moshe on the shoulder. "Thank you, Friend. I'm in your debt."

Moshe nodded once, and Frank turned to climb the stairs. Luke followed, taking them two at a time.

34

120 Miles South of Crete
Over the Mediterranean Sea
March 29
1115 Hours Local Time

Luke whistled as he and Frank settled into the seats of the sumptuously appointed jet. This jet was much nicer than the one he took to Turkey. A private traveling oasis, not some assembly line corporate ride.

"Where did you get this thing?" Luke looked around. In the rear of the plane, he saw a queen size bed.

"Called in a favor. Don't worry about it." Frank was already pulling his dogeared notebook from a tattered brief-case not bothering to buckle in.

"You alerted the Denver FBI field office?"

Frank nodded. "As soon as you called me last night. No one on their watch list matches the names you got. They're still vetting aliases. I don't suppose you have any more information."

The jet shot down the runway and into the air. They

would be in Denver in fourteen hours including one fuel stop.

Luke shook his head. "Get back on the horn with them and tell them the bomb will likely be in a vending machine or something similar. Malls, public transportation, crowded downtown areas. I don't know. DPD needs to beef up presence in their soft target areas."

"Time frame?"

Luke looked hard at his mentor. "Frank, I think he has the uranium. I have it from a good source that the U was already hidden in the US. We have to operate on the assumption that he has it. The time frame is right fucking now. If we can't find those sleepers and bleed them, we're not gonna find this thing until it goes off."

"Agreed," said Frank solemnly. "Who's the source?"

Luke sat back and smiled. "Don't worry about it, Colonel."

The steward, a young Asian man in a tailored gray suit, approached Frank. "We're at cruising altitude. The phone is operable now, sir if you'd like to call."

"Thank you," said Frank. He looked back at Luke. "Got some work to do, son. Apparently, a Canadian and a Spaniard were running around Syria last night shooting everything up." He winked at Luke, then it vanished. "After I'm done icing that cake, I'm going to find out who knew you were in Kiev. When I do, I'll have another job for you."

Luke nodded, grim. "That one you won't have to talk me into."

He stood while Frank moved to the small table and pulled the phone receiver out of the wall panel.

The steward was busy in the back of the plane in the galley kitchen near the bedroom. Luke grabbed his bag and headed back.

"Is there a place I can clean up?"

"Yes, sir," the steward said with practice friendliness. "Into the cabin is the bedroom suite." He pointed to a door at the rear of the aircraft. "Would you like some coffee?"

"Yes, please. And food if you have any." Luke thanked him and pulled the bedroom door shut behind him. He looked around taking in the Brazilian cherry paneling and plush carpet. It must have been a pretty big favor Frank pulled.

He walked into the bathroom. What it lacked in size it made up for in luxury. A solid slab of marble in the shower. He didn't marvel at the opulence for long. A garden hose would feel just as luxurious right now.

Thirty minutes later, Luke emerged scrubbed and clean in his own clothes that Frank had brought. The shower made him simultaneously feel better and so sleepy he could barely speak.

Luke struggled through a cup of coffee and a full English breakfast before Frank gave him a hard look.

Frank put his hand over the phone receiver and said, "Get some sleep."

Luke didn't argue. He stumbled back to the bedroom and fell onto the bed. Fumbling his boots off, he crawled onto the bed and blacked out.

Someone rapped at the door.

Luke sat bolt upright, his brain foggy but the nagging sense of urgency strong.

"Sir?" The steward rapped lightly on the door again. "Sir, we are an hour out."

"Mmky," muttered Luke.

He swung his feet over the bed and immediately felt the soreness from last night's hike through the mountains. His legs ached and his back spasmed viciously. He stretched and twisted a few times trying to loosen it.

Bleary-eyed, he looked at his watch then at the clock on

the nightstand. Then he looked again. After gazing at it for a few moments he realized they were nine hours apart. Colorado was nine hours behind. They flew for fourteen hours, and the clock turned back by nine. It was the same day only nine hours earlier. He'd already had enough of this day and now he had to do it again.

Luke shook his head and decided to take a cold shower. It might help clear the fog.

By the time he entered the cabin, he was wide awake and feeling decent except for the soreness.

He requested more breakfast with a side of ibuprofen and sat across from Frank at the table. Frank was still on the phone, but Luke saw a rumpled pillow and blanket on the recliner in the corner.

The steward placed a china cup of coffee, a water glass, and three gel tablets in front of Luke. He served Frank a cup of coffee then bustled off to get breakfast. Luke swallowed the pills and the entire glass of water, then set in on the coffee.

"Thank you. I'll let him know." Frank hung up. "Simpson's out of surgery. Still touch and go, but he'll pull through. Thanks to you."

Luke drank his coffee and nodded as he worked out the kink between his shoulder blades. Breakfast appeared in front of them. He started eating without a word.

"I'm expecting a briefing call from the ASAC in Denver. They've been working around the clock." Frank scarfed his food down between sentences. "Here's hoping they have something for us." He took two quick bites.

Metal dragged on china as Frank scraped the last bites of egg and sausage off his plate and crammed the toast into his mouth. Then he stood. "Listen for the phone, will you? I'm going to take a shower. I smell like roadkill." He disappeared through the bedroom door.

Luke finished his coffee, his mind already racing, searching again for something he'd missed. Something that gave Arazi away.

Luke heard a shrill beep. His jet-lagged brain was confused as he sat deep in thought. He ignored it, his thoughts still on Arazi.

"Sir, the phone." The steward gestured to the phone by the table that now had a red light blinking. It beeped again.

Luke snatched the handset off the cradle. "Hello."

"Colonel Longer?" A deep voice inquired.

"No, this is Luke Marshall."

The man on the other end obviously knew who he was. "Ah, Mr. Marshall. This is Special Agent Eddie Jackson, Denver office. I've got some information for you and the Colonel. Some of it's good."

"Go," said Luke.

"I think we may have found them. There's a local couple on our watch list. She used the name Damia Ayad once on a job application five years ago. We know her as Miriam Jarwel, married to Issa Abdel-Hakim. They both have Iraqi ties. They've been on our watch list for about seven years, but pretty much only because they've been on the DHS watchlist. They live in a suburb just outside the city." Agent Jackson paused.

"What's the bad news?" Luke knew what the pause meant.

"They've been under surveillance since we found them. About four hours now. We haven't seen any movement in the house despite the fact that they both have 9-to-5s. We have people watching their places of employment too. They didn't show up this morning."

"What do we know about them?"

"They were classified as low threat. I guess that was incorrect," Agent Jackson laughed.

Luke didn't find it funny. "Do they have the ability to build a complicated bomb? Or at least source the materials?"

"I have no idea, but they are citizens. They blend in. They don't dress like devout Muslims. They don't even go to mosque. If they were careful, they could get the components without raising an eyebrow."

"And have they been buying bomb materials?"

There was a short pause.

"Agent Jackson," Luke said harshly. They'd had thirteen hours and almost unlimited resources to work on this.

"We're still checking," admitted Jackson. "Since they were classified as a minor threat we didn't have any surveillance on them. I've got a team of agents on their financials right now, but we haven't found anything. More than likely they paid cash, so we're having to go boots on the ground checking areas hardware and farm supply stores. We've got it out to DPD, but it's gonna take some time."

"Do you have a team on airport arrivals?"

"Yes, sir. We're checking passenger manifests and security cameras. Nothing yet."

"When are you hitting the house?"

"Already got a warrant and working on the ops plan now."

"How long?"

"Maybe an hour."

Luke called out to the steward, "What's our ETA?"

The steward held up one finger and picked up a phone hanging by the sink. He spoke into it then hung up. "Forty-five minutes, sir. We'll be arriving at hangar 46."

Luke turned back to the phone. "We're forty-five out. Do you have a ride for us?"

"Yes, we do. I'm sending a team to pick you up. I'm

assuming you'll come to the house unless you have an alternate location for us."

Luke ground his teeth in frustration. "No, I don't. Send
them to hangar 46."

"Will do, sir."

Luke hung up and rubbed his hands over his face. Then
he walked over to his bag and started rooting through it
looking for his gun and belt that he'd thrown in there before
he fell asleep.

As he picked up his rig, he noticed the pager-sized
personal radiation detector that Romero gave him in Kiev. It
turned his stomach to think about it, but it might come in
handy the next few hours. He snapped the cobra buckle,
fastened the thigh strap, and slipped the PRD into his
pocket.

Thirty-eight minutes later the jet taxied past the
passenger concourses to a large tarmac near the freight
aircraft lots. Through the cockpit window, Luke identified
hanger forty-six by the three black SUV's waiting next to it.
Thanks to Frank's urgent string pulling, they bypassed
customs entirely.

Luke and Frank clicked off their seatbelts. Luke grabbed
both bags as the Colonel went to have a quick word with the
pilot. By the time he came back, the aircraft had swung
broadside to the waiting vehicles and the steward was
lowering the gangway.

A strong white glare greeted Luke as he stepped out. He
squinted as the glaring white stung his eyes. Light snow had
begun to cover the grass beyond the tarmac. Not unusual for
spring in the high desert.

The small convoy of three black Chevy Tahoes sat with
the doors flung open. Luke could see the large yellow letters
on the windbreakers of the men standing around them. He

descended the steps blinking against the morning glare with Frank behind him.

Standing by the passenger door of the lead SUV was a tall, powerfully built black man in a white shirt, and black suit pants. His dark blue windbreaker rustled in the snowy breeze. Luke's days at the Bureau were recent enough that he could still feel the crinkle of the nylon against his skin.

Luke and Frank walked to him and Frank stuck out his hand. "Agent Jackson?"

The man nodded and shook Frank's hand.

Frank turned to Luke. "Luke Marshall."

ASAC Jackson shook Luke's hand in a crushing grip.

"You hit the house yet?" Luke didn't waste any time getting the conversation started in the right direction.

Agent Jackson looked at his watch. "We're going in about ten minutes. Should have the house cleared and secured by the time we get there."

Luke nodded and handed Frank his own bag. There was only one seat left in each of the SUVs. Luke left Frank with the lead agent and walked to the second SUV.

Another three agents in polos and khakis shook his hand quickly then got in the Tahoe. Luke took the back seat behind the driver and stuffed his bag in the middle.

As soon as he shut the door, the vehicle accelerated as the driver floored the gas and they shot down the tarmac.

"I'm Caleb Middleton, this is Natalie Hayes." The driver pointed to the mousy-looking female agent in the front next to him. "The asshole in the back seat is Damian Morton."

Luke nodded to each of them in turn, already forgetting their names. "Have you run threat assessments yet? Do you like any target in particular? We need to focus on the big ones. He's out to make a statement. Somewhere sensational."

The woman spoke. "That's what we figured too. Problem

is, Denver has multiple large venues. The newest one is a concert venue downtown. It's very popular right now, there are concerts almost nightly and on the weekends it gets very crowded. We also have a heavy presence at the zoo, another big draw. If he's after a statement, kids will accomplish that."

The SUV slowed as they approached the guard house. Tires bumped over the one-way tiger teeth, and they shot forward onto the road that skirted the airport. Soon the desert plain spread out in every direction shimmering white in the morning sun.

The caravan took the onramp to I-70 toward Denver and all three activated emergency lights and sirens. They weren't stopping for anyone.

Luke saw the distinctive craggy skyline of the Front Range of the Rocky Mountains to his left. They were headed into the city.

Agent Hayes continued. "Unfortunately your tip about the vending machines applies to all the major venues in town and a ton of secondaries. We can't narrow it down from that. We are trying to cover vending machine service companies, but between the big distributors and mom-and-pop operations, that's going to take time we don't have."

Damian looked over at Luke. "DPD is beefing up security at several places, but neither of us has the manpower to cover all the soft targets in this city. There's just too many."

"Focus on places that have large banks of them. He would have had to get it in, that would make it easier to avoid raising any eyebrows if one was swapped out or an extra one appeared. Malls, theaters, and concert venues are pretty good guesses. The radiation would fill up an enclosed space very quickly leading to a high mortality rate."

"Shit," whispered Damian. "You really think he's going to do this?"

Luke looked at him. He looked young and a little scared. Boyhood ended tonight. He was in the shit now.

"Not if we stop him," Luke said.

The agent gave him a weak smile and reached into the back compartment. "We didn't know what you'd need so I picked some stuff. Take what you want." He pulled a gray duffle and unzipped it to reveal several handguns of varying calibers in holsters, a long gun with extra mags, and body armor.

"Aulden said you wore a large."

Luke squinted at him.

"I went to the academy with Thaddeus." Damian smiled. "I called him as soon as Jackson told us you were flying in." He grinned again. "He also said you need to, and I'm quoting here, 'fucking call him sometime'."

Luke smiled as he translated Damian's words into his old partner's voice. If he made it through this without dying of radiation poisoning, he would call Thad and catch up. Instead of a new gun, he pulled a blue windbreaker from the bag.

"ETA to the house is about 15," said Caleb.

The target house was on a quiet suburban street in Wheat Ridge, Colorado on the other side of Denver. Much like the one Luke grew up in. Every second his father wasn't working, he took his two sons to their rustic cabin in the woods.

Luke grew up in the mountains more than the city. When the snow got too deep for hunting and fishing, they went skiing. Out his window, downtown's jagged skyline came into view, blurred by the flurries.

"Hope you guys got your people out," said Luke, eyeing the city.

"Packed 'em up the second I got the call," said Caleb. The others nodded in agreement.

A handheld radio in the cupholder chirped to life. Agent Jackson's voice came over. "Guys, they hit the house. The couple is dead. Shot execution style."

Luke threw himself back against the seat. The rest of the vehicle sat in stunned silence. Arazi cleaned up, leaving nothing behind. No one to interrogate, nothing to glean. Frustration edged with panic burned up Luke's mind.

Think, Luke. Think.

Arazi, Luke's own bespoke terrorist, would make it personal. Very personal. Luke looked around the cabin of the Tahoe. The other three agents sat in silence looking straight ahead. They had all expected him to give them direction, but he couldn't. That bomb could be anywhere, and Luke would have to sit back and watch his hometown become a war zone, powerless to stop it. As powerless as Arazi all those years ago when Luke came to his hometown.

The front end of the Tahoe nosed up as they drove through the I-20 interchange. At the highest point on the interchange, downtown spread out to Luke's left. The lights over Coors Field blazed, cutting through the dissipating white haze.

Luke looked at his watch. "There's a game today? It's 11:30."

"Season opener at noon. I was supposed to take my kid," said Caleb.

Something in Luke's chest squeezed tightly. He reached forward and clutched the seat. Was it possible?

Luke squeezed his eyes shut as he tried to recall the scene that night. Had he? Had his partner yelled his op call sign in front of Nasir Al-din Arazi that night? He couldn't remember, there was a lot of yelling, but Arazi called him 'Slugger' when he called Luke in Kiev.

He still held the record for strikeouts in a single season and the nickname Slugger followed him into active duty.

Operational code names weren't included in after-action reports. They certainly wouldn't have been declassified. How would he have known Luke's call sign if he hadn't heard it that night?

Beside him, Damian said quietly, "What is it, Mr. Marshall?"

"He's going to hit Coors Stadium."

35

———

I-70 Westbound
Denver, Colorado
March 29
1132 Hours Local Time

The sign for the I-20 exit to downtown was just ahead. Luke pointed at it and yelled in the driver's ear, "Go to the stadium."

"Wha...," Middleton said, flinching.

"Fucking do it." Luke launched forward and snatched the radio as Caleb yanked the wheel and the Tahoe darted across two lanes of traffic barely making the exit ramp.

The Tahoe behind them wobbled as the driver was caught off guard and couldn't make a decision. He barely made it onto the exit, leaving a swath of pissed-off drivers behind. Frank's lead car continued on I-70 to the suburbs.

"Frank. Frank, are you there?" Luke yelled into the radio.

"Son, what are you doing?" Frank's voice sounded pinched like he was turned around to see why the SUV behind him veered wildly off course.

"Frank, he's going to hit the stadium. He knew it, Frank. He knew my call sign from the op. He called me 'slugger'.

There was a moment of radio silence before Frank came on again. "Are you sure?"

"Yes. The season opener starts in half an hour."

"Alright, we're turning around."

"No, Colonel, keep going. I need you to tear that house apart. You need to get eyes on any intel you can. The stadium may have to be collateral damage. We have to stop that U from getting airborne."

"I don't like it, son."

"I know, Frank. But if we swarm the stadium, he'll see us coming and blow the device, maybe before he planned. Notify DPD, but they are not to respond to the stadium. They need to start evacuating the surrounding areas. We'll brief the officers and security that are already at the stadium, and start looking for Arazi, quietly. Give them a basic description. And have EOD stage near the stadium."

"Alright."

Everyone but the driver threw a hand to stabilize themselves as the Tahoe veered off the exit ramp at seventy miles an hour onto the exit announcing, 'Coors Stadium'.

"Cut your siren," ordered Luke.

"Go around back." Hayes pointed past the parking garage to a paved access road. "There's a service platform where they make all the deliveries and take out the trash and whatnot."

Everyone looked at her. She shrugged. "What? You never snuck into a baseball game before?"

Damian slapped her on the shoulder.

"Who is this guy?" She twisted to look at Luke. "He doesn't sound like a garden variety jihadist."

"He's the son of a dead terrorist. I killed his father in '06 in Mosul," Luke told her.

"Well, shit," she said.

Middleton brought the SUV to a screeching halt at a platform large enough to accommodate three semi-trucks. The rear Tahoe screeched to a stop beside them. Next to a bank of dumpsters, steam roiled out of a grate on the brick wall, and large metal doors led down a utility corridor. Inside the stadium, a woman was singing the national anthem to a cheering crowd.

They all slipped out and gathered around Luke.

"Take off your jackets or turn them inside out. We need to keep a lid on this as long as we can. He's cleaning up after himself. He knew we would find the couple, so we have to assume he knows we're coming. Remember he wants me to see. I think he'll blow it when he knows I'm close. We have to use that window."

Everyone nodded and pulled off their jackets. An old man pushing a large rolling garbage bin pushed through the door. He stopped and stared at the armed group huddled together.

"Um, who are we looking for? We never got a picture," said someone from the second SUV.

"I don't have one," said Luke. "He's a twenty-seven year old middle eastern man with a jacked-up eyebrow. If you see him, don't challenge him. Try to blend and follow. I don't know what kind of detonator he has. I doubt it's on a timer, if he really wants me to be here for the show, it's probably a remote trigger. If it is, he'll have to be close for it to work. There's a lot of concrete in there. Hang back and follow him."

Luke glanced around. "I don't want everybody looking for Arazi. You four," he pointed to Middleton and Hayes and two other agents whose names he didn't know. "Go to the concessions office first. Get a list of all the vending machine locations in the stadium. Start with machines that have been replaced or repaired within the last two weeks. I'm assuming they do maintenance before the season starts. That would give Arazi an opportunity to sneak it in. It's a place to start."

They nodded.

Luke continued, "It won't be one of those clear front machines. The machine's guts have to be removed, so focus on machines that aren't see-through. Oh, and the machine won't work, so that's a clue.

"The rest of you start pushing machines out from the walls. If the guts were removed, there should be signs. Stay orderly, bottom levels working up, and make sure you cover all of them."

The group nodded again.

"Morton, you coordinate with security and make sure these guys aren't disturbed and get them tipping machines over as well. Just don't tell them why we're here. Tell them it's drugs or something. Everybody clear?"

"What are you doing?" Damian turned to him.

"I'm going to find this asshole."

"By yourself?"

"Yes." Luke looked at him daring him to argue. He didn't.

"Okay," said Middleton. "Let's go be heroes." He led them through the utility doors left open by the trash man. The security guard sitting on the stool at the inner door grew wide-eyed when he saw the group bearing down on him.

Middleton badged him and began grilling the man about a fraud investigation causing the man's eyes to glaze over. When Middleton asked him about the requisition office, he seemed relieved that was all he needed to know.

"This way," he said, scooting off his stool and opening the door. They all filed in behind him. He broke into a jog for a hundred feet before they ran into another security guard around a corner.

The first guard hurriedly explained the situation then kept going with the agents. Luke hung back and hooked the arm of the second guard.

"Take me to the main security office. I need to look at the cameras," Luke said.

The man nodded and backed up a step as he sized up Luke. Luke wasn't dressed like the other agents, nor did he act like them. The guard hesitated.

"Let's go," snapped Luke.

The man started and squeaked out, "Which one? We have two. One covers the three lower levels and the other covers the top three levels."

Luke tried to put himself in Arazi's place. He would want to be away from the crowded lower levels. Less possibility of interference if someone wanted to play the hero. In a post 9-11 world, citizens took zero shit, and terrorists knew it. High up was a better vantage point.

"Upper," Luke said, obeying his gut.

The security guard turned and began walking. Luke nudged him hard in the back and broke into a jog beside him. The guard complied. By the time they reached the elevator to the fourth level, the pudgy guard was wheezing. He punched the button and hunched over to catch his breath.

On the top floor, they stepped off into the wide concourse with only the nosebleed section above them. Luke caught a glimpse of someone in a Rockies jacket throwing out the first pitch. The crowd cheered wildly as the jumbotron proclaimed "PLAY BALL" in flashing letters. The organ played the rally song. The smell of beer and frying food wafted from the concourse. Nostalgia and dread filled Luke.

He turned right and followed the security guard along the third base line. Moments later they turned off the main concourse down a hall and stopped at a door that simply said '405'. The guard scanned a key card and pushed the door open.

Inside a bank of screens lined two walls. Luke's security guard guide went to a small office at the back to get the supervisor. He brought him over to Luke who was already violating the personal space of a young man with a mop of black hair, trying to view the camera feeds.

"Can I help you?" He heard a harsh voice behind him.

Luke turned to see the nervous security guard standing beside a wiry older man who looked none too happy to see a stranger in his secure room.

"He's with the FBI," the guard whispered.

"You're FBI?" Boomed the man.

"No," said Luke. "Do you have facial recognition capability?"

The man's eyes narrowed beneath bushy eyebrows. Then he laughed. "You're lucky we have TVs to view the cameras on. What are you looking for?"

Luke turned to the bank of screens. "I need you to keep a lookout for a young middle eastern man with a messed up eyebrow. I know it's a long shot."

The man threw his chin and studied Luke. "This have anything to do with the DPD hubbub? Awful lot of fuss around this stadium."

Luke heard radio traffic, likely from a scanner coming from the office. The man was right, there was a lot of radio chatter. "Something like that."

"So there is a bomb."

Luke closed his eyes briefly in annoyance as the two younger men stiffened. "Yes."

"Then we need to begin evac of the complex." The man turned to dart back into his office.

"Stop," ordered Luke. He abandoned the screens and approached the supervisor. "We're not evacuating the stadium."

"Like hell we're not." He squared his body to Luke ready to do battle.

"You start evacuation and this entire city will die. That is the biggest red flag we can wave at this guy. That bomb is sitting on a pile of weapons-grade uranium. If that bomb goes off it will atomize and release over the city. Thousands will die."

The old man's jaw went slack. Behind Luke, the young security guard jumped to his feet like he wanted to run.

"Under no circumstances do you let security begin evacuation of the stadium unless I give you the order. Am I clear?" Luke turned to the security guard that escorted him up. "Give me a radio."

The man took his radio off his belt and handed it to Luke. "Channel four," he said.

"Good. Stay here and help them. Hit me up if you see anything. Anything suspicious at all." He turned to leave.

"Okay. What...what's your name, Sir?"

Luke looked back at them. "Name's Marshall."

He strode to the concourse and out into the middle of the crowd streaming through it. Families passed, oblivious to the danger. Fathers with sons brushed by Luke without a second glance.

Luke's gaze traveled over the concourse now swelling with fans vying to get food. The stadium was packed. It looked like the game was sold out despite the snow. He checked the nearest monitor showing the televised game. It was the top of the first inning and the Rockies were down by one.

He walked to the edge of the concourse and tucked himself into a corner. He looked down at the throng of white and purple in the stands below him, and the stream of people walking by him. It was a fool's task trying to find one man in that crowd, but he looked anyway.

Luke scanned for one thing, behavior. Arazi would be nervous, stiff and unconcerned with the game.

The concourse followed the third baseline and curved toward the outfield. On the field, the game was in full swing. His eyes snagged on something, but it wasn't Arazi.

A woman passed him in jeans and a brown leather jacket. Her dark hair was in a high ponytail. Her head swung left and right as she studied each face with the same intensity Luke did, unaffected by the energy of the crowd.

Luke fell in behind her and followed until they reached a cutout in the concourse. Here the walls met at a weird angle creating a shielded alcove by a food booth employee entrance.

He came alongside and took her arm. Her head jerked toward him, but she didn't look surprised and yielded to the pressure on her arm. He pulled her to the alcove and again she didn't resist when he pressed her back to the cinder block.

"What are you doing here, Sheppard?"

Maisie met his gaze with a little smile. "Helping you."

"How did you know to come here?"

She smiled again. "Police scanner app. Tommy already had it on the phone he gave me. Wasn't hard to figure out from all the chatter. That and I heard him call you slugger."

Luke put a hand around her neck. She didn't fight him.

"Tommy's dead because of you."

"No," she said, her voice even. "They would have killed me too, Luke. And when we're done here, I'm going to finish the job."

Luke released her throat and propped his hand next to her head leaning in, his suspicion of her finally satisfied. She told him about the vending machines. And she would never have come back unless she was telling the truth. "Why did you come back?"

She raised her face to his bringing them even closer together. "You want to talk about this now?"

Luke searched her face.

"I fucked up leaving Tommy. Maybe I should have died with him. This is the only way I know how to repay him," she said softly.

The small radio that stadium security gave Luke squawked to life.

"Mr. Marshall? I think I may have found him."

Luke raised it to his lips, his gaze still boring into Maze. "Go."

"Um. Near the Rooftop Bar. Top deck, outfield. I mean I can't be sure, but it looks like the man you described."

"Sounds like he wants to talk to you," Maisie said, her eyes never leaving his. "Don't take that away from him. Sometimes us bad guys just need you to understand."

Hope flared inside him. The chance was weak but alive. To Maisie he said, "Find the bomb."

"I will."

Luke started to leave, then turned and looked back at her. "What would you do if you wanted to disburse radioactive material and needed clear line of sight to do it?"

She cocked her head and raised an eyebrow. "That's easy. You go high."

36

———

Coors Field
Denver, Colorado
March 29
1153 Hours Local Time

Luke muscled his way through the crowd as he made his way to the highest level. At the top, Luke had a clear view of the field. The sun was beginning to peek through the flurries making the air above the field sparkle.

Wind whipped through the concourse. The thin high altitude air and the strong breeze were perfect conditions for disbursing a substance through the air. The thought made Luke elbow his way through the crowd faster.

The Rooftop Bar, on the opposite side of the field, gave its patrons a commanding view of the game and five miles in every direction. Luke's phone rang. It was Frank.

"Luke, we've only given the house a once over, but there are plenty of IED components in the garage. They don't look like conventional explosives either. We also found several short range walkie talkies. I don't know if that's how he plans to detonate. There are multiple smartphone boxes and smartwatch boxes."

"Can you call from a smartwatch?" Luke looked around him. Everybody was wearing a smartwatch. He felt like an idiot for not knowing.

"Yes. Or send a text, or set an alarm. We're working on shutting down the phone network in that area, but they're telling me most watches can also work off the internet, not just the phone connection, or some such."

Frank paused and Luke knew he was being coached by someone who knew more about electronics. "We're working on shutting off internet service in the city, so more than likely he'll be going for line of sight at least as a backup. We can't shut that down. If that's how he's planning on detonating, he'd still have to be close enough for the devices to stay connected."

"So remote det with a line of sight back up."

"That's what it looks like. You find him yet?"

"Not yet."

"I don't have to remind you what happens if we don't stop this guy."

"I know," Luke said. "Keep me posted."

He hung up and slid the phone into his pocket. The madman he created was in complete control.

Luke ran the scenario in his head as he walked. Line of sight. If they managed to shut down the phone and internet signals, Arazi would need to be within a couple hundred feet. In a heavy concrete structure, maybe closer.

Fifty feet ahead, Luke saw a shock of black hair and shoved his way through the crowd bowling over a group of teenagers.

"Hey," shouted one of the kids as Luke knocked two of them down.

Luke paid no attention to them or the dirty looks he got as he shoulder checked people to clear a path.

When he reached the young man he grabbed his elbow and spun him, his right hand on his gun.

Instead of Arazi, he spun around an Asian man in his thirties. The man looked shocked at being forced around violently by a stranger. Luke released him and pushed back into the crowd.

Luke keyed his radio. "Has he moved?"

There was a maddening pause. "No," came the wavering voice. "He's still at the Rooftop. Sitting at the bar. He just ordered a beer."

Ahead Luke saw a wide set of stairs leading up. He sprinted up the staircase that took him to the top mezzanine past a large bank of vending machines, several food stalls, and large men's and women's restrooms.

He sprinted the length of the mezzanine around home plate, not stopping until he reached a set of cushioned furniture that marked the entrance to the restaurant.

This would be a lot easier if everyone was sitting down, but there were precious few tables. Most fans walked around carrying glasses of beer or baskets of barbecue nachos.

The Rooftop Bar was more nightclub than ballpark food stand. Connected to the largest bar was a VIP lounge on double decks overlooking the Front Range, with a pristine view of the diamond.

No one seemed disturbed by the panting man carrying a radio. Above him, the heavy girders holding up the massive roof angled back and forth. On his right thick metal beams with zigzagged supports created giant ladders up to the stadium lights.

Luke stopped to catch his breath.

The wavering voice came over the radio again. "I see you

now. He's at the far side of the bar. He keeps looking at the camera."

Luke's eyes flew around the bar scanning the crowd waiting for a beer and caught on a young man bellied up to the bar and hunched over a sweating pint glass.

In the standing room only space, he took up a small space at the far corner. Young hip baseball fans jostled around him not giving him a second thought except as an obstacle to a craft brew.

"Copy." Luke put the radio in his pocket.

The young man didn't move. Didn't look up at the jumbo screens airing the game. Didn't look at the pretty girls drinking and laughing around him. He looked at his glass.

Making a V around the bar, Luke studied Arazi from the opposite end. He looked dejected, sad.

Luke retraced his steps and approached Arazi from the rear, grateful the shoulder to shoulder crowd gave him some cover. Arazi was obviously waiting for him, but he still wanted the element of surprise.

The granite was cold under his palms as he planted them on the countertop and leaned in. The harried bartender bustled up and put a cocktail napkin in front of Luke.

"What would you like?"

"I'll have what he's having," said Luke.

Nasir's head came around. His eyes traveled the rest of the way to Luke's face.

Luke felt Arazi's eyes flicking over his features, comparing this new Luke to the one from his memory.

Nasir said nothing.

They let the roar of the game and the buzzing of the bar fill the space. The bartender brought Luke's beer, shooting a questioning look between the two stiff men before bustling off to his other customers.

"So this is what it's like. American ball games." Arazi looked away. He didn't yell over the din. He spoke in a normal tone. Luke had to lean in to hear him.

"No different than a soccer match." Luke too kept his voice normal so Nasir had no choice but to lean in.

"This is very different from a football match," Nasir said looking around the modern urban decor and the Denver skyline.

The kid seemed like he wanted to talk. Maisie's words rang in Luke's ears. He wanted to be heard.

Another bleeding jilted heart that craved to be understood. It was a special kind of hate that brought them together born from brokenness, not dogma. The kind that sacrifices any thought of survival to the completion of vengeance. Luke doubted Arazi meant to survive the day if he was here drinking a beer.

Luke obliged and took a swig of his beer. "Yeah, you're right. It's nothing like football. So you take the game I love to get back at me for killing your father."

Nasir looked up again, but not at Luke. Instead, he stared over Luke's shoulder at the mountains beyond the jumbotron. The strengthening sun on the last remaining flurries glimmered on the horizon.

Nasir gave a small laugh. "I've never seen snow. It never snowed in England, just rain. And it never snowed in Iraq, but you know that."

Luke felt his muscles flex as he tensed for what he knew he needed to do. He was going to have to put two in this kid's chest with the entire stadium watching.

Nasir continued. "My mother told me about it. She went to university in Switzerland. There she fell in love with the snow."

Something in Nasir's tone halted Luke's hand as it crept toward his waistband.

"She promised me she would take me to the mountains one day, but she never got the chance."

"Spare me the pious bullshit, Arazi. You come from a family with the blood of innocent people on their hands." It irritated Luke how reverently Nasir spoke of his family. "And now you're one too."

"My father was a murderer, yes. He was a bastard. And I suppose I am like him." Arazi straightened and looked Luke dead in the eyes. "And like you. You know what innocent blood on your hands feels like, don't you, Lieutenant Marshall?"

Nasir's hand flew to the counter making Luke tense and swing away. His hand was flat against the gun under his shirt.

But Nasir's hand went to his glass and he downed the rest of his drink. "You think she was reaching for a weapon, but she was not. She hated weapons. She was a gentle woman."

Luke shook his head. His mother? This was about his mother? No, that wasn't right.

Nasir kept talking. "She used to tell me, 'The world is cruel but we don't have to be. The weak hate when they are hated. The strong payback in love when they are hated'. She said it every time my father would beat us."

Arazi's face was an ugly scowl now. "She was bound to him against her will as I was. But you killed her like she was a dog."

"You're misremembering." As Luke said it, he wondered if he wasn't the one misremembering.

Nasir shook his head, his calm unnerving. "I lay on the floor beside where my father's rifle fell. She was reaching out for me, not a weapon."

"No," started Luke. There was a pistol beside her. She had reached for it. He remembered, the thought crystallizing in his memory. He saw the gun in her hand as he pulled the trigger. "No, that's not right."

"It's hard to hear that someone you hated was good, isn't it? I had to clean up what you left behind. I cleaned up my own mother's body."

Luke's eyes flew to Arazi's face. His irritated conscience finally calmed. Now he remembered. Ibrahim had sewn up Nasir's scalp in that bedroom. It was Ibrahim that told them about the pistol Amirah kept in her nightstand and the AK the elder Arazi kept under his mattress.

"No," Luke answered quietly. "You were sleeping twenty feet away in the corner." He held Nasir's gaze. "She reached for something, but as much as you want to believe it, she wasn't reaching for you."

Nasir's face twisted with rage. "You killed my mother," he screamed at the top of his lungs, all of his rage focused on Luke. His left hand moved to his right wrist. Luke saw it.

In a flash, Luke grabbed Arazi's right wrist twisting his hand backward. Arazi had no choice but to move to keep his elbow from breaking.

Smashing Arazi's wrist on the granite over and over, Luke finally felt glass crunch as the watch face shattered. Still holding the man's wrist, Luke planted a foot at the heel of Arazi's shoes, grabbed Arazi's jacket collar, and pulled hard. Arazi flipped backward, landing prone at Luke's feet.

Luke was on him. He needed to check his pockets for a secondary detonator, but Arazi recovered and started to fight back. Luke rained down blows on his face trying to take the fight out of him.

Luke cocked his fist back for the lights out blow, but his fist snagged behind his shoulder. Two bystanders had grabbed his arm and several more grabbed him around the shoulders dragging him off Arazi. As soon as his weight was off Arazi, the man leaped to his feet.

Instead of wasting his breath yelling at the do-gooders, Luke whirled and brought his arm up over his shoulder breaking their grip. He drew the USP from his belt and whirled to find Arazi. The crowd parted at the sight of his weapon.

Arazi was gone.

37

———————

Coors Field
Denver, Colorado
March 29
1157 Hours Local Time

Maisie followed Luke keeping his back in view as they made their way upward. At the top mezzanine, she watched Luke talk into his radio and sprint up the staircase to the fancy bar. All around her was constant movement.

She looked around. If Arazi was up there, the device had to be close. She spied a bank of vending machines nestled beside a popup Rockies merchandise store. They were a hundred yards back the other way.

"Good a place as any," she muttered to herself as she jogged to them.

Seven machines stood in a row, with an ice cream machine at the end. Maisie stuck her fingers in behind the first one and yanked as hard as she could. The heavy machine barely moved.

Maisie planted a foot on the wall behind it ignoring the looks it drew as she muscled the vending machine out. By the time she scooted all seven away from the wall, she was sweating despite the cold air. They were all heavy, and none bore signs of tampering.

She moved down the concourse in the direction Luke disappeared looking for more. As she passed a set of large bathrooms, booing broke out in the packed stadium. A stiff breeze whipped her hair.

On her right was a veranda, a short corridor cut into the outside wall ending at a tall metal railing. Beyond it, she saw the skyline. Picnic tables filled the area, crowded with fans seeking shelter from the snow. Families with children made up most of them.

Maisie skidded to a stop when she saw ten vending machines on each side of the veranda. She cursed. It was going to take a lot of time to yank them all out and check each one. Maneuvering her way through the crowd and into the veranda, she spied an 'out of order' sign on an end unit. She ran to it.

Planting her foot in the wall she pushed with all her might. This time it did not resist. The vending machine slid out so easily it nearly hit a woman walking by. Maisie stumbled back not expecting the machine to yield so easily. She slid in behind it and pushed her back into the wall.

The soda machine had a sheet of aluminum for backing, but it was bent outward in the middle as though something was pushing it from the inside. The bolts holding in the corners were black, not the silver she had seen on the others. It had been tampered with.

Nearby a radio squawked. She stepped out from behind the machine and saw several security guards run by. Marshall must have found his man.

She cursed out loud as she watched them run off. If this thing was radio detonated, even the signal from their radios could blow it.

But that was true of any cell phone. She scanned the crowd around her. Sure enough, they all had their phones out. Judging from the looks of frustration, and a few dozen people holding their phones up for a better signal, it looked like the cell networks had been shut down. It might buy some time.

She ran back out to the main concourse, putting some distance between her and the bomb so she could make a call and get EOD started. She ran headfirst into a uniformed DPD officer making his way toward the bar and whatever ruckus Luke had caused. He looked young and fit.

Maisie grabbed his arm to stop him. "Officer, I need you."

He skipped to a stop at her demanding tone and her hand on his arm. "Not now, I...."

I need your help," Maisie said. When he looked like he was about to shake her off, she said, "I found the bomb."

His eyes got wide. "You found the...it?"

She nodded, her voice steady as she gave him orders. "Listen, I need you to check on the status of EOD. I need them up here now."

He shook his head. "EOD is still fifteen minutes out, ma'am. They were deployed downtown. They're on their way."

"I don't think we have fifteen minutes, Officer. Get on the radio, and give them our location, then turn the damn thing off. Until they get here, you and me are going to work on this thing." She pointed to it.

He nodded and followed her into the veranda. "You can disarm it?"

"Fuck, no. But we gotta make it clean." Maisie positioned herself to push and pointed to the front for the Officer to pull. "You take that side. Push."

They turned the machine until the backside was

exposed. Maisie snapped open a small pocket knife and went to work on the top bolt. The knife tip snapped off, but she kept digging at the bolt until it bit. The screw backed out easily. The one below it was crooked and didn't yield so easily.

"Here, use this." The officer produced a metal Leatherman utility tool from his belt.

She took it and went back to work. When she got the second screw loose she grabbed the thick sheet metal and pulled. The officer joined in and they bent the thin metal back to reveal the innards of the machine.

Maisie sucked in a breath. Beside her, the officer swore out loud.

A rat's nest of wires led out from two large metal canisters and two opaque five-gallon buckets, one filled with blue liquid, the other with clear liquid. All the wires ran to a small metal box. On top was a hard plastic container.

There was no watch, clock, or timing device that she could see, but the device was jammed in tightly, barely fitting in the space and she couldn't see behind. She tugged on the plastic box. It had to be holding the U. It didn't budge. It was bolted to the top of the bomb.

Reaching behind it she felt around gingerly. Her fingers ran over a cheap flip cell phone and a small walkie-talkie. Feeling a little more, she realized that each was wired into the bomb. She prayed Luke had the good sense not to let Arazi push any buttons.

Behind her, Maisie heard a soft "fuck." She looked back.

Sweat had begun to bead on the officer's upper lip. The snap of wood on leather clapped over the loudspeaker. The crowd roared and the organ blared. Nearby on the picnic table, several children squealed in laughter.

The world went on. The officer looked back at the field with a glazed look. The surreal scene seemed to throw him.

"Hey, you still with me?" She faced him and put a hand on his shoulder.

He swallowed and nodded, his eyes once again darting from her to the bomb. She could see him physically struggling to figure out how she was so calm. She didn't know either, but panicking had never gotten her out of a tight spot.

"We found it before it went off, okay? We're not doing so bad. The only way out of this shit is through it. Okay? You good?"

He blinked hard and cracked his knuckles. "Yeah. Let's do this."

"Good. Go find a trash can."

"A trash can?"

"With wheels. The uranium is heavy as shit. Trust me. Go."

He ran off.

Maisie turned back to the device and studied it closer. All of the other components were liquid. Ivanov's bomb was more advanced tech than a low-brow fertilizer bomb. More powerful. Built for one purpose.

Everything was secured inside the machine with screws making sure the components couldn't be easily separated. The plastic case sat on top, padlocked. By process of elimination, she knew the U must be in the box on top. She didn't need to open it, just get it loose.

Running her hands around it she located two bolts on opposite sides of the box. Carefully, she went in with the screwdriver and started backing them out. A few moments later she had the first one out.

"Should have hidden your screws, dumbass," she muttered. "You been cutting some corners."

The next bolt was hard to reach. She had to stretch to reach toward the back of the device.

She heard a clatter behind her as she struggled with the last bolt. Now she was breaking a sweat as time seemed to roll out endlessly. This was taking too long.

Finally, she felt the screw loosen. Pinching it, she unscrewed it all the way out. She turned to look at the officer pushing a large trash can on wheels. The look they exchanged was uneasy. Then she turned and placed her hands on either side of the box and pulled.

It yielded under her hand.

"Oh my god," he said.

Exhaling loudly Maisie turned, struggling with the weight of the box, and walked to him. The trash can was half full of napkins and wrappers. She heaved the box in.

The officer jumped at the sight of the U being chucked into the trash can. It landed on the garbage compressing it.

"Fuck," he said softly. "Is that it?"

"What's your name?"

"Dan," he said, still gazing at the uranium.

"That's the football, Dan. Time for you to go."

"What do I do with it?"

"Get it as far away as you can. As fast as you can. If anybody tries to stop you, you shoot them. And don't tell anyone what you have until you get it to EOD."

He nodded and turned, pushing the trash can in front of him.

"Dan," said Maisie. "Stay away from elevators. Good luck."

At her soft tone, he looked up and she smiled at him.

With a glance at the bomb remaining behind Maisie, he turned and broke into a run with the trash can in front.

Elevators.

She looked back the way she'd come. The elevator. She'd passed one not far back. Without EOD, she had no way to render this bomb safe, but an elevator shaft might contain the explosion.

She studied the crowd for a way back to the elevator. A man in a Rockies jersey was frozen to the spot looking past her at the bomb inside the vending machine.

"Time to go home," she said to him.

He didn't hesitate. He scooped up two school-aged children and took off running. Which in turn made others look. A few took off running and a few stood rooted to the concrete.

Ignoring them, she placed her shoulder against the side and pushed with all her might.

The thick feet caught on the rough cement making the machine tip precariously. She gave up pushing and grabbed two corners rocking it back and forth to move it forward. It was maddeningly slow progress and she could hear the liquid inside slashing back and forth, but she kept going.

Around her, panic started to build. Yelling and a few screams mingled with the bumping music playing between batters. Panic was spreading fast through the crowd around her. The guts of the bomb in the vending machine were on full display as she wrestled it out of the veranda. Maisie let them decide what to do with the information and focused on her task.

She looked up gauging the distance to the elevator. It was at least fifty feet away. That the bomb hadn't gone off yet was a miracle. She didn't have time.

Looking the other way, she spotted the men's restroom ten feet away. The wide door left plenty of room to get the machine through. That would have to do. Changing direction she started pulling toward the men's restroom entrance. Sweat dripped into her eyes, but she kept going.

By the time she made it to the bathroom entrance, the crowd around her had thinned, the panic quickly spreading.

Still, the sounds of baseball echoed over the loudspeaker. Only her little corner knew what was happening, but not for long. She pulled harder.

The concrete grew smoother as she waddled the unwieldy machine inside the bathroom. Maisie went to the other side and shoved it hard. It banged to a stop by the bank of urinals on the back wall. A soda machine being pulled into a restroom caught two guys off guard midstream.

"Get out," she yelled at them. They stood frozen, unsure if they should help the woman moving a soda machine into the bathroom or call security on a crazy person.

"Ma'am are you...."

"Get out," she snapped at them.

The man closest caught sight of the contents inside.

"Get out of the stadium." She said calmly. They obeyed instantly, zipping up their pants and leaving.

Maisie faced the bomb. She took a deep breath and let it out slowly. The city was safe. Only the people in the concourse and the sections directly below the first baseline were in danger. This bomb would rip through concrete supports and rebar. Maybe collapse a level or two. But that was a victory.

She didn't have a prayer at diffusing this bomb and EOD was going to be too late. Turning her back on the bomb, she headed out. Starting an evacuation attempt might save a few lives.

Maisie turned and headed out the door. As she reached it, a high-pitched beeping sounded behind her. Maisie threw herself around the corner and tucked next to a concrete beam.

Then everything went black.

38

———

The men around Luke parted at the sight of a gun. He'd lost sight of Arazi.

Behind the bar, a disheveled bartender pulled herself to her feet. Her hair flopped over her face, and her right cheek was swelling. When she pulled her hair back from her face, Luke saw her fear. He headed to her.

"Which way did he go?"

The woman started sobbing when she saw Luke looming over her with a gun.

"Which way did he go?" Luke roared at her.

She pointed down a narrow alley behind the bar stacked with metal kegs. It led to a storeroom.

Luke didn't wait for her to say anything else. He leaped over the bar and pushed past her sprinting toward the door.

He shouldered through it and brought his gun up as soon as he crossed the threshold. It was a large pantry stacked with more kegs and lined with wire racks loaded down with condiments and canned ingredients.

On the other side was another door with the jamb splintered and the knob hanging loose. It had been kicked open.

Luke could see a light coming from inside. He ran to it and pressed his back to the wall beside the door listening. All he could hear was the commotion his presence just caused in the bar.

Pivoting, he nudged the door open with his foot and drove in muzzle first. It was a small closet that contained a welded metal ladder leading to an open hatch on the ceiling. Luke holstered and climbed the ladder. At the top, he peeked through the hatch.

A short distance across the flat roof led to another ladder up a steeply pitched roof. At the top of that ladder, a narrow catwalk curved back toward home base. The catwalk ran through the girders of the main concourse roof. The highest point in the stadium.

It was designed for one purpose; access to the massive light arrays perched on six pairs of thirty-six-inch thick metal poles with metal support girders zigzagging between them. It also gave line of sight to the wide concourse below.

Cold metal burned Luke's palms as he hoisted himself up. In a crouch, he ran over the roof and scaled the ladder to the catwalk. Pulling himself onto the catwalk he knelt to take a look.

Nowhere to hide up here. The skyline of the city lay on one side and the mountains on the other. Beneath him, the green diamond fanned out.

The sun had come out, but the massive awning above shaded him. Shadows cut in every direction across the catwalk.

Luke took a few steps and realized he'd been wrong. There were places to hide.

At every access to a light pole sat a large metal box painted the same color as the catwalk and girders. They were big enough to conceal a large man. He drew his gun.

In a slow jog, Luke advanced down the catwalk clearing each box as he passed. When he reached the third spur, he heard screams below and looked down at the concourse. A secondary roof covered an alcove below him, and he saw people run from it screaming. The panicked crowd flowed into the main concourse and joined the growing exodus from the bar.

It was too far away from the Rooftop. They wouldn't have seen his fight with Arazi. She must have found it.

A clink and a flash on his left came too quick for him to react. From the corner of his eye, he saw a head come from the nearest electrical box. Arazi appeared with his arm raised over his head.

Shifting his weight to his left leg, Luke sidestepped the blade Arazi drove toward his chest. He braced for the pain, knowing he couldn't get completely out of the path of the blade.

Arazi drove a steak knife from the bar into the hollow of Luke's right shoulder. His strong arm went limp and the gun clinked on the metal grating and spun away.

But his left arm worked fine. He brought it around and wrapped it around Arazi's throat in a crushing hold. They fell onto the catwalk grating. Luke tried to get his legs around Arazi to control him, but he misjudged the strength of his opponent.

Arazi twisted the knife still in Luke's shoulder making Luke yell in agony and release him.

Arazi pushed up on his elbow and started squirming. Luke reared back his head and pitched it forward, the thickest part of his skull connecting with Arazi's nose. He heard a crack, then a gurgle as blood from Arazi's broken nose ran down the back of his throat.

Nasir's hands flew to his face.

Luke wrapped his arms around the man's chest and flipped onto his back, pulling Arazi on top. Arazi's back now pushed into his chest.

With one hand, Luke patted his jacket pockets. Nothing. He patted Arazi's jeans pockets. There was something hard in his left pants pocket. The size of a two-way radio.

Luke locked his legs around Arazi's ankles, but Arazi threw his head around and connected with the knife still sticking out of Luke's shoulder. Luke flinched from the pain and Arazi threw his arms out breaking Luke's hold. A hard buck and Arazi broke free of Luke's grip and rolled away.

Slowly, Luke pulled himself to his feet using the railing of the catwalk. He gritted his teeth and yanked the knife out of his pec muscle. He looked around for his gun. Five feet behind him. Then he looked for Arazi.

Nasir stood ten feet away, blood streaming over his mouth and dripping from his chin. He looked unsteady, clutching the hand railing.

They stared at each other for an eternity. The wind whipped around them, small leftover granules of snow stinging their skin. Neither of them felt it.

Luke's right side felt like it was on fire and he couldn't stop his arm from trembling as he watched Nasir who stood with his hand posed over his right pocket. He seemed frozen, which tempted Luke into the same inaction.

Fuck that.

He turned and launched himself five feet to his gun with his good arm stretched out. His fingers curled around the grip and Luke flipped onto his back and spread his legs. He aimed through his knees.

Arazi's hand had made it into his pocket.

Luke pulled the trigger.

The catwalk surged beneath him like a wave tossing him

onto his side. Milliseconds later, a deafening boom hit them followed immediately by the blast concussion.

He felt the metal under him buck and he blacked out. A moment later he opened his eyes and tried to lift his head. It felt fuzzy and his ears rang so loud everything else seemed silent.

Fighting the fog, he tried to figure out how long he'd been out. Fifteen feet away he saw the lump of a body lying on the walk grating, ashen from the fine cement dust now swirling in the air the way the snow had moments before.

Luke pulled himself up relying heavily on the warped railing. He clung to it as he made his way to Arazi. He couldn't have been out for long. His hand still clutched his gun.

As he approached, Nasir didn't move, but his eyes tracked Luke.

The blood on his face mingled with cement dust into a dark gray. His shirt had the same dark gray and red stain in the center of his chest.

Blood bubbled from the corner of Arazi's mouth as he tried to smile, but it was more of a grimace.

Luke couldn't reach his holster with his good hand, so he tucked his gun into the small of his back. He ran his fingers along his belt line hoping it was still there.

A finger brushed over the personal radiation detector Romero had given him. He pulled it off and looked at it.

Air rushed from his lungs and he threw his head back panting. He wanted to laugh, but he couldn't so he settled for looking up at the hazy swirl carried by the wind. A column of concrete dust rose above the stadium.

That crazy bitch did it. She actually did it.

He checked the screen again to make sure. It was the same. The radiation levels around him were normal. No uranium had been disbursed by the bomb. He looked down to see if Arazi was still alive. Arazi was fading, unable to speak.

Luke knelt next to Nasir who had started to convulse and held the display so he could see it.

"The air is clean. You lose, motherfucker."

Then he stood and tossed the PRD onto Arazi's chest as the young man's eyes began to close.

Luke turned and walked away.

The catwalk spun and he reached for the rail to hold himself upright as he shook his head.

Where was she?

The thought ran through his head as he moved down the catwalk. There was something he was forgetting in his blast-addled brain. *Where was she?*

He half climbed, half fell down the short access ladder to the roof of the bar. Picking his way carefully over brick and chunks of concrete, he headed back to the storeroom. Luke's head felt clearer by the second; his brain rebooting after being hit by the concussion.

Halfway down the roof access ladder, his right arm failed. He fell to the floor and didn't move for a minute.

Where was she? Why did it matter, she was probably dead.

The dark storeroom came into focus through the door. Dust swirled around the corners and everything in the room looked like it had been shaken in a snow globe. The stacks of kegs rolled on the floor and jars of food lay smashed everywhere. By now the ringing in his ears had muted enough to hear. He heard no one. No screaming. No yelling. Only sirens in the distance.

Luke sat bolt upright. The alcove. People had fled that area before Arazi detonated the device. That's where she was.

Using the ladder, and his good arm, he pulled himself to

his feet. He couldn't stop a groan when his right side flared with pain, but he kept going.

Down the hall he stopped on the main floor of The Rooftop Bar. Glass lay everywhere, interspersed with chunks of concrete and blown lights hanging from the ceiling. The big jumbo televisions behind the bar were shattered. One hung off the wall. It looked like a war zone.

He began picking his way through the wasteland. Most of the customers were smart enough to get the hell out while the getting was good. He didn't see any bodies.

Then, fifty feet later he saw the first one. A lump of gray chalky dust lay still next to the railing that overlooked the field. Thirty feet later he saw another. Then another.

Luke could feel his throat swell as he looked at the citizens of his hometown lying dead or injured. Some were still, some were groaning. Hot tears cut tracks in the thick dust that covered his face, but he passed them by. Help for them would be here soon. There was something he had to do.

She wore a brown jacket. He searched for anything that looked like a woman wearing a brown leather jacket.

Luke knew he was close to the blast zone when the holes in the floor and gaps in the wall grew larger. Here the dust was so thick it choked him and blotted out the sunlight. He pulled his shirt up to cover his nose and mouth.

Fifty feet from the elevator, a large chunk of the floor had broken off and fell to the level below. Luke picked his way along the remaining narrow ledge of concrete to the other side of the gaping hole.

"Maisie," he yelled into the dim swirling light. "Maisie."

Nothing. Luke pushed ahead peering through the thickness looking for any sign of blood or clothing or movement on the ground.

By the men's bathroom, a pillar had collapsed. The top portion still clung precariously to the ceiling. He pushed himself against the wall as he went under in case it collapsed.

Occupied with the cement stalactite above him, he tripped over a soft rubbery object. It felt very different from the hard, unyielding rubble he'd been walking over. He looked down.

It was a foot. A small foot wearing a black boot, and a leg in denim. The leg stuck out from underneath a chunk of concrete the size of a car door. It was her. She'd been within the blast zone when the bomb went off. It wasn't looking good for Maisie Sheppard.

Luke fell to his knees and started digging. His fingers left blood trails as he cleared the smaller pieces of concrete to reach the edge of the large one.

Luke straddled the leg and grasped the edge of the concrete with both hands. Gritting his teeth against the pain, he squatted and pulled up as he straightened his legs. Fire ripped through his shoulder and he yelled with pain and effort as he slowly shifted the heavy piece over and dropped it.

When she was clear, he fell to his knees beside her. He brushed the tangle of gray matted hair back from her face and leaned over her.

A small puff of ash blew out from her nose. She was breathing. Then Maisie stirred.

"You're alive," he said, almost laughing with relief.

She groaned softly. It was answer enough.

With his good hand, Luke reached underneath her neck and pulled her up until she rested against his chest. She cried out in pain then coughed and collapsed against him.

"We have to go, Maisie," whispered Luke.

He braced his shoulder under her armpit and rose to his feet pulling her up with him. She cried out in pain, as he slung her arm across his neck and wrapped his good arm around her waist.

Next to her, Luke could feel her trying valiantly to stay on her feet. Every few seconds, she lost control of her head and it slumped forward. Together they stumbled down the ruined concourse toward the sound of approaching sirens.

39

Honey Spot Motor Lodge
Idaho Springs, Colorado
March 29
1500 Hours Local Time

Maisie curled into a fetal position on the cold, chipped ceramic. The shower was as hot as she could get it with hands that could barely make a fist. Still, it soothed the raging pain. Inside and outside of her body, there was nothing that didn't hurt.

She'd barely managed to get her clothes off before she ended up on the floor of the grimy tub with a hand over the edge, the gold locket clutched away from the water. She couldn't move enough to wash herself. She lay under the shower until the water stopped running gray and red.

Everything faded to darkness.

Warm. She felt warmth. The dampness of her hair contrasted with her warm, dry body. Maisie stirred and tried to rise to one shoulder, but she couldn't move.

With a massive effort, she opened her eyes. She blinked and the room swam into view. It was dark, then red, then dark. She batted her sticky eyes trying to clear them. The room went red again.

Maisie managed to shift her head to the left. Outside a large window, a blinking neon sign lit the dark room red every few seconds. It came through a narrow part in the curtains over the window. Then it was dark again.

It was night? She must have blacked out. She tried to speak but ended up slurring something even her brain couldn't understand. Why was her tongue swollen?

She tried to move again and realized her body was wrapped up in scratchy sheets and a bedspread that smelled like disinfectant.

Movement by the window caught her attention and she squinted into the darkness.

A shadowy figure rose from a chair. In vain Maisie struggled to get her uncooperative body free of the bedspread as the figure approached her.

"Maisie." A strong arm snaked under her shoulders and took the pressure of the aching arm holding her up.

"Marsh...," she croaked the word out. Her mouth wouldn't cooperate.

"Shhh. It's alright. Drink this."

A plastic cup touched her lips and she tasted chlorinated water. It was the best thing she'd tasted in her life. She slurped at it, but the cup tipped back stopping the flow.

"Not too much."

She swallowed. Her throat hurt less. "More," she whispered.

The cup touched her lips again and she took a satisfying gulp before he could tip it back.

"Easy. You don't want to get sick." He set the plastic cup down as the red light lit up the room.

She saw his face. Worried. He was worried about her.

She was worried about her too. The desire to speak overwhelmed her, but it hurt too much to talk. Instead, a tear trickled down her face.

Exhausted from the small amount of effort, Maisie fell back onto the arm holding her up.

The creaky bed shook as Marshall crawled over her and lay down beside her. With a groan, he pulled her toward him and settled her in the crook of his arm.

The pain eased a little. Maisie's forehead lolled against his neck and the red light didn't blink again.

Luke rested his right elbow on the armrest, as he guided the SUV down the interstate with the left. Even though his left side was uninjured, it was stiff after spending the entire night at the motel cradling a severely wounded Maisie.

All night it felt like she was fading. He'd held onto her and willed it not to happen. Miraculously at first light, she was still breathing. And now she stirred in the passenger seat of the black Tahoe as they wound through the craggy mountain passes.

Luke looked over at her. Maisie opened her eyes and immediately slammed them shut, blinded by the sun streaming through the windshield. She was coming to. This crazy son of a bitch was tough.

With her eyes shut, she turned her face toward the sun like she was savoring the heat. She shifted and groaned.

She was as comfortable as he could make her. The seat was back and he'd wrapped her and cushioned her with blankets and pillows stolen from the hotel. To keep her warm, the heat was up so high he had started to sweat.

Luke knew the pain must be vicious. He was no doctor, but he'd seen his share of internal hemorrhaging from damaged organs. If she didn't get to a doctor soon, she was done. She'd been incoherent for the last twelve hours, slipping in and out of consciousness, but she hung on with the same tenacity and fierceness he'd seen before.

Gradually Maisie began to blink, slowly letting her eyes adjust to the brightness. A confused look screwed up her face as she took in the Tahoe and the rust-colored mountain walls passing by.

Her eyes flicked to him. Luke tucked his injured arm in trying to make it look like it didn't hurt but winced.

"You're hurt." Maisie's voice was hoarse. She cleared her throat.

"Hey, sleepyhead," Luke kept his voice light. "I'm fine."

Maisie took a ragged breath. "It's not fine. Why are you doing this? You'll get in...." She pushed up on one elbow and almost screamed when the pain hit. She forced it into a strangled groan and fell back on the seat.

A moment later he heard whirring and her seat back started moving upright. He couldn't stop an amused smile as she slowly sat upright taking short breaks to breathe through the pain.

Finally, she made it to a mostly upright position before deciding it was far enough. "Where are we?" She looked out the window.

"On our way," said Luke.

She looked confused. "To where?"

"The airport."

"No. I can't...." She raised her hands and covered her face. "Luke, I can't go to the airport. You shouldn't be helping me."

"I'm taking you to Vail," said Luke.

"They can arrest me as easily there as in Denver," she said softly. "But thank you."

It surprised Luke how much he enjoyed giving her good news. He drew it out to savor it. He turned to her with a sly grin on his face. "Turns out you have a guardian angel."

"What?" She challenged him. Something like hope spread across her bruised face.

"And nobody knows where we are. There is a jet coming for you."

Her eyes brimmed with tears and she blinked them back. Her voice wavered when she spoke. "How did you find him?"

"I didn't. He found us." Luke adjusted his arm back to the armrest. "I got a phone call on the motel room landline four hours ago. That's a hell of a friend you've got."

"He's not my friend," Maisie said, struggling to straighten again. She seemed infused with strength at the news. "He's the only family I have."

"Then take care of him. He'll be in the crosshairs if it's known he helped you. Trust me, when you have so few people on your side, it's important to look after them."

Maisie rested her head against the headrest, the fire rekindled in her eyes. "I will."

Luke turned his attention back to the slushy road thinking the conversation was over. A soft touch on his aching arm made him look down, then over at Maisie.

She ran her finger down his tattoo. The small movement exhausted her and her hand stopped moving, resting on his forearm. She kept looking at him.

Luke held her gaze for as long as he could before looking back at the road.

"He was wrong you know," said Maisie.

"What?" The question caught him off guard and he wondered how hard she had hit her head.

"It was just an illusion."

"Sorry?"

"Ferdinand." The tap on his forearm was so light he

barely felt it. "The spirits that Prospero conjured to scare them onto the island weren't demons. Everyone on the ship thought they were real, but it was just a parlor trick."

"Oh," said Luke realizing she meant the quote he'd had inscribed on his body after he left Savannah. "Well, yes and no. The real devils were the people Ferdinand was with. Men that he loved and respected."

He looked at Maisie's drawn face. "Including his own father. They unjustly put Prospero there in the first place, out of jealousy. Ferdinand wasn't wrong about bad guys, he was only wrong about who the demons really were."

She looked away and studied the rock formation passing by. "Is it possible to forgive them?"

Luke didn't answer right away. It felt like she could see inside his soul.

"When someone you love betrays you, does it ever stop hurting enough to forgive them?" She was looking at him again.

Luke gave her side eye. "What do you mean?"

"All those articles barely mentioned her, like she was nothing. But they said enough. You loved her, didn't you? I know that's why you did what you did. Why else would you do such dumb shit?"

She laughed then gasped in pain. "There are some things so stupid, only love could make us do them."

For the first time since he left Savannah with vengeance in his heart, he felt seen. Like someone understood. Even Frank, completely read into the events in Georgia, never really grasped what Luke had lost. Blinded by his own prejudice, he had deeply misjudged this woman. They were made of the same stuff.

"Is it possible to forgive them?" She turned to look out the window again like she didn't want to look at him when he answered.

They drove in silence for a long time.

"No," he said finally. "You can't.

Luke saw her swallow the lump in her throat. "But it does get better. It just…kind of becomes part of you. You get so used to it that, if it went away, it would feel like something is missing. It's a piss poor excuse for relief, but it's something."

Maisie nodded and pushed the blanket down to her waist. She slipped the gold chain from around her neck and held it out. "Here."

"What is that?" Luke asked.

"The coordinates to the remaining uranium. I found them under the photo after I confronted Bressler."

Luke hesitated then reached out to take the locket.

"The file is gone," she said softly, her face pale and drawn. "I burned it. Dad signed the shipping manifest. He was there. So was Adrian."

"I'm sorry," was all Luke said.

"Adrian just did what Dad told him to."

"It's not your fault, Maisie."

"I know. But I was stupid enough to think my father was innocent. I believed it so much that I was willing to sell out everything I believed in. Now I'm a bad guy too. That *is* my fault."

"You already answered that. Love makes us fools." Luke glanced over. "Adrian's body left for DC yesterday. They're going to bury him with honors."

Holding the steering wheel with his knee, Luke opened the locket and a small strip of folded paper fell into his hand. He straightened it. "Somewhere in the fly-over states. Maybe Oklahoma."

"I had it all this time," she said bitterly. "And I had no idea."

Luke tucked the paper into his chest pocket and closed the locket offering it back to her.

She shook her head. "I don't want it."

Luke stashed it in his pocket. She might feel differently one day. "It's better that way, Maisie. Romero would have killed you on the spot if he'd known."

"Maybe that would have been better."

"No it wouldn't," he said with conviction. "I'm sorry I gave you such a hard time. You weren't the only one with blinders on."

"I know." Maisie smiled sadly at him. "I misjudged you too. You're not a boy scout." She groaned as she readjusted in her seat.

"No, you were right about that." Luke put his blinker on and changed lanes. "I follow the rules. It's why I'm so frustrated all the time."

Maisie laughed softly then groaned again.

Luke looked over at her. "Maybe I should be a little more like you."

"That's a fucking terrible idea."

"I'll tell them what you did." He patted his pocket. "It might make a difference."

"Yeah, life in prison instead of the needle." She shook her head. "I don't know. I guess...I guess I just wanted you to know I'm not a completely terrible person."

"There was probably a better way to do that, you know," Luke teased her.

She smiled sadly. "I got tunnel vision. I was just so...sure that I couldn't see the obvious."

"You're not a fool, Maisie."

Luke's harsh tone caught her off guard. Her eyes got big.

"It's impossible for your enemies to betray you, Maisie. By definition, betrayal has to come from someone you trust.

It's impossible to see it coming. You are not the fool," he finished.

Their eyes met and she gave him a weak smile. He glanced back to the road more quickly than he needed to.

"What will you do now?" She asked him.

"Maybe teach surfing." Luke grinned.

Maisie pressed her eyes shut for a moment. "Luke, I know who tipped off Ivanov. Adrian was in on it, but it wasn't him. I know who set us up."

Luke looked over at her, all pleasantness gone.

"I'll tell you, but you have to wait for me to heal."

"Tell me now." His face was stone.

"You're not the only one who mourned Tommy. I've got unfinished business of my own with him and you're going to need a cover. They're already going to charge me with Adrian's murder. Another one on my head won't make any difference."

"This isn't up for discuss...."

"You're damn straight it's not up for discussion. I'm not arguing with you. I won't even tell you until I'm mobile again."

Luke clenched his jaw several times, letting the flare of anger die. She had a right to claim vengeance too. Maybe more than he did.

"Fine. We'll do it together."

An hour later the black Tahoe pulled into a small airport. The single metal-sided building bore a sign that said, 'Vail Regional Airport'. Below it was another sign that announced, 'arrivals/departures'.

Luke drove past the building and out onto the single runway. He pulled to a stop and threw the SUV in park as a silver Gulfstream 350 taxied down the runway. He hopped out and crossed to the passenger side.

Maisie leaned heavily on Luke as he helped her out.

They walked to the front of the vehicle. He tucked the bedspread tighter around her as the mountain wind whipped up.

Together they watched the jet reach the end of the runway and turn around. It rolled to a stop in front of them.

The gangway lowered smoothly to the ground and a beast of a man walked into the brisk cloudless morning. As soon as his eyes landed on Maisie, his face lit up. The look tempered somewhat when he saw the sorry state she was in.

He rushed down the stairs and over to her, eyeing Luke suspiciously.

"Hi, Timo," Maisie said weakly.

In the jet door, Luke saw a thin man walk out leaning heavily on forearm crutches. He surveyed them but did not brave the stairs.

Without a word to Luke, Timo wrapped his arm around Maisie and guided her gently toward the plane. At the bottom of the stairs, she twisted to look once more at Luke leaning casually against the hood of the Tahoe.

Luke lifted his hand to his ears, his thumb and pinky finger extended. "Call me," he mouthed.

She grinned at him. Her rich reclusive friend would get her patched up, then she would.

Luke knew he would be talking to Maisie Sheppard again. He found himself looking forward to it.

40

———

3297 Inglewood Court
Potomac, Maryland
July 14
2245 Hours Local Time

Ralph Fienne took the first sip of the fifty-year-old scotch and sighed. It was as good as promised by the contractor who gave it to him. One of the little joys of the job. A small one, but greatly appreciated.

He needed it. Lately, the job came with plenty of headaches.

As Secretary of Energy, he'd endured intense scrutiny since that bomb went off in Denver almost three months before.

When the uranium signature was identified as coming from the Orchid Project, he'd received an uncomfortable amount of personal scrutiny. He was personally involved as a senior agent at the time, and now he found himself dodging bullets like it was his job.

How much he was involved, they had no idea, and it would stay that way. But the carpetbaggers were calling for his head and he'd worked overtime convincing them he was just as confounded as they were. The investigating Congressional Committee was full of red state hillbillies and they weren't buying it.

He'd considered scattering a trail of breadcrumbs leading to Adrian Romero, but that would reveal too much. Especially with Charles' daughter knowing the truth and running amuck. If his sources were reliable, she'd gotten her hands on that file and killed Adrian. What a pain in the ass she grew up to be.

Fienne eventually decided to tear a page out of the Secretary of State's playbook. Deny the whole thing and make counter accusations until the unwashed masses got worked up over the next news headline. A time-tested classic.

So far it worked beautifully. The hearings had ended, and he was headed to the Hamptons for the next month. He leaned back in his walnut paneled office and took another sip feeling sleepy.

A round of golf with some private investors and the scotch had worn him out. His lady friend would be here soon too. He needed to keep up some energy. She always set his head straight.

The wifey had been at the Hampton's house for two weeks already giving him unfettered access to his mistress.

She wasn't staying the night though. It was time to put his toes in the sand and plan a few upcoming lucrative investment opportunities.

Ralph Fienne sank into the plush leather chair behind his library desk. The only light on in the office was the antique lamp on his desk. Soothing, quiet and insulated, the perfect recipe to recharge for his flight tomorrow. He leaned his head back and closed his eyes.

They flew open when he heard a rustle come from the

shadows in the corner by the built-ins. The family Corgi was in New York with his wife.

"Antonio? Is that you? I told you I didn't want...."

A figure emerged from the shadow and walked into the halo of lamplight. His glass thudded on the desktop.

"You." Scotch and spit flew from Ralph Fienne's lips as he recognized the woman.

"Hello, Secretary Fienne. I hope you're having a relaxing evening," said Maisie.

Panicked, Fienne looked past the woman clad head to toe in black tactical clothing to the open library door.

She shook her head. "Your security guards aren't coming, Ralphie. They're indisposed."

He drew himself up in the chair, indignant. "What are you doing here, young lady?"

"You know why I'm here."

"If everything I've been told about you is correct, you should be in handcuffs."

"Everything you've heard about me is correct," she answered. "Every. Last. Detail. Even the grapevine rumors are true. I found the file, Ralph."

He noticed a limp as she walked toward him. She sat on his desk and swung her leg up to rest on the desktop. Fienne mastered himself quickly like a true professional.

"Then you know exactly what happened and how your father masterminded everything. How dare you come into my house."

"I'm here because there was one name *not* in that file."

"What are you talking about?" Fienne managed to sound indignant despite his fear.

"You haven't heard everything about me, Mr. Fienne. And that is what's going to kill you."

"You're going to kill me? Charles Sheppard's daughter is going to kill me?" Fienne laughed, then his face turned into a nasty sneer. "Why would you kill me? I'm not a Russian spy."

She leaned in and studied him, her smile unnerving. "No," she said. "You're right. I'm just here to ask the questions."

She picked up his forgotten glass and sniffed it. She took a sip. "Um. That's good stuff."

"What questions?"

Maisie put the glass down. "You knew we were in Kiev. Why did you sell us to Ivanov? Why did you care if we found Ivanov or not? You knew he didn't have the U."

"I don't know what you're...."

Maisie dropped her leg and rounded the desk. She backhanded Ralph across the face.

He put his hand over his stinging cheek and gazed at her in horror.

She put a hand on either side of his chair and leaned in. "You sold us out to Ivanov. A good man is dead because of what you did," she said, each word slow and deliberate. "And I'll take a finger every time you try to tell me you 'don't know what I'm talking about'." She mimicked a whine.

Fienne decided it was time for some damage control. "Agent Romero got sidetracked. He was supposed to control you, not get seduced by you. Darn it, he got distracted. He needed a swift kick in the butt."

Maisie cocked her head. "You've got blood on your hands, Fienne, I think you're in the clear to cuss. At least in private."

"Fuck you," he hissed.

"That's more like it," she said, straightening.

"So, what do you want? Money? If you know where the uranium is, I can make you a rich woman."

"You think money can buy a woman like me?"

"Immunity then? I can get it for you. You can get your life back."

Maisie paused and thought. "What do you know about Senator Henry Onessa?"

Fienne's eyebrows shot up at her question. "Henry? What about him?"

"He's very popular with all the right people. I know you hobnob with the same crowd. Surely you have some dirt on him."

Fienne's eyes widened then flicked around the room as he tried to decide if information about Onessa would save his life.

"Tiktok, Secretary."

"There's not much to tell, he's...wait, please. Wait..."

"Horseshit," spat Maisie as she moved to punch him again.

Fienne threw up his hands to shield his face. "Wait. Robert Dunn."

Maisie's hand dropped an inch. Enough to encourage Fienne to keep talking.

"He...he's a candidate for Congress, but he got his start in fundraising. It's how he made all his connections. He worked on Henry's senate campaign."

"What about him?"

"They're close. Very close. They play golf together all the time. It was Henry's endorsement that won him the primary."

"Hmm, sounds like Senator Onessa had a favor to repay."

"Yeah. Yeah, exactly. If you're looking for something on Henry, I guarantee Dunn will have something. Everyone in this town collects secrets. Even on their so-called friends. It's how you survive."

"Looks like you've made the right friends. I've made

some friends recently too, Ralphie. The difference is your friends make you rich, Ralph. They give you this awesome scotch when you play pickleball or whatever. This is awesome by the way." Maisie took another sip.

The old man's look of fear turned to annoyance. It turned into terror a second later.

Maisie put the glass down with a thunk.

"My friends don't make me rich. But they scare the hell out of fuckers like you. Which is priceless to the right people, if you think about it."

As she spoke, a man's form stepped into the light behind her. An imposing form. As the man stepped forward, Ralph recoiled.

"Oh, I see. Him you're afraid of." Maisie feigned annoyance.

Then her face turned up in a dark smile. "You're smarter than I thought." She stepped back and stood by the man who'd said nothing. He held his gun down by his side.

"My friends look out for each other, Ralph. And if someone fucks us over, we make sure the favor gets returned."

"What do you want? I'll give you anything."

"We want Tommy back, you son of a bitch. You're in debt for his life and we're here to collect."

"No...," the old man wailed as he curled into a ball.

"My father paid for his actions. So did Adrian. I'll spend the rest of my life on the run to pay for mine. But you? You sip five-hundred-dollar scotch in your imported library while stadiums blow up around you. There's no evidence you were directly involved in the Orchid theft. You're clean, Ralphie. You did it. You get off scot free."

Maisie walked back to the desk taking off her left glove. She picked up his glass and took another long sip making sure her fingertips made good contact with the glass. Then she set it down.

"Tonight you pay up."

Fienne looked desperately at the man. "But you're a war hero. You were a Federal Agent like me. Heroes don't do this. Please."

Maisie answered instead of Luke. "Amoral men don't define a hero. If anything, men like you turn heroes into the bad guy. Everyone in this room is going to hell. The difference is, we're going to sleep a lot better until we get there."

Ralph looked at Luke, fear twisting his face.

Luke's arm was no longer hanging at his side. It was raised in front of him holding a gun with a suppressor screwed into the barrel.

"Please...," Ralph begged. "I'm not a bad man."

"Yes, Secretary Fienne. Yes, you are," answered Maisie. "Say hello to my father."

Luke Marshall will return in *The Omega List.*

Maisie Sheppard will return in *Overkill.*

Reviews are critically important to authors. If you enjoyed this novel, please leave a quick review to share your experience with other readers. Thank you for reading and supporting independent authors.

About The Author

R. J. Strong is a veteran police officer and Crime Scene Investigator who married into a family of police officers. When she's not writing characters who do bad things for good reasons, she travels, lifts weights, and cleans up dog hair. She lives in Northern Virginia with her husband and son.

Catch up with her at rjstrongbooks.com